THE
COURTSHIP

G·K
Hall
&Co.

Also by Catherine Coulter
in Large Print:

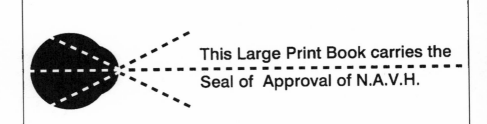

This Large Print Book carries the
Seal of Approval of N.A.V.H.

Catherine Coulter

THE

COURTSHIP

G.K. Hall & Co. • Thorndike, Maine

Published in 2000 by arrangement with The Berkley Publishing Group, a member of Penguin Putnam, Inc.

G.K. Hall Large Print Core Series.

The text of this Large Print edition is unabridged.
Other aspects of the book may vary from the original edition.

Set in 16 pt. Plantin.

Printed in the United States on permanent paper.

Library of Congress Cataloging-in-Publication Data

Coulter, Catherine.
   The courtship / Catherine Coulter.
     p. cm.
   ISBN 0-7838-9032-X (lg. print : hc : alk. paper)
   ISBN 0-7838-9033-8 (lg. print : sc : alk. paper)
   1. Large type books. I. Title.
   PS3553.O843 C675   2000
   813'.54—dc21   00-027585

To my very dear friend, Martha Walker,
Who's finally home where she belongs.
And you were our first birthday celebration in the
Pink Palace.
— Catherine

1

London 1811
May 14
Just before midnight

Lord Beecham stopped dead in his tracks. He turned around so quickly that he nearly tripped over a huge potted palm.

He couldn't believe it. He had to be wrong. She couldn't have said that, could she? He looked for the woman he had just heard speaking.

He parted two huge palm fronds and peered into the Sanderling's library, a long, narrow, shelf-lined room just off the ballroom. Where the library was filled with dark-bound tomes, cobwebs in gloomy corners, and just one small branch of candles casting shadows, the ballroom was overflowing with lit candles, plants, and at least two hundred guests, all of them laughing, dancing, and drinking too much of the potent champagne punch.

The woman he had heard before spoke again. He took a step closer to the dimly lit library. Her voice was rich, tantalizing, filled with laughter. "Really, Alexandra," she said, "doesn't just the simple thought of discipline, just hearing the word, saying it slowly to yourself and letting it caress your tongue as you say it, doesn't it conjure up all sorts of delicious scenes of dominance? Can't you just see yourself? You are completely at the mercy of another, that person is in total control, and there is nothing you can do about anything. You know something is going to happen, you're dreading it, your heart is pounding, you're afraid, so very afraid, yet it's a delicious sort of fear you feel. You know, deep down, that you are anticipating what is to come. You can't wait for it to come, but there is nothing you can do except imagine what will be done to you. Ah, yes, your skin is rippling with the excitement of it."

There was dead silence. Wait, was that heavy breathing he heard?

Lord Beecham, whose very active imagination had conjured up a vision of himself standing over a beautiful woman, smiling down at her as he tied her hands over her head and her legs, spread, to the posts of his bed, knowing that in just a few minutes, he would remove her clothing, one lovely garment at a time, slowly, ever so slowly, and —

"Oh, goodness, Helen. I have to fan myself. I believe my bosom is palpitating. You are far too good at painting word pictures. What you describe — it sounds terrifying and wonderful. It rather makes my mouth water. It also sounds like a grand production that requires a lot of planning."

"Oh, yes, but that is part of the ritual. It is very

important that it be planned perfectly. You are part of the ritual, the most important part, if you are the one in control. It requires that you be constantly inventive, that you don't continue to rely on the same old disciplines. Remember, anticipation of something unknown is a very powerful thing. To be effective, discipline must constantly grow and change. In most cases, it is effective to have other people nearby to witness the discipline. This makes the recipient all the more frightened, his senses more heightened, his thoughts more focused. It is an amazing process. You will have to try it. Both sides of it."

More deep silence.

Try it? He wanted to run into that room this very instant and try everything he could possibly envision or dream about. His fingers were already on his cravat, ready to jerk it off so he could tie the wrists of the woman speaking, together over her head, so she would be helpless, her eyes large and frightened and excited as she stared up at him, her lips parted. Damnation, he had only one cravat, the one he was wearing. He needed at least two. He shuddered, imagining the smooth flesh of her wrists as he lightly wrapped the cravat around and around them, then pulled them bound, over her head —

He heard a deep sigh.

"All of that is well and good, Helen, but what I need are specific disciplines to try. A list of disciplines, if you will. From mild disciplines to the most rigorous."

He realized suddenly that he knew that voice. Good God, it was Alexandra Sherbrooke. He couldn't believe it. On second thought, he pictured Douglas Sherbrooke in his mind's eye, that big, hard man who had reputedly kept his wife happy for eight whole years now. And Alexandra wanted to know about discipline? To try on her husband? What a delightfully wicked idea.

Who was the woman speaking to her, this Helen?

"On the other hand," Alexandra said after a moment, "I would like to know how you know so very much about discipline."

"I have read every book, every article, every paper — both scholarly and secular — ever penned on the subject. I have seen every painting, etching, and drawing of disciplines employed throughout the world and throughout the ages. Now, the disciplines in China — goodness, talk about inventive. The drawings show that the Chinese are exceedingly flexible."

A bit more silence, then Alexandra said, her voice lowered a bit, as if she were leaning closer to this other woman, speaking in confidence, but he could still make out her words. "Helen, you are laughing at me. All right, I accept that you know all about discipline. Now, you must force yourself to come to my level. You have told me how you discipline your servants. You have told me about the ritual, how to build to a climax, how to squeeze out every tantalizing drop of fear

10

and excitement during the discipline to achieve the result you wish.

"Now I want to go directly to the extreme pleasure end of things. I want specifics. I am talking about physical pleasure, Helen. I want to know exactly what you would do to a man to drive him to the brink of madness. Since you have read every tome written about the subject, you must know something that would help me."

Lord Beecham would not have moved if a beautiful woman had stripped naked in front of him and started kissing him. Now this was a kicker. Alexandra Sherbrooke wanted to know how to drive Douglas to the brink of madness? That made no sense. Driving a man like Douglas to the brink would require very little effort on her part. It would probably require an effort of ten seconds, no more. Actually, any man who was still breathing was a suitable candidate. He himself, for example.

Suddenly it simply became too much. He was eavesdropping on two ladies discussing discipline, for God's sake. He was lurking there behind a palm, listening to them, sweating, and ready to remove his cravat. It was not to be borne. Lord Beecham couldn't hold it back. It just burst from his mouth. He laughed — something he didn't normally do because he was, after all, a man of the world; a lazy nod or a slightly contemptuous snicker was usually more fitting. And so what poured out of his mouth sounded a bit rusty, perhaps a tad hoarse to the casual ear, but it was a laugh, a good strong laugh, and it just kept rolling out of him.

He realized they could hear him. That would never do. He tried so hard to stop laughing that he hiccupped. He clapped his hand over his mouth and quickly slipped behind another giant palm tree. And none too soon.

"I know I heard someone, Helen. It was a man and he was laughing. Oh, dear, you don't think it was Douglas, do you? No, Douglas would come right in here and laugh in our faces. Then he would look at me with a smile in his eyes and tell me to forget the thought of disciplining him, that he is in charge. I am tired of his controlling everything. Eight years is a long time, Helen. I want to make him wild first, for once."

"Well, that can't be too difficult. Simply distract him when he is reading the *Gazette*. Start nuzzling his ear, kiss his neck, bite him. Why haven't you done this already?"

Dead silence.

"Oh, dear, you are scarlet to your hairline, Alexandra."

"I have bitten him, Helen, I have. My bites simply take place in a different context. There is no *Gazette* lying about."

"A context that Douglas has provided?"

"Yes. You know, it's just that Douglas has only to look at me, perhaps give me a small touch anywhere with his hand or his mouth, and I lose every shred of thought. I puddle right on the floor, directly in front of him. It just does not stop, Helen. Help me. Oh, dear, what if he is out there, listening? Now he knows what power he wields over me."

"Trust me, he already knows. Now, you're right, of course. If it had been Douglas, he would be standing right in front of us, laughing his head off. But then, perhaps he would have let you lead him off to begin disciplining him this very night — that is, if he didn't decide to discipline you first."

Alexandra sighed.

"Goodness, you mean it? You're serious here, Alexandra? Doesn't Douglas ever let you have control? Eight years of one-sided marital sorts of things? From everything I've read, this isn't good. The Italians, especially, believe that participation in lovemaking should be balanced. You must pull yourself together."

"It's difficult once Douglas turns his attention on me. I would like to read what the Italians have to say about this."

"I will lend you a treatise on it. Now, you cannot allow Douglas always to discipline you first. You must focus your mind, Alexandra."

Alexandra's eyes nearly crossed. She shuddered delicately. "Douglas has never said anything at all about discipline. I'm sure he's never done any to me."

Helen laughed and patted her cheek. "From everything I've read, I'll wager Douglas already performs a lover's standard discipline on you and you don't even realize it. You're just having fun."

"Do you really think so? I wonder what specific sorts of things that Douglas enjoys with me one could call discipline? Perhaps I shall ask him."

"Or perhaps not, at least not yet."

"Whatever he does, it's true that I do sometimes forget to think," Alexandra said, then squared her shoulders, "but that's another problem, one I will have to solve." Her shoulders squared even more and her magnificent bosom achieved new prominence. "I will have to learn how to retain my own control if I want to have a chance of controlling Douglas. I will have to have a specific goal in mind, a course that I will have to follow. I will get the upper hand of Douglas. The brink of madness — yes, Helen, that is where I want to dispatch Douglas. You must tell me specifically what I am to do."

Helen looked down at her fingernails a moment. She knew she should keep her mouth shut, but she couldn't help herself. She said on a deep, wistful sigh, overflowing with exquisite memories, knowing that Alexandra would be enraged within moments, "Ah, even when I was fifteen and I first saw Douglas and fell in love with him, I knew instinctively that he wouldn't be a clod. I knew he would excel, and I wanted to be the female he chose to excel upon. Such a pity that it wasn't meant to be." She sighed again, a sad, forlorn sigh.

Helen watched beneath her lashes as Alexandra's eyes narrowed remarkably, and her

14

voice turned mean and low. "Helen, I will not tell you again. You will forget those early years of infatuation with Douglas. You will forget those tender feelings you cherished for him when you were too young to realize what was what."

"Yes," Helen said at her most humble, her head bent to show how contrite she was, "I will try." She hoped Alexandra couldn't hear the laughter in her voice.

Lord Beecham heard the laughter. And then he realized that here he was, a man of immense *savoir faire,* hiding behind huge green palm fronds, hanging on these women's every word. He hadn't yet seen the disciplinarian, but he could see Alexandra Sherbrooke now. She was looking around, just a bit apprehensively, her fingers splayed over her incredible bosom. It was too bad Douglas insisted she keep all that lovely white flesh more covered than not. It wasn't at all the style. God gave women bosoms to flaunt, and every woman he knew flaunted, except Alexandra Sherbrooke. Everyone had seen Douglas drag his wife into a corner from time to time to pull up her bodice if he thought there was too much white flesh showing.

A pity.

Lord Beecham loved breasts: bountiful breasts like Alexandra's that would overflow a man's hands, small breasts that were ripe and sweet, breasts pushed up to be lovingly framed by a gown's satin and lace. He loved to bury his face in a woman's breasts.

15

He got hold of himself. Who was the other woman, the self-proclaimed mistress of discipline? He knew only that her name was Helen.

Lord Beecham was not normally a skulker, but he had to know who she was. He waited, veiled by the palm fronds, until, finally, the two ladies came out of the Sanderling's library.

He nearly dropped his glass of champagne when he saw Helen. She was the woman he had seen riding in the park with Douglas. He remembered remarking to himself then that he wanted a better look at her. Now he was getting it. She had to be nearly as tall as he was, but there all resemblance between them ended. His imagination soared to Mount Olympus for suitable comparisons. She was sculpted like a goddess, statuesque and beautifully curved, skin so white it was alabaster, and her hair — surely even goddesses didn't have hair like that, thick and pure blond with no hints of gold or red. She wore it twisted atop her head, making her appear even taller, with long, lazy curls caressing the white flesh of her shoulders. Her eyes were bluer than Aphrodite's, her smile so charming, so utterly seductive, it could have belonged to Helen of Troy. He would wager that this new Helen could launch even more ships.

Lord Beecham had just lost his wits. Frankly, his literary-inspired imagination had made him produce tripe. She was a woman, just a woman, and her name was Helen. She might be on the magnificent side, but she was still only a woman, nothing more, nothing less. He had seen women who were more beautiful, had bedded women who were more beautiful. She was not a goddess, not even close to a siren of myth. She was just a very big girl who happened to have very nice hair of a shade that sparked poetry in a man's soul. And she had spoken authoritatively of discipline.

All other things being equal, she was a man's dream.

He watched Helen and Alexandra walk away from him, down the corridor to the ballroom.

She wasn't a young, untried girl of eighteen either, newly released from the schoolroom to prey upon the hapless bachelors of London. No, she had been released a goodly number of years ago, which meant she was well married and knew exactly what was what — and that was surely an utterly excellent thing.

He had always preferred married women. What man didn't? They were safe. They wanted what he wanted — a bit of excitement, a bit of warmth, a new companion to add spice and passion. They didn't usually whine or carp when he was ready to move on. He did not have to worry about their husbands, most of whom were his friends and who bedded other friends' wives just as he did. Many men and women were not discreet, and that sometimes stretched civilized manners to the limit. Lord Beecham, however, never spoke of his conquests. There wasn't any need to even if he had been inclined to bray and brag. For some reason, he could not escape the gossips, no matter how silent he remained.

He tossed down the rest of his champagne as the two women disappeared from his view back into the ballroom.

He rubbed his hands together.

Helen was a very big girl. He spread his fingers out. He thought of her breasts. Were his hands big enough for her? Oh, yes, he thought, his hands would make do quite nicely. He looked at his hands, pictured her breasts, and knew that if he had been speaking just then, he would doubtless have been stuttering.

Why were they talking about discipline? His flesh rippled. He pictured Helen on her back, her white arms pulled above her head, her wrists tied with two of his softest cravats to the posts at the head of his bed.

A woman who was well versed in the art of discipline? She had read everything ever written about it? Had she also employed everything she had learned? Had it all been employed upon her? It was a heady thought, one that made him swallow a bit convulsively.

When he reached the ballroom he looked and looked, but the big girl was gone.

He wasn't worried. He would simply call upon Alexandra and, with his exquisite finesse, discover Helen's address and the name of her husband.

He hoped Alexandra would cooperate. He had stopped trying to seduce her at least six years ago, when one evening in the midst of one of his

18

more effective offerings she laughed at him. It had wounded him greatly. He was a renowned lover — at least that was what the gossips were always saying.

But in the end, he quite liked Alexandra Sherbrooke, despite her appalling preference for only her husband in her bed. He liked her husband as well, all the more so once Douglas determined he wouldn't have to kill him for trying to seduce his wife. It was nothing more than attempted poaching, and that, Douglas had told him some years before, he would let slide. Thank the heavens that there were not all that many couples like the Sherbrookes in London.

Exactly what did the big girl know about discipline? Like Alexandra, he wanted specifics. He couldn't wait to find out. Other than her far-flung reading, had her husband taught her? Or a lover?

Lord Beecham wanted her in his bed, and he wanted her there very soon. He would be a lover who would teach her something altogether new about discipline. He would take his fill of her and when they eventually parted, she would never forget him. Whenever she spoke of discipline after her time with him, she would remember him, and smile.

He rubbed his hands together in anticipation even as he wondered if her hair was long enough to fall over her shoulders and curl lazily around her breasts.

Lord Beecham was a man with a very detailed

imagination. He saw her beneath him, all of her, stretched out, smiling up at him, and her hands were busy, very busy. He was forced once again to swallow. He would bed her soon. Very soon.

Tomorrow night would fit nicely into his schedule.

His fingers clenched at the emerging picture in his mind, a very big picture.

So much white canvas.

2

Sherbrooke Town House
London 1811
May 15
Less than twelve hours
after the Sanderling ball

Alexandra Sherbrooke, Countess of Northcliffe, shook out her dark-green silk skirts and rose. Mankin, the Sherbrooke town house butler for the past eighteen years, was, she saw, growing more and more stooped by the year, but it was not because he worked too hard or that his shoulders were rounding with age. No, Mankin wanted to show off his head in all its perfectly round, glittering bald glory. He polished his head. She had seen him doing it once when she'd happened to peer around the corner into the butler's pantry; he'd been using some of Mrs. Hibble's home-made wax. Today, as usual, he had achieved a high shine.

"Lord Beecham, my lady," Mankin said from the doorway of the first-floor drawing room. He bowed low, bending his head until the very top was in her line of vision. She was nearly blinded.

"Hello, Spenser." She walked to him, her hands out, smiling. She quite liked Spenser Heatherington, much to Douglas's annoyance.

21

"Please tell me that you are here to murmur sweet nonsense into my ears. I do miss that, you know. You just stopped doing it."

He gave her a smooth, charming smile, with just enough white teeth to add a little wickedness. "You laughed at me, Alexandra. How can a man murmur love words when the lady laughs all perky and amused in his face? One's manhood can't survive such a tactic."

"I had forgotten that. Well, that wasn't well done of me. Yes, you must begin again. It always made Douglas red-faced when I told him what you said to me. Ah, but it also made him become ever so attentive. He had to prove, of course, that he could murmur nonsense better than you could. It still riles him no end that I call you by your first name."

"It took me five years to convince you."

"You know very well that Douglas detests the familiarity of it. You do it to enrage him. He says I am the one flirting, that I am the one who is encouraging you to think thoughts you should not be thinking."

He laughed, couldn't seem to help himself. It was his second bout of laughter in under twenty-four hours. He cleared his throat. Was his throat a bit sore from the unaccustomed exercise?

"May I offer you tea, Spenser?"

"Yes, if you wish. Actually, what I would really like is to discuss the finer points of discipline with you."

Alexandra flushed from her neck to her hairline. She pressed her palms to her cheeks and fanned herself.

"What is this? You get overly warm when just the word is spoken?"

"Don't bait me, sir. Dare I ask where you heard about that?"

He gave her a grin so wicked she wanted to smack him, but she wasn't close enough. She watched him lean back against the mantel and cross his arms over his chest. "You were in the Sanderling's library, speaking of discipline with a big girl who — hopefully — has enough soft ribbons to tie a man down by both his ankles and his wrists. She was discussing various philosophical points, while you, Alexandra, you wanted specificity that you could immediately try on Douglas."

"Oh, dear. I thought we were quite alone. No, wait. I remember hearing a man laugh. It was you, Spenser? Oh, goodness, better you than Mr. Pierpoint, who would have collapsed of apoplexy on the spot. I never would have been able to face Mrs. Pierpoint and tell her how her husband passed over."

"Also better my overhearing you than Douglas."

"I am not so sure. Do sit down, Spenser. You have embarrassed me to my toes. As to Douglas, he would have laughed his head off, just as you did." She cocked her head at him. "Now just a moment. You of all people do not need any further instruction on various forms of discipline.

You already know all there is to know, don't you? I would assume a man of your experience would be well versed in it."

He looked down at his hands, his long fingers and well-buffed fingernails. He never allowed a hangnail because he did not want to chance hurting a woman's soft flesh when he was caressing her. His dratted imagination again. He cleared his throat and pontificated. "Just as there are many forms of government, there are also no shortage of approaches to the subject of discipline. I am always eager to garner new knowledge, no matter the source."

She cleared her throat and called out, "Mankin, I know you are standing not two feet on the other side of the door. Your jaw has probably dropped halfway to the floor because you are eavesdropping. Please pick up your jaw, bring some tea, and some of Cook's delicious mince clappers."

They heard a harrumph from the corridor.

Lord Beecham's eyebrow rose a good inch. "Dare I ask? Did you say mince clappers?"

"Yes. Our cook, Mrs. Clapper, is from the far north, just at the southern edge of the Cheviot Hills. The recipe descends from her mother's side of the family, sheep farmers all of them, going back many hundreds of years. It's a special sort of pastry made with raisins, apples, cinnamon, currants, and oranges, all ground together. It is quite delicious, really."

"It sounds rather strange to me, Alexandra.

With all of it ground up, do you think there might be some sheep parts in there she hasn't told you about?"

"If there are, you can't taste them."

"Perhaps I won't indulge in the clappers at this time."

"Now, Spenser, you were just saying how there were many different schools of discipline. There are also many different kinds of pastries to be tried. I expect you to be eager to expand your culinary knowledge. In short, my dear sir, don't be a coward."

"The ultimate weapon, a direct blow to the manhood. Bring on the clappers."

Ten minutes later, Lord Beecham was enthusiastically chewing a mouthful of clapper when, without warning from Mankin, the big girl came sweeping into the drawing room.

"Alexandra, I will have him chasing at my heels by tomorrow evening, at the latest. Meeting him will be so very easy, and —"

She stared at him, her expression so horrified that he laughed. That made him choke on the clapper. She was on him in an instant, slapping his back so hard he wondered if his ribs would burst through his chest.

He managed to swallow the rest of the clapper, but since he was having a hard time breathing, he just sat there, gasping for breath as he looked up at her.

"Are you all right, Lord Beecham?"

"He still can't breathe, Helen. Give him a

minute. Did she cave in your ribs, Spenser?"

Two minutes passed before he had enough breath back in his body to speak. He looked up at the big girl. "You know me?"

"Of course. I imagine that most people know you, particularly the ladies."

Why did she look flushed? He was the one nearly flattened. When he was finally breathing easily again, he cleared his throat, drank a bit of tea, and set the cup back on its saucer. "The reason most people know me is because I have lived in London since I was eighteen years old and quite know everyone." He rose, came to within one foot of her, and stopped. She looked him straight in the eye.

"Douglas is wrong," Alexandra said. "You are at least two inches taller than Helen, just like he is. Douglas was telling her that he was taller than you."

Lord Beecham looked into those clear blue eyes. "I am one of the tallest men I know."

"Douglas is taller," Alexandra said. "By at least an inch. Yes, I can see that clearly now."

"Well," Helen said, "I am surely one of the tallest ladies in all of England."

"You are a very big girl," he said slowly, wanting to eye her up and down very thoroughly but realizing it wouldn't be a good thing to do in Alexandra Sherbrooke's drawing room. Instead, he picked up his teacup and toasted her.

She laughed, a splendid sound that was full and rich and curled through his innards like a snifter of good brandy. He thought about her lying in the middle of his bed with him over her. It would be early evening, not more than six or seven hours away. His schedule was open.

"Not really a girl anymore," Helen said, giving him a beautiful smile, all white teeth and dimples deep in her cheeks. "I am twenty-eight, twenty-nine in seven months. I am quite long in the tooth, my father tells me. Just three months ago he was so enraged with me over something — neither of us would even remember what now — he let fly and yelled that I was on the shelf. Whenever I provoke him, he is capable of moaning to the heavens what an unnatural child I am. I am not unnatural, it is just that I am . . ."

She stalled, and Lord Beecham smiled. "A big girl."

Helen gave him that brilliant smile again. "That, too, I suppose." She stuck out her hand. "I am Helen Mayberry. My father is the eccentric Viscount Prith, the very tallest gentleman in all of England."

Lord Beecham straightened to his full height — a good two inches taller than Helen — took her hand, and turned it as he leaned down to kiss her wrist. He felt the quiver in her hand. Excellent. Perhaps, if he were suave and a bit lucky, he would have her naked on the sheets in the very early evening, perhaps even in the very late afternoon, exchanging discipline recipes with her while he kissed her silly.

"I am Spenser Nicholas St. John

Heatherington," he said. "You can call me Spenser or Heatherington or Beecham. I was named after Edmund Spenser, of *Faerie Queen* fame. My mother admired Queen Elizabeth and thus chose to name me after Edmund Spenser, a man the queen admired to perhaps an immoderate extent. Who knows? My father even told me it was just possible that I was a very distantly related descendant."

"It all sounds like nonsense to me," Helen said.

He grinned at her, toasting her again with his teacup. "I agree, but it makes for an amusing tale. You are telling me you have not yet found a man who suited you to your doubtless quite lovely toes, Miss Mayberry?"

"Perhaps for a relatively short period of time. You know the problem — there are so many boring very short men in England, and it seems that my dear father is acquainted with all of them. I really do not mind short, but boring I cannot accept."

"I don't mind short, either," he said.

"And boring? You don't mind boring ladies?"

"Ladies are never boring, Miss Mayberry. Not if they are treated properly."

"I wonder if I should approve of what you just said."

"When you have decided, you will tell me. I believe you wished to meet me, Miss Mayberry?"

It was a shot in the dark. Still, when she had

come flying into the drawing room talking about meeting someone, looked at him like she could not believe he was actually sitting right there, choking, he had known in his gut she was talking about him.

Instead of acting embarrassed or chagrined and thus tongue-tied, Miss Mayberry nodded. "I don't know how you managed to figure that out, but it's true. It is a pleasure to meet you, my lord. What is even better is that I don't have to bother with any machinations now, although the one I had in mind was really quite efficient."

He looked at her, fascinated. Say six and a half hours until the early evening, perhaps just five and a half hours until late afternoon. He had enough time. "What were you going to do?"

"I was going to ride you down in the park."

"You mean trod me under your horse's hooves?"

"Oh, no, I don't want to hurt you." She paused for a delicate moment, her voice so demurely wicked he nearly swallowed his tongue, particularly when she added, "At least not in that way."

Had she really said that, right here in the open, right in front of him and Alexandra? He thought about having her naked on the sheets with the mid-afternoon sun streaming through his bed-chamber window. Would she insist on disciplining him? He devoutly hoped so.

"I was going to pretend to lose control and my balance and just happen to fall on you."

"Depending on your momentum, you might

well have smashed me flat."

"Oh, dear, I hadn't thought about that. I might have driven you right into the ground, like a stake, or broken your ribs. Ah, but then I would have knelt beside you and held your hand until you managed to get your wits together again. It would have been just fine. You would have smiled up at me and lifted your hand, weakly, to touch my cheek. Yes, that forms a pleasant picture in the mind."

"Only your end result. I would have deplored the process. Men do not like to be weak, Miss Mayberry, ever."

Alexandra cleared her throat. "I know you are much enjoying yourselves, but I must tell you, Spenser, that Douglas grows livid whenever Helen talks about meeting you. He rants, Spenser. He insults you. He grinds his teeth. He ordered Helen to steer a wide berth."

Helen laughed. "Douglas fears for my virtue with you in the vicinity, Lord Beecham."

It was very warm in the middle of the afternoon. There would be no need for a fire in his bedchamber even with the both of them naked. He mentally put his mouth and his hands on her. He rose and held out his hand to her. "Well, then, to spare Douglas's teeth, I will simply remove Miss Mayberry from the premises before he returns home."

"Where would you remove me to, Lord Beecham?"

"To Gunther's. For an ice."

He had never seen a woman glow so much in his life.

"That would be wonderful. It is my favorite treat since I came to London. How ever did you know?"

Lord Beecham looked over at Alexandra, who was looking just a bit shell-shocked. "Tell her, Alexandra, that I am a man of vast and varied experience. I have the gift of looking at a woman and clearly reading her deepest desires."

"Perhaps that is true," Alexandra said as she bit into a mince clapper. "However, I did not know you could guess as deep as Helen's endless desire for Gunther's ices."

"Now you do." He was still holding out his hand to Miss Mayberry. "Shall we?"

Helen winked at Alexandra even as she closed her hand over his forearm. "Tell Douglas I have succeeded."

"What was that all about?" Lord Beecham asked as Mankin opened the front door for them and then bowed very low. Sunlight streamed through the doorway and glittered off his bald head.

Unfortunately, neither Lord Beecham nor Miss Mayberry noticed.

"How have you succeeded? By meeting me? Surely that would not require you running me down in the park."

"Are you acquainted with Gray St. Cyre, Baron Cliffe?"

"Certainly. What of him?"

"He got himself wedded not too long ago."

"Yes, I know. What about him?"

"He and his bride happened to be near my inn after Jack had escaped from Arthur Kilburn. Unfortunately, Gray had gotten himself thrown and cracked his head against an oak tree."

"You own an inn?"

"Yes. It's called King Edward's Lamp. It is the premier inn in Court Hammering, a market town an hour or so northeast of London."

"Arthur had kidnapped Gray's bride? I had not heard of this. Her name is Jack?"

"That's right. In any case, once we resolved everything, my father and I came back to London to attend their wedding. It was quite charming, really, and quite small and private, and so you weren't there. I saw Douglas again."

"And you were infatuated with Douglas when you were fifteen," he said, staring at her, his fascination growing by the word. He forgot for a moment that he wanted to bed her by two o'clock in the afternoon.

This afternoon. No later than three.

"So you were the man who overheard Alexandra and me talking in the Sanderling's library."

"Oh, yes. Discipline is a subject that is dear to my heart."

"I am not at all surprised."

He was smiling at her, wondering if it was too soon to kiss her, perhaps lightly touch his fingertips to her throat, feel her pulse quicken.

"Yes, Douglas was a lovely young man. But that was a very long time ago. I have assured Alexandra that I am over my tender feelings toward her husband."

"That's good. It wouldn't please your current lover all that much if you weren't over Douglas Sherbrooke. Was Douglas your first lover?"

3

She gave him a cocky smile. There didn't appear to be a single embarrassable bone in her body. His fascination continued to climb. "Now, that is very straight speaking, Lord Beecham."

"Of course. You strike me as a woman who prefers straight speaking." He helped her into his carriage. He said to his driver, "Babcock, drive us to Gunther's. I must feed this lovely lady an ice or two before she begins to fade away."

"Aye, my lord," Babcock said, eyeing Helen with awe since she was a good nine inches taller than he was. Lord Beecham noticed that Babcock straightened his shoulders as he jumped up into the driver's seat.

"Hurry, Babcock," Helen called out of the window. "It will be a close thing. I did not have my luncheon today."

Lord Beecham laughed, he just couldn't help it. Surely what she had said wasn't all that funny. He coughed and followed it with a harrumph.

Helen settled herself opposite him, smoothing down her skirts. "What's wrong?"

"Nothing, nothing at all. So you didn't let Douglas bed you?"

"Actually, I fear he wasn't at all interested." She sighed. "I was just a little girl to him. I believed him a god. I would have gladly wiped a rose-water cloth over his brow, peeled grapes for him before respectfully popping them into his mouth. I would have —"

"That's quite enough." Lord Beecham frowned at her as he pulled on his soft York tan gloves.

She grinned shamelessly back at him.

"You were telling me why Douglas would be annoyed that you had found me," Lord Beecham said. "You still haven't arrived at the reason, what with all the drivel you've been spouting. Why did you bring up Gray's name?"

"Douglas, Alexandra, and I were visiting with them. Alexandra brought up your name as being marvelously degenerate and lecherous, in short, a man of vast competence and talent. She thought you could take Douglas's place in my mind. But Douglas said your reputation was exaggerated, that you purported to be a better lover than any dozen men combining their experience, but that it wasn't true. You were, in short, a very distant second to him.

"When I looked even more interested, Douglas said in his lord-of-the-manor way that I was to stay away from you, that you would corrupt me and leave me in a ditch.

"When I pointed out that he claimed to be your superior in lechery and that he had not left Alexandra in a ditch, he said that she was simply too pathetic, that is why he'd had no choice but to remain married to her and keep her safe and

35

smiling. He does, you know."

"Does what?"

"Douglas keeps her smiling. Now, Alexandra likes you. She told me about how you wanted to be her shepherd."

He whacked his cane against the carriage floor. "You damned women. You can't wait to tell each other all about a man's failures, you never forget them, even though this particular failure happened eight years ago. She was newly wedded to Douglas. He was being an ass, nothing all that unusual for Douglas. She was ripe for the plucking, so I thought. But instead, she clung to the tree. She was utterly green, naive, and, unfortunately, adorable." He frowned over those words and shrugged. "Over the years we have gotten in the habit of exchanging friendly conversation. It is no longer as unnerving as it was at the beginning. I quite like her."

"You mean you found it strange to like a woman you'd failed to seduce?"

He gave her a look of acute dislike and crossed his arms over his chest. It was intimidating, and he knew it. "Exactly. I can even pass a good half hour now in her company without staring at her breasts." There, he thought, pleased with himself. He wasn't going to let her be more provocative than he, the brazen twit. He would keep the upper hand. Time was growing short. Two o'clock in the afternoon was only an hour from now. He wasn't going to have time to get her into his bed. He lowered the sun in the sky, thinking of twilight. It was a lovely time of the day, soft lights caressing a woman's body. He cleared his throat.

"Thirty minutes?" Helen said. "Not a single look? For a man, that has to be close to sainthood." She gave him another dazzling smile. "So you can see why I wanted to meet you. I want a man who can control himself, who can decide what to do and get it done. I want a man of charm and a bit of wit and endless experience. I want a man who can set a goal and figure out how to gain it, a man who can separate the chaff from the wheat."

"What does that mean?"

"That, Lord Beecham, was a metaphor. It means you know what is important and what is not. Alexandra recommended you. You have just shown me that you are very comfortable bandying about women's parts that no other gentleman of my acquaintance would bandy about in front of a lady, and that shows, I suppose, that you know you are fluent enough so that you won't get shot. Actually, I do exactly the same thing with men and I haven't been shot either."

"You mean we are both fluent?"

"Oh, yes. I believe in fairness."

He couldn't think of a single thing to say. He realized that she wasn't taking in the passing view, no, she was taking him in. She was giving him a thorough examination from his ears, to the toes of his boots, to his hand holding the head of his cane.

"Alexandra told me you were handsome, not as handsome as Douglas, naturally, but still, more than adequate. She said you don't have excess flesh as many men do after they pass their thirtieth year. Er, you have quite passed your thirtieth year, haven't you?"

"I am thirty-three, two years younger than Douglas."

"Douglas has no excess fat either. It's refreshing to find at least two gentlemen who look quite well enough to encourage a lady to take a second look, perhaps even lightly place her palm over their bellies, to feel the hard smoothness of their muscles."

It took all his control not to take her down to the floor of the carriage right that instant. He could have her breasts free of her gown in a second. Damnation — not in a carriage, not the first time he took her. He wanted her happy after they finished, not sore from being tossed about between two carriage seats.

He cleared his throat. He was being overly enthusiastic. At thirty-three years of age, he had sublime control. She'd said she knew he had control. Well, he did. What was happening here? "You must be from the country, where the squires parade around with their bellies sticking out."

"Yes, indeed. I cannot tell you how exhilarating it is to be here in London." She crossed her hands over her heart.

She had smacked him with a goodly dose of sarcasm that he undoubtedly deserved.

She leaned a bit forward now. "I do think that you, Lord Beecham, will be perfect for my purposes."

He was the man. He was the hunter. He was the supremely experienced lover. Did this woman have no shame? No reticence? No modesty? It appalled him.

He knew that if she were married, her husband would be equally appalled. What would he say if he knew his wife wanted to seduce another man? He cooled down his voice to throw her off stride. "Look at me. Of course I'm not fat. Only a man who is a complete fool would have a paunchy belly. Ladies don't like paunchy bellies."

"That's true enough."

"What are your damned purposes?"

Babcock pulled up the carriage in front of Gunther's on St. James. It was a narrow building, painted white, quite lovely in the bright sunlight — sunlight that was a relief, since they had endured solid rain for the past three days. Helen gave him her hand as he helped her down from the carriage. "This is utterly delightful, my lord. I thank you for so graciously accompanying me here. I do love the ices."

She was wearing a rich emerald-green walking dress, very simple and elegant. She had a small bonnet on her head adorned only with three leaves from some bush or tree he didn't recognize, all intertwined just over her left ear. She looked sophisticated, very much a lady, until you looked at her eyes. He saw intelligence, humor, and a good deal of knowledge. About her fellow man? He liked intelligent women, in small doses. They tended to want to examine things after lovemaking, pick things apart until he wanted to sink into a stupor. He also enjoyed humor in a woman, if it was a proper sort of humor — that is, a humor not directed at him.

Twilight, he thought. Twilight still looked possible.

He cleared his throat and escorted her into the charming interior. A young man wearing a huge white apron wrapped around his middle was immediately at their side, offering them a small round table. Lord Beecham helped her sit down. He smiled down at her, his eyes filled with the knowledge of her, a woman. "Don't eat too much. A gentleman doesn't like a paunchy lady either."

"I never change size," Helen said as she looked at the table next to them, not at the people, but at the ices in front of them. "Vanilla," she said. "I adore vanilla."

It was his favorite as well. He ordered chocolate.

He said no more until their bowls were set in front of them. He said no more until she had downed a good half dozen bites, closed her eyes, and moaned in bliss. He still didn't say anything until he had finished his own chocolate ice. He wouldn't mind at all feeding her an ice after making love to her. It would, at the very least, keep her quiet. The only thing was, he wouldn't know if the ice gave her more pleasure than he did.

He said suddenly while she was looking about the room, "What purpose do you have for me?"

"You are much sought after, are you not?"

"Yes."

"Why?"

There it was again, this damned attempt to swamp his boat. He would not let her control him. "Use your eyes," he said, his feathers all ruffled. He didn't want her to know that she had riled him, and so he smiled at her, showing lots of straight white teeth. "Use your ears. You yourself spoke of my fluency. I am not a stupid man."

"No, you are not at all stupid, are you?" Helen said after a moment. She was looking longingly at a huge bowl of some fruit-flavored ice set in front of a gentleman with a huge belly.

"Don't even think it," he said. "You have spooned quite enough down your white throat."

"It's the oddest thing," she said. "Do you know that I become very relaxed when I eat a Gunther's ice?"

Lord Beecham raised his hand instantly and called to the waiter.

He fed her two more bowls of ice cream. On her third spoonful of the third bowl, she said, "Who is that couple just over there? She is

41

wearing that rather alarming blue dress and the gentleman is obviously displeased with her?"

Lord Beecham looked, then studied his nails. Finally, he said, a bit of tolerant contempt in his voice, "Mr. and Mrs. Crowne. Only a year they've been wedded, and yet they flay each other regularly, even in public. That is why, Miss Mayberry, a smart man never jumps into that black pit. Marriage is the end of the road, the end of reason, the end of any contentment a man may lay claim to."

He looked as if he were suffering from excess bile when he said the word. Helen just smiled at him, understood him down to his socks, and was not only pleased but vastly relieved. She took another bite, savoring the lovely burst of cold filling her mouth and the cold, soft, slick cream sliding down her throat. "I quite agree with you, Lord Beecham. Marriage is only for weak-minded fools."

He didn't like that. A man, by his very nature, was supposed to evade marriage, but not a woman. He managed to keep his displeasure with her from showing. "Tell me, now. What is your use for me?"

"We do keep getting off the subject, don't we?"

"Yes, but no more. Talk to me. Tell me what I may do for you."

Helen wasn't a fool. She saw clearly in his brilliant, dark eyes that he wanted nothing more than to pull her gown away and make love to her.

42

"You obviously find marriage distasteful."

"Yes, as would any reasonable man. Unfortunately women must bear a man an heir, so at some date before his death, he must produce the requisite male child. I do not plan to pass to the hereafter until after my fiftieth year. When I am forty-nine, I will wed and beget an heir. Then I will die with a smile on my face. Perhaps my pregnant wife, who will be puttering around my country estates, will also have a smile on her face. The country estate in Devon. It is charming."

"I have found that every nobleman has a country house and every one of them has a name. What is the name of this one in Devon?"

"Paledowns."

"Unusual." She leaned toward him. "It is a bit more difficult for a woman, don't you think, Lord Beecham? A woman doesn't have a man's freedom unless she simply does what she wishes to do and ignores what society says about her."

"Women rule the world, Miss Mayberry. If they are smart, they can control a man with but a look."

"What if the woman doesn't happen to be passably pretty, Lord Beecham?"

"Then she will obviously not rule many men."

"And if she doesn't have money?"

"Then she will sell her services and rule the fellow who has paid for her."

"I do not think I have ever met a more cynical man," Helen said, her ice forgotten.

"I am only a realist, Miss Mayberry. I trust you don't complain about women's dreadful lot on this earth. You would look like an idiot and a hypocrite were you to whine even the least bit.

"Your father is a peer, you have doubtless led a raft of short young men around by the nose, you are young and quite independent to boot, and you are more beautiful than you probably deserve. No, I don't want to hear a single plaint out of you about the unfairness of a woman's life on this damned earth. To sum it all up, Miss Mayberry, you look far too happy and robust to be anything other than deliriously pleased with your lot in life."

"That certainly puts me in my place."

"And a very good place it is."

"What about this poor wife you will procure when you are forty-nine years old? She will have no say in anything. You just want her for breeding purposes, like you would breed animals. She will have needs and desires and hopes, and you will treat her like a sheep in a pen."

He laughed at that. "What a picture you paint, Miss Mayberry. Please don't ignore the facts. This lady will want to marry me. She will gain my title, my money, and she will have anything she desires, except a lover, at least until I am passed to the hereafter. She will be the mistress of Paledowns and three other properties as well. After she buries me, she will be rich, her son will be Viscount Beecham, and she can bed every

44

gentleman from Pall Mall to Russell Square.

"No, don't feel sorry for the future Viscountess Beecham. Now, I will agree, Miss Mayberry, that most women, just like most men, aren't rich, aren't particularly toothsome, and aren't particularly intelligent. And since they aren't men, they must endure more than men.

"However, since I am not a woman and I cannot do much about their plight in our society, I see to my own people. I am responsible for their welfare and I take my responsibilities seriously. I do my best not to cause any particular pain or difficulty for another human being, man or woman, just as I imagine you do."

"Give me just one example of your goodness, Lord Beecham."

"More sarcasm wafting toward me? Very well. Last month one of my maids was raped by a footman in a neighboring house. I met with the mistress of the house and was told in no uncertain terms that my maid was a trollop of no moral fiber at all and that it was she who had seduced their poor footman, a brawny Irishman who was a bully.

"I beat him to a pulp. My maid got to kick him herself once in his ribs. She spit on him. She is fine now, didn't become pregnant, thank God."

She just stared at him. He watched her long fingers stroke the silver spoon handle.

He frowned, not looking up from her fingers. "I don't know why I told you that. You will contrive to forget it. It is no one's affair. Are you quite through? Your ice is melted and looks revolting."

Helen watched him pay for their ices. When they reached the carriage, she said, "May we drive in the park, Lord Beecham?"

"Why? Haven't you yet decided if you want to use me?"

"You are very smart. That's it exactly."

4

Lord Beecham shouted up to his driver, "Babcock, to the park. Drive slowly."

"Aye, my lord."

They had taken a full turn when Helen leaned forward on the opposite seat. "I would very much like to walk a bit."

Lord Beecham shouted out the window to his driver, "Babcock, pull over."

"Aye, my lord."

It was the middle of the afternoon, still on the early side for all the ladies and gentlemen to venture out for their social hour in the park. The sun was spilling out bits of light and warmth, Helen thought, looking up, but it was still chilly, the feel of dampness lingering.

"You just shivered. Are you too cold?" He was drawing on his gloves as he spoke.

"No, I was just thinking. You know, Lord Beecham, I have wanted to meet you for the past week."

"But you still don't wish to tell me why?"

"A bit more conversation, perhaps? We were speaking about women and perhaps about your uses for them."

"My favorite species."

The black shadow of bitterness coming through, she thought. But she said nothing, just smiled at him.

He shrugged. "Truth be told, Miss Mayberry, God set us upon this stage to play our roles and so we play them, pathetically for the most part, but we try."

"Our roles are infinite, Lord Beecham. We may stumble and bumble about, but you are right, we do try."

"What role are you playing now, Miss Mayberry?"

"I am Diana the Huntress."

"And you are after my fair self. I am not certain that I wish to be caught. You are not married. I much prefer women to be married. It simplifies things."

"Good heavens, why? Oh, I am being obtuse. You believe that an unmarried woman wants to use you only in order to marry you."

"If a man is rich, yes, that is the way of it."

"You are very jaded, sir. If I were to tell you, for example, that all I wished from you was your company involving only a certain activity, you would automatically disbelieve me?"

"If you are speaking of taking me as a lover, then, yes, Miss Mayberry."

"You would be wrong, Lord Beecham."

She saw the contempt again, the incredulity, but all he said was, "Time will tell."

There was a bench on the side of the path. Helen sat down.

Lord Beecham leaned toward her. His eyes were brilliant, knowing. "What is your use for me, Miss Mayberry?"

She knew exactly what he wanted. Knew exactly what he imagined she was thinking. She ran her tongue over her bottom lip. He stared at her tongue, leaning a bit closer to her.

"Don't do that," he said, still staring at her mouth. "If you don't want me to very gently place you on the ground right next to this bench, you will not do that again."

"Very well. I apologize. You are renowned as a debaucher. You have made love to more women than I have meted out discipline to men. Do you have any bastards, Lord Beecham?"

"No. Not a single one. I would never do that to a woman, to a child, if it happened to survive."

"I understand it is not always possible to prevent conception no matter how careful the man and woman may be."

"I am so careful, Miss Mayberry, I would sooner wager that the sun wouldn't rise than that I would impregnate a woman. You're doing it again with your tongue."

He pulled her very gently against him and kissed her. She had been assaulted by a man's mouth only once since Gerard. No, she wouldn't think about Gerard. She recalled she had taken a good bite of that gentleman's tongue, before she hit him in the jaw and knocked him unconscious. But this was gentle, an exploration, a tantalizing invitation. Well, it should be. He was a master at this.

It was he who pulled back from her.

She didn't want him to stop, but she didn't try to hold him when he ended it.

"Tell me, Miss Mayberry," he said in the most delicious dark honey voice she had ever heard in her life, as he lightly rubbed his thumb over her eyebrow, "what is your use for me?"

Helen never lost control. She wasn't about to now, even though she wanted very much at this moment to hurl him to the ground and kiss him until he was begging.

"Perhaps," she said, swallowing, "just perhaps I still don't know you well enough to tell you yet. I am just not certain. There was something else Douglas said about you."

"And what insult would that be?"

"Not an insult. He said there were shadows in you. He said you had a dark soul."

He looked away from her as he rose. "Not so dark anymore. Time shifts and blurs and changes things, Miss Mayberry. No, not so very dark anymore. Now, where are you staying? I shall be delighted to see you home."

"You are angry because I'm not falling all over you immediately." Helen stood beside him, staring him right in the eye. "It isn't becoming for a man to get in a snit simply because he does not get his way. It's childish."

He laughed, the third time in under two days. Or was it the fourth? He stopped abruptly, touching his fingers to his mouth. He cleared his throat.

"What's wrong?"

"Nothing," he said, frowning right into her beautiful blue eyes. "Nothing at all. I am not in a snit. You misunderstood. You are a woman. Women frequently misinterpret a man's silent deliberations."

She snorted.

"You may look like a goddess, Miss Mayberry, but I assure you I can exist quite well without you."

"A goddess?"

"Also women hear only what they wish to hear."

"You have a point there. Oh yes, my father and I are staying at Grillon's Hotel."

He turned around and yelled, "Babcock!"

Leonine Octavius Mayberry, Sixth Viscount Prith, looked down his straight, narrow nose at his only child.

"I have known you all your life. I actually felt you while you were in your mother's belly. I know all your games — at least I have until now. Tell me why you have invited Lord Beecham — a man of many parts, most of them dangerous — to dinner."

Helen raised her hand and lightly touched her father's cheek. "I ordered champagne."

"At least we will see if the fellow's a real man. If he desires some of that filthy brandy instead, I will boot him out of here myself."

"I will assist you and apply my own slipper."

"You mock me, girl. Why is he coming?"

51

Helen slowly walked away from her father, who stood a good head taller than she. He was, in fact, quite the tallest man she had ever seen. She couldn't wait to see what Lord Beecham had to say when he craned his neck to look up at him. She walked to the lovely little bow windows in the parlor of their suite. She pulled back the curtain. The month of May was glorious even in London, she thought. At least today was. So many people, all in such a hurry. She hoped they knew where they were going. Sometimes it was very difficult to know.

"I have a use for him, Father. But I just don't know him well enough. The fact is, I want to see what you think of him. If you do not wish me ever to see him again, you will tell me, and I will show him to the door."

He beetled his thick arched brows, sleek and white. "I have heard all about Lord Beecham. I have heard no scurrilous tales about him. He appears honorable, though he is a renowned satyr. At least he is tall, I'll give you that. He's rich, but you don't care about that. Are you thinking you'll marry the fellow, Nell?"

"You know I don't wish to wed, Papa."

He looked at her thoughtfully for a long time, then turned and said over his shoulder, "I'll order two bottles of champagne."

Of course he had not thought to order the dinner with the champagne. She smiled as she rang the bell for their butler, Flock. Flock, so small he fit quite nicely under her arm, could deal well with the Prince Regent himself were the need to arise. He said to his mistress, "Miss Helen, I understand that Lord Beecham is a very intelligent man."

"Yes, I have heard that too, Flock."

"You will not worry. I will speak to him when he arrives. If he impresses me with his wit, I will give you a single wink. If he does not impress me, I will open the windows so Lord Prith may toss him out."

"I could do it just as well, Flock," she said mildly.

"Yes, I know, but I fancy you will be wearing a lovely gown and I wouldn't want you to wrinkle it."

"Very well, Flock." She couldn't wait to see whether she got a wink or an open window.

Helen spent more time than usual on her appearance that evening. When her maid Teeny fastened pearls around her neck, Helen said to her image in the mirror, "Have you decided to marry Flock?"

There was a big sigh behind her. "Oh, Miss Helen, I can't do it, I just can't."

"Why ever not? He is an excellent man. He is kind, he is competent. He is ever so forceful, and I have seen you shudder in delight when he tells you he will discipline you if you don't do as he wishes. He would take good care of you."

"I know all that, Miss Helen. But don't you see — my name would be Teeny Flock. It makes my teeth ache just to say it."

"Good God," Helen said as she rose and smoothed her skirts. She leaned down to give Teeny a hug. "I hadn't realized. Let me think about that. It is an obstacle, you're right about that, but it is not insurmountable."

When Flock announced Lord Beecham, Helen was already on her feet. Why the devil was she nervous? It was absurd.

Flock gave her a wink.

Lord Beecham, wearing evening clothes that perfectly complemented the arrogance of the man, strode into the room, spotted her, and was before her quickly. He bowed over her hand but didn't kiss either her hand or her fingers or her wrist. He just smiled at her and stepped away to shake hands with Lord Prith.

"I had the great pleasure to see you once, sir, in White's. May I inquire the height of your wife?"

"Ah, my sweet Mathilda, named after the conqueror's wife, you know. She was just a slip of a girl when I met her. No taller than my elbow when I married her. I swear, though, that she grew through the years just to keep up with her daughter. Helen, how tall was your mother?"

"My mother, Lord Beecham, was perhaps an inch taller than I. She swept through East Anglia, gentlemen in her wake, begging for her attention, but then she saw my father, and she stopped sweeping."

"It is just the same with you, Nell," Lord Prith said. He added to Lord Beecham, "So many fellows wanting to marry my little Nell. Sad thing is, though, most of 'em are short, more's the pity. Short men take one look at Helen and swoon. Of course, neither Helen nor I see them when they collapse."

"Because they're so short."

"Exactly," said Lord Prith. "Flock, bring on the champagne."

Now, Helen thought, with a smile toward her father, they would soon see what Lord Beecham was made of. She didn't know what Flock used to measure a man's wit, but to her father, it was, and always had been, champagne.

Lord Beecham eyed the beautiful goblet filled to its very brim with perfectly chilled champagne. He smiled at Flock as he shook his head. "Forgive me, but I would very much prefer a brandy."

Lord Prith choked and spewed champagne bubbles.

Helen shook her head sadly. "Are you certain, Lord Beecham? You don't care for champagne?"

"It isn't that I don't appreciate it, it's that champagne, particularly very fine champagne like this obviously is, makes me very ill. When I first drank it at Oxford, I believed I would die, I became so very ill. I tried one other time since then. It was not a pretty sight. It is an even worse memory, still."

"Here is brandy, my lord," said Flock. "It is the finest French brandy, smuggled in to a very private cove on his lordship's estate."

"Lord Beecham may decide to inform on us, Flock," Helen said as she sipped her champagne.

"No, he won't," said Lord Prith slowly. "He may be dangerous, but he's tall and he's straight. A pity about the champagne, though. There is nothing more splendid than a half dozen glasses — that quite sees you through the darkest times."

"So I have heard, sir. However, I have found brandy an excellent substitute. I may have dark times, but I am not dangerous, sir — at least not in the normal course of events."

"It is better for your reputation if you don't disagree with that," Helen said, and poked him lightly in the arm. She looked glorious tonight, her gown a soft ivory, the lovely pearls around her neck luminescent. Her hair was piled high atop her head, making her taller than he, which amused him.

"Very well," he said, "I am so dangerous that highwaymen see my carriage and ride directly to the magistrate." He wondered what she would taste like. Her gown wasn't cut particularly low, just low enough so he could see the lovely roundness of her breasts.

"Stop that," she said under her breath.

"If a woman did not want a man to admire her attributes, why then would she wear a gown that was halfway to her knees?"

"I selected that gown, sir." Lord Prith paused then and looked at his only offspring. "I say, it is somewhat revealing, Nell. Perhaps I could give you one of my scarves to tie around your shoulders. Flock! Fetch one of my wool scarves to cover Miss Helen."

"Hoisted on my own petard," Lord Beecham said and drank down the rest of his brandy.

"Papa has excellent hearing. One must always think before speaking if he is anywhere in the vicinity. Hearing even a whisper isn't beyond him."

"I will be more careful in the future." Future? It was possible he would not see her again after tonight, but he wanted to. He wanted to bed her, nothing more to it than that. Sweet, simple lust, a fine thing, something a man could see to without much difficulty, and then it was over and done with and a man could go about his business again, unburdened for a goodly number of hours.

"Dinner is served, Miss Helen."

When Flock opened the dining room door, frowning because it was closed in the first place, he stared in perfect horror.

The small dining room was fast filling with smoke.

"Oh, dear," said Flock. "Oh, dear."

Lord Beecham quickly moved Flock to one side.

"It's the buttock of beef that's burning," Lord Beecham said. He picked up a bottle of wine and poured it over the roast. He then removed a silver dome from another platter and set it over the meat. There was a hissing sound. More smoke gushed out from beneath the dome, then it stopped.

"Open the windows," Lord Prith said to Flock. "How did this happen?"

"It is the hotel, my lord," Flock said as he pulled the draperies back and shoved up the three side-by-side windows. "The chef is extremely voluble and quite French. His name is Monsieur Jerome. He saw Miss Helen when we arrived, lost his head, and has begged me to allow him to cook for her. This is his latest attempt to impress her. He called this his *feu du monde.*"

"World fire?" Lord Beecham said and coughed. He picked up a napkin and began flapping it against the smoke. "I don't suppose the chef is short?"

"Yes, my lord. Jerome doesn't even come to Miss Helen's chin. I do, however, pass her chin on most occasions."

"Eh? What does that mean, Flock?"

Flock said as he rubbed the burned spots on the lovely white linen tablecloth, "It means, my lord, that Miss Helen is safe from me. I define a short man as not coming to Miss Helen's nose. I am there, my lord. Nearly."

Helen was batting at the smoke as well. "I thought you told him that I was married, Flock, and thus his ardor was sufficiently cooled."

"He informed me that if you weren't married to a Frenchman, you had no idea what *l'amour*

58

could possibly be like."

Lord Beecham laughed and lifted the dome from the blackened buttock of beef. More smoke wafted out. "Miss Mayberry, regard a Frenchman's masterpiece. World fire — it is too much."

"I don't think I will ever look at a buttock of beef again the same way," Helen said.

There was a stain of ashes on her nose, a small streak down her cheek. Lord Beecham lightly rubbed it off with his fingertip.

He said close to her hair, which smelled a bit like smoke, "Not only am I to your nose, I can even see the ribbons you've threaded through your hair."

Flock cleared his throat. "I believe, Miss Helen, that you should repair once again to the drawing room. I will bring what food is edible and you will dine there. However, I must first go outside, where Monsieur Jerome is very probably pacing nervously, the poor Frog, to tell him that his *feu du monde* was an unexpected surprise."

"Bring more champagne," said Lord Prith. "It is one of those dark moments."

5

Lord Beecham stretched out in his bed, his head pillowed on his arms, and watched the thin, lazy light from the one candle beside him curl upward to form vague outlines of exotic shapes above his head.

It was the strangest thing. Tucked in among those weaving, ever-changing shapes above him he again saw Helen Mayberry with her father's bright-red wool scarf tied around her neck, the knot right in the middle of her breasts. He had wanted to laugh his head off, but managed to hold back, nearly choking when he swallowed the wrong way.

She had worn that ridiculous scarf the entire evening, tied between her breasts, its tails hanging down nearly to her thighs. They had finally dined on potatoes, beautifully stewed and smoked, three different oyster dishes, also richly and unintentionally smoked, and some dressed green beans that looked gray. Lord Prith had sighed. The damned Frog chef was always making Helen oyster dishes, he told Lord Beecham, to tantalize her more base desires. He supposed that Helen had base desires, but understandably he did not like to think of his only precious little girl in that light.

"Poor Jerome," Helen had said, taking her father's words in affectionate stride. "Flock said he has written to all his relatives in France to learn more recipes for oysters. Since we are at war with France, I doubt he will be receiving additional cooking instructions anytime soon, at least, I hope, not until after we have left London."

Lord Beecham nearly laughed again, but caught himself in time. "Perhaps he needs a touch of discipline," he said after swallowing a singularly doughy bite of a roll that was so filled with smoke it turned the butter black.

"Eh?" said Lord Prith. "What is this, boy? You know about discipline?"

"Certainly, sir. I am an Englishman."

But there had been no further discussion of discipline because Flock had come into the drawing room at that moment to inform his lordship that it was time for their walk. Lord Prith shook Lord Beecham's hand and bade him good night, kissed his daughter and bade her sleep well, straightened the red wool scarf around her neck, and left the drawing room, whistling. It was close, but Lord Prith's head missed the lintel by a good inch.

"Flock and my father take a twenty-minute walk every night that it isn't raining. It was getting late and Flock needs his sleep. Nine hours a night, he tells my father."

She laughed, shook her head, and showed him out not five minutes later.

And now he was in bed, lying there, seeing her

twining in and out of those damned smoky shapes over his head in his bedchamber. She was still wearing her father's red wool scarf and he was still thinking about inching his fingers down beneath that lovely ivory gown of hers to touch her warm flesh.

"She will give me excellent sport," he said, blew a kiss to Helen in and among the shadows overhead, blew out the candle, and smiled as he watched the dash of candle smoke explode into the air.

Lord Beecham knew women. He knew strategy. He was a master hunter.

He made no effort to see Miss Helen Mayberry for three days.

On Thursday afternoon the small park across from Lord Beecham's town house on Grosvenor Square was rioting with spring flowers — sunny daffodils, pale lavender lilacs, creamy red azaleas. There were other richly bloomed flowers peeking out here and there, but he didn't know what they were called. It was a beautiful day, and he decided he had worked enough on the estate accounts. He informed his secretary, Pliny Blunder (an unfortunate appellation that the man did his best to overcome by working harder than any three secretaries in London), to leave him alone, that he was pale from being locked up in this damned estate room for so long and that he was going riding.

Pliny didn't want him to quit working, however, having produced a thick pile of accounts and correspondence that would surely prove his worth, if only his lordship would put off — for just another hour, maybe two — his quite unnecessary ride in the park.

"My lord, you are not at all pale. Look yon at the accounts for Paledowns. Well, not really that many accounts from tradesmen and that sort of thing, but I have many recommendations, my lord, that have added excellent bulk to the pile."

"Recommendations, Blunder?"

"Yes, my lord. Your aunt Mabel is so very frugal that now she is refusing to buy new sheets even after Lord Hilton put his foot through one when he was visiting just last month."

"Prepare a very civil letter to my aunt Mabel telling her that you are ordering new linen and it will be delivered to her."

"But my lord, I know nothing about linen."

"That is why God created housekeepers, Blunder. Speak to Mrs. Glass. Now you will leave me alone. You may torture me tomorrow morning, but not before ten o'clock, do you understand me?"

"I understand, my lord, but I cannot be happy about it."

"Get Burney to saddle up Luther now, Blunder. Run to the stables — you are on the pale side yourself — to inform him. I am leaving right now. My eyes are crossing, my fingers are numb, my brain is an ascending balloon — all hot air. Leave me alone."

Pliny Blunder sighed deeply and, taking his master at his word, ran out of the estate room. For the first time, Lord Beecham noticed that his secretary was on the short side. So short that he would fall in love on the spot with Miss Helen Mayberry, as it seemed all short men who saw her did?

Lord Beecham threw up his hands, snagged his riding crop and jacket from his acting butler, Claude the footman, because Mr. Crittaker, the butler at Heatherington House since before Lord Beecham had come into this world, had finally died peacefully in his lovely room on the third floor with Mrs. Glass on his left side and Lord Beecham on his right side. All the other servants were ranged in a line according to rank, from right to left at the foot of his bed. Mr. Crittaker's last words had been: "The upstairs maid should not be standing next to the tweeny, my lord. Claude, you must do better than this."

"Er, have a nice ride, my lord."

"Thank you, Claude. How are you doing with the polishing of the silverware?"

Claude's narrow shoulders rounded themselves. "My fingers are rubbed raw, my lord. It is beyond me how Old Crit ever got those spoons so shiny you could see your own dear ma's heavenly soul shining back up at you."

"Keep trying, Claude. Speak to Mrs. Glass."

"Old Crit always said that a housekeeper, being a female and all, had no notion of how to provide a good polish, my lord."

"Old Crit was from the last century, Claude. Bring yourself up to modern times."

"Mrs. Glass doesn't like me, my lord. She will not tell me the proper silver procedure."

"She simply misses Crittaker. She will adjust, if you are properly deferential."

"But Old Crit said —"

I am surely in Bedlam, Lord Beecham thought, waving Claude away. He walked down the front steps of his town house and turned right toward the small stables, set beneath newly leafing oak trees, some twenty feet from the house.

Lord Beecham would say one thing for Blunder — when he set his mind to something — he got it done quickly. Luther, his big, mean, graceful gelding, was saddled and waiting for him.

He was enjoying the cool spring air on his face as he cantered through the park. He waved to friends, paused to speak to ladies, who laughed and waved at him from their landaus, and then spotted Reverend Older. The two gentlemen reined in and rode side by side for a while. Reverend Older was a distinguished and popular churchman, a fine orator, an eccentric, and a horse-racing fanatic, who, Lord Beecham had heard from a St. Jude sexton whom the reverend had fleeced, spent some of the money from the collection plate to wager on the races. Reverend Older had called it a rotten lie and given the sexton a bloody nose.

"I am thinking about traveling down to the McCaulty racetrack next week," Reverend Older said. "Not on Sunday, of course. That is the one day I am simply too busy."

"True enough," said Lord Beecham, trying not to laugh between Luther's big bay ears. Was this the way it would be from now on? There would be a laugh behind every tree to ambush him? He supposed he could accustom himself. "I didn't know you had any interest in the cat races, sir, just horse races."

"Ah, the little nits can run faster than the wind, my boy. The trick is to keep them focused, many times difficult since they get distracted so easily. Have you ever attended a cat race?"

Lord Beecham shook his head. "Not yet. Perhaps one day. A friend of mine, Rohan Carrington, Baron Mountvale, is one of the major patrons of the cat races."

"Yes, indeed. His racing cats win regularly. Also two of the preeminent cat trainers, the Harker brothers, are gardeners at Mountvale's country estate. That is certainly to his advantage."

Everyone had heard of the cat races at the famous McCaulty racetrack. Actually, huge sums of money were won and lost at the cat races. Lord Beecham, however, couldn't imagine such a thing.

Lord Beecham had been to one horse race in his life — at the racetrack in York — and had found it a dead bore. He had even won a hundred pounds betting on a horse he had never heard of, but the horse's name had appealed to him. It was Muddy Boy, a huge, rawboned gelding who looked more vicious than his great-aunt Honoraria when she had caught him as a lad walking behind her and pulling stuffed birds out of the massive wig she wore.

"True enough. I once stayed with Rohan Carrington for the cat races. Nearly lost my clerical collar when a thin little white tube of a cat streaked past the favorite — and the racer I had laid fifty guineas on — in the home stretch."

They rode alone together for some minutes before Reverend Older, sawing on his horse's reins, shouted, "Oh my! I very nearly forgot. The dear ladies of Montpelier Place are giving me a tea this afternoon and I must attend. I can't disappoint the sweet dears. I am even thinking of marrying one of them."

Now this was a shock. Reverend Older also had something of a reputation, not for debauchery, naturally, but the fact was that over the years, the good reverend, in addition to all his other achievements, had become an accomplished flirt.

"Which good lady, sir?"

"Why Lilac Murcheson, Lady Chomley. You remember Chomley, don't you, Spenser? He was a loose-mouthed codbrain who thankfully croaked it before he had gone through his fortune. As I recall, he fondled a man's wife in the very nave of my church, and the husband was forced to call him out. Put a bullet neatly through his forehead. Lilac's son gave her a neat little stud in Wessex. I fancy I will retire there when the holy words dry up in my brain, and breed my own horses one of these years."

Lord Beecham just shook his head as he watched Reverend Older canter away, his bottom bouncing up and down on the saddle. It had to be painful. He couldn't imagine the reverend no longer exhorting sinners from his pulpit, then laughing when the choirmaster tripped on his gown and fell into the organist, who brought forth a chord that had the entire congregation covering their ears.

He just could not understand how his own father and Reverend Older could have possibly been friends. The reverend Older was eccentric and enjoyed betting perhaps a bit too much, but he seemed to be awash in good humor and honor, unlike Gilbert Heatherington, Lord Beecham's sire.

He breathed in deeply as he turned Luther off the well-trod path into an area of the park that would allow him to gallop for just a bit. "All right, Luther," he said close to his stallion's ear, "do what you will."

Luther, nothing loath, stretched his neck, kicked back his hind legs, and shot forward. Lord Beecham laughed aloud, a good clean sound and he liked the feel of it. He leaned down close to Luther's neck, breathing in his horse's clean wild sweat. "I might enjoy watching you race," he said. "You could have raced that damned Brutus into the ground. If you do ever race, I will ride you myself."

He was thinking that perhaps he should give racing another chance when suddenly, without a hint of warning, a female body slammed into him from out of nowhere and sent him crashing to the ground.

He saw white bursts of light. He couldn't breathe. A weight was crushing him.

The lights dimmed. He swallowed. He slit open his eyes, all he could manage. Miss Helen Mayberry was all in a heap on top of him. A thick blond braid was wrapped around his face. Her riding hat tipped over her right eye. Her nose wasn't an inch above his.

"Oh, dear, are you all right, Lord Beecham? Please say something. Can you look at me?"

His wits were still on the jagged side, his brain hovered in the ether. He couldn't quite breathe yet and he wondered if his leg was broken. But he was a man of strong parts, strong will, and he realized his leg wasn't broken, thankfully, just twisted a bit. Finally, not two minutes later, he managed to blink a couple of times and focus on the lovely face above his.

"Did I not tell you that I wouldn't care for the process of you bringing me down, Miss Mayberry? Just the end result?"

"But, sir, my horse threw me. I was riding happily along, saw you out of the corner of my eye, started to wave at you, and just in that split second, a bee stung my poor mare on the neck, she raced up close to you, and then tossed me right into you. It was all a ghastly accident. I haven't broken anything, have I?"

"My leg was in question for a bit, but I think no bones are snapped in two. Please remove yourself, Miss Mayberry. If you remain where you are, then I will probably get myself back together well enough to start caressing you. My hands are very close to your hips as we speak. Do you want to be caressed in the park? Or would a lady from East Anglia shrink from that?"

"It would be a novel form of discipline," Helen said slowly, still not an inch from his face. She felt all of him beneath her. He felt quite nice.

He lightly touched her chin with his fingertips. "Actually, I would call it discipline only if the pleasure you took from me was balanced by the imminent chance of discovery by one of society's matrons, say, for example, Sally Jersey. Have you met Sally?"

"No, but I fancy that my father would like to meet her. I understand she adores champagne."

"It's true. I can even see them together. Yes, there he is, carrying her under his right arm, and she has a bottle of champagne tucked close. Now my body has recovered from its appalling shock, Miss Mayberry, and is more than eager to commence."

"I had no choice, Lord Beecham. I had to act. You have kept your distance for three days. I suppose you were punishing me."

He lightly touched his hands to her hips. She jumped, then didn't move a muscle. "Not at all, Miss Mayberry. It is psychological discipline. I am a master at it."

She felt him against her belly, felt his large hands now caressing her bottom, and quickly rolled off him. She imagined he was a master at many things. She came up, clasping her arms around her knees.

He took a very deep breath, then whistled. Luther, cropping grass some ten yards away, looked up and whinnied. "No, stay there, boy," he called. "Where is your horse, Miss Mayberry?"

She whistled through her teeth, just like a boy, louder than he had whistled. A chestnut mare with a white star on her forehead and four white socks cantered over to within a foot of them and pulled up sharp.

He had never heard a woman do that before in his life. She had whistled louder, he thought, than he had been able to, even as a boy, when no one could best him at it.

No, surely that was impossible. She was a big girl with big lungs, but he was a man. He decided he would practice when he was alone. "Your hair is falling down," he said, pulling up a spike of grass and chewing on it.

She calmly wound the thick braid of hair round and round her head, tucked it into itself, then smashed her riding hat down over it.

"My mare's name is Eleanor, named after the

wife of King Edward the First."

"You are a historian, Miss Mayberry?"

"In a manner of speaking, sir."

"I was lucky this time, Miss Mayberry. I don't believe you broke anything when you landed on me. Come now, what did you really do, hurl yourself off Eleanor's back?"

"Yes. It gave me a bit of a scare. I was surprised you didn't hear me."

"I was hunkered down against Luther's neck, breathing in his sweat and thinking about my mistress and the many ways she teases me to distraction."

Her voice was colder than the wooden floor beneath his bare feet in February when she said, "You don't currently have a mistress."

"Why don't you give me a list of your sources and I can provide them accurate information for you?"

She waved her gloved fist under his nose. "Why haven't you come to see me, damn you? Why haven't you even sent me some nice posies, a poem praising my eyebrows, anything that gentlemen regularly do? It has been three days."

He chewed on the grass, gave her a lazy smile, and leaned back, bracing himself on his elbows. "I am a man, Miss Mayberry. I do the chasing."

She rose very slowly to stand over him, her hands on her hips. "There was no chasing. You weren't doing anything at all."

"Psychological discipline. I would have acted when I felt it was appropriate. I am much better at this form of discipline than you are, Miss Mayberry. I would never take the chance of killing my prey, as you just tried to do. A mathematician could have told you that the weight of such a big girl hurtling through the air would flatten most poor mortals, rendering them beyond earthly cares. Behold me. Even I am nearly expired, and I am a very large male mortal."

"You are no such thing. I mean, you are large, but you are not nearly dead. You are whining, Lord Beecham. It is not appealing."

He sighed. "I fear you are right. The next time you choose to do the chasing, however, I would ask that you consider something along a more intellectual, rather than physical, approach."

"I didn't have time to think of anything else. You see, my father informed me over breakfast this morning — yes, the dining room still reeks of smoke — that he wishes to return home next week."

"Ah, then, that certainly changes things. That forces my hand." He rose, dusted himself off, and straightened her hat, tucking more hair beneath it. Three small grapes decorating her bonnet had come untwisted and were hanging by the side of her cheek. He gently pulled them off and slipped them into his jacket pocket. "Very well, Miss Mayberry, would you like me to bed you and teach you a bit about my sort of discipline before you hark back to the country to all your potbellied squires and all the various and sundry short men who swoon at the sight of you?"

Her mare lightly pushed her nose against her back. Helen laughed, turned, and patted her. "It's all right, Eleanor, he is just being outrageous and intriguing me. I would be disappointed with anything less." With those words, she turned back to him. "Lord Beecham, I don't want you for a lover."

A dark eyebrow shot up a good inch. "I beg your pardon, Miss Mayberry? You wanted to meet me, you threw yourself at me; your ease with men and all their aberrations is remarkable, at least for a woman. Of course, you are rather long in the tooth, so you have had time to hone your skills. If you don't want me for a lover, then what do you want me for?"

"I want you for a partner."

6

Now this was a kicker. A woman's partner? He couldn't imagine such a thing. "How very odd. A partner, you said, Miss Mayberry, not a lover? Did you happen to rattle your brains when you crashed yourself into me?"

"Not at all. I have been thinking about this since the first time Alexandra Sherbrooke mentioned your name. I thought, a man with such a demanding sort of life must be quite excellent at devising strategies and organizing details and proper plans so he does not ever find himself at the end when he should be in the middle. You must perform continually at the most rigorously high standards to keep yourself in business, so to speak."

"You won't accept that I am simply quite gifted?"

"Oh, yes, there is no doubt in my mind about that. I daresay it's a talent that most men would barter all their earthly belongings to have in a quite small measure. You have talent aplenty, Lord Beecham. But don't you see? Your gift, your talent, is only the beginning. You must have all the other attributes as well to keep your reputation at such a high level."

"Let me see if I have got this correct. You want me to be your partner because I am a fine strategist, I can organize details well, and I always perform at a high level. Does that cover it?"

"Very nearly."

"I assume you are referring to my performance with the fairer sex?"

"Naturally. But what's most important, Lord Beecham, is that you set your sights on a goal and you won't give up until you have attained it. I am right about that, aren't I?"

"There is no way you could know that," he said slowly, staring her straight in the eye since he was only two inches taller than she. He suddenly felt as if he were walking down the street, stark naked, holding an umbrella over his head. Everyone was pointing at him. Everyone knew exactly who and what he was — and what he was was decidedly strange. "That is ridiculous. You are merely guessing."

"Well, you see, I met your Mr. Blunder two days ago. No, don't go home and thrash him. Mr. Blunder holds you in such high esteem it nearly made my stomach cramp. His worship of you positively spews from his mouth. All he needs is a listener. He admires you vastly."

"The damned man wants to work me to death."

"He told me it was amazing what you could grasp with only the most scant of explanations."

"I am beginning to feel ill myself."

"He said when you set your sights on something, normally — in his experience at least — it was a lady. But if it wasn't a lady, then it could be a problem you wished to solve, a situation you wished to resolve, two enemies you wished to bring together to become friends, a political compromise to keep two sides together, whatever. He said you never faltered, never settled for half measures or defeat. Mr. Blunder believes you can do just about anything, my lord."

"Ah, I see now how you so easily pried him open. You took him to Gunther's, didn't you?"

"Why, yes, his favorite ice is raspberry. I saw him standing there, in front of Gunther's, with the look of a man who would give his last guinea for just one lick. He was very easy, truth be told. He kept eating and talking. And I kept ordering more ices for him and listening. Perhaps I ate an ice or two myself."

"When I came riding today," he said slowly, looking around at the half dozen people strolling through the park around them, "I hadn't expected any of this. Even Reverend Older, a delicious old eccentric, doesn't compare to you. I am not used to surprises of this sort, Miss Mayberry."

"Just wait until your birthday, my lord."

He laughed, a full, rich laugh that wafted through all the splendid old oak and maple trees surrounding them. It was getting easier, sounding positively natural now, this magnificent laugh of his. Luther raised his head and snorted. Eleanor started toward him. He lifted his hand and she rubbed her nose against his palm.

He looked over at Miss Helen Mayberry — her dark-blue riding skirt stained and wrinkled, her riding hat askew, the little bunch of grapes in his jacket pocket — and said, "What if I told you I would prefer to be your lover rather than your partner?"

She took a step closer to him and stared him straight in the eye. "Have you no curiosity, my lord? Don't you wish to know what this is all about? Don't you wonder why I, a woman of infinite resource, am in need of a partner?"

"No."

It was her turn to laugh. "I will say this for you, sir — you are certainly not short."

"As in I haven't swooned at your feet?"

"I can't imagine you ever swooning at anyone's feet."

"I haven't. Now, tell me what use you have for me, as your partner."

She was searching his face, for signs, he supposed, that he would give her a full hearing. "Talk to me, Miss Mayberry."

"This will take a while. May we sit over on that bench?"

She walked beside him, her stride as long as his, at least in her riding habit. Blond hair was creeping out from beneath her riding hat. He stopped her and tucked it back under. Then he took her chin in his palm and turned her to face him. He studied her upturned face. He rubbed a bit of dirt from her cheek. He brushed his palm down the back of her riding habit, smoothing out

78

wrinkles. There were also wrinkles down the front of her that needed smoothing, but he controlled himself. "There, you are once again presentable. A partner — something I had never considered. What possibly could a lady involve herself in that would require a partner?"

She sat down, smoothing the front of her own gown and skirts. "It isn't that I really need a partner, it is just that I need a pair of new eyes, and behind those new eyes I require a very sharp brain that would bring new ideas, new perspective. You would bring me that and possibly more."

"Tell me what you are involved in, Miss Mayberry."

"I told you that I own an inn in Court Hammering called King Edward's Lamp."

"Yes, you told me. Somewhat unusual occupation for a lady, but I suspect you would try your hand at whatever interested you. Why do you call your inn King Edward's Lamp?"

"I knew you would immediately peel the bark from the tree. I knew I was right about you. There is such a lamp, you know, called King Edward's Lamp. At least I believe with all my heart there is. I discovered the myth of the lamp when I was still in the schoolroom. My father happened to come across this ancient text in an old chest shoved into the corner of a friend's library. The friend had died and bequeathed all the contents of his library to my father. It was written in very old French, but I finally managed to get it translated."

She was thinking about that manuscript and that lamp, he thought, looking at her face. She was looking beyond him, beyond the park, to something he couldn't see or feel, something that moved her unbearably.

"Tell me," he said quietly.

"Actually, I don't know all that much, but enough, truly. It was an account written by a Knight Templar toward the end of the thirteenth century, telling how he had broken his vows to his order because of his love for his infant son. It seems that King Edward saved the boy's life when three Saracen warriors were going to spit him and his servants on their swords. The boy was wounded when Edward rescued him. The king took the boy up before him on his war horse and rode with him back to his camp, which wasn't far from a huge Templar stronghold.

"The Templar wrote that when he arrived at the king's camp, he found his small son in the queen's arms, being fed by her own hand, his wounds attended to. Such was his gratitude that he broke his vow of secrecy he wrote, giving the king a golden lamp that would make him the most powerful man in the world.

"Then he took his son and left the king's encampment. The last line written in the manuscript was the plea for forgiveness for his crime against his order."

"I remember hearing of a golden lamp," Lord Beecham said slowly, looking down at his clasped hands between his buckskinned knees, "very, very old, that came to England and then was lost. Some old scholar at Oxford spoke of it to me. I had forgotten. But, Miss Mayberry, even that scholar was not at all certain that it wasn't just another myth, a strange tale woven in, like so many other strange tales, with all the happenings in the Holy Land."

"I am willing to concede that the Crusades were extraordinarily brutal, that what men did to men will never again happen. But this is magic."

"I don't believe in magic."

"I know it exists," she said, leaning closer, her gloved hand on his arm. "I do not know if it is indeed some sort of magic, but I believe it to be. Otherwise why would the Knight Templar give it to King Edward? If not magic, then what is the lamp? Surely he would not give the king a simple lamp to thank him for saving his son. More than that, where is it?"

He continued to look at her, one eyebrow raised, saying nothing.

She drew a deep breath. "I finally found another reference to it six years ago. It was in the old Norman church in Aldeburgh that sits atop a cliff right above the sea. I have made friends with a good many churchmen and scholars over the years, telling them only that I am fascinated by myths that relate to the crusade made by King Edward the First.

"The vicar, Mr. Gilliam, in Aldeburgh told me that he and his curate had been digging through the remains in the old Norman church after there was a mud slide. He said he had found some very old parchments he believed would interest me.

"They were written in Latin. Finally, I was able to translate them well enough to realize that they were about the lamp. I tell you, Lord Beecham, I thought my heart would burst I was so excited. Robert Burnell, the secretary to King Edward, wrote them. I know all about Burnell. He was very smart, cynical yet tolerant of his fellow man, very devoted to the king. He says the king didn't know what to do with the lamp, that he was at once afraid of its power and on the other hand disbelieving that it was anything more than just a Saracen lamp that was old and worn, that for some reason had come to be prized by the Templars and hidden away by them. He said he had never seen the lamp do anything at all until —"

"What have we here?"

They looked up to see Jason Fleming, Baron Crowley, standing right in front of them, lightly tapping his riding crop against his right boot.

Lord Beecham didn't like Crowley, an older man who knew too much and appeared to make a lot of money off what he knew. He drank too much, gambled too much, and wenched until he should have dropped over dead from the French pox, but he hadn't yet done so. He habitually wore a sneer that made Lord Beecham want to smash him in the nose.

He gave the man an emotionless look,

nodded, and said shortly, "Crowley."

"Who is the lovely lady, Beecham?"

"No one to interest you, Crowley. Your horse looks restless."

"I have seen you, my dear. I believe it was just last week at the Sanderling ball. You were with Alexandra Sherbrooke. Everyone remarked upon your rather obvious attributes."

Helen, who had not entertained a single notion about like or dislike of this intruder, said immediately, "My attributes might be obvious, sir, but your rudeness is even more apparent. Indeed, it is rather transparent."

Lord Crowley took a step back. His well-formed mouth grew ugly in its sneer. "Is this your first assignation with Lord Beecham, my dear? I beg you to have a care. Beecham is a dangerous man. He won't treat you as well as I would." He bowed. "I am Crowley, you know. And you are?"

She smiled up at him, showing lots of white, locked teeth. "I am a lady, sir."

"Go away, Crowley. The lady and I are busy."

"Busy doing what?"

Lord Beecham rose slowly. He eyed Lord Crowley for a very long time. The man fidgeted. "Actually I will tell you, Crowley. The lady and I are partners."

"Partners in what?"

"That is not any of your affair. Go away, Crowley."

"You begin to interest me, Beecham." Then

he gave a small salute to Helen with his riding crop, turned, and gracefully mounted his horse.

"Stay away from him," Lord Beecham said, looking after Crowley until he disappeared from view. "I have the reputation of a seducer, surely a harmless pursuit when all is said and done. Lord Crowley has a flair for evil."

"What sort of evil?"

Lord Beecham said briefly, "He feeds on helplessness. Now, where were we?"

"Robert Burnell and the lamp. He said he'd never seen it do anything save just sit there and let the king and queen rub it endlessly until Eleanor grew violently ill in the fall of 1279. Some sort of fever was raging through London, and the queen, along with three of her ladies, became very ill. All of the ladies died. The king was distraught. He took the lamp — it was a last resort, Burnell wrote, because the physicians had given up — and he put it in Eleanor's arms." She shuddered.

"Well, what happened?"

"She survived."

Lord Beecham said slowly, "As I recall, Queen Eleanor bore more children that I can count. If she could survive all that childbirth, it seems to me that surviving a fever would be nothing to her."

"She was pregnant nearly every year," Helen admitted, "but still, the fever was virulent, and it did kill all three of her ladies. Don't be so cynical, sir."

"What did Burnell write about that?"

"He claimed that the king wrapped the lamp in a bolt of exquisite crimson velvet from Genoa and set it beneath glass. He proclaimed the lamp magic and set guards around it. Then one morning, the king unwrapped the velvet to look at the lamp.

"It was gone. In its place was a silver lamp, ugly and quite new. The king went on a rampage. The guards were questioned, brutally. No one admitted anything. Then, the next morning, the gold lamp was back. Everyone believed that the guard who had stolen it had been so frightened that he simply returned it.

"But you see, it happened again the next week. One morning the gold lamp was gone and in its place was the ugly silver lamp. The following morning, the gold one was back."

"Where did the lamp go?" Lord Beechem asked. "What magic made it disappear only to reappear?"

"King Edward brought in scholars, Burnell wrote, but none of them could figure it out. The king himself even slept by the lamp for a week, to guard it. The same thing happened. The lamp disappeared, then reappeared. Everyone proclaimed the lamp to be magic. Churchmen said it was evil. They wanted it destroyed. The king refused, saying it had saved his queen.

"Finally, Burnell wrote, the king, because of the pressure from the Church, buried the lamp near Aldeburgh, right on the coast. Supposedly when the queen was ill again, he sent men to fetch it. They reported that they could not find it. The queen died. It seems that the lamp disappeared."

"Which of Burnell's versions do you prefer?"

"I believe the king buried it in Aldeburgh. Why else would Burnell write about its being there? I think the men who were sent to bring it back simply didn't go to the right place. It only makes sense, don't you think?"

"The lamp could simply have disappeared again. You have searched?"

"I bought the old Norman church and the land surrounding it."

He raised an eyebrow to that.

"No, my father didn't buy it for me. I earn my own way, Lord Beecham. I run an excellent inn."

"How do you propose that you and I proceed? You have found two accounts about the lamp. I will concede, for the sake of argument, that it did exist; its properties, however, are quite murky. You have doubtless sifted through every grain of sand to find more clues. What now?"

"There is something else, but I don't want to tell you until you agree to be my partner. I haven't even told my father."

She had caught him with that bait. He sat forward, his eyes intent on her face. She was reeling him in quite nicely.

"What is it?"

Helen looked at him for a very long time, then

said, "Will you be my partner? Will you help me find the lamp?"

He thought about his life until his thirty-third year. There were black clouds strewn throughout the years, particularly the young years, when his father had been alive. But surely everyone had tragedy or appalling situations to deal with. Perhaps his were blacker than most, carved more deeply into his soul. Perhaps his endless, relentless search for pleasure and its immediacy and its anticipation, its urgency, had kept him from succumbing to the black pit that he knew yawned at his feet.

No, he was being a fool. His life was in his control now, at least most of it. He enjoyed his pleasures, the women who favored him with their attention and their bodies.

He sat there and pondered. A magic lamp given to King Edward I by a Knight Templar. The chances of such a lamp's even existing in the first place were very close to none at all in his mind. And this same magic lamp that couldn't possibly exist was hidden somewhere in England, now, in modern times?

It was impossible. It was a chimera, a dream, nothing more. And he shook his head even as he said, "I will be your partner, Miss Mayberry. Now tell me what else you have discovered about the lamp."

She stuck out her hand and he shook it.

"All right. Now, tell me."

7

Helen leaned very close to him and whispered, "Not three months ago when I was in Aldeburgh, again searching as I have searched for the past six years, there had been a vicious storm that had destroyed parts of the beach just the week before. It had even torn away parts of cliffs. I found a small cave, uncovered by the storm.

"At the very back of the cave an iron cask had been dumped over onto a ledge. There was a hole in the wall where it had been hidden. Inside the cask was a rolled piece of leather, barely holding itself together. I don't know what language is written on that scroll, but it is very, very old."

"You've taken it to none of the medieval scholars at Cambridge?"

"Oh, no, that would surely be my last resort. I want you to look at it, Lord Beecham. I want you to translate it. It would be your first act as my partner."

He said very slowly, "How did you find out that I spent two years at Oxford studying the medieval parchments and manuscripts vaulted there, specifically the ones brought back from the Holy Land to England? You are not thinking about laying this at Blunder's door, are you? He couldn't have told you about my studies at

Oxford. He has no idea."

"One of the churchmen once told me about you. His brother taught you at Oxford some twelve years ago. Sir Giles —"

"— Gilliam," Lord Beecham said, looking inward, remembering those exciting days when there was a discovery around each corner, on each page of some precious bit of parchment that Sir Giles had managed to unearth from the Oxford vaults.

"Yes. His churchman brother is Lockleer Gilliam, a vicar in Dereham. He married my father and mother once, about two years before she died."

"What are you talking about?"

"Oh, I forgot. My father is a vastly romantic gentleman. He wed my mother on three different occasions. Vicar Gilliam is a man of flexible mind and infinite kindness. He and my father became great friends."

"But why did you not simply take the writings to Oxford to Sir Giles Gilliam?"

"He died last year."

"I didn't know," Lord Beecham said, and he felt a blow of guilt so swift and powerful it nearly bowed him to his knees. He hadn't heard. No one had bothered to tell him because — because he was nothing more than a pleasure-seeking nobleman who didn't give a damn about anything other than his own gratification. He looked down to see her hand on his arm.

"I'm sorry," she said. "I met Sir Giles once at

his brother's vicarage in Dereham. He was always talking, only it wasn't to any of us. He was conversing with people who lived back then, in thirteenth-century England, and he was explaining to them that he needed to know more about this or that. Then, and I swear this to you, he would pause and it seemed that he was listening to someone speak who wasn't there.

"The vicar told me not to pay any attention to Sir Giles. He said, however, that after Sir Giles's conversations he wrote the most remarkable documents."

Helen clearly saw Sir Giles, his head cocked to one side, listening intently to a shelf of books, a picture on a wall, a carpet at his feet. "It was disconcerting. When Sir Giles finally realized I was there with his brother, he said, and I will never forget this, 'How magnificent you are. But that is not important. What is important is that you not allow your mind to become mulch.' "

Lord Beecham laughed, a free, full-bodied laugh this time that resonated throughout his head and into the air around him. It brought back marvelous memories of a young man of twenty, so very eager to learn everything Sir Giles knew. And Sir Giles had even told him once, patting his shoulder, that he was so very bright, and that Sir Giles was thankful that Spenser had given his brain over to him, Sir Giles. Ah, the medieval mind, there was nothing like it, Sir Giles would say, then drink down a snifter of delicious smuggled French brandy.

But Spenser hadn't remained at Oxford. His father had died, and he had become seventh Baron Valesdale and fifth Viscount Beecham.

He had left Oxford at the age of twenty-one. And become a nobleman.

"I remember," Lord Beecham said, his voice rich with memory, "Sir Giles once telling me that the Catholic Church was quite wrong. A man didn't need to give up lust in order to be obedient and holy and committed to God. He needed only to truly mean both his vows to God and his vows to a woman, and his life would be balanced and no part of him would ever wither."

"I fancy that his brother, Vicar Lockleer, is relieved to be Church of England," Helen said, smiling. "He has two children. His wife died last year, but he loved her very much. He is also a very practical man, unlike his learned brother.

"He didn't know how to begin to translate the scroll. That was when he recommended you. What do you think, Lord Beecham?"

He was silent for the longest time. The big girl sitting beside him jumped up once, patted Eleanor's nose, then returned and sat down. She began to tap her foot. She whistled.

"I have forgotten so very much," he said at last.

"It won't matter. You'll see," she said, still now, all her attention focused on him. "The vicar now has many of the translations, texts, and notes his brother made at Oxford. Perhaps there will be enough to help you remember."

He said as he turned to take her hands between his. "I have never been a woman's partner before. This should prove interesting. I want to see that iron cask and the leather scroll."

"The iron cask is old, very old. Medieval? Very possibly. Perhaps even older. As for the leather, I am very afraid that it will crumble if we work with it very much."

"We will take the greatest care."

She rose and shook out her skirts. She gave him a brilliant smile. "Let's go home to Court Hammering."

Lord Beecham and Miss Mayberry elected to ride, since it was a beautiful, warm day. Lord Prith and Flock followed in the carriage behind them. Engulfed in their carriage dust in the second carriage was Lord Beecham's valet, Nettle, and Teeny, Helen's maid. He had given Pliny Blunder a short congé, telling him to exercise his wit on the seashore in Folkstone, where his parents lived. Lord Beecham had noted before they left that Nettle was casting interested looks at Teeny, much to Flock's annoyance. At least Flock was riding with his master. That should keep poor Nettle safe.

As for Helen, she just couldn't seem to stop singing. Everything was working out so very well. Her enthusiasm was catching, and even her father, Lord Prith, said to Flock, "There is a song in the air, Flock. It makes my thoughts turn to champagne and the trappings. I fancy to attend another wedding. The last one was charming, surely it was, and the champagne was excellent. I just wish I'd known the participants."

"Ah, it was Lord and Lady St. Cyre."

"That's right, Gray and Jack. Flock, you must find me a wedding where the principals are known to me so that I can trade jests with the bride and groom while we are drinking champagne. Then I will be dancing about and singing at the top of my lungs, just like my lovely little daughter is right this moment. It was always so. Put Helen atop a horse, provide a sunny day, and she's singing."

"Consider it done, my lord," Flock said, looking out the carriage window to see Miss Helen laughing now, her hand on Lord Beecham's arm. He didn't think the sunny day was the main reason for Miss Helen's high spirits. Lord Beecham was a man of vast experience, a man who knew what was what, particularly when the what had to do with women. On the other hand, it didn't make much sense to worry about Miss Helen. She had three fellows working for her at her inn. All of them held her in awe. All of them, he suspected, were also deliciously afraid of her. If there was going to be any goose or gander sauce, he would lay his groats on Miss Helen.

He turned back to his lordship, whose head was only half an inch from the ceiling of the carriage. Whenever the carriage hit a rut, there was a pained grunt.

"I hope that damned Frog chef, Jerome, isn't sniffing after our trail, eh, Flock?"

"I left the Frog in his kitchen, my lord. I doubt he will intrude on us again."

"Delicious oyster dishes he prepared, though," Lord Prith said, and sighed as he folded his arms over his chest.

"His aim with the oysters wasn't your culinary pleasure, my lord — rather it was his attempt to seduce Miss Helen."

"I know that, Flock. The poor fellow. My father used to say that you should always be careful what you wished for. Just imagine Miss Helen setting her eye on the Frog because he got her attention with his oysters."

"It fair makes my scalp itch, my lord."

Lord Prith actually shuddered.

About twenty feet ahead, Lord Beecham was saying to Helen, "What have you told your father about my entry into your lives?"

"I told him the truth, naturally. The only secret I have ever kept from my father was when I struck young Colton Mason across his shoulders with my riding crop because he had tried to take liberties with my eighteen-year-old person. It was the oddest thing — he really liked it, begged me to hit him again."

"I have heard that some people, men mostly, like that sort of thing, particularly if a woman metes out the blows. If there is a desire for anything at all, you'll find it in the fleshpots of London."

"I believe that is where poor Colton ended up."

"I hope you are not confusing that sort of strange sexual fervor with the application of good clean discipline?"

"Oh, no," she said, her eyes twinkling wickedly at him. "I'm not a fool. At eighteen I realized I was on to something. Certainly whipping is part of it, but there is so much more, don't you agree?"

He would have her explain that to him in great detail, later. "You told your father that I was a medieval manuscript scholar here to translate your leather from the iron cask to help you find King Edward's Lamp?"

"Oh, yes. He just looked at me and finally said, 'Lord Beecham has the look of a man with too much knowledge crammed into his head. I do not know just how ancient that knowledge may be. He is dangerous as well as valuable to you, my girl, make no mistake about that. He is bound to want something other than some dented, hoary lamp.' "

Lord Beecham laughed. "Not so much crammed in my head anymore."

"I believe he was commenting on your current state of knowledge, my lord."

"Fleshpots again."

"Very probably. Do you think you will require something of me other than the lamp?"

He looked thoughtfully between Luther's ears. The road ahead was straight and flat. On either side of the road, the fields were laid out like rich green and yellow squares on a nicely sewn quilt. Yew bushes lined the stone fences that marked the boundaries. It was a warm, breezy day. Every once in a while the strong scent of sheep wafted through the air, just to remind you that this wasn't a beautiful painting or an idealized setting.

"Actually, truth be told, when I first saw you, I wanted you in my bed by early afternoon. It was sunny that day, and I had a very clear picture of you lying naked on your back, your arms out to me. However, when it did not happen, I was not cast down. I decided it would be all right to have you in my bed by nightfall. When that did not happen, I was forced to forgo poor Jerome's remarkable smoked oysters, else I would have become quite mad with unfulfilled lust."

She was laughing so hard that Eleanor whinnied in response and took several side steps.

"You find that amusing, Miss Mayberry? My physical discomfort doesn't make you regret not complying with my very understandable man's lust?"

"I am on the shelf, Lord Beecham. I beg you not to make such jests at my expense."

"I really don't believe you had the gall to say that. You, my girl, know very well that you are quite the most magnificent woman to grace three counties. Your pretense at old age makes me remeasure your level of guile."

"I have no guile to speak of. I am straightforward. I will not give you coy speeches about bedding you at noon or at twilight or at the rise of the moon. No, I will tell you very honestly exactly what I thought when I first saw you, Lord Beecham. I saw you standing in front of me. I stripped off every article of clothing covering your doubtless magnificent self, beginning with that very artfully arranged cravat of yours. I was all the way to your boots before I was pulled from my very pleasant fantasies."

His eyes were nearly crossed.

"Where is your father's carriage?"

"Not more than twenty feet behind us."

"There are quite a few maple trees off just to my left. We could find privacy." Then he sighed deeply; he shook himself. "No, this is ridiculous. I am a man with a man's control. I will not be drawn into your damned woman's fantasies. I will enjoy my own. I can control them more readily."

"Very well," she said, her voice as demure as a schoolgirl's. "Goodness, if I just close my eyes a moment, I see myself now bent over in front of you, and you are sitting down. Your left boot is in my hands and I'm nearly ready to pull it off. I'm looking over my left shoulder, smiling at you, and —"

"You will hold your tongue or I will send Flock out to ride with you and immure myself with your father."

"Victory over a man is nothing at all," she said, and began whistling. "You are such a simple species. Paint you one small picture and you are slavering and shaking, ready to swoon."

He laughed, there was simply nothing else to do. Then he turned in the saddle and gave her a very slow smile. "Trust me, Miss Mayberry. When I have you away from your fond parent, I plan to introduce you to a very intriguing course of discipline."

It was his turn to see her eyes go vague and watch her swallow. He picked a small bit of lint off his riding jacket. "I have always thought that ladies were such easy creatures. They think of me mastering them and I invariably find myself with a very excited female in my arms, begging me to do my worst." He smiled at her. "You may be the discipline mistress of Court Hammering, Miss Mayberry, but I am the master of London. Don't try to compete with me. You will lose."

"I will compete with you," she said slowly, "but just not yet."

"Very well. I agree, not yet. Now, let us see where this ancient leather scroll leads us, Miss Mayberry. As to the rest of it, I will let you know what I wish to do with you, and when."

"Men love to be mastered more than women do."

A dark eyebrow shot up a good inch. "Where did you hear such nonsense as that?"

"It's true."

"We will doubtless see. Someday. If I wish it."

He had routed her. Helen had never before in her life been routed. She had never before met his like, either. He had reduced her to an idiot. She couldn't think of a single thing to say that would improve matters, so she pulled Eleanor back until she was riding beside her father's carriage.

Lord Beecham heard Lord Prith's booming voice asking Helen what the devil she wanted with an old man like him when she could torment a handsome young devil like Lord Beecham. He didn't hear Miss Mayberry's reply, but he could not imagine that it was very complimentary to him.

He began whistling. It took him a good mile before he could get his brain back in harness and focus it away from Miss Helen Mayberry's sublime self.

King Edward's Lamp.

What was it? He had little doubt that some lamp somewhere once existed. Hanging about for six hundred years, however, was a vastly different matter.

King Edward's Lamp was a specific lamp that a Knight Templar gave the king, telling him it would make him the most powerful man in the world. But the only thing that had happened was that Queen Eleanor had gotten well, and the lamp could possibly have had something to do with it.

The only other lamp Lord Beecham knew about was Aladdin's Lamp, a magic lamp from a tale in the *Arabian Nights*, a collection of stories to come out of the Middle Ages. It was one of the thousand and one tales that Queen Scheherazade had told her husband to avoid being put to death after her wedding night. Lord Beecham believed that the royal husband was eventually so overwhelmed by the woman's creative stamina that he canceled the death order.

When Helen rode beside Lord Beecham again, her equilibrium doubtless restored to its usual level of confidence, he spoke aloud what he was thinking. "If we are talking about Aladdin's Lamp, historically it all fits. Back in the Middle Ages, stories like this one were immensely popular all over Europe. It is old, I know. I just don't remember how old."

"It's Persian," Helen said. "From the Persian *Hezar Efsan* or 'Thousand Romances'. I think the magic lamp was based on a real story that had floated about for a good long time before it was ever recorded. And I suspect that the relic we know as King Edward's Lamp is the item that inspired the tale."

He felt something deep inside him, something he had believed long buried, begin to unfurl. It was excitement, the excitement of discovery, of seeking something that wasn't immediately available.

He leaned forward and scratched just beneath Luther's left ear. The horse whinnied and shook his great head. "He likes that. I keep forgetting to do it. The real lamp, without the genie, the shiftless lad, or the evil magician, ended up in the Knight Templar's storehouse of riches in the

Holy Land, only to find its way into the hands of King Edward of England. It made a very long journey."

"Lord Beecham, you are living proof that debauchery doesn't necessarily rot the brain, at least until after you are thirty-three."

"Miss Mayberry, are you mocking me?"

"No, not really." And she was thinking that the slant of his right eyebrow, currently arched at her, was quite fascinating.

"For God's sake, we are having an intellectual discussion here and I am showing off some of my remembered erudition. Did I tell you that I read *A Thousand and One Nights* many times because I set myself the task of learning Arabic?"

"Vicar Gilliam did not know that about you. Arabic? I am very impressed."

"You are mocking me again. I had hoped that after your return from your father's company, you would have dismissed your delightful thoughts of pulling off my boot while you're smiling at me over your shoulder."

"I'm trying."

"Is my other foot set against your bottom?"

"Not yet. I will consider that."

"Good. Now, Miss Mayberry, just perhaps there might be other things to life than simple lust." He laughed aloud and rubbed his gloved hands together. "Bedamned, Miss Mayberry, I do believe I am enjoying having my brain stretched."

She was giving him an odd look. "You really

sound quite different. Splendid, in a way. I know all this, naturally, since I've slept with most of these facts under my pillow for a goodly number of years."

Lord Beecham said, "I even find that I can consider that this lamp, whose origins we don't know, has some sort of magic property. Why not? As Hamlet said, 'There are more things in heaven and earth, Horatio, than are dreamt of in your philosophy.'" He continued after a moment. "I believe in the Holy Grail, after all, in its powers, even though it has been out of our experience since Joseph of Arimathea so carefully hid it.

"But there is a huge difference between the chalice the Lord passed around to his disciples at the Last Supper and a simple lamp that was supposedly hidden in a cave for a shiftless boy to retrieve. It is not cloaked in religious trappings, in the power of the Almighty. There is no higher magic with this lamp, none of the awesome might with which the Holy Grail is imbued."

"Yes," she said and sighed. "I cannot help but agree. Who in the world would make an old lamp magic? For what purpose? That is what I cannot explain."

He found he didn't like her to fold her tent so quickly. "On the other hand, perhaps it is based on something that is real, something that isn't a lamp, but something else."

"Oh, how I hope so." Her voice was very serious. Then she thrust up her chin. "But what?

Oh, the devil, I know it exists, and that is good enough for the present."

He smiled at her. "All right. I will settle for that as well. Now, even if we prove the existence of the lamp, how the devil are we going to find it?"

8

Lord Beecham watched Flock elbow Nettle out of Teeny's path. He had never seen Nettle look so vacuous. He turned away, shaking his head, reached up and clasped his hands around Miss Mayberry's waist and lifted her down, no mean feat.

He said close to her ear, "You are indeed a big girl, Miss Mayberry. But you know, I don't feel a single twinge in my back. Is it happenstance that your weight didn't drop me to my knees? Let me see." And he clasped his hands around her waist again and groaned as he lifted her in front of him. He let her back down very quickly. "At least two inches off the ground. I will say that this time was perhaps more precarious for my poor back, but regardless, I am still smiling, still looking at your mouth, still not bowed like an old man carrying too many sacks of flour. Now, tell me if I will have to protect poor Nettle from Flock. Do you think Flock is going to challenge Nettle to a duel for looking like a half-wit at Teeny? I have never seconded a valet before. It would prove interesting."

"Flock is not only very territorial, he is also desperately in love with Teeny, but she refuses to marry him."

"Why the devil not?"

"Just imagine it, Lord Beecham. Her name would be Teeny Flock. She managed to say it aloud, although she shuddered as it came out of her mouth. I will tell you, she has a point."

"She can change her name to Elizabeth. Elizabeth Flock sounds quite charming."

"I suggested something like that. She said that Teeny was her dear old grandma's name, and she swears that the old witch will drop a hefty curse on her head for the rest of her life if she dares to change it."

"What's her last name now?"

"Bloodbane."

He could only stare at her, repeating slowly, "Her name right now is Teeny Bloodbane?"

"Yes, a very old, very proud name, she told me. So, you can forget any droll comparisons, Lord Beecham, as to which would curl a listener's toes more readily."

"Teeny Bloodbane," he said yet again, as if savoring the feel of the sounds on his tongue. "Tell me, Miss Mayberry, do you believe she will live in sin with Flock?"

"Oh, no, Teeny and Flock are both very religious. I overheard Flock telling my father that he fancied he was meant to be a Tristan to Teeny's Isolde — an ill-fated love that would never result in marital fulfillment."

"I think that both Flock and Nettle are far too old for Teeny. What is she, eighteen?"

"Yes. She told me that older men, like Flock, look at her differently, even speak to her differently from young men. She said she quite likes the older guzzards."

"Guzzards? Good Lord, am I nearly a guzzard, Miss Mayberry?"

"I would say you have a good half dozen years before you reach the guzzard level, Lord Beecham."

"My lord."

"Yes, Nettle? What is it?"

"I pray that you will not desert me in my time of need."

"Naturally not, Nettle. What need specifically do you see looming?"

"Flock is looming, my lord. He just told me he would pull my gullet out through my ear if I even so much as smile at Miss Teeny again."

"Don't worry, Nettle," Helen said. "I will discipline Flock if he steps over the line."

Lord Beecham gave her a look of great interest. "Just how will you do that, Miss Mayberry?"

"I am not in the habit of giving out free advice on my specialty, Lord Beecham. Now," she said, turning away from him, "go about your business, Nettle, and don't smile at Teeny. It is possible that Lord Prith, not Flock, might challenge you to a duel. He is very fond of Flock.

"Look beyond Teeny's left shoulder, not at her face. Save yourself from my father, who could smash you if he simply decided to sit on you."

"He won't be a broken man for long," Lord

Beecham said as he cynically watched his valet wander away into the taproom of the Wet Sexton's Inn in the middle of Henchly, a small town not far from Court Hammering. They were stopping, Lord Prith had shouted out his window to Helen, because he wished to taste the ale that the inn's owner, Mr. Clappe, had made just three months ago, a new recipe that might please his lordship exceedingly.

"My father also likes ale," Helen said, following her sire into the inn.

As the three entered the low-beamed taproom, Lord Beecham wasn't surprised to find Flock already against the wall with his arms crossed over his scrawny chest, making certain that no one dared treat them with less than boot-licking respect.

"It is not a badly run inn," Helen said as she sipped the new ale that Mr. Clappe, all good humor and fat belly, carefully and respectfully placed in her hands. "There's a bit too much grease ground into the tabletops, but men seem to feel comfortable with a certain amount of filth. Mr. Clappe is attentive, but perhaps he is a bit too effusive with you, Father."

"You mean as in he toadies, Nell?"

"Yes, Father. Mr. Clappe toadies."

"He can toady all he likes," Lord Prith said, wiping his hand across his mouth, "so long as he keeps this ale coming. Clappe! I want a cask of this excellent ale. Two casks. See to it." He turned back to his daughter and Lord Beecham and beamed. "Best inn in England other than my dear daughter's. Only thing, though, Nell, you don't let men drink as much as they'd like to. You turn off the spigot just when they're beginning to shuck off their worries."

"Nonsense, Father. If I let them, the men would drink until they dropped dead on the floor."

"You shouldn't try to change men's habits, Nell."

"I'd rather haul them outside into the inn yard rather than watch them retch in my taproom. Also, I don't want them to spend all their shillings on ale. Most of them have families, you know."

"If they keep coming back, sir," Lord Beecham said, "then whatever she is doing must surely work."

"There is no other inn in Court Hammering that serves such excellent victuals," Lord Prith said.

"Indeed," Helen said. "I feed them well and don't let their innards corrode with too much drink. I do a favor to all the wives in Court Hammering. Come to think of it, perhaps you could consider me something in the manner of the patroness saint of food and drink in Court Hammering."

Once two huge casks of Mr. Clappe's ale were firmly secured atop Lord Prith's carriage, they were off for the final seven miles to Court Hammering.

"Actually, we live at Shugborough Hall, just east of Court Hammering."

"I have never heard that name before."

"My great-grandfather built Shugborough Hall back in the early part of the last century. It is really quite beautiful, particularly with the sun bright behind it. You see, it is all creamy brick quarried over at Pelton Abbott. It just softens more and more as time passes. What with all the wildly growing ivy climbing over the walls, it is probably the most charming manor house in the area.

"The grounds are quite spectacular, since my father enjoys flowers and gardens and thick hedges everywhere. The various lawns stretch from the hall a good fifty yards in every direction, lush green."

"How many gardeners does your father employ?"

"At last count, I believe it was thirteen. There is a head gardener, of course, and four under-gardeners. There are three men who do nothing else but scythe the lawns. Oh, yes, there are even two peacocks strolling around the grounds. Father calls them, originally, Peacock and Peahen, or, when they're making too much racket, he just yells out, 'Pea and Pea, shut your beaks!' "

Lord Beecham's first view of Shugborough Hall fulfilled what she had said. Not only was it a graceful manor house, it was also set atop a gently rolling hill that sloped down on all sides, the incredible green lawn ending only at the edge of a fast-flowing stream that ran east to west. Massive old willow trees framed the stream, with oak and lime trees dotted over the rest of the lawn. The home wood beyond was a thick collection of maple trees. The carriage drive was narrow, an afterthought, Lord Beecham suspected — that, or no owner had ever wanted a graveled drive to cut into the beautiful flowing green lawn. The ivy on the cream brick walls was kept neatly trimmed. No danger of it overwhelming the house.

"It is very nice," he said to Lord Prith when they were both standing in front of the manor.

"Thank you, my boy. A snug little property, if I do say so myself. Been happy here. So was my Matilda, God bless her beautiful soul." He gave a lusty sigh, then yelled, "Hinkel! Get your scrawny buttocks out here to help with the luggage."

"Our long-suffering footman," Helen said close to Lord Beecham's ear. "The thing is, he is very skinny, especially from behind."

"Sort of like a windowpane?" He turned to smile at her. It still made him start that he didn't have to look down at the sound of a woman's voice. No, she was right there, her mouth on a level with his, not more than five inches away.

"Exactly."

He did not realize he had been staring at her, but she did, and leaned even a bit closer. "Shall I tell you about what I fantasize you to be doing

110

while I am pulling off your right boot?"

"Yes," he said, his eyes glazed.

She gave a merry laugh and went into Shugborough Hall.

One hour later, after a light luncheon of sliced chicken topped with apricot chutney, crunchy fresh bread with the sweetest butter Lord Beecham had ever tasted, and orange and pear slices sprinkled with roasted almonds, enjoyed with Lord Prith's favorite drink, champagne, a treat that Lord Beecham declined, he found himself sitting at Miss Helen Mayberry's charming gilt-and-white Louis XV desk in a sunny back chamber that didn't enjoy the presence of many gentlemen, she had told him. It was her estate room, where she conducted all her business. It was also her library, where she read and thought and dreamed about the lamp and what it *really* did.

She carefully placed the iron cask on the desk in front of him. "It's very old. But solid. After all these hundreds upon hundreds of years, it is still strong."

"I wish there was some way we could tell just how old it really is," he said. Slowly, with infinite care, he pulled the fraying leather strap off its hook and lifted it, then gently raised the domed lid. He breathed in deeply. It was an ancient smell, he thought, ancient and something else. Not only did it smell very old, the hundreds of years leaving a vaguely yeasty scent with perhaps just a hint of the smell of olives, but also it didn't seem quite to belong here in this modern world where everything was explained by science and there were no more mysteries, no more magic, no more strange phenomena that boggled a man's brain.

Olives, he thought. Yes, there was the faint but distinct smell of olives. And something else as well. It nearly overwhelmed him, this feeling that the cask was, in and of itself, important — very important. He felt it deep inside himself. It was also frightening because it did not feel to him as if it was of this world.

What did he mean by that? That this cask had somehow floated down from another world? One of the millions of stars he looked at in the heavens? It had come from one of them? Oh, certainly not. Just breathing in the smell of this ancient cask with its scent of olives and yeast was making him more fanciful than Helen's little jest about pulling off his boots had done.

"I wish," he said, "that we could find a person who has been around something magical, something exquisitely different from everything we know. He could perhaps explain, just breathing in the air of this cask, just touching it, how old it is and where it came from."

"Yes, and what it is doing here. Hidden in a wall in the back of an old cave in a cliff beside the sea."

"Do you smell the olives?"

She nodded, "When I carried the cask out of

the cave and gently set it on a rock, I looked at it for the longest time before I could bring myself to open it. I don't know if I expected some sort of genie to float out. When I did open it, the smell of olives nearly overwhelmed me it was so strong. It has grown weaker over time, allowing the other smells to come out."

"The smell of age."

"Yes. I felt too as though I were in the presence of something ancient and powerful, yet very strange, very different from me. The smell or the feeling of this thing hasn't changed. Don't you think that odd?"

He slowly nodded. He had no words. Slowly, with infinite care, Helen gently lifted out the scroll of leather. "You can see how very fragile it is."

She unrolled it while he held down one side. It covered a third of the desk. There were four paperweights, each set carefully upon a corner, to hold it down. "Did you measure it?"

She nodded. "It's twelve inches by nine and a half inches."

He lightly touched his fingertips to the old leather as a blind man would. "There was probably something tying it closed?"

"Yes, but it disintegrated long ago. It must have been tied for a very long time, because when I found it, the scroll was still tightly rolled."

Only then did he allow himself to look down upon the old leather. It was the color of dried blood. The writing was black. The person had pressed the inked tip hard into the leather. It wouldn't have mattered if the leather had turned completely black over the years. The deep grooves and shapes were still perfectly clear.

Reading what was written, however, was a different matter.

"Do you have a magnifying glass?"

"Yes, right here."

The silence grew long and thick. Helen walked away from him to the French doors of the small estate room, which gave onto a private walled garden.

She looked back at him, leaning over her desk, staring down intently at the leather scroll. He was frowning.

"What is it, Lord Beecham?"

"I believe," he said at last, turning to look at her, "that it is time you called me by my given name. It's Spenser."

"All right. You may call me Helen."

"Helen is a good name. This scroll — it is not Latin or old French or anything like that."

"What is it?"

"It is something along the line of ancient Persian." He straightened. "Does your father have any texts about languages?"

"Yes, but Persian? I doubt it."

Lord Prith had nothing at all ever written east of Germany.

"It's time we went to see Vicar Gilliam," Helen said. "It will take us about an hour to ride there."

Lord Beecham looked back at the leather scroll atop the desk. "I'm thinking that we should oil the leather, make it more pliable and more resistant to cracking and splitting, particularly when you and I touch it." He paused a moment, then said, "You know, Helen, the chances are that this says nothing at all about the lamp. In fact I would say the odds are very much against it."

She was shaking her head even as she said, "No, I don't believe that. I believe that King Edward hid the lamp near Aldeburgh and that is where the cask was buried. The lamp is nearby, I know it is. What is the purpose of the leather scroll if not to explain the lamp? That must be it, don't you see?"

"Then why would the scroll be written in ancient Persian and not in French, if it is indeed some sort of explanation about the lamp?"

"Robert Burnell, the king's secretary, was vastly learned. He must have done it. He must have wanted the lamp to be difficult to find."

Lord Beecham didn't think that was the case, but he said nothing.

They used the almond oil that Helen poured into her bath. "I thought the scent was somewhat familiar," he said over his shoulder as he gently rubbed his thumb in the oil and lightly touched it to the leather. He lifted his thumb to his nose. "It smells like you."

"Keep rubbing, Spenser."

"Just look at that," he said after a moment. "It's working."

Together they oiled the leather, going very slowly until, finally, it was done. There were only three small tears and perhaps a dozen places where a single touch would split the leather and destroy some of the words.

They covered the newly softened leather with a clean cheesecloth, locked the door to the estate room, and remounted their horses to ride to Dereham to see Vicar Lockleer Gilliam.

They didn't make it.

9

From one minute to the next, as happened so often in England no matter what the season, the sky went from a soft, misty gray to the near black of nightfall, only there was no moon to light the way, just heavy black clouds rolling and tumbling in low, right over their heads.

"Oh, dear," said Helen, looking up. "This is a new riding habit. One of your London modistes made it for me just last week. You would not believe what the peacock feathers cost."

"Which modiste?"

"Madame Flaubert."

"She is rather conservative, I have found, but the quality is excellent. Actually, given your size, I like the cut. Simplicity is —" He didn't have time to finish his thought because at that precise instant lightning struck an oak branch that stretched over the narrow country road. Smoke billowed out as the branch snapped off and struck the ground not three feet from their horses. Thunder ripped through the silence. Luther, maddened beyond control, reared up on his hind legs.

"Helen, hold tight!"

Lord Beecham didn't have a chance. When Luther twisted sideways and hurled his hind-quarters in the opposite direction as he kicked out his hind legs, Lord Beecham flew off his back to land headfirst in a thick hedge on the side of the road. He heard her yell to him.

As for Helen, she had her own difficulties. Luther, his eyes wild and rolling in his head, slammed into Eleanor, who had already backed away, tripping over her own hooves. Luther bit her neck. Eleanor whirled about and skidded to a dead stop. Helen yelled as she went flying over her mare's head. She landed at the edge of a ditch and rolled down to the bottom, coming to a stop on a carpet of luscious wild daffodils in full yellow bloom.

Lord Beecham, just slightly winded now, no bones broken, climbed down to her and went down on his knees beside her. He lightly slapped her cheeks. "Are you all right?"

She was lying flat on her back, a bunch of daffodils sticking up between her riding boots. Her left arm was over her head, showing the huge rent beneath her right arm.

There were two of him weaving above her when she managed to get her eyes to open. "Stop moving, it is making me dizzy. Please, just hold still."

"All right. I am perfectly still now. Is that better?"

"Yes, thank you. Oh, dear, my riding habit, is it quite ruined?"

"Helen, I am worried that you might have broken something or hurt yourself internally, and all you can do is cry piteously about your damned riding habit. I will buy you a new one. I will even select the material and the style. Forget the habit. Yes, there is a big tear under your arm. It looks like you put a boot through the hem. Nothing important. Now, attend me. How do you feel?"

"You have dirt on your face." She raised a hand to flick it away. "You've got a small cut beside your right ear. I don't feel any particular pain. Did you rattle your brains?"

"No. Luther very kindly tossed me into a thick hedge that cushioned my fall. I saw you go right over Eleanor's head. Both those damned ingrates are probably trotting happily back to Shugborough Hall. At least I hope that Eleanor will lead Luther back there."

"Luther was so maddened that he bit Eleanor's neck. Or maybe he is in love with her. If that's the case, you can be certain he will follow her as closely as he can."

He would never be able to explain why he did it. Perhaps it was all the unexpected danger, the utter relief that both of them were still alive. It didn't matter. Blood pumped wildly through his veins, his heart pounded deep, heavy strokes, and he felt ready to burst out of his skin. He leaned down and lightly nipped her neck just above the lace on her white blouse.

He drew back, holding to a thread of control. "I did see Luther eyeing Eleanor's flanks earlier today."

"You did not. Forget mimicking your horse

any further. You may not bite me there next. Now, I am getting myself together again. Yes, I am very nearly together. How did my neck taste?"

At that moment the black clouds burst open.

"Oh, no, my poor riding habit." She tried to pull him down over her to protect her habit. Lord Beecham was laughing so hard he got a mouthful of rain. But he ended up lying on top of her, all of her beneath him, a perfect fit, like no fit he had ever experienced in his entire adult life.

"This is a goodly dose of nature's discipline," he said, leaned down and kissed her mouth.

She turned to stone.

He raised himself up just a bit so he could look down at her face. "What's wrong? I didn't slide my hand under your riding skirt to stroke my fingers over the soft flesh behind your knee. I didn't nibble at your neck again. I haven't headed anywhere near your flank. No, I just kissed you. Nothing of any import, really, just a touching of mouths. What the devil is wrong with you, Helen?"

He was lying on top of her, balanced above her on his elbows. Rain was coming down so hard she knew the ditch would fill up very quickly, but she didn't say anything. She just stared up at him.

"Are you thinking about pulling off my boots again?"

She shook her head.

He leaned down and kissed her again.

"This is ridiculous," she said into his mouth, locked her arms around his back and pulled him so tightly against her that no rain could even get between them. His hands were in her hair, pulling at the riding hat, with its broken, drooping peacock feather, and his tongue was in her mouth and he was panting, beside himself, but perhaps Helen was even further gone than he was. She managed to open her legs and he was between them, and he was hard and ready and this was indeed ridiculous, just as she had gasped into his mouth.

He jerked away from her and hauled himself to his feet. He grabbed her hand and pulled her upright. "It's raining hard. We have to find shelter. If we are possibly so lucky as to find anything at all that will provide even a dollop of protection, I am going to be inside you in a matter of moments."

He started pulling her up the side of the ditch. "Where are we?"

She was looking at him like a half-wit.

"Helen? Get ahold of yourself. Stop thinking of what I'm going to do to you. Or are you thinking of what you're going to do to me? Think. Where can we go for shelter?"

She raised her arm, the one with the big rip in the armpit, and pointed. "There's a wreck of an ancient cottage through the woods, there, to the east. Perhaps it's only a quarter of a mile away."

They struggled to the top of the ditch and

found an opening through the thick line of trees that clustered near the country road. The foliage was so thick that it at least protected them from the worst of the deluge.

Lord Beecham stopped for a moment, aware that his right leg was drawing up on him. "Well, damn." It was something of a sprain, but not too bad. He looked at Helen, who was breathing hard, her beautiful blond hair flattened wet against her head and face, a long sheet of hair down her back. "How do you feel?" He cupped her face in his hand.

"Better than you. Do you want me to help you?"

He shook his head. "No, it isn't that bad, just a slight sprain. Which way?"

They slogged their way through the forest until Helen stopped and looked around. "It's near here. Just over there, to the right. There is a small clearing."

They stepped into the clearing in another three minutes.

"Thank God it hasn't collapsed in on itself," Helen said as she ran toward what once had been a dilapidated cottage and was now a relic. "At least a part of the roof is still up there."

"Stay here," Lord Beecham said and carefully pulled the rotted door open. It creaked and groaned, and the hinges scraped and loosened even more.

"Come inside," he said over his shoulder as he stepped into the most appalling excuse for a shelter he could imagine. Half the roof was gone. Three beams held up the other half of the room. There were still wooden floors, of a sort, mostly rotted, undoubtedly dangerous.

But bless the munificent Lord — there was one dry corner. They were laughing as they eased down very slowly and carefully onto the wooden floorboards and leaned back against the wall. It creaked loudly, then stilled.

They grew quiet. The rain pounding on the roof over their heads sounded like hails of bullets. As for the roofless part of the single room, the rain came down in a thick gray sheet.

He looked at her mouth. "Come here, I want you right this minute."

"I've been thinking about this," Helen said, not moving an inch. "I don't think it's a good idea. We are partners in this exciting venture. In my experience, the minute a man is tired of a woman or vice versa, the last thing they want to do is spend more time together."

He raised a dark brow. It made him look utterly insolent and arrogant. He brought his knees up and wrapped his arms around them. "Just tell me about all this experience of yours."

"Men aren't always reasonable or logical."

"Neither are women."

"My point exactly. Let's not muddy things up with physical sorts of things."

"What is your experience, Helen? I know you are the prominent mistress of discipline in Court Hammering. I know that the men who work for you tremble in delicious fear of your discipline threats. I know I can see you pulling off my left boot, your bottom thrust toward me. And the smile on your face as you're looking over your shoulder at me is decidedly wicked, filled with knowledge of pleasure and how to dole it out."

She stared straight ahead at the pouring gray sheet of rain not six feet away. The rain splashed to within two feet of where they sat. It was chilly. She was wet clear through, and all she wanted was to have him bite her neck again, perhaps even take a nip or two of her flank. She turned to say something, but the words never made it out of her mouth. He was on her, pressing her onto her back. Thank God there were no leaks in the ceiling over them.

She was not the least bit cold, not now, not with his hands on her upper arms, caressing her shoulders, her neck while his mouth was heavy on hers, drawing her into him and his urgency, into his wild need for her, and she made a decision she knew had already been made in her own mind the first time she saw him. She gave him her mouth, gave all of herself to him, pushing and bringing him tightly against her, her hands frantic on his back, coming between them to the buttons of his riding breeches.

The heat of him amazed her, drew her even deeper, so quickly now, arching up when his hands were on her breasts, and then on the buttons of her riding jacket.

"Helen, now," he said into her mouth, his

breath hot and wild. "I can't believe this." He was panting as he reared up over her, stared down at her for just a fraction of a moment before he jerked up her riding skirt and her petticoats. When she was naked to the waist, he sat on his heels and stared down at her. Slowly, with her watching him, he stretched out his hand, let it hover a long moment over her belly, then ever so slowly let his palm lie flat against her soft flesh.

He was looking at his hand resting on her belly and she knew he was looking at his fingers as they slowly moved downward, so slowly, savoring every bit of her until at last, he was cupping her.

She arched upward and grabbed his shoulders to bring him down on her.

"No, Helen, not yet. Good Lord, not yet. Once I kiss your mouth again I won't be any good to you at all. I'll spill my seed and then you will believe me the greatest clod in England."

"Spenser."

She whispered his name on a soft sigh as he slid a finger inside her. He nearly lost himself right then, right there. His breathing quickened, his heart was pounding out of his chest and he knew it was all over for him. She was so very hot and soft and she wanted him. Her face was flushed, her lips parted, and she was staring up at him like he was the only man in the entire world and the only man she wanted.

"Helen," he said again, jerked down his

breeches, lifted her hips, and came into her, deep and hard.

She screamed at the pain of it, then screamed again at the pleasure of it. He was on top of her now, his mouth on hers again, and his tongue was touching her lower lip, then easing into her mouth, and she accepted him and kissed him until she thought she would die with the power of the feelings that were so deep inside her. He was moving now inside her, so deep, so much pressure, filling her, and it was delicious and she wanted him there forever.

But it wasn't to be. He knew he was almost gone. He hadn't given her a woman's pleasure. He tried, he truly did, to draw out of her, to put his mouth and his fingers on her, but for the first time in as long as he could remember, he simply lost every shred of control. He threw back his head and yelled to the pounding rain.

He was flat on top of her, his face in her wet hair beside her head. He had been stomped into oblivion by the greatest pleasure he had ever experienced in his adult life. He had been stripped of all control. He had soared to the heavens by himself — in short, he had been a bore.

"I'm sorry," he said, coming up on his elbows. "I'm very sorry, Helen. You are so bloody beautiful." He couldn't help himself and leaned down to kiss her again and found that he was again hard inside her.

"I am thirty-three years old," he said between kisses. "I want you again immediately. You're a witch. You're incredible." And he pulled out of her, throbbing and hard but not as hard as his heart was pounding. He was panting as he kissed her, his fingers finding her to begin a rhythm he did so very well, but the simple touch of her flesh beneath his fingers, the softness, the heat of her, but no, it was something more than that, and it flooded through him and he wanted desperately to see her pleasure. He kissed her and loved her until he felt the tension near to overflowing in her, and he lifted his head to look at her face when she arched against his fingers, her eyes frantic and vague, and she screamed as her own pleasure flooded through her, his fingers the focus of everything that was swamping her. She screamed again, this time into his mouth.

He kissed her more deeply, not at first aware that she was struggling to get away from him. When it finally got through to him, he blinked in confusion, his mouth open, but she screamed again. "Oh, my God!"

She wrapped her arms tightly around his back and pressed him hard against her. She rolled with him on the rotted floor. He heard the crashing of beams and ceiling not six inches behind him, exactly where they had been lying. It was a horrendously loud noise, so close it chilled him to the bone.

Then the silence of the thick rain enclosed them once again.

They were lying facing each other, still pressed very close. "The ceiling," he said. "My

God, the ceiling crashed in."

Her eyes were closed. He leaned forward to kiss her. Her mouth didn't move beneath his. "Helen?"

He pulled back just a bit.

She was unconscious. And damn him for a beast, he was still hard, deep inside her.

10

Lord Beecham came up beside her and carefully rolled her onto her back. He saw the blood now, seeping through her wet hair just behind her left ear.

Something had struck her. He looked up. The sleeting rain was so close, the rubble flattening beneath its force. He pulled down her clothes, fastened his breeches, and sat back on his heels.

He shrugged out of his riding jacket and covered her with it. There was nothing else he could think to do. He was afraid to move her. But just lying there like that she would surely get chilled, and that could be dangerous. He eased her as far away from the rain as he could. His back was pressed to the wall. He stretched out beside her and pulled her tightly against him. "I'm sorry, Helen. You saved my lustful hide and you're the one who got hurt. It will be all right now. We will just stay here until you come back again." He kissed her ear and pulled his jacket more firmly over her.

They had been on their way to Dereham to find a text on ancient Persian. Now they were lying pressed against each other, soaking wet and Helen was unconscious, with a collapsed roof not two feet away.

It was at that moment that he realized it was

getting toward late afternoon. It would get colder as the hours passed. What if it did not stop raining? He closed his eyes, his cheek pressed against hers.

He knew he could carry her, but not all that far, surely not far enough to make any difference. He doubted he could even get her back to the country road. And if it continued to rain like this?

No, they had to remain right here. No choice. He slipped his hand between them and pressed his palm against her breast. To his relief, her heart was beating slowly and steadily. He could do nothing but wait.

He thought about his reaction to her, and was still amazed. It had been too much, far too much. He had simply never felt anything like it, the urge to have her so powerful, so very urgent, that nothing else had existed for him in those moments, just Helen and being inside her, holding her tight and tighter still until they were joined so deeply neither of them could feel anything apart from the other.

What had happened — he distrusted it profoundly, now that his body had calmed from its incredible need. An aberration, he thought, just being here in the rain, in this ruin of a cottage, seeing her beautiful blond hair straggling around her face, and he had lost all sense. He supposed that she had as well. He had enjoyed many women over the years. He had always been the one to set the pace of things, but this time he had lost himself in the dust. And he had spilled his seed inside her, something he never did. He wanted no woman pregnant by him. But with Helen, he had simply leapt off a cliff, screaming with the joy of it, and hadn't cared what parts of him had landed where.

She had quite simply stunned him.

A woman rarely got pregnant with just one mistake. Actually, he would have spilled his seed deep inside her a second time if the roof hadn't fallen in on them.

At least she'd had pleasure in those moments before it had happened.

He kissed her temple.

He felt her move. Relief surged through him. She had been unconscious for only about four or five minutes. "Helen," he said against her cheek. "Helen."

He felt her moan deep in her throat.

"Helen, open your eyes. Come back now, Helen."

She opened her eyes.

He lightly touched his fingertips to her cheek. "Welcome back."

He said nothing more, waiting for her to gather herself. Her eyes were vague, just as they had been when she'd been on the edge of her orgasm. He pulled back a bit more so he could see her more clearly. To let her focus on his face.

"What happened?"

A skinny little thread of a voice, he thought, and smiled at her. "It's all right. You saved us from being smashed beneath the collapsed roof. However, something hit you behind your left ear. There's just a bit of blood. Tell me, how many fingers am I waggling in front of your face?"

"Too many."

"Close your eyes, just think about nothing at all. I'm here and we're safe. But don't go to sleep. Whatever struck you knocked you a bit silly. Tell me when you want to count fingers again."

"I've never done that before."

He leaned down and kissed her pale mouth. "Never been hit on the head by a falling roof? Or saved the man who just lost his head over you?"

"That, too. I'm sorry, but I don't think I'm quite ready to race you back to the country lane. What are we going to do, Spenser?"

"Nothing at the moment. Don't worry about a thing, Helen. I'll do all the worrying. Now, how far are we from a village or a farmer's house?"

She was shivering. He wrapped her more tightly against him. "I know you're wet. Unfortunately I am just as wet, so I can't help you." He thought a moment. "Here's what we're going to do. I'm going to get all those clothes off you and strip myself as well. Then we're going to get so close we'll be hot as oven bricks in no time at all."

Helen moaned, but said nothing. He stripped her, something he had done to many women many times in his adult life, but it wasn't fun this time. Her clothes were wet and sticking to her, she was shivering, her teeth chattered, and her eyes were closed against the pain any movement brought her. "I'm sorry, Helen, nearly there now. Did I tell you how very beautiful you are? No, perhaps now isn't time to talk about bodily sorts of things. Now, these clothes are wet. You'll have my body against you in just a moment. Hold on just a bit longer."

Finally they were both naked and he managed to pull Helen's petticoat directly over them. The petticoat was just damp, so it wasn't quite so bad. Then he layered all their other clothes over the petticoat.

It wasn't bad at all.

"You're hotter than the old brick oven my father had installed in his hunting box near Leeds."

His eyes were crossed. He was hard against her belly, he just couldn't help it. He kissed her temple. "Don't pay any attention to me, Helen. I can't control that part of me. Just ignore it. Are you feeling warmer?"

"Oh, yes," she said, her breath warm against his throat. "You feel very interesting against me, but it doesn't matter. I'm very tired, Spenser."

"Blink your eyes and look at me. Yes, that's it. Now, Helen, you're not a fragile little miss. Don't you dare go to sleep. Wrap your arm around me. Yes, that's right. Is your back warm enough?"

Since he was stroking his hand up and down

her back, over her buttocks and as far as he could reach down the back of her thighs, she was growing very warm, very quickly. And because he was a man, he probably spent more time stroking her hips. "This isn't something you could have planned, is it, Spenser?"

"The roof collapsing?"

"No, I was thinking about all of it, each thing that happened that triggered the next. It is almost as if you put into motion a perfectly executed form of discipline. Except for me getting hit on the head. A master of discipline wouldn't want that to happen."

"No, the master wouldn't." His hand was on her buttocks, his fingers splayed. He was pushing her against him, and he was desperately hard again, nearly shaking with it. What was wrong with him?

"Just ignore me," he said again against her ear.

"That's rather impossible. You're shoving me against you. My head is better. Yes, and I'm warm now. Oh, goodness, this is nonsense. I've never lost my head like this before. I don't like it, Spenser, I don't like it at all." And without any shoving from him, she moved against him.

He didn't care about liking it or disliking it. He just wanted her now, and it was as strong and prodding as it had been the first time. He rolled on top of her. "Helen," he said, and began kissing her. He was between her legs and then he was inside her, her arms clasped around his back.

134

It was fast and hard, and when she yelled to the roofed sky that still held steady over their heads, he reared back and did his own yelling.

He didn't want to leave her, and so he didn't. He managed to cover them again and to his surprise, he went to sleep, his head beside hers, still inside her.

Helen looked up at the narrow slice of roof that covered them. She wasn't cold now and her head didn't particularly hurt. She was so surprised, so utterly bewildered by what had happened between them, that when the incredible feelings began to build again inside her, she just sighed deeply and kissed him back. She felt his fingers on her, and he didn't stop his beguiling rhythm until she was panting hard into his mouth. He smiled down at her as he moved slowly, fully, and it didn't take long, even this time, the third time, and he realized vaguely as he spilled his seed deeply inside her that surely this was something amazing, to want and want. He wasn't a randy boy; he was a damned man and he was thirty-three years old.

When his brain turned outward, finally, he said against her left ear, "I really don't want to expire in a ruined cottage, wallowing in the rain."

"I'm well enough, just a slight headache. It will be dark in an hour. I should be exhausted, but I'm not. I feel marvelous. I can walk now."

Actually, he himself could have leapt up and danced an Irish jig. His body pulsed with incredible energy. He didn't want to, but finally he managed to make himself pull away from her. He rose and looked down at her. His face was hard with satisfaction. He gave her his hand and pulled her to her feet.

"No," he said, "Helen, don't look at my mouth or I'll toss you back down again. We must dress. We must find shelter."

She hated the layers of clothes that chilled her to her very bones. When she sat down to lace up her boots, he was leaning over trying to pull on his own boots.

She laughed. He looked at her and grinned. It wasn't raining quite as hard when they made their way back to the country road, but it still took them an hour to return to Shugbourgh Hall.

"Oh, my God," Lord Prith said when the two of them strolled like bedraggled urchins into the entrance hall. "I shall heat some champagne immediately."

Lord Beecham begged for brandy and got it. Lord Prith shooed him off to his bedchamber, where Nettle was already pouring hot water into his bath. He stripped his lordship in a minute flat and wrapped him in a dressing gown. Lord Beecham added wood to the fire while Nettle nearly broke into tears over the state of his Hessians. When he was in the tub, leaning back, his eyes closed, he saw Helen, naked, beneath him, arching up when his fingers caressed her, and he saw himself leaning down to kiss her as she screamed out her pleasure.

Three times he'd taken her.

What the hell had he done?

As for Helen, she realized much sooner exactly what she had done, and she cursed the air blue. Teeny paced in front of her tub, back and forth, wringing her hands, completely misunderstanding why her mistress appeared so angry she could spit.

Teeny said, "There is no reason for you to be mad about all the blood on your head, Miss Helen. I will be upset for both of us. It's real blood, Miss Helen. Let me call in the physician."

"I'm not mad, Teeny, you are. Now listen to me. I would have to be dead before I would let Ozzie anywhere near my person."

"But you have said that he never tries to kill people."

"Yes, that is true, but he fancies himself in love with me. No, he cannot come near me. Come now and help me wash my hair. We'll get the blood out, don't worry."

Yes, Helen knew what she had done. What she had done three times. And it had been glorious. She cursed herself as she walked down the stairs to dinner.

Luther and Eleanor were home in the stables, having returned even later than she and Lord Beecham had, which was why, her father told her, no one had been in the least concerned.

"What were those damned horses doing if they

didn't come back here after they threw us?" Lord Beecham asked the table at large as he felt the rich turtle soup slide all hot and tangy down his throat. Was that a hint of lemon he tasted?

Helen cleared her throat and said to the potatoes on her fork, "They were probably taking shelter, just as you and I were, Lord Beecham. Don't worry, Father. I can see you puffing up to worry in the worst way. I drank the warmed champagne and it cleared my head to such a degree that the past three hours could never have happened."

She looked Lord Beecham straight in the eye. "Indeed, those three hours are fast becoming a blur in my mind. Yes, now all I remember is Lord Beecham and me riding away from here to Dereham. Then everything is a complete blur. There must have been rain, since we came back wet, but for all the in-between?

"It is gone from my mind and my memory. Now, everything is as it was. Nothing is any different. Nothing at all."

Lord Beecham should have heard that with relieved ears. But he didn't. He didn't know why, but it enraged him. She wanted to forget he had given her immense pleasure three times? He cursed into his soup.

Helen rose when she finished her dinner. She looked directly at her father. "I am going to bed now. I hope you and Lord Beecham will excuse me. Whatever happened this afternoon has made me very tired.

"Lord Beecham, I will see you in the morning. If it isn't raining, we can once again endeavor to reach Dereham."

What was he to say? What he wanted to do was push back his chair, rise slowly, never taking his eyes off her, walk to where she stood, and put his hands around her white neck. He didn't know how hard he would squeeze. Certainly hard enough to gain her attention, curse her. He flexed impotent fingers as he watched her leave the dining room. She was dressed in soft gray silk gown that draped very nicely over that delicious white body of hers.

He had made love to her three times, given her his all, actually more than his all, simply because, for no reason he could fathom, she had hauled it out of him. She had completely possessed him, emptied him, and now she wanted to forget it?

Not if he had anything to say about it.

He and Lord Prith played whist. Lord Prith talked about how his sweet little Nell was the very picture of her soft, very gentle mother. If it had not been for Flock hovering close, Lord Beecham would have choked to death on his brandy.

He lost sixty pounds and had drunk too much delicious smuggled French brandy by the time Flock fetched his lordship for their evening walk.

11

"Damn your eyes, Helen, you will talk to me about this. Women always love to talk after making love to the point of rendering a man insensible. Usually a woman starts chattering immediately, when the man is lying there, felled, still utterly witless. I will admit that our surroundings yesterday were perhaps not all that inspiring, and thus you wished to wait to talk everything to death and in great detail. Now it is time. We are in pleasant surroundings. Now you may speak to me."

Nothing from Helen.

He persevered. "You may now feel free to thrash everything over, Helen. You may complain about certain minor digressions or perhaps omissions."

But Helen, curse her beautiful eyes, began whistling.

He jerked on Luther's reins, and his horse reared back, nearly unseating him. He turned to her and yelled, "Damn you, stop that. All right. I will accept that just perhaps not everything that happened between us was necessarily perfect during those hours yesterday that you are claiming to forget."

"Goodness, Spenser, whatever are you talking about?"

He ignored that bit of goading. He was a reasonable man. Sometimes a woman needed to be eased into spilling her innards. She had to trust a man, know that he admired her, particularly if she wished to praise him. Of course she knew he believed she was utterly delicious. She also knew, damn her, that he'd given her wondrous pleasure. He could still feel her hot breath in his mouth when she moaned her climax. He had felt it to his toes. His breathing hitched for a moment. Perhaps she was just embarrassed to tell him how spectacular a lover he was. That had to be it. "If you wish to speak of how immensely well suited we are, you may do so now. I will listen. I will attend you."

Helen continued to whistle. A robin redbreast answered from a maple tree to the side of the country road. Rage was building up inside him, nice, bubbling rage, but still he held his voice calm, the epitome of male reason. "Listen to me. We are alone, there is no more bloody rain today, the sun is shining down quite brightly on our heads, our horses are clipping along at a fine rate, and I am ready to listen to you.

"It is all right, Helen. I understand you now. You want me to wrap every pleasurable thing we did yesterday all up in a poetic and soulful package."

She gave him a look of female amusement, a look that could shrivel a man's manhood. "Since we did not do anything at all yesterday afternoon — at least nothing worth mentioning that I can

141

remember — then you may take all your soulful packages and dump them in a ditch."

"You will stop trying to enrage me. This so-called memory lapse of yours is laughable. When I take a woman, she never forgets it. Never. If I ever take a woman three times, her life changes utterly."

Curse her all the way to China, she laughed. She looked over at him and laughed. He pulsed with rage.

Then, suddenly, she stopped her laughter and looked all sorts of bored, even indifferent. She looked down at her tan leather riding gloves that had Eleanor's reins wrapped loosely around them, looked down at her black riding boots that could have been polished to a brighter shine, but she didn't have a valet like Nettle, so what was she to do? She looked all too ready to continue with her show of bored indifference.

He was ready to leap off Luther's back and take her to the ground and — his mind balked at what followed then. She turned to look at him again and said in an unruffled, calm voice that reeked of martyred female patience, of which there was no other kind in his experience, "There is no need for you to sulk, Lord Beecham. You should learn how to control your wounded male vanity."

"Damn you, my name is Spenser."

"Very well, Spenser, I will use your given name until you behave like an ass — again."

"Helen, do you want me to throw you to the

142

ground and show you yet again that my taking you — three times, mind you — was one of the greatest experiences in your damned provincial life?"

"Goodness," she said, shaking her head at him, her tranquil self still firmly in place, and rubbing his nose in it, "you certainly have an exalted opinion of yourself, Lord Beecham. I wish that you would simply forget all that nonsense of yesterday and strive to remember that you are my partner, not my lover."

"I want to be both. I am both. There is no reason to discontinue either one or the other, particularly the other. I want to continue what we started. I regret that you were struck on the head by some falling roof, that you were wet through to your bones, that the rotted wooden floor wasn't quite as comfortable as a bed, but all of that aside, regardless, you enjoyed yourself immensely. Three times. And I was the man to give you all that pleasure."

"Yes, I did, and so you were. So what?"

So *what?* He could but stare at her, his brain at half-mast. No woman had ever said that to him in his male adult life.

So what? She had actually said *so what?*

He was primed to yell. He stopped himself. He drew a deep, steadying breath. He even smiled at her as he said, "That was quite amusing. What do you mean, 'So what'?"

"I mean, sir, that yesterday afternoon was a very short amount of time when one but considers the possible age of the universe, for example. It was barely a spit in the ocean of time.

"You and I are involved, sir, but not in a trivial sort of enterprise. We, sir, are involved in a mystical quest. We were only temporarily derailed because of the weather. The weather is lovely this morning so there is nothing else to distract us.

"Pay attention to the road, Lord Beecham. Luther has an eye on that delicious thick goosegrass over there."

"Luther," he said very quietly to his horse, "you will not act like a bloody woman and hare off on your own, particularly with me on your back."

His horse snorted and Helen laughed.

There were times when a man had no other viable choice but to cozy up to defeat. Lord Beecham cozied up for the remainder of their ride to Dereham.

Vicar Lockleer Gilliam, a distinguished gentleman of fine parts who was also a father of two grown children and a widower pursued by every unmarried lady over forty years of age in his flock, ducked his head into his own small study, which currently housed his brother's manuscripts and books, a nobleman who had studied at Oxford with his brother, and Miss Helen Mayberry, a strapping young woman he would have courted with all the passion in his soul if only she had not been only eight years old twenty years before.

Lord Beecham and Miss Helen Mayberry were both absorbed in what they were doing — namely, poring over those old parchments, mainly shaking their heads because they had not yet succeeded in finding what they were searching for. Dust had formed a light sun-streaked film in the air.

Helen was on her knees in front of a huge parchment manuscript spread out on the lovely Flemish carpet given to the vicar by Lady Winfred Althorpe, who was now, thankfully, re-married. "This isn't it," she said. "It's close, but not close enough."

Lord Beecham looked over. "Yes, it is close. It's Aramaic."

"A cup of tea, my dear?"

"That would be marvelous, Mr. Gilliam," she said, blinking up at him. "You are very kind. Oh, dear, look at all the dust we've raised in here."

He waved her back when she started to get up. "No, you two remain doing what you're doing. I will see Cook about the tea."

Thirty minutes later, their empty teacups set aside, Lord Beecham shouted, "I've got it, Helen. Eureka, I've got it!"

She was on her feet in an instant. He was bending over the vicar's desk, a very old vellum book open in front of him.

"What is it?"

He looked up at her, his dark eyes even darker now with excitement. There was no indolent, world-weary nobleman in his look now. Lord

Beecham was fascinated, he was exhilarated. He was, in short, thrilled to his toes.

"I've found it. I'm sure of it. Look, Helen, just look, and tell me if you don't think this is it."

She looked over his shoulder. She hummed while studying the script. "I think so," she said. "See that strange-looking figure that is repeated many times? It's identical. What is the language?"

"It's called Pahlavi. The alphabet developed from the Aramaic, which is why it looked so similar. Pahlavi was the writing system of the Persians around the beginning of the second century B.C. It lasted until the advent of Islam toward the seventh century A.D. The Avesta — that's the Zoroastrian sacred book — is written in a form of Pahlavi called Avestan. Oh, God, Helen, this is just amazing. To find something like this —" He broke off, gave her a big grin, and clasped her around the waist. He lifted her over his head and swung her around. "We found it. Imagine: Pahlavi, a language so old that it has long been gone from this earth. Just to say the word makes me want to laugh and shout. Think about it: someone actually wrote the leather scroll more than a thousand years ago and we have it here with us, today, in modern times."

He let her down, kissed her mouth, then immediately released her. He was soon bending over the text before him.

She stared at him for a moment, then looked down at the book with the strange writing that was surely identical to the writing on the leather scroll. He was talking to himself as he trailed his long fingers lovingly over the words.

"Tell me about it," she said. "Can you translate our leather scroll?"

"I'm going to try my damnedest. It will be difficult, very difficult, because it was the Pahlavi custom to use Aramaic words to represent Pahlavi words. So take our word 'king.' It's *shah* in Pahlavi, but it's spelled exactly like the Aramaic word *malka*. And the thing is, you have to read the Aramaic word and translate it instantly into Pahlavi, and read it as *shah*. So you're always having to go back and forth in your mind to find the right words. It makes it very difficult to translate, much less simply read. But I can do it, Helen. Given enough time, I can translate the leather scroll."

He turned, grinning from ear to ear. "What's wrong?"

"What if the leather scroll has nothing at all to do with the lamp?"

"Come, Helen, you always knew that was only a remote possibility, despite that you found it on the east coast of England. Why should it? But don't despair just yet. The fact of the matter is that we know the lamp came originally from the Holy Land. We are in roughly the right geographical area. Whatever it says, it will be fascinating, an incredible find, and you, Helen, you are the one who found it and gave it to the world. When it finally comes out, I can imagine scholars from all over Europe coming here to see it." He rubbed his hands together, gave her a vague pat on the shoulder, and looked down once again at the parchment pages.

"But why would a Pahlavi scroll be buried in an iron cask in a cave on the east coast of England? If it was brought here by the Romans when they invaded England, why would it not be written in Latin?"

"I don't know, but we will find out. Don't worry. Your partner is an able fellow."

They spent the next two hours searching for more manuscripts that would help Spenser translate the leather scroll. "There," he said at last, rising and brushing his dusty hands on his riding breeches. "We've got three sources. It is more than I expected to find. It will do."

It was late afternoon when they left the lovely mellow peach brick vicarage, set just behind the old church amid a beautiful wild garden. There were three ladies having tea with the vicar. "The poor man," Helen said in a low voice. "He is mercilessly hunted. His poor wife died just thirteen months ago, around the same time as his brother and your mentor, Sir Giles Gilliam."

"I would say that vicar Gilliam is enjoying himself immensely."

Lord Beecham didn't lose any more of his guineas to Lord Prith at whist that evening because immediately after dinner Helen told her father that Spenser was her partner and she needed him.

Lord Prith said only, "I understand he is your

partner in this lamp business, Nell, but the dear fellow is such an excellent loser at whist."

"You can filch his guineas when he is of no more use to me, Father."

"Ha," said Lord Beecham, but his step was energetic, excitement rippling through him. He couldn't wait. They'd had only a few moments when they'd arrived back at Shugborough Hall to look at the leather scroll before changing for dinner. They had looked just long enough to be absolutely certain that the scroll was written in Pahlavi.

When Helen left him at eleven o'clock that evening, he was still hunched over the manuscript, sometimes writing, sometimes cursing, sometimes humming with pleasure. She doubted that he had even heard her close the door.

She fell asleep immediately and dreamed she was holding a lamp tightly against her chest. She couldn't breathe. She squeezed the lamp harder. Suddenly a strange thing happened. The lamp became a man, a large man who was smiling down at her even while he caressed her flesh. The man was Spenser.

She roared upright in her bed, her breath whooshing out. Oh, goodness, she thought. Every detail of the previous afternoon stood out stark and magnificent in her mind. She was shaking with the power of all those details. She swung her legs over the side of her bed.

It was one o'clock in the morning when she

slipped into her study to see Lord Beecham fast asleep, his head on the desktop, not an inch from the leather scroll, the three manuscripts from Vicar Gilliam's covering the remainder of the desk.

A candle was nearly gutted at his elbow.

There were pages on the floor beside the desk. She went down on her knees and picked up the top sheet. Written in his strong hand was:

From King Faval to his . . ? . . in Alexandria . . . . . . ? . . a holy man sought to secure my soul for his master . . ? . . the lamp is not real, it is from the other . . ? . . is it a gift from God or the devil? . . . he died screaming blasphemies, he cursed me for his end but he killed himself . . .

"Helen, why are you crying?"

"It is the lamp, Spenser, the manuscript is about the lamp. I'm crying because I'm so happy. It is good or evil? It isn't real, it is from the other. . . . Oh, goodness, look at all you have accomplished."

She jumped to her feet and threw herself onto his lap. He caught her to him as the chair collapsed and they sprawled onto the floor, Helen lying on top of him.

He was laughing so hard he couldn't catch his breath. "I've never laughed like this in my benighted life. Get off me, woman." His arms went around her. "No, I wish to change my order. Don't move." He grabbed a fistful of her loose hair and pulled her face down to his. He kissed her, lightly, then he rolled over on her. It quickly became something else, something urgent and frantic, and he wanted her so much that he knew, simply knew, that he would fall lifeless in a heap beside her if he couldn't have her *now*. He didn't stop kissing her as he jerked up her nightgown. His warm hands were on her thighs, her belly, caressing her. "Oh, my God, Helen, I must have you now." He got his breeches open and reared over her.

His fingers were on her, her scent swamping him. He managed to focus in that moment on her face. Her eyes were the blazing blue of a stormy summer day. Her lips were parted, damp from kissing him. Her breasts were heaving.

And she whispered, arching up to him, "Spenser."

He nearly went over the edge just looking at her, just hearing her say his name like that. He gritted his teeth, lifted her hips, and came into her hard, so deep he thought he would die from the power of it. Her arms were tight around him, but he had enough sense, enough experience, to pull out of her, breathing so hard he thought his heart would burst from his chest, and caress her with his fingers. He was staring down at his fingers, at her, his look so intense, so filled with the pleasure of it, that in a minute, no more, she yelled out his name, heaving against his fingers, and he watched her face in those precious moments, her pleasure tearing through him as well through her. He came into her again, deep and hard, wondering how he had survived all these

151

years without her, and soon, too soon, it was over, and he knew he'd given his all, there was nothing else in him, and he was content. They were pressed tightly together, panting, and he was still kissing her, unable to stop.

He was still breathing hard, his breath hot in her mouth, and she whispered even as she licked his chin, "I don't believe this."

He reared up over her, balanced himself on his elbows, and said, "This isn't what I am used to, either. No, that is ridiculous. Of course I am used to this, it is just that something has happened, something —" He stopped talking, just stared down at her, and frowned. He was also still deep inside her. He looked to be in pain. "Oh, Helen," he said, and moved, arching his back with the instant power of it. "My God, Helen." And he began moving again, deeply, and then, suddenly, he pulled out of her, lifted her hips, and gave her his mouth.

Helen arched and twisted as if she'd been shot. He held her firmly until she gave it up, yelled his name, and collapsed even as he came into her again.

"No," he said, panting as if he had just run all the way from Court Hammering, "I don't believe this. A man doesn't do this every three seconds. It is madness. I will topple into an early grave. No, I must control myself. No, Helen, don't you dare move. Oh, no, it is too much."

"It was at least three minutes," she said. She didn't move. Actually, she doubted she could move if this roof fell in on her. She was sprawled beneath him, pinned down by him, and she clasped her hands around his neck and brought his mouth back down to hers.

12

At least ten minutes passed this time before he was once again moving deeply in her, more easily now, but soon enough it quickened, and he was a madman once again, his mind splintered, all his focus on her and how he couldn't get enough of her or get deep enough inside her. He wanted to possess her, to brand her, to imprint her, it was that simple, that final. He caught her cries in his mouth, felt her nails digging into his back, and climaxed as wildly as he had the first time.

"I will die now," he announced to the silent, small room, his hot breath in her left ear. Her hair was tangled around her face, over her shoulders, her mouth red and swollen, her nightgown bunched up about her breasts. He was still inside her, but not so much now — after all, a man had to retreat sooner or later.

It was definitely later.

"Yes," she said, "I will, too." The sound of her frantic heartbeat was not so loud now in her ears. As for his heartbeat, it pounded deep, steady thuds against her breast. She said, her voice both surprised and bewildered, "I never imagined there could be anything like this. I have read many different books, looked at many different drawings. Never was there anything written or drawn that contemplated what you have just done to me so many times in so few minutes."

"You mean what you and I have just done together," he said. "I promise you that I could not have done this without you." He sounded as baffled as she did, but she also heard something else.

She said, "I don't understand."

"Understand what? That you are a passionate woman? That I am an immensely excellent lover?" The austere male arrogance was suddenly back, and she saw the blatant satisfaction stamped hard on his face, heard it in his voice.

"No," she said slowly, rubbing her hands up and down his back, feeling his muscles, his bones, the warmth of his flesh, the wondrous smoothness of him through his fine lawn shirt. "I don't understand why you are scared."

He jerked out of her and was on his feet in the next instant, pulling up his breeches, buttoning them. He stared down at her, sprawled naked, her white legs apart, long and sleek, so utterly beautiful, so soft in the gentle candlelight. "Damn you, I am not scared. You are a woman. Stop drawing absurd conclusions based upon your own weak female notions. I am not scared."

She slowly sat up and slowly pulled her nightgown over her legs. She was very wet with him. It was strange, this wetness. It had been a very long time since she had felt such a thing.

Since yesterday.

She stroked her fingers through her hair to pull out the tangles. She looked up then to see that he was staring at her fingers pulling through her hair.

She saw his own fingers clenching at his sides. "I am not scared. That is ridiculous. It is nonsense."

She looked over at the broken chair, a lovely Louis XV, all white and gold, that had belonged to her grandmother. One leg had broken off cleanly. The other leg had splintered badly. With care, perhaps, the chair could be repaired, but that one leg would be difficult.

She looked over at the pile of pages beside her on the floor. They had both been so focused, so urgent, that they hadn't even moved much, just gone mad together in one spot. The pages hadn't been touched.

"I don't like this, Helen."

She sighed and stood up. Her legs nearly gave out on her. She grabbed the edge of the desk, waited a moment, then slowly straightened again. She said, her eyes focused just beyond his left shoulder on the narrow bookshelf in the corner that held her novels, "I am going back to my bedchamber now. I think you are doing a magnificent job on translating the scroll. It is about the lamp. I knew it just had to be. But how?"

He shrugged and tucked his shirt into his breeches. "I agree. I would have thought that since it is about the lamp, then the lamp would have been in the iron cask with it. Why was a letter or a message or whatever it is sealed up all by itself? What is the point? Where is that bloody lamp?"

"It is possible," she said slowly, lightly touching her fingertip to the leather scroll, "that someone found this cask much later, perhaps even after the lamp was here in England with King Edward. Perhaps this someone knew where King Edward had buried the lamp in a general sort of way, and buried the cask nearby. Then if both were found, the scroll would explain about the lamp and all would be known. There was nothing else in that small cave. I looked very carefully. But perhaps close by, not too far away from the cave —"

"Helen."

She raised her head and stared at him. He looked tough in the dim, spindly candlelight, tough and hard and dangerous. She had the sudden urge to fling herself on him and take him down to the floor. It was a floor she would never look at again in quite the same way. She smiled then. He had made love to her with his boots on.

"Don't smile at me. Listen, I am not scared. But I will tell you this. It must stop. This has never happened to me before, this complete loss of what I am and what I'm doing. Not once did I think to withdraw from you, not one single time, either yesterday or now. If this continues you will become pregnant." Just saying the word made his eyes nearly cross, and, strangely enough, not with abject terror. No, in that instant, he saw her belly rounded with his child, and she was laughing and telling him something that made him kiss her and laugh as well. And his hand lay over her belly, over his child. Then it was gone.

He didn't know what was wrong with him. It was the bloody lamp. Whatever it was or wasn't, it was making him quite mad.

She looked away, toward the windows behind her desk, where the pale yellow draperies were tightly drawn. Her shoulders were slumped, her head bent. She said, "That need not worry you ever."

He didn't know what she was talking about. He saw her again, her eyes sparkling, their babe in her belly, and his hands, they were all over her now.

"What don't you wish to worry me?"

"Your staying inside me is not a problem."

"Spilling my seed inside of you isn't a problem?" No, he thought, it was not a problem at all. He said, "Are you mad, woman? Of course it could be a problem. I have no bastards because I have always been very careful. With you, it's been different, somehow."

"I am barren."

No, he thought, that wasn't right. There she was, so clear in his mind, her belly pressing against him when she kissed him. The babe was due soon. "How the devil would you know that?"

"I was married, once, a very long time ago, when I had just turned eighteen. My father be-

158

lieved I was too young, but I was desperately in love and thus he gave me my way. My husband, a man of nearly your advanced years, wanted an heir very badly." She shrugged. "He was killed when the war started again, just after the Treaty of Amiens collapsed."

"That was a long time ago."

"Yes. We were only married for two years before he died. I came back to my father's house and took my own name again."

"I didn't know."

"Why should you? It isn't common knowledge."

"I remember I asked you if you had been married. You didn't really answer me, now that I think about it."

"I would not have told you now, except you are very scared that you have made me pregnant. Well, you haven't. I am barren."

She turned without another word and walked out of the study.

Lord Beecham slowly bent down to gather up the papers on the floor. He barely glanced at the translation he had managed so far. He laid the pages atop Helen's desk, snuffed out the candle, and left the room.

It was nearly three o'clock in the morning. When he fell asleep, he saw Helen again, so very clearly, and she was naked and he was kissing her mouth, her breasts, as his hands stroked her big belly, then he was kissing her belly, feeling his babe kick against his cheek when he pressed his face against her.

He jerked awake and sat up in bed. He was not a superstitious man. He did not believe in visions or in portents. Then he thought, If Helen birthed a girl, she would be an Amazon, a beautiful sharp-tongued Amazon. And a boy? He would be a big man, confident, a leader of men.

He smiled fatuously into the darkness.

I am losing what few wits remain to me, he thought as he pillowed his head against his arms. Helen was his partner. The rest of it was lunacy. All right, so she was both his partner and his lover, and even she must accept that now. They would do their best to find this lamp, whatever the thing was.

But there was this madness with her. When he had been a randy boy there had been the fire in his gut, as lust was spoken of in young males. But he wasn't a boy now. He was a full-grown man, a man of control and experience.

Only he had no control with Helen. It wasn't what he was used to. Usually, sating himself with a woman sent him into sweet dreams almost immediately, but not this time, not with Helen. He had been beyond sated, nearly unconscious, yet, at the same time, he had a very strong feeling that if Helen were to stroll into his bedchamber right this minute, he would want her as much as he had the first, the second, the third time he'd taken her on the floor of her study two hours before.

When he fell asleep again, he didn't dream of

Helen. He dreamed of a man who held a gun in a very white hand. He could not tell where that gun was pointing, but he knew he was afraid. Then the man turned and Spenser saw that a black mask covered his face. He laughed, aimed the gun at Spenser, and pulled the trigger.

Spenser came awake abruptly and bolted straight up in bed, his heart nearly bursting out of his chest. There was Nettle, standing not two feet from him and he was screaming at the top of his lungs.

"Nettle, shut up. Good God, man, what's the matter?"

"My lord, you must help me, quickly, quickly! That madman will be here in just a moment and I know he is carrying an ax over his shoulder and he wants to chop my poor head from my neck. Please, you must help me, my lord."

And Nettle bolted under Lord Beecham's bed.

Not two minutes later, Flock appeared in the now open doorway to Lord Beecham's bedchamber. He wasn't carrying an ax over his shoulder. However, he did have a gun in his right hand, and there was a very determined expression on his face.

"Where is the little rat, my lord?"

Lord Beecham said mildly, "Flock, do you know what time it is?"

"It is a good time for that little bastard you employ as your valet to meet his maker, whom I believe to be the devil."

"Flock, get out of my bedchamber."

"Goodness, Flock, you will stop this now or I will send you to my inn and discipline you with all my lads there."

"Miss Helen," Flock said with great dignity, which was difficult since Helen towered over him, "his lordship's valet, a man of no moral fiber whatsoever, was kissing Teeny on the back steps. She was even carrying a bucket of hot water for you, Miss Helen. She even set down that bucket to return the bounder's kisses. I must kill him, Miss Helen."

"I don't see him in here, Flock," Helen said. "You have disturbed his lordship, who, I must tell you, was working very, very late last night."

"It wasn't all work," his lordship said.

"In any case, you awoke him because of all this melodrama. Go away, Flock. Do you want me to discipline you, in a way you won't like at all?"

Flock's gun hand shook a bit. Finally, he whispered, "No, Miss Helen. Your stable lad at the inn told me what you did to him after he had started a fight with the butcher's cousin and bloodied his nose."

"Good. Worse will happen to you if you do not give me that bloody pistol immediately and go see about Lord Prith's breakfast. You know how hungry he is by seven o'clock in the morning. If you don't hurry, he just might be awaiting you to wring your neck."

"Yes, Miss Helen, but I am not happy about this. I already warned that little codpiece, you know that. If he believes that he can seduce my

Teeny without retribution, I am sunk."

"I will speak to Teeny, Flock. I will find out what is going on here, and I will tell you when I have all the information I need. You will not be sunk. Go away now."

Once Helen had closed the door behind Flock and set the pistol down upon a dressing table, she eyed Lord Beecham, who was sitting up in his bed, the covers coming only to his waist, his hair tousled, and she called out, "Nettle, you will show yourself immediately, or it will be the worse for you."

Nettle crawled out from under Lord Beecham's bed.

"An excellent hiding place," she said. "Even Flock at his most ferocious would not have dared to peer beneath Lord Beecham's bed. Come here and sit down."

Lord Beecham had never before been awakened to such wonderful comedy. He settled himself back against his pillows, crossed his arms over his chest, and prepared to be entertained.

"That's right, clean yourself off. I see that I will have to speak to Mrs. Stockley. Dirt and dust under the bed. She will likely chew on the maid's ear about that. All right, now, Nettle, you look well enough. Sit." She pointed to a chair not far from Lord Beecham's bed.

Nettle sat, but he wasn't looking at Helen, he was staring beyond her, at the bedchamber door.

"Why were you kissing Teeny on the back stairs when she was carrying a bucket of hot water?"

Nettle crossed his small white hands over his chest. He looked soulful, or bilious, depending on the eye beholding him. "I am in love, Miss Helen," he announced then, having set his stage to his satisfaction.

Helen said, "What is your last name, Nettle?"

"Why, it is Nettle, Miss Helen."

"Your first name, then?"

"Bloodworth, ma'am. Bloodworth Nettle."

"You are jesting."

"No, ma'am. It was my ma's name before she married my pa and became a Nettle."

Helen's voice was faint. "That would make Teeny and Bloodworth Nettle. It curdles the belly."

Lord Beecham rocked with laughter. The covers fell even lower. Helen looked resolutely away. She needed to solve this problem. "I try to use a bit of blood whenever I call for him," said Lord Beecham.

"That's right, ma'am. His lordship calls me bloody Nettle or bloody scoundrel or bloody baboon. Something along that line, you understand."

"Yes, I quite understand."

"It would be simply Teeny Nettle, ma'am."

"No, Teeny is very sensitive. There is too much blood in the names. It will never do."

Lord Beecham remarked to the room at large,

"There is also the matter of Teeny becoming a small weed."

She ignored that. "How old are you, Nettle?"

"I am only thirty-five, Miss Helen."

"Flock is thirty-eight," she said, and sighed.

"Not much difference there," Lord Beecham said. "What's a poor big girl to do?"

Helen said as she walked to the bedchamber door, "I am going to introduce Teeny to Walter Jones, the young man who works in his father's mercantile shop in Court Hammering. He is only twenty-two, and there is no blood in any of his names."

"Oh, no, Miss Helen!"

"Don't do that, Miss Helen!"

Nettle leapt to his feet. Flock flung open the bedchamber door, nearly knocking Helen sideways against the wall.

Lord Beecham leaped out of bed, stark naked.

Helen whirled about to look at him, blinked, then resolutely turned away. "Lord Beecham," she called out over her shoulder, "return to your bed. I have things well in hand." She got herself together, straightened her skirt, and poked a finger at Lord Beecham's valet and her father's butler. "I have had quite enough of this. Neither one of you will ever win Teeny. Flock, your name simply will not do. Teeny Flock — it is impossible. She cannot be a small herd.

"As for you, Nettle, in addition to Teeny being a small weed, your first name will not do at all. As a couple, she would be Teeny Bloodbane, and you would be Bloodworth Nettle. It will not work.

"As I told his lordship here, there is just too much blood flowing about. Now, both of you might as well set your sights elsewhere. Teeny Jones sounds marvelous and that is the way it will be. Teeny and Walter Jones. I have also decided that both of you are too old for Teeny. Walter is just right. Now, both of you get out of here."

"Er, Miss Mayberry, may my valet remain and assist me?"

"You are a grown man, Lord Beecham. I have never understood why a grown man can't assist himself."

"And your Teeny?"

"You, sir, have no notion what it is like to have buttons marching up your back. Now, out of here, Flock. You may remain for the moment, Nettle, but no more scurrying under his lordship's bed. You will maintain a modicum of dignity."

With that, Helen whisked out of his bedchamber, her pale-blue muslin skirts dancing around her ankles.

Lord Beecham crossed his arms behind his head. He eyed his valet, who looked to be on the verge of tears. "I don't believe I've ever been quite so entertained at seven o'clock in the morning. Fetch me some bathwater, Nettle. Don't cry, man, you'll get over it soon enough. Didn't you see the downstairs maid?"

"No, my lord. I doubt I could see her even if I looked directly at her, what with all the tears from my broken heart filling my eyes."

Lord Beecham rolled his own eyes.

At the breakfast table with Lord Prith, Lord Beecham even managed to avoid sipping a noxious mixture of apple juice and champagne, but he watched Lord Prith vigorously down a glass. Lord Prith ruminated a moment, then admitted, "I must say, this concoction would send a warning to a man's liver. What would you think of a mixture of elderberry wine and champagne?"

Lord Beecham nearly gagged.

13

The roof of the cave was so low that both Spenser and Helen had to bend over. Helen, leading the way, holding a lantern in front of her, said over her shoulder, "The floor slopes down in a few more steps. Then we can stand up, barely."

Spenser hated caves, avoided them like the plague, always had since the time when he was nine years old and a young neighbor girl had gotten lost in one and he had had to go in to find her. Her echoing cries, like dying breaths of tortured souls, overlaid with the cold, wet air of that cave, were forever imprinted on his brain.

"How big is the cave?" His voice sounded hollow, thinning as the echoes used the sounds until his words dissolved throughout the cave. He wondered if his voice would even be recognizable in a few more steps.

"Another twenty feet or so. It is like a long loaf of bread. There are no side chambers." She sounded vastly disappointed. As for Lord Beecham, he was more relieved than he could say. The little girl had wandered off into a side chamber, and that was where he had found her all those years ago, huddled beneath a narrow ledge. Not two feet from the little girl lay a skeleton, something he doubted either of them would forget for the rest of their lives. The faded, tattered clothes, of excellent quality and at least one hundred years old, that still hung on those bones were so old they disintegrated completely when the men collected them for burial.

It wasn't quite as damp and clammy in this cave because it was smaller, but still, inside, it was blacker than a villain's dreams.

Helen paused a moment just ahead of him. He saw her tilt her head in the glittering light of the lantern as if she was listening to something. He stopped as well. He could hear his heart beat just as it had so many years before. The beat was deafening.

"It is nothing," she called out, "just bats settling in." She continued forward, the lantern held high.

Bats, he wondered, as he had always wondered about things for which man had no explanation. How did bats manage to see in the dark? He remembered that Sir Giles Gilliam had known the answer to many things, but he hadn't known a thing about bats. No one at Oxford knew much about bats.

The ground was sloping downward now. Another two steps and he could stand straight with a good two inches between the top of his head and the ceiling of the cave.

Helen stopped. She went down to her hands and knees and carefully set the lantern on the ground beside her. "After that big storm, I was exploring in here. You can see that the wall there caved inward, spilling out a lot of dirt and the cask." Her voice was low and deep, and the faint echo made her sound mysterious, perhaps not even of this world. It flashed cold over his flesh. He said aloud, "The echoes, even here, when we speak quietly, very close together, they spread throughout my brain. I believe I am becoming mystical, Helen. Perhaps soon I shall begin to chant in strange tongues."

She looked up at him, the glow from the lantern making her face look like a white plaster death mask. "I know. Caves make me feel the same way. When I am by myself, I usually sing so I do not scare myself to death. When I am not shivering from fright, I am laughing at myself."

"I will have to try that." Lord Beecham came down beside her. "So the storm shook something loose and sent the cask spilling out of the wall. Look at this." Pressed against the wall of the cave was a small ledge, no higher than a foot and a half off the ground. "It is perfectly flat, and that means that someone carved it this flat to hold something." Now that he looked more closely, he added, "No, the ledge isn't natural to this cave. I think perhaps some people built the ledge here specifically to hold that cask and then changed their minds. Too exposed, better to hide it, to bury it in the wall of the cave. And they left the ledge, why not?"

There were two narrow slabs of stone holding up the ledge.

"Goodness," Helen said suddenly, nearly falling over with surprise. "I had not noticed this

170

before." She picked up the lantern and held it close. She pulled a handkerchief from her cloak pocket and began wiping down the stone. "Carvings, Spenser, or writing of some kind."

He came down beside her. As she held the lantern, he took the handkerchief and finished brushing away grit and sand until the carved letters showed themselves to be deep and well chiseled. "Well, now," he said slowly, "this certainly isn't Pahlavi or Latin." He turned to look into her shadowed eyes.

He said, "It's Old French."

"The French Edward the First spoke?"

"Oh, yes."

"Just a moment." Helen set the lantern down and reached into her cloak pocket. This time she pulled out some ribbon-tied papers and a chunk of charcoal wrapped in a white cloth.

"Are you always so prepared, Helen?"

"I sketch," she said. She gave him a quick sideways look. "I had thought perhaps that later I would draw you on the beach, just over where the tide pool is."

"I should like that," he said. She looked down then. Was she mayhap embarrassed because her level of skill wasn't sufficient? He was pleased, very pleased.

"Naked. Perhaps standing with your hands on your hips, staring out to sea, the tide pool flowing over your bare feet. What do you think?"

He stared at her, mesmerized. "Be quiet. I prefer you pulling off my boots."

She was grinning as she smoothed out a piece of foolscap on the ledge. She held the charcoal, waiting for him to translate.

"The words are written on top of each other. This won't be easy." He read slowly, translating as he went, " 'It is blessed or it is nothing. It is here and yet it is not here. It is the light of his dawn.' " He paused, frowned.

"Yes," he said, staring at that word, "it does say '*his* dawn,' not '*the* dawn.' "

Helen was tugging on his sleeve. "Hurry, Spenser."

"Let me think a moment. Oh, yes. 'It is powerful but it cannot be proved. It is something other, but no one knows what. Whatever truths it holds we do not understand them. We fear its power. We bury it and pray that its spirit survives. If it is evil, withal, we pray it journeys back to hell.' "

Spenser looked up. "That's all of it. I think I got most of it right. Have you gotten it all down?"

"Just a moment, a bit more. Now, let me take a few moments and copy down the original as well."

He watched her very carefully copy down the Old French. When she was finished, she looked up at him and shuddered. "I'm cold. It's from the inside out. What can it mean?" He rose slowly, then gave her his hand. "Why was this with the leather scroll?"

He just shook his head.

"Where is the lamp? Why wasn't the lamp here? Surely this Old French speaks directly of the lamp."

"Yes, it does. There is nothing else that fits."

"Then where is it?"

"I begin to think that the Templar who gave King Edward the lamp presented it to him in the iron cask along with the leather scroll. I do not believe that anyone could have translated the scroll back then. I think that when the king decided to hide the lamp, perhaps at overwhelming urging from churchmen, he simply placed it back into its original cask, with the scroll, then buried it in the cave wall. He had someone write on this ledge — giving some sort of explanation, some sort of reasoning."

"But none of it makes any sense. It seems it was just as great a mystery to them as it is to us."

"Possibly. But perhaps they did understand a bit of it, enough to be frightened of it. Who knows? It is said that the medieval mind was a labyrinth with more twists and shadows than we modern folk can begin to comprehend.

"Or, Helen, perhaps someone found the lamp hundreds of years ago and simply removed it. He left the cask and the scroll behind because he perceived no value in them."

"Yes," she said slowly, "that sounds reasonable." She looked as if she would cry. "Then the lamp is gone, found by someone long ago, perhaps disposed of again, and now there is simply no trace of it."

"No, I could easily be wrong. The lamp could have been hidden elsewhere. Perhaps the scroll instructs that the lamp should be kept separate from it. That would mean, then, that someone did translate the scroll. If that is true, then the scroll will have to speak of it." He saw that she wanted to believe him. He wasn't at all sure what he himself believed at this moment. A riddle in Old French engraved on a ledge at the back of a cave. And out of the wall of that cave, just above that ledge, had fallen an iron cask that held a leather scroll with writing from before the birth of Christ.

He was beginning to feel chilled, the damp of the cave burrowing through his clothes to his flesh. "We can't believe anything just yet, Helen. There are a number of possibilities. We will discover the truth, I swear it to you."

"You are an excellent partner," she said, and tried to smile.

He dismissed the lamp from his mind and lightly cupped her cheek with his palm. "Three weeks ago, Miss Mayberry, I was quite happily absorbed in doing not much of anything, simply enjoying all those delightful little pleasures of life. Then I heard you speak of discipline to Alexandra at the Sanderling's ball, and my life flew out of my control."

"Lord Beecham," she said, all stern and hard, "I am the one who has been made love to six times in the past two days. Pray do not speak to me of life having flown out of control."

174

He laughed deeply, a black sound in the damp darkness that echoed like chortling demons around a midnight fire. When they reached the narrow mouth of the cave and stepped into the sunlight, he turned to her and wiped the dust from her face. "When I became your partner, I had not expected such adventure."

"I have a feeling," she said slowly, staring at him, "that the adventure is just beginning."

They stood together for a moment on the promontory just south of Aldeburgh and stared up the long, narrow beach. The small cave was ten feet below them, a shadowed black mouth in the side of the sliding rubble of a cliff. It was a bit treacherous getting to it because of all the strewn rocks and loose dirt.

"It's the most beautiful place on the earth," Helen said. The tide was rising, sending swirling waters to break and fan out higher and higher onto the dirty brown sand. Countless black rocks, piled atop each other or standing alone, were covered with sea lettuce, bright green beneath the bright morning sun overhead. There were scattered piles of driftwood with seaweed woven in and over the broken branches and stems, like tangled green ropes. Shallow tidal pools were filled with limpets, beadlet anemones, periwinkles, barnacles, and sponges, all clinging to the small rocks within the pool. Lord Beecham wondered which one Helen wanted to flow over his feet when she sketched him naked.

Marram grass stuck up in thick clumps on low

sand dunes, along with lady's bedstraw and restharrow, pink and violet blooms that looked delicate but were as tough as a man's mother-in-law. And the pink of those dainty blooms reminded him of Helen's mouth, and so he looked at her mouth, all softly plump and pink, and he shook.

Lord Beecham breathed in deeply and looked at the scores of birds, particularly the one sanderling who was just a bit slower than his brothers. On one of his races with the waves, he was going to lose. He watched and breathed in the smell of the sea, the drying seaweed, the scent of the wildflowers, and he didn't look at Helen's mouth.

"Just look at the avocets," Helen said, pointing to several birds sitting in among the bedstraw and restharrow. "Those long, skinny, black beaks can go very deep to stab food. See how they turn up at the end? And there are so many black-headed gulls here. Most of all I love to watch the sandpipers hopping along the sand, racing the water both in and out."

Somehow he wasn't surprised. But he said nothing, just kept looking at all the birds. There were more kinds than he could begin to count, all of them hungry, all of them yelling, crying, squawking, yipping. He watched some small oystercatchers and gray plovers racing a fast incoming wave. The water feathered out more quickly this time than just the time before, and the sanderling he had been watching, lost the race. It got soaked and nearly tottered over.

"My family home," Lord Beecham said, "as I told you already, is Paledowns, near the coast in North Devon. You can stand on the cliffs there and look toward Lundy Island. There are more birds mating there than you can even begin to count. They cover the sky during the spring. Puffins — my favorite as a boy — and razorbills, and kittiwakes — ah, so many different kinds, all of them loud and rowdy. If they're not shrieking at each other, they're flying over anyone who chances to be outside, their noise deafening, and naturally you're running for cover. It's a fascinating time of year."

"I have never been to Devon. Where is Paledowns, exactly?"

"Between Combe Martin Bay and Woody Bay, by the village of Bassett. The sea cliffs there about are covered with shags and cormorants. There are days I remember as a child when there were so many fulmars diving and whirling about overhead that you couldn't see the sky. Just fulmars gliding and swooping about, and even when one flew away you couldn't see the sky because another moved in to take its place."

She was looking at him as though he was a stranger to her. She said slowly, looking at his mouth — she didn't know why, but his mouth pleased her — "I hadn't imagined that you would be so familiar with birds and such." She shrugged. "One thinks of a gentleman and one pictures a stack of playing cards, a bottle of brandy, and an unbuttoned waistcoat."

"And a red nose? Perhaps a woman bending over him, her breasts nearly falling out of her gown?"

"It is the likeliest image."

He supposed that was fair enough. A man of his proclaimed habits wasn't necessarily given much credit for having expanded horizons. "Helen, a man who is a noted lover can appreciate other things as well. Life is not all drink and playing cards and women's soft flesh."

He had silenced her for the moment, he saw that, and it pleased him. He stared toward a small group of pink-footed geese who couldn't seem to decide whether to stay on the wet sand or soar up to the cliff top. Even geese had to have a leader, and so he said, "A woman, even a strong woman like you, Helen, needs a man to assist her over the cracks in the roads of life."

She stared at him, her head cocked to one side.

He pointed upward. "See the geese, now soaring upward in a nearly perfect formation? Well, they need a leader to get anywhere at all. So does a woman. She needs a man. That's what I meant."

"If I could fly," she said, shading her eyes with her hand and staring after the geese, "I wouldn't need anything at all. Even without a leader, I would be free."

He looked again at her soft mouth and said, "Perhaps. To be truthful, a man prefers to be in bed with a woman rather than philosophizing about geese needing leaders or studying the eating habits of the leach's petrel. However, when the man — such as myself — is very intelligent, then he can do many things at once, all of them well. Freedom for a woman, Helen, is being led by a man like me."

Helen bent down, pulled up a yellow-horned poppy, and threw it at him.

He caught the small flower, shook off the dirt, and brought it to his nose. "Not much smell. Time for more truth — I would rather be breathing in your scent while I'm kissing your white belly."

She turned away from him, and he imagined quite correctly that she wanted to smash him but good, but she controlled herself, saying as she pointed, "Pay attention, Lord Beecham. The land flattens out south of us. There are salt marshes that are covered with waders at low tide, estuaries that snake in and out of the low-lying land, very bad-smelling stretches where the water is trapped for long periods of time. I doubt you would appreciate that particular scent. But along here we have a more interesting coastline." She opened her arms wide. "I own a lot of this land."

It wasn't worth much, he thought, but he wouldn't mind owning it either, just for its incredible beauty. He said, "This land is like the biblical lily of the valley, Helen, it provides neither food nor a way to grow it. There is no arable farmland, no place to build homes, not even decent grazing for sheep or cattle, just the vast stretches of marram grass, pink sea bindweed, and dunes covered with yellow evening primroses."

"I bought it because I know the lamp is here, somewhere."

He nodded. Perhaps he would have done the same thing. The only thing was, anyone could come on this land and search. There were no fences, even though fences wouldn't make any difference to a treasure hunter.

"There are even some rich pink marsh orchids sticking up here and there," Helen said. "You wouldn't enjoy it if I threw marsh orchids at you. But mainly, as you can see, there is just the harsh green shingle flora covering most everything. Yes, this is my biblical lily of the valley. I do not expect it to return anything to me, except the lamp."

"A rather large expectation."

"Just the search makes it worth it," and he believed her. Actually, it would make it worth it to him as well. He watched her reach down and snap a flower off its stem. "It's wild chamomile," she said, straightening. "Just breathe in the smell of it, Lord Beecham. Mrs. Stockley makes a marvelous tea with it."

"The scent is not bad, but on the other hand, it's not you."

Did her hand tremble at his words just a bit? Probably not. She said, "Lord Beecham, you will attend me. Now is one of those unexpected times in your life when you must attune your brilliant mind to matters other than carnal passions."

"You wish me to forget that soft white flesh behind your knees?"

"You have never known the soft white flesh behind my knees."

"True, I've been too frantic, too crazed with lust, and thus neglected the less dramatic yet still quite delicious treats that you have to offer me. I will try to find more control the next time." He took her hand and couldn't help himself. He stared at her mouth. "But the problem, Helen, is that I want to be inside you immediately. I want to be so deep inside you that when you tighten around me, I feel like I will fly apart and there is no more wondrous thing in life to do than fly apart inside of you. And your long legs, Helen, around my flanks, squeezing me. And just before you scream your pleasure, I love to kiss that wild beating pulse in your throat."

"You are very fluent with words that create very vivid images, but I am not listening to you, Lord Beecham. The words you have just said have flown away on bird wings, thus, to me, they never even existed.

"There will be no next time. I have given this a good deal of thought. You will be my partner, no more, no less. Anything else makes no sense. I am serious about this, Lord Beecham. Now, it is time to get back to Shugborough Hall. It is time for luncheon, then time for work."

He lightly stroked his fingers over her cheek, tucked a windblown piece of hair behind her ear, and leaned forward to touch his mouth to hers. It nearly undid him, but not quite.

He drew back, smiled at her, patted her cheek, and whistled as he walked away from her.

"You need discipline," she called after him, her hair whipping into her mouth.

He turned and gave her a long, thoughtful look. "Discipline, if dished out by an expert, is a very fine thing, Miss Mayberry. Perhaps I should reconsider having a competition with you. What do you think? Could you possibly devise anything close to what I eventually will do to you?"

"You will probably be shot before that can happen."

He laughed and laughed. It was beginning to feel familiar to him now, this laughter thing. He rather liked it. It made his innards feel warm and somehow more connected to something outside himself. It brought that something closer to him, and whatever it was, he liked it.

Helen prepared to leave him at the turnoff to Shugborough Hall. "I must find Walter Jones, the young man who will be marrying Teeny. Also, I must see that all my lads are doing their jobs correctly and that Mrs. Toop is controlling Cook and Gwen. I will be home soon."

"What if the lads are slackers?"

"They will be sorry for it." She paused a moment, then gave him a sloe-eyed smile that made him instantly randier than a goat looking at the first grass of spring. "They know all about punishments, Lord Beecham. It is rare that they would dare not pull their weight. It is only when there is a rumor about a new punishment that they do their jobs poorly just to see what it is."

His eyes nearly crossed. She gave him a little wave and rode Eleanor, snorting and flinging her head about, toward the west to Court Hammering. Her laughter floated back to him.

"Wait," he called after her. "I wish to visit this inn of yours."

14

The market town of Court Hammering was just three miles east of Orford and two miles south of Shugborough Hall. Had there been any high promontories about, he fancied he would be able to see the sea. But the land was gentle rolling hills, thick stands of oak and maple trees, and stone fences older than the Druids.

Court Hammering wasn't a particularly beautiful old town, but it had an air of satisfaction and stolid durability, a lovely old stone church built from the local pale-gray stone, and a small green with a pond in the middle and at least three dozen birds of all sorts hanging about in the willow trees that hung over the water. Not a bad town, he thought, to nurture the mistress of discipline.

Unfortunately, King Edward's Lamp, the premier inn of Court Hammering, was currently overrun by a group of boisterous young men from Cambridge, here for a touted mill being held over near Braintree way. They were also here to drink themselves stupid in Helen's taproom, something that would not have been allowed were Helen present.

Lord Beecham saw the blood in her eyes as she walked into the inn. He was grinning from ear to ear. He couldn't wait to see what she would do.

The taproom was long and narrow, low-ceilinged, with heavy dark wooden beams, a highly polished oak floor, and a large fireplace with a wide stone hearth. There were four long tables with benches and three smaller tables with chairs and a row of windows across the back of the room. There was an open door on the far side of the taproom that gave onto the kitchen.

It felt cozy and warm as a mother's womb, safe from the dangers of the world, a man's haven. The air was thick with the rich, yeasty smells of ale and baking bread.

But what struck Lord Beecham when he stepped into that open doorway was the ear-shattering noise. When he had been at Oxford, had he made this kind of racket? Probably so.

One young man was standing on top of a long table, singing at the top of his lungs, his shirt free of his breeches. Another young man was cursing at the barmaid while his friend was trying to pull her onto his lap and put his hand up her skirt at the same time. One very pale young man was lying on his face close to the table, perhaps unconscious. Dice were being thrown at another table. There were shouts of triumph, moans when the dice came up snake eyes, and the general wild-eyed fever of youth.

In the short moment after Lord Beecham arrived in the doorway of the taproom, he would swear that it got noisier.

Any other woman in the world, and he would have ordered her to remain in the corridor while

185

he dealt with the drunk young men. But it was Helen, and there wasn't any other woman like her in the whole world.

He smiled, folded his arms over his chest, and watched her stride into her taproom. By all that was good and right, he thought, she would look magnificent with a sword in her hand. But, truth be told, she didn't need one.

She went directly to the young man who was pulling the barmaid down onto his lap.

Helen stopped directly in front of him.

The barmaid, Gwendolyn, saw her first and yelled over the din of young male voices, "Miss Helen, help!"

"I am here, Gwen." She closed her hand over the young man's shirt collar and lifted him straight up. He dropped Gwen and gawked at the goddess who had him by the neck.

"What — ?"

"You stupid young codfish," Helen said calmly, jerked him off the bench and shoved him against the wall. She grabbed his neck in both hands and slammed his head back once, twice, against the wall. She quickly stepped back and watched him slide slowly to the floor, uncon- scious. She said to Gwen, who was straightening her apron and cap, "Go fetch the lads from the stable. We need to clean all these little giblets out of the taproom."

"Hey, you big woman, what are you doing?"

It was the young man who had been cursing a blue streak. Helen turned on him, grabbed the oversized lapels on his bright-yellow jacket, and jerked him to his feet. "I think the buttons on your jacket are too big. You need a new tailor."

"I paid my last quarter's allowance for this jacket," the young man yelled in Helen's face. "I know it is prime style because my father hates it."

"Hmmm," Helen said. "I see your point. Very well, then just reduce the size of those silver buttons."

The young man looked suddenly uncertain and a good ten years younger. "You really believe they are too large?"

"They are wearing you, not the other way around," she said, saw that his wits were probably too addled from her fine ale to understand, and said, "You are the tail and your clothes the dog." She turned away then, saying over her shoulder, "Cursing makes you look dull-witted." She then turned to the rest of the young men, most of whom were just staring at her, bleary-eyed. She was so big and beautiful, not to mention commanding. He could imagine they wondered if they weren't dreaming they had died and gone to the Vikings' heaven.

Lord Beecham saw another young man, this one so drunk he was frankly surprised the fellow could even coordinate enough to walk, but he managed it. He also looked furious, his sharp features flushed scarlet. Lord Beecham didn't like that. He took a step forward, stopped, and said quietly, "Helen, behind you."

187

"Oh, yes," she said, smiling at him as she turned slowly. "You mean this little turnip with a face so red I'll wager he looks just like his father in a rage?"

"My father's dead," the young man said. "It's my mother. She turns redder than I do just before she flies at me." Then the young man raised his fists and ran toward her. Helen sighed and said aloud to the room at large, "Why do children have to repeat the horrible behavior of their parents? This fellow is probably too drunk to reason with." She sighed again. She knew that all the other young men were staring, waiting to see what would happen. When he got close enough, she turned slightly to the side. When he went past her, she smacked her hand on his back. His momentum together with her hit sent him flying, and he slammed into the wall not six inches away from Lord Beecham. Lord Beecham watched as the young man stared up at him, sighed then fell, all boneless, to the floor.

"He's not red anymore," he called out to Helen.

She had all the young men's attention now. They were staring at her, uncertain what to do, since their wits were numbed with too much drink, but they knew enough not to attack her. The young man who had been singing stopped. He began tucking his shirt back into his breeches and making a hash of it.

Helen, hands on her hips, stood in the middle of the taproom. "Listen, all of you. You are a flock of dead-brains. Your innards are awash with my very good ale, and it is a pity because my ale deserves better innards than you young rogues have."

Lord Beecham wanted to tell her that she had used the wrong word. Every young man wanted to be called a rogue.

"You will all walk out of this taproom and go to the courtyard. Oh, yes, and take these two who are lounging on my very nice oak floor with you."

Still they simply sat there, staring at her, disbelieving, Lord Beecham thought, what had happened to two of their number.

He stepped forward. "Out," he said quite pleasantly. Unfortunately he remembered all too well that on a number of occasions he had been just as drunk, just as rowdy. Dear God, but they looked young.

"Now listen here, sir, we —"

"She's got no right to order us out of here."

"I still have some of my ale left."

"She has every right to do anything she pleases with you," Lord Beecham said to another red-faced young man whose eyes were more vague than a man lost in a fog. "She is Miss Helen Mayberry. She is the owner of this inn, just as she said. Go along with all of you now. Ah, here are some lads coming to assist you out of here."

"But we don't want to leave," one young man yelled, and he turned to Helen. "I can smell that bread baking and I want to eat it."

Another young man said, "You're bigger than I am but I know I can make you sing with happiness," and he lurched toward her, his arms held wide to embrace her. "I could be more of a rogue if you would just give me more of your ale."

Helen simply stuck out her foot and tripped him. He sprawled onto his face, lay there a moment, then flopped onto his back, and blinked up at her. "Does this mean that you do not want me?"

"Not at this precise moment, no." She grabbed his collar and dragged him to the tap-room door. Her three lads were standing there. "Pick this spirited young scoundrel up and bring him into the yard. Treat him tenderly, boys."

The young man was yelling now, "No, I want her. I want all that blond hair covering me." He was trying to grab Helen, struggling mightily, but he was too drunk to do other than flop about.

The lads dropped him on the grass-covered courtyard. Helen picked up a horse bucket full of water. The moment they let the young man drop to the ground, Helen dumped the bucket of water over him.

He yowled.

"Help them all outside, one at a time," she told her three lads.

"I can't remember the last time I was so diverted," Lord Beecham said to Gwen, the barmaid who was watching the young man who'd manhandled her being dragged out now by two of Helen's lads.

"Little bounders they be," Gwen said. He watched her march to Miss Helen, take another filled bucket from her, and say, "I weren't thinking aright, Miss Helen. I was silly enough to be afraid. Now I can see that they're all jest pathetic young'uns. It won't happen again." She looked down at the young man. "Next time you will ask the lady first to allow you to stick your hand up her skirts," and she threw the water on him.

He lay there choking and coughing, and moaning because his head still hurt from being slammed against the wall.

Within five minutes, eleven young men were all in the yard, sprawled on the large expanse of grass or on the circular gravel drive, all of them soaking wet. Helen stood off to one side and said, in a very proper, disciplining voice that had Lord Beecham ready to collapse in laughter, and, at the same time, nearly go on point: "You are very lucky that none of you got ill in my tap-room. If any of you had, then your punishment would be severe and not at all pleasurable.

"As I said, you were fortunate. Now I will tell you that I enjoyed this young man's singing. He sang with his heart. The rest of you, however, have not endeared yourselves to me. You all need disciplining. However, there are too many of you and not enough time to do it properly.

"You will all remain out here in the yard until you have sobered up and are dry enough so that you won't drip on my lovely floors. You may

191

remain at my inn if you wish to. But there will be a limit of three glasses of ale. No more. When you accept any future ales from Gwendolyn, you will thank her politely. If you ever feel ill, you will immediately excuse yourself and come out here into the yard. The taproom will close exactly at midnight. Does everyone understand?"

There were grunts, nods, and groans. The one young man whom Helen had complimented, opened his mouth and started singing again. One of his friends threw the empty water bucket at him.

Helen dusted her hands, gave Spenser a brilliant smile, and went back into the inn. She left her three lads standing guard in the yard, watching the young men as they tried to get their wits together again.

"Helen," Lord Beecham said, awe in his voice, "that was really well done. It was inspiring. You left all their collective manhoods intact, yet gave them a goodly amount of food for thought. I doubt they will forget this day anytime soon."

"My father told me how to go along with young men when I first bought King Edward's Lamp six years ago. They're not bad, just wild and young and have too much money. That mill in Braintree — I had forgotten all about it. If I'd remembered I would have been here to deal with them." She straightened her gown, twisting around just a bit, and his eyes fastened onto her breasts.

She said, "Thirteen years ago would you have

192

perhaps been one of their number, Lord Beecham?"

He gave her a slow smile. "I would have been the one singing. You would have tried to seduce me."

And she wondered if perhaps he weren't right about that.

Lord Beecham strolled about the inn while Helen spoke to Mrs. Toop, Gwendolyn, and her taproom man, Mr. Hyde, who, Helen told him later, was an expert ale maker, but, unfortunately, also a coward, whimpered whenever anyone spoke a harsh word to him, and hid behind the ale barrels when there was too much commotion and too many raised voices. He was still behind the ale barrels when Lord Beecham came back into the taproom, leaned over, and ordered an ale.

He was impressed. Everything was clean, in good repair. The inn boasted two private parlors, each with a small fireplace and windows that gave onto the courtyard. The inn wasn't overly large, though — two stories high, a stable to the left, cobblestones covering the outside yard in a great sweep. There was thick green grass where there were no cobblestones, a huge elm tree between the inn and the stable, and flowers everywhere. Her father had said that Helen's victuals were the best to be had at any posting house in the entire area. The smells of baking bread from the kitchen made his belly growl.

An hour later, with Mrs. Toop ready with a skillet should the young men not obey Miss Helen's instructions, Lord Beecham and Miss Mayberry left King Edward's Lamp and went to the butcher's shop. Helen remained in close conversation with both the butcher and his very handsome young son, Walter. When she came out, she was smiling and rubbing her hands.

"I've got him," she said as Lord Beecham tossed her onto Eleanor's back. "Walter is a very reasonable young man. He will treat Teeny very well. His father is fulsome in his appreciation that his family will be linked with mine through his son's marriage to Teeny. 'Teeny and Walter Jones' — it sounds pleasing to the ear. Now, we can get back to business."

He pored over the Pahlavi leather scroll until his eyes were nearly crossing with strain. It was nearly five o'clock in the afternoon, teatime. He rose, stretched, and took himself to the drawing room.

While he and Helen drank tea, Lord Prith downed a glass of champagne and a luscious raspberry tart.

"I don't know about Walter Jones," Lord Prith said after Helen told him of her machinations. "He is said to have relieved at least six young girls of their virginity in the past year."

"Oh, dear," Helen said, and choked on a scone. Lord Beecham leaned over and lightly thumped her back. His hand stopped and he looked at his fingers, saw them twitching to caress her. He resolutely put his hand back on his thigh and drank more tea.

"He is too pretty," Lord Prith said. "I don't know about marrying our Teeny off to him, Nell."

"I will give this more thought, Father. Thank you for your information. Oh, dear, I suppose I will have to accompany Teeny when she meets him, as her chaperone."

"Oh, no," said Lord Prith. "Send Flock with her."

"He would certainly protect her virtue," Helen said, grinning. "Of course he would also probably stick a knife between Mr. Walter Jones's ribs." She turned to Lord Beecham. "You are looking too tired, sir. Would you like to stroll around the gardens with me?"

"The gazebo," he said. "I want to see the gazebo."

It was a lovely warm afternoon. Lord Beecham smiled fatuously when he saw that lovely little gazebo sitting atop a small rise to the east of the hall. Helen was still thinking about Teeny with that lecherous young man, of whom she had absolutely no doubt she could make the most ardent and faithful of husbands, or she would have seen that smile of his.

"My dear grandfather built that gazebo," Lord Prith had told Lord Beecham earlier while he consumed two glasses of champagne. "He used to say that my grandmama liked to sit there and watch the geese wheeze and paddle to the pond just beyond while she did her tatting. But I don't know if that was true. You see, there was always this strange sort of smile on his face when he talked about that gazebo."

Yes, Lord Beecham thought, taking Helen's hand to pull her more quickly to that gazebo. Tatting of a sort was just what Miss Mayberry needed.

15

All Helen could talk about was the Pahlavi scroll and the Old French they had copied from the ledge in the cave. That is, it was all she could talk about until he jerked her against him and kissed her, his hands on her bottom, kneading her, pressing her against him, hard. He didn't have to lift her, she fit against him perfectly. He nearly swallowed his tongue.

It didn't even occur to him that he wasn't behaving with her as he normally did with a woman. With any other woman, he would have gone slowly, easily, his charm overflowing, his wit smooth and fluent, his kisses deep and drugging. His master's hands would be touching her everywhere, testing, assessing what pleased her most until she was wild and ready and so eager she reached her pleasure and was asleep from exhaustion before he'd managed to hie himself over the edge.

But not with Helen. He was moaning into her mouth, kissing her jaw, her nose, back to her mouth, deeply, then teasing her with his tongue, and his hands were everywhere, rough and fast, and then he pushed her back onto the chaise that was in the gazebo, jerked up her gown, and nearly lost his seed at the sight of those long white legs of hers. "I simply cannot deal with this, Helen," he said, wondering how he even managed to place those words together in a logical string. "I am just a man. I can't deal with it."

"No," she said, "no, I can't either. Hurry, Spenser, oh, please, hurry." She was trying to unfasten his breeches, and he slapped her hands away. This time he wanted at least to pull his boots off. He managed it, but just barely.

He was on top of her, pushing her legs open, lying between them, breathing so hard he knew his heart would burst out of his chest. "It's been too long," he said into her mouth, "much too long." His palm slid over her belly and pressed down over her and she cried out, a thin wailing cry that nearly broke him. "Just a moment, love, just a moment," he said over and over into her mouth even as his fingers were on her soft flesh and he felt the building heat of her, the easing of her, the utter giving of herself to him, and he began a rhythm that was natural to him, thank God, because he was in such a bad way, he doubted he could have realized what to do next if it hadn't been second nature to him. She was tensing, arching beneath him, and he knew, as a man knew always, somewhere deep inside him, that she would reach her pleasure at any moment. He wanted to be with her, not watching her, not controlling her, and so he kissed her hard, reared back, and came into her fully and deeply, groaning because it was nearly painful now, this urgent need of his, the wild pounding of his own blood, faster, harder, burning him with its heat. His whole body tightened as he pushed deeper, deeper until he pressed against her womb. She nearly bucked him off her, arching and twisting, nearly taking them to the floor. He managed to pull them back. He was desperate, throbbing, moaning into her mouth. When her muscles tightened around him, making him bellow with the exquisite agony of it, he knew he couldn't hold back any longer. To his delirium, he felt her pleasure cresting, knew she was bursting with it and he was giving it to her, and he smiled as he threw back his head and yelled to the crossbeams in the gazebo ceiling.

Helen was gasping, still twisting beneath him, still straining against him, and he knew, simply knew in that moment, that it was all over for him. When, finally, she stilled, he kissed her, and sent his fingers into her beautiful hair, pulling it free, burying his face in it, then pushing it back and nibbling her earlobe. He lay fully on top of her, his weight pressing her into the soft chaise cushion. He finally managed to raise himself on his elbows and look down at her. That was all it took, just looking down at her flushed face, her parted lips, the banked wildness in her eyes. And then she had the gall to raise her hand and lightly touch her fingers to his chin. "You have just a bit of a dimple. I've always liked chin dimples."

That was all it took. He sucked in his breath, began kissing her again, and in a remarkably short time, he was moving inside her again, and it no longer surprised him at all. He wanted to make it last longer this time, and it did, at least a full minute longer before he was jerking above her like a palsied man and she was heaving, so frantic that it seemed to him in one single sane moment that she wanted him all at once, just as he did her. When his hot fingers found her, she cried out into his mouth, her breath hot and fierce, and he poured himself into her.

"I want you on top of me," he said into her ear when he could draw a breath. She said nothing, not that he expected her to. She was utterly relaxed beneath him, probably asleep, he thought. Then he simply collapsed, his head beside hers. It was as if someone had slammed a door down on his head, only it didn't hurt at all, and his sleep was very deep and profound. He just winked out, holding her tightly, still deep inside her, her arms holding him hard against her. He felt her hands on his back, warm even through his clothes and he realized in some part of his brain, that he'd just pulled his breeches down and that he still had on his shirt and his jacket.

He was a pig, but he would think about it later.

He awoke at the touch of a wet tongue on his left ear. "Spenser," she said, then licked him again. He reared up over her, balancing himself on his elbows and looked down at her face.

She looked dreamy, vague, and excited, a combination that ignited him instantly, no delay whatsoever.

"Spenser," she said again, and when he leaned

down to kiss her mouth, to taste her, to revel in her, she said, "I've seen pictures of the woman on top of the man. I would like to try it. You don't believe I am too big, do you?"

"Oh, no," he said. "But not just yet, Helen, not just yet. I'm sorry, but I just can't. I'm an old man, Helen —" And then he was moving deep inside her again, growing harder and harder by the moment as her mouth was on his, and she was biting him, licking him, and his world once again spun out of control.

"I'm going to die," he said when at last they were both breathing hard, pressed hard together, his face only an inch above hers because he didn't have the strength to push himself up higher. "I am thirty-three and I'm going to die. Helen, I may be a man of interesting habits and experiences, but this goes beyond anything I've ever known in my life. I'm tired now. Would you like to sleep for just a little while with me?"

She drew a deep breath and closed her eyes. There was a slight smile on her mouth. He kissed her, then once again they were asleep in Lord Prith's gazebo.

Lord Beecham awoke to realize his butt was bare and he was cold. It was twilight. He slowly eased off Helen. He fastened his breeches and pulled on his boots. He stood over Helen, just watching her breathe. Her legs were glorious, long and white and sleekly muscled, his seed smeared on them, and he groaned with the feelings that flooded through him. He hadn't asked for this. Life had been perfectly pleasant.

Of course life had been pleasant. What had he done to make it unpleasant? He had enjoyed himself, done precisely what he wanted to do whenever he wanted to do it. He wasn't vicious or petty, but it was rare that he saw things outside his pleasant existence.

He looked down at Helen.

She wanted him for a partner. She wanted to find that damned lamp more than anything else in this entire world. He didn't doubt for a moment that she wanted that damned lamp more than she wanted him, except for the few moments when he touched her and she touched him and they came together as fast, as violently as a winter storm lashing out of a midnight-black sky.

He lightly touched his palm to her thigh. Slowly, very slowly, she opened her eyes. She didn't move, just looked up at him. She smiled at him. "I didn't get to be on top," she said.

His muscles nearly went into a spasm. "Next time, I swear to you, next time."

"It is too much," she said then. "Simply too much. This cannot continue."

He had thought the same thing, recognizing the strangeness of this immense need for her, so different from the other women who had come into his life. But to hear her actually say the words made him go right over the edge. It made him nearly wild with rage.

He jerked up and removed his hand from her leg. He straightened. His voice was colder than a delicious vanilla ice at Gunther's. "You don't know what you're talking about. Of course it will continue. It is too much, but we will figure all that out sooner or later. Keep these inane conclusions to yourself, Helen. I have promised that next time you will be on top."

She frowned at him. She cocked her head to one side, regarding him from beneath her lashes. Then she sat up and looked down at herself. She said blankly, not looking at him, "I am wet with you. Very wet."

"Yes." He handed her his handkerchief. He turned away to walk to the narrow arched entrance of the gazebo.

"I'll return your handkerchief to you tomorrow."

"Yes, do that, since I imagine that you will be needing it again."

She didn't say anything at all, just walked around him, down the gazebo steps, across the vast expanse of lawn and into the library entrance on the east side of the hall.

He didn't move, just watched her. At first her steps weren't all that steady, and he knew it was because of the special strain he'd put on her muscles, something she wasn't used to. He smiled. He realized something else then. This proud, very independent woman was fighting him for all she was worth. *It cannot continue.* Like hell, he thought.

At that moment, he realized that he himself had lost all perspective on this situation.

It was a mighty lust, a lust the strength of which he had never experienced before in his life. And perhaps that was all it was — lust, an incredible lust, a lust that would bring a man to his knees in short order, or simply smite him dead from overindulgence.

This had to be dealt with. He knew there would be no dealing with anything as long as she was beside him, just there so he could make love to her, and not stop.

He had some soul-deep thinking to do. It could be that the conclusion of his thinking just might end up changing the course of his life.

The thought of taking a wife didn't freeze the blood in his veins. Odd that it didn't. He was thirty-three years old. He would have thought that life would have settled into its lifelong pattern by now, but, Lord love him, it hadn't.

Life had seen him coming around the corner and smacked him between the eyes.

Whatever had happened between them, repeatedly, and even more repeatedly after that, he was prepared to face head-on. He just couldn't face it with her anywhere in the vicinity. Seeing her, listening to her talk, looking at her, any of it, all of it, turned him into a cock-hard fellow with no thought of anything at all but being inside her and hearing her yell out his name when she clenched and shuddered beneath him. Ah, the pleasure, that gut-deep, nearly painful pleasure. He had promised her that next time she could be on top. He nearly swallowed his tongue at that thought and the incredible image it brought clear to his mind.

After Lord Prith and Flock had left for their evening walk, Flock bemoaning his fate — namely a future without Teeny being his wife — all the while Lord Prith was walking out the front door beside him, Lord Beecham said to a very silent Helen, "I am going back to London tomorrow. I need to go to the British Museum. I need to speak to scholars I know there. I am at a standstill with the scroll."

She didn't like it, he could see that plainly, but what didn't she like, specifically? Him leaving her? She wanted him with her? He began to glow.

"I don't want to let the scroll out of my sight," she said, and his innards tightened alarmingly. The damned scroll. He stopped glowing.

"I will make a copy of it," he said, all clipped and cold, as he rose.

"You are my partner. I don't want to let you out of my sight either."

Partner, she said, not the man she'd willingly lusted with nine times in three days. He thought in that moment that he would simply burst with rage. He was on her in an instant, his hands hard around her upper arms and he was shaking her. Not that he could shake her very much because she was nearly as tall as he was, and strong. But she didn't retaliate, just stood there and let him shake to his heart's content.

"You don't trust me, is that it?"

"I don't know you all that well."

"Damn you," he said, "you have made love with me nine times in three days." It felt excellent to just say it, yell it actually, right in her face. "You don't know me? Jesus, Helen, you know me all the way to my toes. Yes, I did manage to get my boots off before I fell on you this afternoon. You think I would steal this wretched scroll and go haring off on my own? Steal from you?"

"I know that you are a passionate man. In that, you are true to your reputation. As a partner you have been superbly satisfactory to date."

"But?"

She just shook her head. "It is so very important to me, Lord Beecham."

More important than I am? he wanted to ask, but he managed to keep his mouth shut. He ground his teeth and left her then, without a backward glance, and went to her study. He spent the next hour carefully copying the leather scroll. He oiled it again, smoothing down the cracked humps in the leather, then gently laid the cheesecloth on it once more. When he came out of the study, Helen was on the third step of the staircase.

"Do you wish me to take this copy or not?"

Very slowly, she nodded.

Lord Beecham left Shugborough Hall at six o'clock the next morning, damp fog enclosing everything in filmy gray, his luggage and his valet Nettle with him.

16

"I heard you and Reverend Mathers had your heads together," Reverend Older said to Lord Beecham two weeks later when he collared him on St. James Street just beneath the bow window of White's. He leaned close, looked around furtively to ensure that no one could overhear them, then loosed his hot, excited breath in Lord Beecham's face.

Lord Beecham raised an eyebrow. He wasn't used to a furtive Reverend Older. He felt excitement rippling through the man. What was going on here?

"Don't fret yourself, my boy. Old Clothhead Mathers told me all about this find of yours — an ancient leather scroll written in Pahlavi that speaks of a very old magic. This is a wondrous thing."

Naturally, Lord Beecham thought, he and Reverend Mathers had agreed to keep all of this between them. He had believed the man would hold silent — indeed, Reverend Mathers had sworn himself to silence because, as he had told Lord Beecham, "this incredible scroll, my lord, it makes up for all the miserable years of mediocrity I have known. To be a part of this, ah, it will give all of us proud modern men amazing insights upon the ancient world. I thank you with all my heart. No, sir, no one will ever learn of this from me."

Lord Beecham had known Reverend Mathers since his Oxford days. An honorable man, a scholar, a man more attuned to the mysterious ancient past than to a present he found unimaginative and trivial. Lord Beecham had been a fool, and he hated the bone-deep feeling of betrayal. Because he was not a man to spill his guts at the first attack, or even the second, for that matter, his expression remained impassive, his eyebrow elevated. He looked faintly annoyed. But his heart was pounding, slow, deep strokes.

Reverend Older leaned forward, patted Lord Beecham's sleeve and dropped his voice to a near whisper, "Now, don't you worry, my lord. None of this will go beyond me, Reverend Mathers, and his brother. You see, Reverend Mathers didn't willingly tell Old Clothhead, no; it seems that my friend talks in his sleep whenever he is unduly excited or worried about something. Old Clothhead said his brother spoke of strange and magical things and this ancient old scroll written in Pahlavi that would tell all about it. Of course, Reverend Mathers would have brought you to me eventually. I am renowned for my knowledge of old myths that have a grain of truth to them. I searched you out, my boy. I am here. You may now ask for my assistance." Reverend Older finally pulled away a good six inches from Lord Beecham's ear and beamed at him.

"Yes, I propose that we be partners, my lord," he continued. "I can assist you in ways you never dreamed possible. We will explore all those possibilities together. Now, do tell me all about it."

The man talked in his damned sleep. Lord Beecham wanted to laugh at the vagaries of fate, but his uppermost reaction was vast relief that Reverend Mathers had not intentionally betrayed him. And apparently he had not said all that much specific in his sleep, thank God, which was why Reverend Older was here, now, trying to whisper in his ear. He smiled down at Reverend Older and said pleasantly, "No. There is nothing to tell. This is all a fabrication by Old Clothhead. You should not encourage him to drink so much brandy."

Lord Beecham had seldom if ever seen a frown on Reverend Older's face. There was one now, deepening the lines alongside his mouth. "Come, my boy, you don't wish to be the coy one here."

Yes, now he could hear the frustration, the burgeoning anger.

"I can help you. I can do incredible things for you. Now, where did you come across the scroll? Have you managed to translate all of it yet? Does it give exact details about any sorts of magical instruments or objects?"

Thank God Reverend Older didn't really know anything, just about the scroll, but no specifics. But he knew about magic, and so it was greed that was pushing him. It was a disappointment, but Lord Beecham wasn't unduly surprised. His fellow man rarely showed honesty, much less honor, be he churchman or not.

"Ah," said Lord Beecham, shading his eyes from a barely existent sun's rays, "I believe I see Lady Northcliffe, just over there on the walkway, speaking to her husband. Excuse me, Reverend Older."

"Wait! You must deal with me, my lord!"

Lord Beecham turned slowly back to the man he had always liked, had always admired, a man who frankly amused him. "There is nothing to tell you. There is no strange scroll, no ridiculous magical anything. Old Clothhead is spinning yarns. You have approached the wrong person. None of this has anything to do with me."

"But Old Clothhead told me he followed his brother because he was acting so mysteriously. He said his brother met with you at the British Museum, in one of the small back rooms. He knows who you are, my lord. Come now, don't cut me out. I need to be in this, I surely do."

"Good day, Reverend Older." Lord Beecham dodged an earl's carriage, a dray filled with ale kegs, and three young bucks riding horseback, and made it intact across the street. He wondered cynically if Reverend Older had made an unwise wager at a horse race. He bowed to Alexandra Sherbrooke and turned to her formidable husband.

"Good day to you, Douglas. You are well?"

"I passed my thirty-fifth birthday in the warm

bosom of my family. Of course I am well. Do you now believe I am too old to be well? What do you want, Heatherington? Stop staring at my wife or I'll bash your pretty face and knock you into the next street."

Alexandra Sherbrooke, roughly half the size of her husband, nudged him aside and took Lord Beecham's hand. "How are you, Spenser? Ignore poor Douglas here. He fancies that he found a gray hair this morning and is trying to blame me for it, all because I enraged him last night by taking Ryder's side in an argument."

"My brother was wrong about that ridiculous notion of his, Alexandra. Imagine, letting children decide whether or not they wish to work in the factories, whether or not they wish to be assigned to be apprentices, or to be given schooling. It is the parents' choice; it must be, else there would be chaos and havoc. Can you imagine our boys being allowed to make any kind of decision? It is utter nonsense. You will retract your support when you see him next."

Alexandra Sherbrooke just laughed and leaned closer to Lord Beecham. "Now, about this gray hair of Douglas's. Perhaps now, if you continue to bait him, he will consider you as the cause of this gray hair. Who knows?"

"Hello, Alexandra."

"Why must you continue to call this damned dog by his first name?"

Alexandra patted her husband's arm as she continued speaking to Lord Beecham. "It is

211

good to see you. I don't suppose you know anything about Helen Mayberry?"

"You know very well that I am now Helen's partner and that I returned with her and her father to Essex, to Court Hammering."

"Yes, but you are here and she doesn't seem to be. Where is she?"

"She is at home. I am back here to use better minds than mine at the British Museum."

"Oh, goodness, Spenser, does this mean that you have found anything about King Edward's Lamp?"

"It is all bloody nonsense," Douglas said, his dark eyebrow raised higher than any of Spenser's eyebrows.

"Well, Douglas, actually it isn't," and with those few words, Douglas Sherbrooke was all ears. He stared at Spenser Heatherington. "It is surely a myth," he said slowly, "a silly tale that just won't die. Don't say there is something to it."

"Just perhaps there is."

Douglas began a tapping rhythm with his cane on the walkway, a sure sign that he was getting excited. "Yesterday I heard that lecherous old reprobate, Lord Crowley, telling some fellows who were nearly ready to fall down dead drunk that he was on the trail of something fantastic, something that would make him very, very rich. I never considered that it could have anything to do with the lamp. Was that what he was talking about?"

"Well, damn." Lord Beecham sighed. "I hope it wasn't, but with my blasted luck, I'll wager it was." He sighed again and this time streaked his long fingers through his hair, making it stand on end. Alexandra raised her hand and smoothed down his hair.

"Please don't, Alexandra," Lord Beecham said, taking a step back. "Else your fierce husband will pound me into the walkway. I'm too young to be pounded, only thirty-three. Now, I just managed to escape Reverend Older and he had already heard about it from Reverend Mathers's brother, whom he refers to as Old Clothhead. Other than you and Alex, Reverend Mathers and me, no one else in London should know about this. But it turns out that Reverend Mathers talks in his sleep and his brother told Reverend Older and God knows who else. Damnation, is there nothing at all sacred? Nothing that a man can depend upon to remain only his?"

"Yes," Douglas said absently, stroking his jaw, "his wife. You mean all this started with Reverend Mathers talking in his sleep about it?"

"I fear so. And now Lord Crowley — damnation, that man makes me want to scrub my soul after I am forced to be near him. On a good day, he might even be worse than my father, who was bad enough, let me tell you. Hell's bells, I don't like this. I'll wager he knows a bit now. At least it is not specific, but he will burrow about, you know his reputation. Perhaps half of London knows what he knows now, at least the scurrilous half. I would not be surprised now if some of these buffoons ended up in Court Hammering trying to threaten Helen. Damnation, now I must think of some way to protect her."

"Protect Helen?" Alexandra said, her left eyebrow going up. Her cloak then fell open. Her husband's eyes glittered before he pulled the cloak shut again and said to her, "You will go to your modiste, tomorrow at the very latest, and you will instruct her to hoist up this blasted gown a good three inches. Just look at Heatherington. The fellow has nice teeth. I would hate to have to knock them down his dog's throat were he to ogle you, and he would find the temptation well nigh impossible to deny. He will be moaning on the walkway soon, his jaw broken, if you continue to flaunt yourself."

"I see," Alexandra said, ignoring Lord Beecham and eyeing her husband. "Let me see if I have this exactly right. You feel sorry for the gentlemen because I am forcing myself upon them."

"Yes," Douglas said. "Perhaps you can go to the modiste this afternoon."

"Look, Douglas. All you can see now is my fist closing over my cloak. May we return to more interesting matters now?"

"The gown isn't cut all that low, Douglas," Lord Beecham said mildly.

"Just how the hell would you know that, you damned scoundrel?"

"I swear to you I am jesting with you, nothing more."

"I don't believe you. If by some small chance you are telling the truth, it would mean that you are clearly not yourself, Heatherington. Something is wrong with you. Come, what is it? I know it can't be this lamp business. I still don't believe such a thing can actually be real — real, as in you and I could actually touch it and make something incredible happen."

"I'm not sure that I believe in it either, but it makes me furious to know that scoundrels are now on the scent. You know Crowley. If he even had only the veriest smidgen of belief, he would go after anyone. I know he would find out about Helen."

Douglas eyed him for a while longer. "You are really worried about this?"

Alexandra eyed the two men and said, "In all truth, knowing Helen, she will take one look at Crowley and put him in the stocks she has at the back of the stables."

"Stocks?" Lord Beecham said, staring at her. "As in a man or a woman has to put his head and his hands through these holes and is locked in? And he or she has to just stand there in the middle of a street for all and sundry to come by and taunt him or her?"

"Oh, no," Alexandra said, and giggled, "the stocks are behind the stable, not in the middle of the street. Helen says taunting is nothing, it is far too lenient a punishment."

Both men's eyes were nearly crossed, particularly since Alexandra had flushed to her hairline.

"No," she said firmly. "We can discuss stocks once this is over. Now we will figure out what to do. I am worried about Helen as well, despite her prowess. What if there is some danger? Since things are now getting about, what if some bad man goes to Helen's house to force her to tell him about the lamp? Perhaps Spenser is right. We need to protect Helen. She is still at home?"

"She is at home, minding her inn and setting up a marriage between the butcher's son and her maid, Teeny. Flock, who appears to do everything for Lord Prith, is very loud in his pain over this. My valet, Nettle, must needs share in this unrequited love with Teeny, and he looks like a wounded dog.

"Helen is fine, Alexandra, surrounded by more people than any of us ever are. I imagine she is trying her very best to decipher the leather scroll." He paused just a moment, then added, his eyes narrowed, "She is very smart. Given time, I'd wager she could do it."

Douglas said, grinning, "Helen could snap the neck of just about any scoundrel I could pick off the streets in Soho. This stock business, Alexandra, I do want to speak more about this later, perhaps tonight in bed, perhaps —" Douglas cleared his throat, then continued, "Besides being beautiful and big and strong, Helen is also smart. I agree with you about that."

"What is this, Douglas?" his wife said, coming

right up to him, rising on her tiptoes and staring at his chin. "You're going on and on about Helen again, and it distresses me. I know you admire her, Douglas, but it would be wise of you to keep it to yourself. But I will still know even if you do keep it to yourself because I am a part of you, so you must get Helen once and for all out of your mind. Forget about stocks and Helen. Do you hear me, Douglas?"

Douglas was staring at his wife's once again open cloak. He swallowed, lightly stroked his fingers down her nose, and said, "I know where my bread is buttered, my sweet. I am merely attempting to reassure Heatherington here."

"I don't need any reassurance," Lord Beecham said. "Well, I do, and I shall write Helen this very day and warn her to take care. Besides, I have been gone from her nearly two weeks now, and I have learned quite a lot. Perhaps it is time I returned to Court Hammering. Then we will decide what to do."

"Not until you tell us all about what you and Helen have discovered." Douglas began to elbow Lord Beecham along the walkway toward his carriage. "You can even ride with me and Alexandra."

"I want to know why Helen isn't with you, Spenser," said Alexandra. "I cannot imagine she would let you out of her sight if it came to her precious lamp."

"It was a close thing," Lord Beecham said. He wasn't about to add that Helen wasn't with him because he needed time alone to come to grips with himself about her. He had made up his mind. Since he did not yet want a wife, since Helen was a lady, since he could not continue making love to her three times a day, he had to remove the lustful part of himself from her beautiful premises. He had to become her partner, pure and simple. He had thought about it a lot. He knew he could do it.

Well, damn. He had been gone from Helen for nearly two weeks now, and no matter how busy he kept himself, he still felt, at odd moments, like he had left part of himself back in Court Hammering — possibly the most important part, which was ridiculous. He was simply suffering withdrawal pains, and that didn't mean a thing in the long stretch of things. Still, it was disconcerting. He would avail himself of an opera girl, perhaps this very evening, and take her until he fell down dead. It wouldn't be three times either, it would be five, perhaps even six, which would surely ensure any man's demise, including his.

It was the newness of Helen, the splendor of her magnificent legs and — he had seen her breasts only once, in that rotted relic of a cabin when he had helped her to strip off her wet clothes. He nearly swallowed his tongue remembering that day. He had been so frantic he hadn't even kissed her breasts. He had to stop this. Tonight, he would sate himself with someone new. Three times at least, in fifteen minutes, no more.

Lovemaking, once a favorite sport, was fast losing its joy. Lovemaking should not be hard work, and suddenly he realized he wasn't looking forward to any new girl, to taking her three times. He sighed, dropped his chin onto the top of his cravat — not so perfectly tied today, since Nettle was distraught over losing Teeny and wanted his master to be well aware of it.

"Spenser, what is the matter with you? You're looking off at that lamppost and there is this strange expression on your face."

"He is probably just thinking about his latest conquest," Douglas said.

"Actually, he's right," said Lord Beecham. "Now, I have an appointment with Reverend Mathers at the British Museum. Since the good reverend talks in his sleep, it also might be wise of me to send him to Grillon's Hotel, so if he babbles in his sleep his brother won't be anywhere near to hear him. Douglas, Alexandra's gown doesn't need hoisting. If you wish, I will see you two later and tell you more about that bloody lamp."

"Oh, no, you don't, Heatherington. You move one step and I'll flatten you."

17

Alexandra cleared her throat. "Actually, Spenser, what Douglas would like to say is that he and I would both like to accompany you to see Reverend Mathers. We would very much like to insert ourselves into your adventure."

Douglas raised a dark brow at his wife. "Of course he knows that's what I said. Yes, we would rather come with you, Heatherington, than go to Richmond. Lady Blakeny may cast me her sloe-eyed looks another time."

"Lady Blakeny is tall," Alexandra said. "Not as tall as Helen, but still tall, curse her."

Douglas beamed at his wife, assisted her into the carriage, stepped back for Lord Beecham, then swung himself inside.

Lord Beecham looked out the carriage window to see Reverend Older still standing there in the walkway just outside of White's, staring after them. He did not like the look on the man's face.

"Perhaps you should find another scholar," Alexandra said as she arranged her skirts around her.

"He is the best," Lord Beecham said. "The very best. He and my mentor at Oxford, Sir Giles Gilliam, were excellent friends. I can remember sitting quietly on a stool in a corner of

Sir Giles's rooms, listening to them argue over some ancient text. It was fascinating." He could remember not wanting to leave even to relieve himself.

"I don't like seeing this different side to you, Heatherington, one that smacks of intellect and admiration of something that isn't warm and soft and ever so delightful."

"He's referring to the ladies, Spenser."

"I know, Alexandra."

"I prefer you to be simply a rakehell with no redeeming qualities. I detest having to alter my opinions, particularly when I am convinced they are perfectly right."

"I know," Lord Beecham said. "But Douglas, those other parts of me — they have been dormant for a very long time. They are just now coming back into being. No reason to fret yourself about my changing on you just yet."

Douglas cleared his throat. "I have decided to help you, Heatherington here. I will even help you remove Reverend Mathers to Grillon's Hotel. Yes, you need me, Heatherington. Others might horn in, like Crowley, and the good Lord knows you are gullible. I want to make sure that no one takes advantage of Helen either. Yes, I will make certain that you don't get your knees cut out from under you by any charlatans and, of course, will ensure that you understand exactly what is being said and exactly how to respond. I have known Reverend Mathers since I was a boy. He won't mind that I am with you. I will even counsel him how not to talk in his sleep."

Lord Beecham said, "I appreciate that, Douglas, I surely do. I am also certain Helen won't mind having two more partners. Now, have either of you heard that Reverend Older is having particular difficulties, at present, paying his gambling debts?"

"That conniving old bookend?" Douglas was once again closing his wife's cloak over her bosom, frowning as he added, "You fear he will continue trying to insinuate his way into this business?"

"Yes, I know he will."

"He was at Ascot a while back and lost some five hundred pounds on a horse from the Rothermere stud that went lame nearly at the finish line. The Hawksberrys were very upset about it — not about Reverend Older, of course — but about the horse.

"He knows a lot of people, does Reverend Older. We will continue to pay attention to him. I will have one of my footmen follow him about and see if he meets with fellows like Crowley. What do you say?"

"I think that's an excellent idea. Let one of my boys change every other day with yours, Douglas. That way, it won't always be the same face Reverend Older would see."

Alexandra said, "I think you should have men following Lord Crowley as well. He seems the more dangerous of the two."

"She's right," Lord Beecham said. "I have

only one bully boy footman. I shall simply hire another."

"I will as well," Douglas said.

Alexandra said, "I have heard that Reverend Older has this knack of sniffing out money."

"He sniffs everything," Lord Beecham said. "A very cunning man, is Reverend Older. I believe he is quite the best orator I've ever heard. I have always liked him. I hope he isn't a scoundrel."

"You gentlemen should see him flirt. He is really quite accomplished at it. I fear to tell you this, but once he did ogle me, just a bit."

Lord Beecham said, "The last time I saw him, he told me he was going to marry, retire, and manage the lady's stud in Wessex. He told me he wants to breed horses."

"That old lecher. No, not about buying a stud, Heatherington, but about looking at my wife's bosom."

"Whom does he wish to marry, Spenser?"

"Lady Chomley."

"A lovely woman," said Alexandra, then she frowned.

"What? What is it?"

Alex said, "I have heard it said that Lilac enjoys the more titillating sorts of lovemaking."

Her husband gave her a ferocious frown. "What the hell does 'titillating' mean? Something that you and I don't do on a regular basis? Are you keeping some new and perverse sort of pleasure from me, Alexandra?"

She went red to her earlobes. She pressed her palms to her cheeks. She took an extra moment to clear her throat. "I don't wish to pursue it at this time, Douglas. Now, Spenser, let me tell you about the twins."

After five minutes of hearing about the most brilliant, most beautiful twosome of children in all of England, Lord Beecham said, "If I were some other man, perhaps I should not mind having twins. One to sit on each knee. One to hold with each hand."

Both Sherbrookes stared at him.

"If they yelled their heads off," Douglas said, "what would you do if you were this other man?"

"What do you do, Douglas?"

"I take them riding."

Lord Beecham frowned as he looked out the carriage window. He didn't know why he had said that. It didn't matter. It was not relevant to him or his life, at least for another ten years or so. Forty-five would be a good age to bring his heir into the world.

The British Museum was vast in size and very dim inside. Every footstep on the stone floors replayed itself a dozen times all around, each new echo more menacing than the last. It was also damp. There was no need for Douglas to tell his wife to keep her cloak shut, she was fisting it tightly beneath her chin.

"It is better in the back rooms," Lord Beecham said. "There are fires and many branches of candles. It's downright cozy in the room where I usually meet Reverend Mathers."

"A few more windows might make this place less dreary," Alexandra said. "Perhaps some warm draperies."

"Only very serious gentlemen come here," Douglas said, nodding to the porter. "They need only their intellectual fervor and they're content. Show the stoics a warm drapery and they would doubtless shudder."

It took them five more minutes to walk through the large rooms, all of them empty as gourds. They paused every couple of steps to look at some artifact on display, but mainly, it was so dreary and chill, they just kept walking. There were perhaps a dozen men dotted throughout the rooms, speaking in small groups or hunched over manuscripts.

Lord Beecham veered off to a small room off the main sweep of the museum. The door was shut. Lord Beecham lightly knocked, then opened it. He was suddenly haloed in warmth. He saw the brisk fire burning in the fireplace, casting shadows throughout the room.

"Reverend Mathers?"

There was no answer.

They all stepped into the room. There was a long table running along the entire side of the room, several branches of candles set at intervals along the table. There were dozens of books, in haphazard stacks, some piled neatly by a clerk's hand, others sitting alone, one very ancient tome still settling in its dust, its pages parted as if fingers had just roved through them to find a certain section.

"Oh, dear," Alexandra said and stepped back against her husband.

Reverend Mathers was seated at the far end of the bench, in the shadows. He was hunched forward over a blood-red, very large vellum-bound book. But he wasn't studying or reading or writing with the sharpened quill held loosely in his right hand.

He looked to be sleeping, but they knew he wasn't.

He was dead, a thin stiletto stuck out of the middle of his back.

"Lord Hobbs will be here any moment," Lord Beecham said quietly to Alexandra and Douglas. "He became a magistrate on Bow Street not long ago. He is a good man, intelligent enough to know when he doesn't have the experience to deal well with something, and he doesn't give up. Do you remember the theft of Lady Melton's ruby necklace some six months ago? Lord Hobbs came himself, spoke with everyone present, then assigned one of his runners to ferret out the facts of the case."

"Were the rubies recovered?" Alexandra asked as she took another drink of very strong India tea. She was sitting in on a pale-green brocade sofa, her husband next to her. Lord Beecham was watching a tall, very thin man, dressed all in a soft pearl gray, being ushered into the drawing room by his acting butler, Claude, who was looking particularly tight about the mouth. "A murder," Lord Beecham had heard him whisper to himself earlier. "What will become of all of us with the master involved in a murder?"

Lord Beecham stepped forward as he said to Alexandra, "Oh, yes. The Bow Street Runners, for the most part, are canny and know all the villains and criminals who roam the London alleys. Lord Hobbs is one of the gentlemen who keeps them assigned to cases."

"Lord Hobbs."

There were pleasantries, always at least twoscore polite words before one eased into things, Lord Beecham thought, as he mouthed his own feelings about King George III going mad for the last time and his eldest son, yet another George who was a fat, very unpopular buffoon, being appointed Regent.

There was no chance to continue on to Reverend Mathers's murder, for there was Claude, clearing his throat at the drawing room door.

"My lord."

"Yes, Claude?"

"Goodness, Claude, just stand aside. This is very important. Move!"

And there was Helen, dressed in a sky-blue pelisse, a matching bonnet atop her blond hair. She was flushed, impatient, waving her white hand at Spenser's acting butler.

He couldn't believe it when she came dashing through the door, his beautiful big girl, his

Valkyrie, his own angel who was surely an Amazon. She was actually here. He had not realized how very much he had missed her.

He stood there and nearly bowed in on himself with bone-deep pleasure.

Something had happened to bring her here, but he didn't want her to spill it in front of Lord Hobbs.

"Welcome, Miss Mayberry," he said.

18

Helen immediately saw him, and no other, and went right to him, her hands outstretched. "Spenser, oh, dear, I had to come myself. Oh, you will not believe this, I —" She broke off at the sight of the tall, austere gentleman dressed all in gray. She looked him up and down, blinked, and said, "That is a charming affectation."

Lord Hobbs, known among the Bow Street Runners as a man with ice in his veins, froze, sputtered, then laughed. "Why, thank you, ma'am."

"Miss Mayberry," Lord Beecham said easily, "I would like you to meet Lord Hobbs, a magistrate from Bow Street. He is here because something very bad has happened."

"A pleasure, Miss Mayberry," Lord Hobbs said, and smiled at the incredible creature staring him right in the eye. He bowed, kissed her hand.

Lord Hobbs was not the least bit on the short side, Lord Beecham thought, and wasn't certain whether he should be worried or not.

"Yes, my lord. Why are you here? You are a magistrate from Bow Street? What has happened to bring you here, of all places? Spenser, are you all right?"

"Yes, Helen, I am fine."

"Yes, Miss Mayberry, I am indeed from Bow Street."

"Douglas? Alexandra? What are you doing here? What is happening?"

Douglas rose, patted Helen's arm even as Alexandra said from behind him, "We are all here to assist you, Helen. The four of us together can overcome anything. Stop fretting."

Douglas said in that low, soothing voice of his that always settled down the twins, "Helen, calm yourself."

"All right, I am now calm. Spit out everything."

Lord Beecham managed to sort everyone out, get them seated, and order tea from Claude, who was still standing stiff as a statue in the drawing room doorway, the way old Crit had taught him.

"Now," he said pleasantly, drawing everyone's attention, "I will go through what happened. Sir, feel free to interrupt if you have questions. You as well, Miss Mayberry. Now the earl and countess and I were to meet Reverend Mathers at the British Museum. When we came into the room we saw him slumped over the worktable, a stiletto sticking out of his back, right between his shoulder blades. He was still warm, though that might not mean that he had just been murdered. It was very warm in the room and the door was closed, keeping all the heat within."

Helen sat in a pale-blue brocade chair, her hands folded in her lap, speechless. She was staring at him, at no one else in the room. Her face was flushed. A single long tress of blond hair had come loose from the pile of plaited braids on her head and was trailing down her back. She looked shocked, terribly shocked. Not frightened, just disbelieving. He knew exactly how she felt. He just shook his head at her.

Lord Hobbs said, "I know you remained with the body until one of my runners arrived, Lord Beecham. Since you were the one working with Reverend Mathers, did you search to see if anything was missing? Something taken by the murderer?"

"Yes," Lord Beecham said, realizing there was no reason to withhold basic information from Lord Hobbs. "Reverend Mathers and I were working on the translation of a very old scroll that Miss Mayberry here had discovered close to her home in Essex. Reverend Mathers had made a copy so that he could work on it by himself. It was gone."

Helen turned paper-white. "Oh, no," she said. "Oh, no."

"This copy of the scroll — did it contain information that was valuable?"

"It is possible," Lord Beecham said. "Its importance lay in its remarkable age. It is an immense archaeological find, sir, one of tremendous value for that reason alone."

"Perhaps," Lord Hobbs said thoughtfully, unable to look away from Miss Helen Mayberry, "it was a colleague of Reverend Mathers who became jealous of this find? They perhaps argued and he stabbed him?"

"If it were a colleague," Helen said, sitting forward, "would he not want the original scroll and not a simple copy?"

"Yes, you are right, of course," said Lord Hobbs, and the look he fastened on her held far too much admiration for Lord Beecham's taste. Lord Hobbs turned his formidable attention back to him again. Lord Beecham said, "What is most likely is that some people believe the scroll the key to finding a vast treasure. Is this true? None of us has any idea if it is or not."

Lord Hobbs studied his long fingers, the short, well-buffed nails, then he looked at Miss Mayberry. "Ma'am, where did you find this scroll?"

"In a cave right on the beach."

"I see. You have no idea why it was there? No idea what the scroll might contain?"

"None. It is written in an ancient language that I could not read."

"And that was why I was working with Reverend Mathers," Lord Beecham said.

"I see," Lord Hobbs said again. "You will give me names of men who you believe wanted to know more about this scroll, Lord Beecham."

"I know of only two names, sir. Reverend Titus Older and Jason Fleming, Lord Crowley."

To everyone's surprise, Lord Hobbs cursed very quietly under his breath. He saw Lord Beecham's raised eyebrow and said, "Reverend

Older is probably sunk in debt again. Curse the man, I will have to find out just how deep a hole he finds himself in this time. And Lord Crowley, not a good man, my lord. A very bad man, if one were to believe just some of the gossip about him."

"I would imagine," Douglas said, "that at least eight out of ten of the stories told about him are the truth. Some three years ago, Lord Crowley tried to swindle a consortium put together to build a canal up near York."

"What happened, my lord?"

"When I discovered he was lurking in the shadows, I immediately investigated. I myself had some five thousand pounds invested. I did not want to lose it."

"You unmasked him?"

Douglas nodded. "He managed to escape blame. Everyone knew what he had done, but the proof conveniently disappeared. One member of the consortium ended up dead, supposedly suicide, but we all doubted that it was. Again, there was no proof that Crowley was the murderer. You are right, Lord Hobbs, he is a very bad man. He also bears grudges."

"One is toward you?"

"Oh, yes. Some four years ago, he wanted to marry my sister, but she, a very smart girl, simply told him that he was much too old for her, and that he gambled. She would never marry a man who gambled. He wasn't happy with this outcome. I heard it said that Crowley decided that no female could speak her mind like that, and thus he believed that I had put the words in her mouth and, fortunately, blamed me and not Sinjun, my sister."

Lord Beecham said, "He is forever in need of money. He has buried two wives, both of whom brought him sizable dowries."

"Do you believe he killed his wives?" Lord Hobbs asked.

"It wouldn't surprise me," Douglas said. "His luck at cards is rotten, not at all a surprise, given that he has the gambling fever. He cannot make himself stop."

"Yes," said Lord Beecham, "he is always convinced that his luck will change with the turn of the next card."

Lord Hobbs rose and began to pace the length of the lovely Aubusson carpet. "So it is possible that both of these gentlemen could believe that the scroll is the key to vast wealth?"

Everyone nodded.

"I hesitate to believe that Reverend Older could stab a man in the back. He is a man of God no matter his lapses."

Douglas said, "Man of God or not, I have put one of my footmen to follow Reverend Older. Lord Beecham has done so as well. We will also have Crowley followed."

Lord Hobbs nodded. "That is very wise. I will assign one of my canniest runners to this case. He can work with your men, direct them, if you will. Solving this case is vital. It doesn't look good for a man of the church to be murdered in the British Museum. Mr. Ezra Cave will come to introduce himself to you so you will know who he is. I bid you good day." He stopped to stand directly in front of Helen. "I hope to see you again, Miss Mayberry." That cold, deep voice of his had miraculously turned as warm as a mild spring day, Lord Beecham thought — the poaching bastard. "Are you currently residing in London?"

Helen, distracted, merely shook her head, saying, "No, I am just here to see Lord Beecham."

"I would like to hear more about your discovery of the scroll. May I call upon you?"

That got Helen's attention. "I don't know where I will be, my lord."

"Helen, you will stay with us," Alexandra said.

"Then later, Miss Mayberry," Lord Hobbs said, gave her a long look, and finally took himself off.

"You will not see Lord Hobbs alone," Lord Beecham said, frowning after the man who had ice in his veins, not passion. "For some reason he intends to try to attach you. I will not allow that."

"What do you mean 'for some reason'? What am I, a troll?"

"Trolls are really quite small. No, don't turn your cannon on me. I meant nothing. It merely came out of my mouth that way. You won't ever be alone with him. I insist upon that, Helen."

"For heaven's sake, Spenser, who cares?" Helen jumped up and waved her fist in his face. "You are worried about Lord Hobbs when everything is falling apart around us?" She smote her forehead with her palm. "I can't believe I let you distract me with all this troll business. Reverend Mathers is dead, all because of that wretched scroll I found. He's dead! What are we going to do?"

"You are hysterical, Helen," Alexandra said in the voice of a Mother Superior. "Get a grip on yourself."

Helen blinked, drew a deep breath, and pulled back her shoulders. She removed her bonnet and worked the thick blond tress of hair back into its plait. "There," she said. "I am all together again."

"Well done," Lord Beecham said. "Tell us what has happened."

He watched her jump up and begin pacing the drawing room. Long strides, long, strong legs. He saw those legs of hers so clearly, felt them squeezing tightly against his flanks, that he nearly fell to the floor in a swoon.

"Oh, goodness," Helen shouted, "this is perfectly dreadful. A man murdered here in London, and no matter what you say, it is all my fault."

Alexandra shouted back at her, "Helen, you are slipping again. Get ahold of yourself. You did not stab Reverend Mathers. An evil person did. It is not your fault."

236

Lord Beecham, who had managed at the last moment not to swoon, walked to her and took her gloved hands into his. He looked into her eyes, as blue and rich as a summer sky. He felt her fear now, her anxiety, her disbelief. It was he who got hold of himself. This was serious business. He said, "It will be all right. Now, what happened at home?"

"Someone tried to break into Shugborough Hall. The thief would have succeeded if it hadn't been for Flock. He has taken to roaming around all through the night, to prove to Teeny that he is heartbroken so that she will pity him and perhaps overlook the name issue."

"Name issue?" Douglas said.

"Teeny Flock."

"It sounds like a very small assembly of sheep," Alexandra said.

"Would you prefer Teeny Nettle?" Lord Beecham said.

"A very small weed? No, both give one the shivers."

"Exactly," Helen said. "In any case, Flock was roaming about the house, trying to deepen the shadows beneath his eyes, no doubt, when he saw this figure trying to break in through the drawing room windows. He raised the alarm. The man got away, but it was a close thing. He would have stolen the scroll if Flock had not been there."

Helen drew a very deep breath. "Our secret is out, Spenser."

"It could have been a common thief, after the silver," Douglas said.

"It is possible," Helen said, "but I don't think so. Common thieves wouldn't come to Shugborough Hall. We have a reputation, you see."

"I can only imagine," Lord Beecham said. "I am sorry for this, Helen. Still, Flock saved the day. I hope Teeny is better disposed toward him?"

That made Helen grin. "She was mumbling beneath her breath about the utter embarrassment her future children would feel whenever they had to say their mother's name."

Douglas said, "No one really knows all that much about anything at this point. But the lure of hidden wealth is enough for many men to break into a house and murder a man of the Church."

"And that means," Alexandra said, "that someone discovered that Helen was involved and has moved very quickly."

"I don't like this at all," Douglas said. "I am going to have my brawniest footman, Kelly, begin immediately to follow Lord Crowley."

"I shall assign Crimshaw to Lord Crowley as well," Lord Beecham said. "He was raised in the stews and is tougher than an old boot. This Bow Street Runner, Ezra Cave, we will tell him to hire two more men to follow Crowley."

"I will see to this right away," Douglas said and gave his hand to his wife. "You, my sweet, will come with me. I have this feeling that Heatherington and Helen here have a number of things to speak about."

"Yes," Alexandra said slowly, looking from one to the other, "I do believe you are correct."

"You will keep us informed," Douglas said and took his countess out to their carriage.

Lord Beecham turned to Helen, who was staring at him, her eyes so intense he wondered if she was seeing directly into his brain, "As for you, Miss Mayberry, I have just decided that you and I are going to return to Court Hammering. But first, we are going to visit Old Clothhead Mathers, Reverend Mathers's brother."

Old Clothhead was drunk when they arrived at Reverend Mathers's small town house near Russell Square.

" 'Tis near to puking on my clean carpet 'e is," said Mrs. Mappe, Reverend Mathers's housekeeper whom Lord Beecham had met the week before. "Och, my poor master, all kilt by some evil bastid."

"You already know of this, Mrs. Mappe?" Lord Beecham asked.

"Oh, aye, milord, I know. Jest look at ye!" she said, beaming at Helen. "Ain't ye a purty big girl."

"Lord Hobbs came?"

"Aye, strange feller that, all dressed in gray like a man what knows 'e's got to dress special to 'ave folk pay attention to 'im."

After ten minutes of weaving in and out of Mrs. Mappe's very fascinating but nearly unintelligible English, they were shown in to see Old Clothhead.

"I killed my only brother," wailed Old Clothhead, who was curled into the fetal position on Mrs. Mappe's clean carpet. "I told anyone who paid for a mug of ale all about what he was doing. I killed my brother. He was always warning me about hell being at the end of my road. I have no chance at all now."

Lord Beecham came down to his knees beside Old Clothhead, a skinny little man who looked as if he hadn't eaten a good meal in ten years. "Give me the names of the men you told, not just the common variety of alley criminal, but the important ones, the men with money."

He had to repeat the question three more times before Old Clothhead understood. "Reverend Older, not that he ever has a groat in his pocket. Titus filled my gullet with brandy, not ale, he was so thrilled about this scroll, though, perhaps his last groat. Then there was Lord Crowley and James Arlington and —"

Old Clothhead didn't vomit on Mrs. Mappe's clean carpet, he just passed out in midsentence.

Lord Beecham rose and looked down at the unconscious little man.

"He's pathetic," Helen said, "and he is right. He is responsible for his brother's death." She drew back her foot to kick him in the ribs. Then she stopped and covered her face with her hands. "Oh, no, I am as guilty as he is. I found the damnable thing in the first place. Who are these people, Spenser?"

He put his hands on her, drawing her ever so slowly against him. He kissed her temple. "It will be all right, Helen. I'll tell you about all of them. Well, no. I didn't know that James Arlington knew anything about this."

They discovered an hour later that Lord James Arlington, fourth son of the Duke of Hailsham, was dead, shot, it was rumored, in a duel with Lord Crowley because Arlington had been caught cheating. Dueling was outlawed in England, but since no one would speak openly about it, it remained buried. Evidently the duke, Lord James's father, had shrugged when told the news of his son's demise and said simply, "He always did cheat. His mother taught him. He obviously cheated the wrong man." And it was over. Had Crowley killed him in a duel?

Lord Beecham said, "It's time for us to go home, Helen."

They rode horseback for the hour and a half. It was a lovely afternoon, summer flowers coming into bloom, the trees spreading their green canopies over the narrow country roads. "I forgot to tell you," Lord Beecham said, "we have two more partners."

"Douglas and Alexandra?"

He nodded, then leaned over and patted his horse's neck. When he straightened, he kept his eyes firmly fastened on the road between his horse's ears. "Before you arrived, I had other plans for tonight," he said at last.

She didn't even seem interested. "Hmmm."

"I was going to bed an opera girl and take her three times in under fifteen minutes."

"Hmmm."

He eyed her now with growing frustration. "You were new to me, that is all."

No more humming, just bored silence.

"If you had stayed the night with Douglas and Alexandra, I would probably have climbed up to your window and taken you three more times. What do you think of that, damn you?"

"I am sorry, Spenser. I was distracted by the lovely honeysuckle. Did you say something?"

"Helen, do you want me to thrash you?"

"I would do you in if you tried it. You know that. What is wrong with you? We are in the midst of a dreadful mess. We don't know anything more about King Edward's Lamp than we did two weeks ago when you insisted upon leaving me and coming back to London. I might add that London is only an hour and a half's ride from Court Hammering, yet you never even once came for an afternoon or an evening, even one simple meal."

Now was the time. He had to do it, else he would be lost. He ignored her complaint and said, "Listen to me, for I mean this. I have decided to be only your partner, nothing more. Ever."

She didn't acknowledge that he had spoken.

She didn't even acknowledge that she had heard him. She simply clapped her heels in Eleanor's sleek sides. Eleanor streaked off down the road. Helen said nothing more to him the rest of the ride.

It rained the final half hour.

19

Nettle followed in a carriage behind his master. Lord Beecham turned around to see him leaning out the carriage window, his face a study in ecstasy even though a sullen rain was dripping over him. "His heart is soaring," he said to Helen, who wasn't speaking to him and in fact was a good twenty yards ahead of him on the road. "Soon he will see his goddess, Teeny."

To his valet's immense distress, Lord Beecham elected to stay at the King Edward's Lamp. He did not want to be in Helen's home, with her coming downstairs in a nightgown and him all weak in his resolution upon seeing her, with the more than likely result that he would lose his head. No, the inn was safer. She never took her clothes off at the inn. She would never look at him provocatively at the inn.

Then he thought of the gazebo and that rotted old cottage. Her wet, sodden clothes — no provocation there, and it hadn't mattered. Ah, but at the gazebo, he had known and she had known as well exactly what would happen. And of course it had, with no particular reflection at all.

He hoped staying at her inn would prove a good idea, one that would keep him on the path of celibacy.

He would be her partner. Not her lover. He

would. He was determined. He would not hurl himself from the path of righteousness again.

Helen escorted him to the inn's largest bedchamber, an airy, high-ceilinged large corner room on the second floor, overlooking the marketplace. She had a trundle bed brought up for Nettle, who looked at it and nearly wept. "It will be all right," Helen said, lightly patting his shoulder. "You will find another girl just as sweet as Teeny. Forget her, Nettle. She was not meant to be yours."

Lord Beecham eventually sent Nettle down to the taproom to buy himself some ale, telling him that three mugs was all Miss Helen would allow to be poured down any one male gullet. "Drown all your feelings about Teeny," he called after his valet. "Well, at least get them wet."

Then Helen stood in the open doorway of his bedchamber, hands on hips, and said, "Now what?"

"You are my partner," Lord Beecham said, and then he said it again: "You are my partner." He walked to her, closed the door, and locked it. "Helen," he said and locked his arms under her hips and carried her to the big bed in the middle of the room. A warm breeze fluttered the light curtains over the windows. There were few sounds now, for it was dinnertime, and most people were at home in front of their own hearths.

And he was here, with Helen, and she was on her back and he was over her, kissing her, pulling

245

the pins out of her beautiful hair, kissing her more, her nose, her earlobe, her chin. "My God, I've missed you," he managed to say between kisses. "Your breasts. I've never seen your breasts. I saw them in the cottage when I got you out of all your wet clothes, but I didn't really look. I touched your breasts once, but not like I want to. I have imagined your breasts, imagined kissing them and caressing them, my hands, my mouth — oh, God, Helen." He reared up, standing beside the bed over her. "Your riding skirt, Helen, your damned riding skirt. Then there's the rest of all those bloody clothes you women insist upon wearing to slow men down to the point of near expiration." He got her out of her riding skirt in just about thirty seconds, then realized that he was still dressed, all the way down to his Hessians.

"I want to do it right!" he yelled to the bed-chamber ceiling, but he simply couldn't wait, just couldn't. He fell on her, yanked up her chemise, and left her boots and stockings on. He opened his britches and yelled when he drove into her. Helen screamed.

For the briefest instant, he believed he had hurt her. He managed to raise himself on his elbows, to see her eyes closed, her lips parted. She was breathing hard, her hands jerking at him, and she was twisting beneath him, so frantic that she nearly bucked him off her.

He watched her pleasure flood through her, watched her eyes open. She stared up at him in astonishment, then he was with her, so beside himself that he knew the end had to be near. A man simply could not bear this sort of thing. He moaned into her mouth, then his mouth was trying to keep kissing hers, but his lips were numb. He was gone. He collapsed.

"I continue not to believe this," he said, his voice deep and rough, when breath and brain finally returned to his body. He rolled onto his side, bringing her with him. Their boots tangled together. He smiled at her, kissed the tip of her nose. He was still inside her, just barely, but still a part of her. He knew he had to leave her now, this instant, or it would begin again, and he didn't want it to. He couldn't allow it to, or his once-firm resolve, now hanging by a single stingy thread, would melt like candle wax touched to flame.

He closed his eyes, and slowly, so slowly it was near to killing him, he pulled out of her. She fell over onto her back again. She opened her eyes when the bed gave. He was standing there by the bed, his britches open, his hair standing on end where she had pulled it and stroked it and streaked her fingers through it, mad with wanting him. His chest was still heaving as if he had just run a very long race.

He looked immensely beautiful.

She watched him fasten his britches. She watched him straighten his clothing. She watched him walk to the window and stare out of it, down at the now empty market square.

She was lying there on her back, her legs spread, her chemise tangled up around her waist. Her stockings were still in place above her knees, held with lacy black garters. Her boots were still on her feet. Then she laughed, couldn't help it. She was still wearing her riding hat.

"It's amazing," she said, coming up on her elbows. "Do you realize that this time you actually managed to get me out of my skirt before you ravaged me?"

"Yes," he said, turning slowly to face her. "It is amazing. I remarked to myself about that when I had it done. What I really wanted was your breasts. I have yet to see your breasts, Helen, the way I want to see them.

"Ah, but I did get your skirt off you. I can no longer remember just how I managed to do it. It took nearly thirty seconds, took that thirty seconds away from me being inside you." His breathing hitched. His eyes went wild and dark, and he stared at her spread legs. "No," he said. "No. I will control myself."

He turned back to look down into the market square again. "Where is the scroll?"

Helen blinked. He was trying to keep himself away from her. On a very intellectual level, she supposed she appreciated his efforts, but as she looked at him, her body still pulsed with the heat and strength of him, and she wanted him, powerfully.

"I have hidden it here at the inn. No one would ever find it." She rose slowly and walked

248

behind the screen to clean herself. When she came around the screen, her clothes were back in place. "I didn't want to put my father in any more danger, our people either. It is quite safe here." She pulled on her riding skirt. She walked over to the narrow mirror beside the armoire. She looked demented, her riding hat askew, her mouth red from kissing him at least a hundred times, her eyes vague and soft.

She was shocked to the soles of her goodly sized feet. Miss Helen Mayberry's eyes were never vague and soft. She was the taskmistress of Court Hammering. This was her inn, where she and she alone ruled. She was in control, she was decisive, she was always the first one to know exactly what to do about anything at all.

She had just ravished a man without a by-your-leave, had done it quickly and very well. Well, perhaps he had been a good part of that ravishment as well. She straightened herself as best she could, pinned her hair back under her riding hat. She still looked like she had been kissed silly. And other things as well. Anyone looking at her would realize that. She slapped her cheeks, then turned to face him when he said, "Reverend Mathers and I did manage to decipher a bit more of the scroll. It was very slow going. Would you like to see what we have now?"

A glimmer of the old excitement came back into her brain, not all of it, but enough. Passion was a strange thing. It simply wrung you out and left you feeling like you were lying in the clouds, your brain empty, your body glowing, your heart filled. "Yes," she said, "but first, would you like to dine?"

It meant leaving this bedchamber. It meant being in a private dining room with servants and guests not many feet away. It meant it would be next to impossible to toss up her skirts and position her on the dining table between the roasted hare and the poached trout. He would be safe from her and she from him. If he was truly a good man, there would not be a lock on the parlor door for him to click tight and then haul her up on the table. There would be no temptation like that.

"One time," he said as he followed her out of the bedchamber. "That is a vast improvement."

"I suppose it is," she said, "but I hated it when you left me. I wanted you again." With those words slamming into his brain, burrowing into him to his very bones, he followed her down the inn stairs.

Her three lads were busy in the yard because there were guests arriving for the night. She spoke to Gwen, to Mrs. Toop and to Mr. Hyde, who was tasting his own ale. When Gwen carried covered platters into the small parlor, Lord Beecham moved to the fireplace, where a small fire burned, and stuck out his hands to warm them, for there was an evening chill to the air.

He looked at that table and he saw the food, but he also saw Helen lying on her back and he saw himself nipping at her mouth as he eased his hands beneath her hips to slowly pull her to the end of the table. He saw his hands lifting her legs, parting them and he was coming close and closer still, and coming into her right there. He was yelling and so was she and — and then the door was flying open and all her lads were standing there staring at him ravishing their mistress, their mistress who disciplined them, the mistress whom they half feared and doubtless adored and would kill for.

"Spenser, what is wrong? You look like you just got shot."

"Close enough. Maybe food will help."

When he took a bite of shepherd's pie, Mrs. Toop's premier family recipe, he realized vaguely that it was delicious as he chewed. Then he swallowed. He couldn't continue this any longer. He drew a very deep breath and took the plunge, in his own fashion. "Put down your fork, Helen. Thank you. Now you will attend me." He took another deep breath. "Here's the truth of it. I just can't be around you, I simply can't. I thought that I could. I thought that here at your inn with all these people about — your people — I would be able to control myself."

She stared at his mouth and said, "I thought I would be able to control myself as well, but you grabbed me, and I wanted you more than anything."

He shook with her words. Then he was shaking his head vigorously. "I did not hear that. I couldn't survive if I had really heard what you just said.

"Now, I don't know what has happened to me, but whatever it is, it has happened very hard. I simply cannot deal with it." Then he looked up, and despite his suffering, he managed to smile at her. "Perhaps you should punish me by putting me in the stocks."

She choked on her asparagus. Her eyes went wide, seeing him at what she'd designated a Level Seven. She went perfectly still, once she caught her breath.

"Tell me, how do you punish your lads in the stocks?"

"If the miscreant merits a Level Five punishment, he is stripped to the waist, his head and hands locked in and the women torment him."

"How?"

"It depends on the nature of the crime committed. For tardiness in assisting a guest, the women will whip him with small bunches of hollyhocks."

"This doesn't make the man want to be tardy all the time?"

"Oh, no. Hollyhocks are very irritating. They make you itch for a good week. It is really quite effective. Actually, to be fair about this, it was the former vicar's wife who devised that particular form of punishment discipline."

"Oh, God," he said and jumped to his feet, toppling his chair. "I truly wanted to be your partner, just your partner." He grabbed a good-sized piece of bread, and fled the small parlor, leaving Helen to sit there, staring after him, wondering how he would look in those stocks, naked — completely naked. She wouldn't let anyone come near him, just her, and she wouldn't have a silly bunch of hollyhocks in her hand. No, she would use her mouth and her tongue and — Helen sighed deeply and took herself to the inn's kitchen to help Mrs. Toop peel apples for a pie.

Lord Beecham marched across the inn yard through the small gate to the stable. He didn't bother with a saddle or bridle, just grabbed Luther's mane and swung himself up on his back. He chewed his bread as he rode, without stopping, directly to Shugborough Hall. Flock opened the door to him. "My lord, what is amiss? Is that a piece of bread clutched in your hand?"

Lord Beecham ate the bread.

20

"My lord, you look maddened now that you have swallowed the bread. Have you been attacked by highwaymen? What is amiss?"

"I am amiss. Where is Lord Prith?"

Flock walked to the dining room, Lord Beecham on his heels. He stepped back just in time to prevent Lord Beecham from walking over him.

"Help me, sir," Lord Beecham said to Helen's father, who was seated in isolated splendor at his own dining table, a glass of champagne in his hand. Flock came to stand behind his master, ready with the champagne, his eyes down, his ears wide open. "I am done for, sir, you must help me."

"Oh, dear," Flock said suddenly, stepping forward, "you didn't bring that poaching Nettle, did you, Lord Beecham? I don't have my gun."

"Now, Flock, can't you see that his lordship is quite alone? That he suffers? From what, we will doubtless learn in good time. Were I to venture a guess at this very moment, I would say that he is hungry. Sit down, my lord. Flock, serve his lordship a bit of baked pheasant covered with jellied apricots."

"Yes, sir, I am very hungry," Lord Beecham said. But he didn't want food, not really. He wanted to weep. It was all over for him. He had fought it, fought it with all his might, fought a good fight. He had thought of his father, and continued to fight it. But even the darkness of his memories had not diminished in the slightest what had happened to him, what he was helpless now to fight against.

He jumped up from his chair, nearly knocking it over. He began to pace. "Sir," he said, striding up and down the dining room, the oak planking creaking beneath his boots. Thank God, he had not taken the time to pull his boots off. He just might have forgotten them altogether. He might have ridden Luther here in his bare feet. The humiliation would have been rather staggering.

No, thank God, his boots had been on his feet the whole while he had made frantic love to a woman. He had never made love to a woman before with his boots on, except Helen. Had he ever taken his bloody boots off? It wasn't to be borne. He sucked in air and looked like a wild man.

"I just left your daughter at the inn."

"Oh? My little Nell is accounted an excellent hostess. What displeased you?"

"Myself, this damnable situation. Sir, there is no hope for it. I am undone. I suppose I simply must marry your daughter. I had not planned to marry until I was almost dead because my own parents gave me a powerful distaste for marriage. Actually, my father's example with each of his three wives made me determined to avoid taking a wife of my own. But now I see that it doesn't have anything to do with me or with Helen. It is other people, not us. It doesn't seem to matter anymore.

"I must have Helen. I cannot continue without her. Well, it is not exactly without her, but this other, it's madness, and it has to stop or I will hurl myself over a cliff, and then where would I be?"

"I believe you would be dead, my boy."

"Not at all a good finish. Please, sir. Have I your permission to court and wed your daughter?"

Lord Prith stared at him. "I have heard of your sire. His name was Gilbert Heatherington, was it not?"

"Yes."

"My dearest Mathilda was a friend of his second wife. Poor Marianne died within five years of her marriage to him."

"Yes, sir, I was there. My father was obsessed with building a dynasty. But I am the only child of his loins who survived. He had no caring at all for women, none really for the children except that they live, which they didn't." Lord Beecham stopped. There was no reason to continue this. His father was dead, all three of his wives, including his own mother, dead as well, and the innumerable offspring.

"I am not like my father."

"But you speak of marriage as if it would be your downfall. Why would you consider marriage a bad thing just because your father mucked it up?"

"He humiliated my mother. He kept her pregnant every year until I could hear her begging him not to take her, not to force himself upon her, that she would die with the next pregnancy, but he just laughed and forced her, and that last time she did die, cursing him, but he didn't care. I believe he was with a mistress at the time. But I was there, sir, and I heard what she said. I heard her death. I despised him. I swore never to impregnate a woman, but then I realized that I had to have an heir, so I decided to wait, wait until it was almost the end of my time, and then I would take a wife and beget an heir."

"How old were you when your mother died?"

"Ten." He stared at Lord Prith. He couldn't believe at all that he had blurted that out of his mouth. It was said. It couldn't now be unsaid. He waited.

Lord Prith sat back in his chair. "I am sorry for that, my boy."

Lord Beecham continued to stare at the man he hoped was his future father-in-law. He had spilled every bit of blackness in his soul, laid it all out for Lord Prith to examine. Now Lord Prith would realize that he wasn't the man for his beloved daughter. He had been stunted and embittered. He wasn't worthy of someone pure and wholesome, the only woman to make him beg to give his all to his marital duties until he was called to the other side.

But he wasn't worthy. It all came down to that. He waited to hear the ax drop on his neck.

Lord Prith said, "At least you are not short. That bodes well for you. Helen turns down short men."

He blinked. Lord Prith was considering him? His confession had not set him irrevocably against him? He cleared his throat, and said, "No, I am two inches taller than Helen. She tries to pretend that I am not, but it is true. Two inches, perhaps even a quarter of an inch more than two inches."

"You and Helen will have magnificent children. It is difficult, as you well know, my boy, not to impregnate a woman. You will not kill my daughter with too many birthings, will you?"

Even as Lord Beecham shook his head and said "No, I will not," he remembered that Helen couldn't have children. She was barren. He felt a very deep shaft of pain, but he felt it for just a moment. In the grand scheme of things, his second cousin, a ship captain who lived in the colonies, in a place called Baltimore, could have his title, or one of his cousin's male children could have it. He was a good fellow, he wouldn't blight the Heatherington escutcheon.

But truth be told, Lord Beecham didn't care what sort of a man his cousin was. He wanted Helen and he wanted her forever. It was the oddest thing. He was standing in Lord Prith's dining room, Flock likely behind him in the shadows, not moving a muscle for fear of anyone realizing he was still in the room, and it didn't matter a single whit. He felt wonderful. He felt whole.

"I will protect Helen with my life. I am not a pauper. She will have everything she could possibly desire. I have a beautiful country estate in Devon. Paledowns. She will love it there, all rugged hills and valleys and the coastline, all jagged and old, sir, so very old." He shut his mouth on his poetic outpourings. He was losing what few wits remained to him. He would make his summation pithy. Show the depths of his ardor with a few witty words. He cleared his throat and opened his mouth, and what came out was, "I have never met a lady like your daughter. She is radiant, sir. I cannot imagine how I could be so very lucky as to have her leap at me from her horse's back in Hyde Park and hurl me to the ground." He cleared his throat. What had that come from? "Ah, Paledowns, sir, she will be happy there. She will also be happy in London. I have three other houses as well dotted over the northern landscape. She will doubtless approve of those as well. If she doesn't, she can discipline the caretakers and change things until she is pleased.

"I will worship her, sir, until I cock up my toes and pass to the hereafter."

Lord Prith said comfortably, "You don't have to worry about things like that, my boy. My dearest Nell nests wherever she happens to find herself. Your home sounds like an excellent place for her, any and all of them. You know, now that I reflect upon things, my little girl did seem a bit on the quiet side whilst you were gone, my boy. Dare I say that she moped? Flock, are you still about, your ears all sharp?"

"Yes, my lord, but I have been staring at the epergne, my lord, wondering how best to clean all the little hidden crevices amongst all the grapes. I have barely heard a word anyone has said."

"Good. Do you think that Miss Helen was moping — or is that too strong a word?"

"Miss Helen moped as I have also moped, my lord. I perhaps taught her through example how to mope properly. It is not too strong a word."

"Good, I didn't think so. She was also distracted. I would catch her looking off into nothing at all, as if dazed. One of her lads at the inn let a thief steal several bridles from the stable. She disciplined him, but her heart wasn't in it, all could tell. She has lost flesh, which isn't good for her, since she is well nigh perfect just the way she is."

"Yes, she is perfect."

"Hmmm," Lord Prith said, drank more champagne, and looked off toward a painting on the wall. Lord Beecham glanced at the painting, a line of rabbits hanging from a skinny rope in a sixteenth-century kitchen, ready for the cooking pot. He didn't like paintings like this though they were so very popular in nearly every dining room in London. They always put him off his feed.

"Helen isn't perfect, my boy," Lord Prith said. "I must be honest with you, since it appears that you see her only with honey flowing from her mouth. She is her own woman. Perhaps one could call her occasionally obstinate and, rarely, just sometimes, a bit on the stubborn side. Those words aren't too strong, are they, Flock?"

"They are perhaps shaded by your loving parental eye, my lord."

"She is used to doing precisely what she wants when she wants to do it. She is strong-willed and strong of limb as well. I have seen her knock a suitor from one side of the room to the other when he chanced to offend her. She didn't break anything, but the fellow had a black eye for a week.

"She has opinions, my boy, opinions that are her own, not necessarily gently formed by her dear father. She is interested in all sorts of things, as you very well know, what with this lamp business. She is a mistress of discipline. Yes, even I know this about my dearest Nellie. Her lads always strive to please her, but when they run afoul of what is right and proper, she does discipline them. Come to think of it, they sometimes beg for it, but she is fair in her judgments and doesn't always give them what they want.

"She won't let you tread on her like a rug, my boy. In short, my sweet little Nell is a handful, just like her dearest mother, my precious Mathilda." Lord Prith looked over at Flock, an eyebrow arched in question.

"Well and accurately stated, my lord."

"Thank you, Flock."

Lord Beecham couldn't help himself. He asked, "Have you ever seen any of her lads in the stocks?"

"Certainly. Other villagers rent the stocks from her to carry out their own punishments. She is considered a goddess of justice in Court Hammering. Wives adore her because she won't allow their husbands to drown their livers in her taproom."

Lord Beecham said, "She is much more than a goddess. I must have her, my lord."

"Yes, I can see that you must. Very well, you have my permission. Do you agree that you know what you're getting into? That you aren't all afloat in a man's lust and blind to the very few nearly meaningless foibles my sweet Nellie occasionally exhibits?"

"No, not really, but I know enough to realize that I want to find out everything about her and each of her foibles during the next fifty years. Perhaps I will even wed her again upon occasion."

"A charming thing to say, lad. Very well. Champagne, Flock. Bring a fresh bottle. Ah, and for my future son-in-law here, some brandy, nasty stuff. We don't want to force him to drink champagne and have him puke on Helen's slippers, now do we?"

21

Geordie had spilled twenty pounds of oats into a huge mud puddle. He knew he would be punished, he was whimpering in a corner, knowing it would happen, and here Helen just didn't appear to care. She was just staring off at nothing at all. Actually, Helen couldn't stop thinking about why Spenser had grabbed that hunk of bread and run out of the inn. Then Gwen said, "Miss Helen, the stupid clumsy lout deserves at least a Level Six."

Geordie shuddered with both anticipation and dread.

"What? Oh, a Level Six, Gwen? Isn't that a bit on the harsh side?"

"Twenty pounds of oats, Miss Helen, feed for the mud, not the horses."

"Very well, then. Level Six." Helen turned and walked back into the inn. It was nearly nine o'clock at night.

There was enough of a moon so that Geordie was clearly visible to all who wished to watch his punishment. When she heard Geordie yell, then moan, she just shook her head and went back into the small private dining parlor. She built up the fire. She took a cup of hot cider and sat there in her wing chair staring into the flames, seeing him striding out of the small parlor, practically reeling.

"Helen."

She turned very slowly to see him standing in the doorway. "You ran away, with the bread."

"Yes, but I came back. I ate the bread."

"What do you want, Lord Beecham?"

"There is a naked man in the inn courtyard. His wrists are tied by a rope looped over the lower branch of that immense elm tree, and Gwen is whipping him. There were three other women in line, waiting their turn. They have switches, not hollyhock bunches."

"Yes. Geordie spilled twenty pounds of oats in a mud puddle. It demands a Level Six punishment. Gwen believed that was appropriate."

"I see. It all makes sense now. Will you marry me, Helen?"

She dropped her cup of cider. She sat there, stunned, watching the cider snake over her exquisitely polished oak floor toward the small rectangular Aubusson carpet. She moaned, jumped to her feet, and looked wildly around.

Lord Beecham untied his beautiful white cravat and handed it to her.

He watched her go down on her knees and wipe up the cider. She continued to wipe long after the cider was gone.

"Helen, it is all clean now." He held out his hand. "You will rub the wood away."

She ignored his hand and jumped to her feet, tottered a bit because she was dizzy, then sat down heavily back into her chair.

"I didn't run away from you. I rode to Shugborough. I have just returned from there.

Your father gives me his permission to court you. Actually, he also gives his permission to marry you. Will you do me the honor of becoming my wife?"

There was another yell from Geordie, followed by a deep moan. Helen said absently, "That was probably Miss Millbark. Did you notice how the moan was louder than the yell? She always teases before she strikes."

"Helen, I don't care about Geordie's discipline at this particular moment. How many strokes does he get?"

"Only ten. Then he is forced to stand naked in front of the inn, holding a lamp, for three hours, unless it rains, in which case it is postponed until it is sunny again."

"I see. Will you?"

She was shaking her head at him, saying, "This makes no sense. You desire me, I will grant you that, since I feel the same about you. But you don't love me. How could you? You don't know me."

"Don't know you? My God, woman, if ours is not a marvelous beginning of knowing, I don't know what is."

"That is something I still don't understand. I am coming to believe that you are a sorcerer, sir. You have but to touch me and I am suddenly mindless."

"Yes, it is rather nice, isn't it?"

She looked suddenly lost.

He was at her side in an instant. He came

down on his haunches beside her chair. "Helen," he said. "I know we only met each other a month ago. I know that I never wanted to marry, at least not until I was nearly ready to cork it. But now everything is different. We are different. Marry me, Helen. We will deal well together. We will find this bloody lamp and perhaps become joint rulers of the world through its magic. What do you think? Is that enough power? There are lots of mysteries in the world, just waiting to be discovered. We can search out our fair share of them. Say yes, Helen."

"I am as strong as you are."

"Possibly." He grinned up at her.

There was another very long yell and a short moan.

"Who was that?"

"The vicar's wife, Mrs. Possett. She enjoys more the pain end of things. I believe she is seeing the vicar in Geordie's place. He isn't a very tolerant man. I have heard her gnash her teeth."

"Tell me yes, Helen."

"I was married before." There was a deep and dangerous pause. "I didn't care for it."

"You were young, your exquisite mind unformed. The man was an idiot. But it doesn't matter now. He is long dead. You and I are different, Helen. We are no longer children. We know what we want."

"No."

He looked like she'd shot him. He rocked back

on his heels. He rose slowly then and stared down at her. The shadows cast off by the fire made a halo around her blond hair. She looked like an angel. She had just had the gall to turn him down.

He felt disbelief. He felt outrage bubble and roil in his belly. "This makes no sense at all. You want me out of my britches all the time."

"Yes, well, that I can't seem to help. Come, Lord Beecham —"

"Damn you, call me by my given name — Spenser."

"Spenser, admit it. It is lust, boundless, mindless lust you feel for me — just as I do for you — nothing more, nothing less. Just lust. What would happen if we married and in six weeks you were over your lustful cravings? What would you do then? We would be bound together forever. No, I don't want that."

"You have written an amazing tale, madam. You have plucked an ending out of the ether that has no substance or meaning or validity. I devoutly pray that our lust for each other wanes just a bit or else we will never get anything accomplished outside of our bedchamber.

"Now, let me propose quite another ending to your amusing tale. We will love and fight and yell and laugh and have a very nice time of it well into the foreseeable future. What do you think about that?"

"It is a good ending," she said, sighed, and looked away from him, into the fire.

"And have you had other lovers, madam? Other men who gave you such pleasure?"

"No."

He wished he could think of more to say. "Why are you saying no to me, Helen? What is it I cannot give you? I don't for a moment believe that ludicrous tale you have spun. I believe you would very much like to become my wife. We would be partners and lovers for life."

Her hands were folded in her lap. She wasn't moving, just sitting there, staring down at her hands. "I don't wish for another husband. I don't want to lose what I have, what I am."

"For God's sake, what kind of a man do you think I am? I wouldn't take anything from you. I would hope that what I would give you would enhance your happiness."

She didn't look at him, simply shook her head.

He was so frustrated, so disbelieving that she would actually turn him down, and for no good reason that had yet come out of her mouth, that he was momentarily speechless. Then, finally, he said, "I wish that were all there was to it." He threw himself down on the chair next to hers. He leaned his chin on his fist, stretched out his long legs, and stared into the fireplace.

"There is nothing else to it. Just lust, nothing more."

"You're being a blockhead, Helen. Obviously this man you were married to, when you were too young to have even the beginnings of a brain, gave you a very bad opinion of men and of mar-

268

riage. It won't be anything like that between us. Use your sense, woman."

She shook her head.

"I too have always had a very bad opinion of marriage, given the utter devastation my father wrecked on three women's lives, but it fades into the shadows when I think of having you at my side, in my bed, sitting across from me at the breakfast table. Why don't I banish your bad experience from your mind, Helen?"

She was shaking her head even before he had finished speaking. He wanted to strangle her. Instead, he rose, walked to the dining room door, shut it, and to his immense delight, there was a lock and a key. He turned it.

"Now," he said, turning around. "Now."

He heard her breath whoosh out. She stood, made to run, then stopped, her hands fists at her sides. "No, Spenser, I don't want to make love with you. You will not coerce me in that way. It is low."

"Not as low as I'm able to get if the circumstance calls for it."

In less than three minutes, Helen was on her back on the table, and he was gently pulling her toward the end. She was trying to grab him, to bring him over her, to kiss him, but he was holding her legs apart, staring at her, trying not to expire on the spot, and then, in the next instant, he was inside her, to the hilt, and he was moaning and pushing, and then he heard her crying out, soft, deep cries that went right to his sex, and he fell over her, kissing her until he was breathless, and he felt her muscles tighten around him, felt the immense power of her climax as she twisted and held him so tightly he wondered if he would be black and blue in the morning. He laughed then, raised his head, and yelled to the beams in the small private dining room.

Geordie gave a final mighty yell from outside.

"That was his last stroke," Helen managed to say, then bit his shoulder. She was panting so hard she could barely draw a breath. He didn't leave her, just waited, and it wasn't at all long before he was moving inside her again. "Your breasts," he said. "This time I have some control. I want to taste your breasts."

He was pulling at her gown, but he didn't have the time. She lifted her hips, and it was all over for him. His fingers found her and she bit his neck this time and it both stung and made him wild. Her hot breath was fast and slick on his flesh. This time he took her lovely moans into his mouth. As for himself, he pressed his mouth against her neck and yelled against her soft flesh.

"There," he said, every shred of male arrogance sounding loud and clear in his voice. He straightened between her legs, still inside her, and he laid his hands on her white thighs. "Open your eyes, Helen. Look, I am still inside you. I am part of you. Now, there will be no more of your wrongheadedness. You will consent to marry me. I am the only man for you. You and I

270

belong together. Together we will find this damned magic lamp. Together we will create a life that will make us stronger as two than what we are now singly. Perhaps, in five years or so, I will have enough control so I will be able to kiss your breasts, and that's just the start of it." Slowly, he pulled out of her, never looking away from her face.

Helen managed through pure force of will to sit up on the table. She was so very wet with him, and with herself, she supposed. She looked past him into the fireplace. There were just two or three small embers that were glowing with any light at all now.

She nearly fell when she tried to stand up. She batted down her skirts. At least she was not wearing her riding hat. That would have been simply too much.

"You are mine, Helen."

That stiffened her backbone. "I will see you in the morning, Lord Beecham," she said and walked to the door. It took her several moments to get the damned key to turn in the lock.

"And will you be thinking about us, together? Forever?"

She didn't say anything, just walked out of her inn, saw that Geordie was standing there in the moonlight, six or so women around him, and several men as well, and he was holding the lamp between his bound hands. He was stark naked.

She nodded to him. She heard him whimper. He didn't sound very distressed to her.

One of her lads saddled Eleanor for her. She was home in twenty minutes. Her father and Flock, thankfully, were out for their nightly walk. She heard her father yelling at the two peacocks. She heard Flock sigh over Teeny. It was later than usual for their walk. It must have been Spenser's visit that threw off their schedule.

Teeny, unusually quiet this evening, helped her undress and pulled the covers over her once she was in bed. Teeny blew out all the candles. She stopped at the door and said, "Miss Helen, Flock told me all about Lord Beecham's talk with your father. He is in a very bad way, Flock said. His eyes were nearly rolling in his head. He would have even drunk champagne if your father had demanded it of him. You should marry him, to save him, to give him back his charming boldness. He isn't short, Miss Helen."

And Teeny left her alone.

That night Helen thought of poor Reverend Mathers and who could have killed him. She fell asleep seeing a man whose back was to her lean over Reverend Mathers and plunge the stiletto into his back. If only she could see his face.

The next day Helen didn't go to the inn. She remained at the hall, alone, brooding. Her father remained silent, which she appreciated. Flock did a good deal of sighing whenever she appeared, but she ignored him.

Lord Beecham didn't come. She waved her fist in the direction of Court Hammering — and was relieved.

In the middle of the following night, when the chill was heavy in the air and the moon was starting to fall toward the horizon, there was a slight rustling sound just outside Helen's bed-chamber window. She stirred, but there was silence again, and she stilled, settling again into a dreamless sleep.

A black shadow filled the window. Slowly, ever so slowly, the window went up until the black shadow eased a leg over the casement and entered her bedchamber.

22

Lord Beecham rather liked the romance of wearing all black to kidnap the object of his affection. He smiled as he stood by her bed, looking down at her. Her beautiful blond hair was spread over the pillow. The moonlight made her face look luminous. Because he wasn't a fool, because he knew well enough that if she were peeved with him, she could inflict a good deal of damage to his person, he dampened the white cloth he held in his hand with the contents of a small vial. He pressed the cork back into the vial, then he leaned over and pressed the cloth over her nose and mouth.

She came awake, tried to jerk up, but he had braced himself and so managed to hold her still for another ten seconds. Then it was too late for her because her strength was gone. She fell back against the pillow, seeing the shadow over her, feeling the sickly sweet scent fill her nostrils, seep into her mouth, filling all of her eventually. She wasn't afraid, there was no time. Just this growing lassitude, just the slow, inexorable withdrawal of consciousness.

She sighed and closed her eyes.

Lord Beecham straightened, folded the small square of cloth and put it and the vial into his pocket. He looked down at the woman he fully planned to marry and smiled a man's smile, a hard smile that was wicked and determined and shouted that he was ready to do anything to get her to a vicar.

He paused only twice while he dressed her, to kiss her breasts, finally, and to admire them as much as he was able in the shadowy light. He just couldn't help himself. Her breasts were incredible, all soft and white, beautifully full and round — and her taste, it made his breath hitch. As for her belly — he had to kiss her belly as well, and he had to close his eyes because it was just too much.

And then she moaned softly deep in her throat, and he nearly fell on top of her.

It took another ten minutes to pack clothes in a valise. Lots of lacy silk things. Because he knew he couldn't very well take her to the vicar wearing only her chemise, he selected a pale-yellow gown that he liked very much, a petticoat, and a chemise. He found a pair of slippers and stockings. He had done well. He was a man of experience and decision. The stockings even matched the slippers and the gown. He didn't bother with a bonnet. Enough was enough. Both of them could be married bareheaded.

Yesterday had undoubtedly been the busiest day of his entire life.

He had thought about carrying his big girl and her packed valise over his shoulder and out the second floor window, three steps down the foot-wide ledge and then climbing down the sturdy trellis, covered with a thorny rosebush, without the both of them crashing down to the flower beds below.

Yes, he had thought about it and just laughed, but now he wondered if he would make it without killing both of them. He thought of the folded letter he had left on her pillow and smiled yet again. The romance of it should surely appeal to her father. If Helen wished it, he would marry her three times during their life together.

It was a close thing, climbing down that thorn-covered trellis with Helen slung over his shoulder, too close for Lord Beecham's peace of mind, and when he finally got both his feet firmly on the ground, he raised his eyes to the heavens and offered up a very sincere prayer of thanksgiving.

He had his big girl. She wasn't trying to kill him because she was blessedly unconscious. He realized he didn't have all that much time. He didn't want to tie her up, at least not just yet.

He carried her all the way past the front entrance to Shugborough Hall, all the way to where the night shadows were deepest, to where he had hidden a carriage. He heard one of the peacocks bleat after him. He was breathing very hard.

He was, he thought, as he gently closed Helen inside the carriage, an amazing man, strong of back, mighty of will. He had wrapped her up in three blankets on the floor of the carriage, and tucked pillows around her. He hadn't wanted to take the chance that she would roll off the seat. He was still breathing hard when he climbed up onto the box and click-clicked the sturdy gray gelding forward. Both Eleanor and Luther were safe and snug in the Shugborough Hall stables.

He whistled into the soft night air as he drove the ten miles to the small hunting box he had rented yesterday morning at ten o'clock from Lord Marchhaven, who had asked Lord Beecham if he was planning on entertaining a hunting party. Spenser had just shaken his head and smiled. "Ah," said Lord Marchhaven, nodding. "I am pleased that it is a nice house."

"I will require it for perhaps a week," Lord Beecham had said.

Again Lord Marchhaven merely nodded, then said as he and Spenser shook hands, "I have learned that sometimes in life a man is forced to do something that sits perilously close to the edge of scandalous to obtain the indispensable. Enjoy yourself, my lord." It was obvious that Lord Marchhaven sniffed a week's worth of wickedness. Lord Beecham should have told him that he intended a lifetime of marital wickedness.

Well, as he figured it, Helen was indispensable to him. He believed, deep down, that he was also indispensable to her. Why had she refused him? It didn't make any sense.

The Marchhaven hunting box was an elegant little Georgian brick house, all stiff and starchy, nearly a perfect square, two stories high, ivy twining in and out of the red bricks. It was set on the edge of the Houghton Forest, much of it owned by the Marchhaven family, for hunting parties. No one was there at present.

When he finally carried Helen into the house, he was still whistling, thinking of how he had wheedled and pleaded and even drunk a glass of champagne with Bishop Horton to obtain a Special License, but he had done it. He whistled louder, so pleased with himself that he nearly dropped Helen on the stairs. His back hurt a bit, but he discounted it.

The house was simply set out. Upstairs there were four bedchambers, the master's bedchamber at the end of the hall. It was nice and big. So was the bed, at least large enough to hold six men side by side. Helen would be quite comfortable here. The headboard was slatted, a truly convenient thing for him.

He shook off the blankets and his cloak and gently eased Helen under the covers. He whistled while he lit three branches of candles, then started a fire in the large fireplace.

He looked around the bedchamber. It was excellent, just excellent. It was an ideal place for a man to bring the woman he'd kidnapped, the woman who must need learn that not marrying the man she bit on the neck wasn't to be tolerated.

He had given it a good deal of thought. Helen wasn't a milksop. If she could, she would brain him at the first opportunity. He couldn't allow her any opportunities, but accomplishing this did set many problems in his path.

He went back to the carriage, brought up the two valises, the second one his, and took the nice old gelding to the small stable to stick his nose in a trough of oats. Back in the bedchamber, he pulled out four of his cravats.

She would awaken soon enough. Ah, that marvelous potion Mrs. Toop had given him, stars in her eyes when he had pleaded his case, giving in quickly because of the glorious romance of all of it. "Just imagine," she said, her hands over her large bosom, "my mistress will learn more about discipline. Oh, goodness, she will, won't she, my lord? Do you promise?"

Since this seemed inordinately important to her, Lord Beecham had quickly nodded and given her endless assurances that he had more to teach Miss Helen than any other man in all of England, and she would enjoy herself immensely, he gave her his word. Mrs. Toop had given him the vial of chloroform and told him how much to use on her sweet mistress.

His last view of Mrs. Toop was her standing at the inn door, her rheumy eyes glittering beneath the lamp that Geordie had proudly held up for three hours the previous evening.

Everyone, it seemed, wanted Helen to marry him. It was up to him now to convince her. He was prepared to do whatever it took.

He gave the smoking fire a big grin, added a couple more small sticks, turned on his heel and walked back to the bed.

Helen awoke slowly, which was strange, because usually her eyes opened and she was ready to bound out of bed, her body and brain thrumming with energy. But her eyes were slow to open. When she finally opened them she saw that it was daylight, bright daylight, with the morning sun shining through the uncurtained windows just to her left.

But she didn't have windows to her left. They were to her right. Something was wrong.

Her brain seemed on the blurry side, the way it felt just after Spenser had loved her until all she had left was a silly grin on her face.

She tried to sit up. She couldn't move. That was surely odd. She tried again. Then she realized that her hands were tied above her head. Tied?

She blinked at the sound of his voice.

He cupped her cheek in his palm. He kissed her mouth, lightly. "Good morning, Helen. I hope you're feeling more alert now? You've been moaning a bit for the last several hours."

"Spenser?"

"Yes," he said, lightly stroked his fingertip over her eyebrows, leaned down and kissed her mouth again.

She kissed him back before she quite realized what she was doing. She blinked up at him. "Why are my hands tied above my head?"

"So that you won't try to kill me. That is, you

could try, but I don't believe that even you, my dearest, could manage it."

"Why would I want to kill you?"

"The complete truth is that I have kidnapped you. You are quite alone with me. I have tied you down to my bed. In short, my sweet little Nellie, you are completely and thoroughly at my mercy."

She did try to bring her arms down to punch him in the nose, but even though the bonds around her wrists didn't hurt or rub, and she realized they were his soft cravats and thus there was just a bit of pull in them, she couldn't get free.

Her feet. She tried to bring up her legs to smash him in the back. He had secured her ankles as well, again with those lovely cravats of his.

She stopped and just looked up at him.

He was smiling down at her. It was a smug smile, one also filled with joy — an odd combination, but it was so. She didn't know what to think, but she knew that she could not allow it to continue.

She tried not to grit her teeth, but it was difficult. She had to start somewhere, and so she said, "You will release me this very instant."

"I don't think so, dearest. You would try to pulverize my liver."

"No, I swear I won't. I won't even destroy your bloody manhood. Let me go now."

"That is a lie of considerable width and

breadth, Nell. Now, we do have a bit of a problem, and I want you to know that I have given it a lot of thought. When you must need relieve yourself, I will release both ankles and the wrist that's right here closest to the side of the bed. I will bring the chamber pot close to the bed. You will be able to manage. To assure myself that it could be done, I myself tried it earlier this morning. I was successful.

"You have slept a long time. Now, before you have your breakfast that I have myself prepared for you, let me release your hand and your ankles. And, Helen, don't be foolish. Relieve yourself, no more than that."

She didn't say a word. To be honest, she was still too befuddled. She was alert, but befuddled.

"You kidnapped me?"

"Yes, that's exactly what I did. I even carried you and your valise over my shoulder, out of your bedchamber window. I didn't falter even once. I am still standing tall, at a minimum at least two inches taller than you."

"But why? Why are you doing this to me?"

"Mrs. Toop wants me to teach you more about discipline."

He released her right wrist and her ankles. He rubbed feeling back into them. "There. Now, I am not going to leave the room because I know you will immediately try to undo the knot on your other wrist. I will be right here."

He patted her cheek lightly and walked back to the fireplace.

She used the chamber pot. He turned to see her begin to work on the other wrist knot. He grabbed her free hand and pulled it back above her head. "Lie down, Helen. Don't fight me."

It was like telling a maddened tiger not to attack the nearest moving creature. She yelled and kicked with her legs and tried to jerk her hand free of his. She got a couple of good licks with her feet, but he finally managed to find the exact position to do away with any leverage she had. He tied her wrist back against the thick headboard.

He stood over her. "That was a nice try. Now, would you like your breakfast?"

"I will kill you, Spenser."

He leaned down and kissed her hard, jerking back before she could bite him.

He smoothed her nightgown over her legs. Then, almost as an afterthought, and before she could fight, he pulled her right ankle out and tied it again. He had her now. "Very nice. Now let me tie your left ankle." She tried to kick him, but couldn't manage it. Soon, her legs were nicely spread.

"After breakfast, dearest, we will enjoy dessert," he said, and whistled his way out of the bedchamber.

He heard her yelling after him, hurling curses laced with various animal parts — all in all, not very creative — and he smiled.

She didn't have a chance.

23

Fifteen minutes later Lord Beecham brought his captive some warm scones, sweet butter, apricot jelly, and a pot of tea he had made himself.

"The scones are not completely fresh. Mrs. Toop made them yesterday, at the inn, just for this special occasion. However, I did build a fire in the fireplace. The scones are all softened up, nice and hot."

"What did you mean by dessert?"

He loved her mind. "Discipline, my sweet. Everyone seems anxious for me to teach you more about this very interesting topic. Perhaps you have become too predictable in your approach, too unimaginative. It is time to infuse new ideas, give new perspective."

"What do you mean by everyone?"

"I must keep my sources private. I believe there is a fear of possible retaliation."

"Spenser, you must let me go. If you do it now, I swear not to hurt you."

"That's nice that you're calling me by my given name again. Does that mean you are no longer trying to hold me at arm's length?"

She jerked on her arms. Nothing happened. She was becoming very red in the face.

He patted her cheek, sat down in the chair beside her bed, and said, "Would you like butter and jelly on your scone?"

"I would like to feed myself."

"All right." He released one hand. He watched her flex her fingers, bend her wrist back and forth.

"Would you like butter and jelly on your scone?"

She nodded. At last her attention was on the food and not on killing him.

She ate two scones, both slathered with the apricot jelly, then lay back against the pillow and sighed. "That was delicious. Thank you. Mrs. Toop makes the best scones in the area. Now, I should like to be back at my inn by luncheon. May we leave now?"

"Would you like some tea now? Lemon? Milk?"

She got the very same look in her eyes as when she had confronted all those drunk young men from Cambridge in her taproom. It was blood. She had blood in her eyes.

He never should have given her the tea, particularly with added milk. She threw it in his face. Then her face scrunched up. "Oh, dear, I didn't think. I should have taken a drink first."

"Probably so," he said, and rose to clean himself off. "That," he said to her from the far side of the room as he dipped a cloth into the bowl of warm water atop a commode, "will gain you punishment, Helen. What do you think? Level Five?"

"Don't be ridiculous. That was nowhere near a Level Five." She realized what she had said and closed her mouth fast.

"All right," he said, a man so agreeable, so reasonable, so ready to compromise, that the air reeked with it, and if she could have, she would have kicked him across the room. "What do you think is fair? Level Three?"

"You will not make sport of me, Spenser."

"At least you are still using my given name."

"If I call you Lord Beecham, it is horridly embarrassing. I am lying here in my nightgown, on my back, with my arms and legs tied down."

His eyes nearly crossed. He closed them and patted his face dry. He pulled his wet shirt out of his britches and unfastened it.

He knew she was staring at him. He wasn't wrong. There was lust in her eyes if he wasn't mistaken — and he wasn't. That was nice.

When he was naked to the waist, he spread his shirt over the back of a chair to dry, then walked back to the bed. "You like me, Helen?"

"You are a man. What is there to like?"

"You were staring at my chest. Now you are having a very difficult time keeping your eyes on my face. What do you think? Do you like the way my manly parts are put together?"

"I'm thirsty."

"If I give you another cup of tea, do you promise to drink it and not hurl it at me?"

He saw it was a struggle, but finally, she managed to say, "Oh, all right, I promise."

He kissed her mouth, straightened, and poured her another cup. He didn't add milk or

286

sugar. He helped her sit up. He handed her the cup.

She drank slowly, not looking at him. When she finished, she handed him the cup. "This is madness, Spenser. You cannot keep me here tied down to this damned bed."

"Why not?"

He nearly laughed at the utterly blank look on her face. Finally, still staring at him, she said, "Well, I don't know. It isn't right, I guess. Besides, there is nothing more about discipline that you could teach me."

It was amazing how very certain she could sound. "You think not, do you?"

She retrenched; he saw it, and was amused by it. A little over a month ago he'd had no idea that a Miss Helen Mayberry even existed. Now he could not imagine not having her here, near him, tied down to his bed.

She cleared her throat. She took another sip of her tea. "Didn't you tell me that you wanted to give me everything I could possibly want?"

"Not that I remember."

"You did, or something very close, something that was vastly romantic and utterly outrageous. You said you thought we would deal well together. I am not dealing well right now. I am tied down. I don't like this."

He gave her a slow sweet smile. "All you have to do is tell me you will marry me and we will be on our way to Vicar Lockleer Gilliam within the hour."

"I could agree, then leave you and Vicar Gilliam alone at the altar."

"You could, but that would be very disappointing, Helen. Your father gave me a fairly complete list of all your weaker points, all your pesky little character flaws, your minuscule little foibles, as he called them. He never said you were a liar."

"I'm not, blast you."

"Good. Will you marry me?"

She chewed her bottom lip. He saw that her lips were chapped and he frowned. He walked over to the dressing table and began opening the drawers. He found cream in the second drawer.

He sat beside her on the bed, dipped his finger in the thick white cream, then began to rub it into her lips. She just stared at him, not moving. She had a free hand but it just lay there beside her on the bed.

"Thank you," she said when he was finally finished.

"You're welcome." He kissed her again, tasting the cream that was rather like licking the bark on an oak tree. "Now, will you marry me?"

"No."

"Very well, are you ready for your Level Three punishment for tossing your tea in my face?"

"It isn't more than a Level One."

"Just what do you consider a Level One punishment?"

"It is being left alone for two full hours, in a darkened room, with no one to talk to, no water to drink, nothing to eat. I usually use the tack room in the back of the stable. It is quite dark."

He sighed. "Well, it isn't at all titillating, but I suppose what's fair is fair."

He pulled the draperies closed. He firmly tied her other wrist again to the headboard. He pulled the covers to her chest, patted her cheek, then kissed her mouth. He rose, looking down at her for a moment. He began to whistle. He removed the tray and left her alone. She heard his whistle as he retreated down the hallway.

He did not come back.

Helen decided as she lay there that this simple punishment was much worse than she had ever imagined. It was a Level Three, at the very least. She would have to reevaluate her discipline scale.

Surely nearly a day had passed when finally the bedchamber door opened. Helen could have leapt on him, she was so glad to see him.

He pulled a chair close to the bed and sat down, steepling his long fingers, tapping their ends together, rhythmically, slowly. She found herself staring at those fingers of his, remembering where they had touched her, and she shuddered, not enough for him to notice, but enough so that she felt it to her toes. And speaking of touching, why wasn't he all over her? In the normal course of things, he couldn't wait to be all over her. Here she was, laid out like an offering, and he was just sitting there, tapping his wretched fingers. What was wrong with him?

"One of the most efficacious disciplinary techniques I have ever discovered is what I call, as of this moment, 'not quite ecstasy.' "

Helen's heart began to pound, slow, deep strokes. Her face was alight with excitement. Spenser cleared his throat. "You see, Helen, you and I together are something I have never imagined happening in my life. I touch you and you become utterly wild."

"I am not the only one here with no control. What do you do when I touch you?"

He nodded. "A good question. It is quite possible that I lose a good deal of my flawless technique, not that you would notice, since you want me so badly. I have considered this and discovered that it makes me smile, even laugh. Don't you think that's strange?"

"Since I have never even observed this flaunted technique of yours, I don't know if laughter is strange or not."

He sat forward, knowing he was going to goad her but good. "Well, you see, dearest, you are so utterly, well, I do hesitate to use so uncomplimentary a word, but it applies perfectly here and I wish to be honest. You are very easy, Helen. Compliant and submissive also apply. Perhaps even docile? There is no challenge to you at all. I have but to look at you with just a dollop of interest in my eyes, and you begin licking your lovely chops. I kiss you — all it takes is just a meager little kiss — and you're ready to hurl yourself on your back and pull me down over you.

"You have, in short, given me no reason to assay a bit of my masterful technique. It is a bit depressing, all this utter easiness of yours, and it presents no challenge at all, and I do not believe one should be wasteful with one's abilities and talents." He sighed. "But, dearest, since I admire you so much, I am trying to adapt."

He waited. He enjoyed the waiting, anticipating what she would do. He loved her outrage, and that was just what she delivered to him. Her face was flushed, her eyes glittered, and her lips became a thin line with cream on them. He wanted to kiss her silly, taste the tree-bark cream, but he merely sat there, his fingers steepled. He wasn't about to unsteeple them and let them touch her, anywhere. He waited.

Then she looked him straight in the eye and said, "You are right about all of it. I am a creature with no will or control at all. It is very possible that any man could make me feel what you do. What do you think?"

He stared at her. He began to quake with his own outrage, which was filling him to overflowing, making him want to yell. "You," he said very calmly, "are a blockhead, Helen. You don't know anything. I plucked you out of the provinces and taught you how easy you are, but only with me. No other man who plucked you would find you remotely easy. You would probably knock anyone else across the room.

"It's true. You're an idiot. If you weren't, you would realize that I am the only man in the world

291

who can make you feel easy and compliant and willing to do just about anything I wish."

She yawned. "Well, Spenser," she said, "now that I ponder it, I have come to the conclusion that all those wild feelings you made me feel never really existed. I think they were probably not much of anything. At the most, they were accidental, on the very edge of meaningless."

"That is truly what you think?"

"Oh, yes. Certainly." She snapped her fingers. "Nothing at all."

"I am so glad you said that."

He rose, pulled off his boots, looking over his shoulder at her. "Soon, perhaps you will do this for me?"

"Perhaps," she said, and he shook. It was the most difficult thing he had ever had to do, but he made himself hold steady.

"Then," she said, "I will spit you on the end of my father's sword."

He heard the excitement in her voice, saw the excitement in her eyes that she couldn't hide from him. And perhaps, there was just a dollop of fury at him because he'd made her helpless. Ah, the woman had been fashioned by a beneficent God just for him. He began whistling. He walked in his bare feet to the windows and pulled back all the draperies. Brilliant sunlight splashed into the room. He looked over at her and smiled. "You know, my sweet, I'm coming to grasp all your precious little peculiarities."

He sat down beside her. He leaned over and

began to pull open the ribbons of her nightgown. He saw the pulse pounding in her throat. His own excitement, he discounted. If he acknowledged it, he just might end up making love to her as he had the other ten times: fast, hard, and demented. No, he was set on his course. He was going to punish Helen, not love her silly, at least not yet.

He pulled apart her nightgown, baring her breasts. "Ah, now I can take the time to appreciate all the bounty you are offering me."

"You pig. I haven't offered you anything."

He lightly touched a fingertip to her mouth, then he leaned down and kissed her breast. She was trying to hold herself stiff as a board, but it wasn't going to work. Well, perhaps for another ten seconds. She trusted him implicitly, he saw it in her eyes, and so she was able to enjoy herself completely. And this was exciting her, no way to hide that, at least not from him.

It helped that he had his britches on and that he had made a vow to his face in the mirror not an hour before that he wasn't going to take her, not once, until she was married to him. He might want to slit his wrists, but he would hold firm. "Now it is time for your punishment. Since you're tied down and can't attack me or distract me, I will give you a taste of my incredible technique." He heard her suck in her breath even as he began kissing her breasts and caressing her until she was nearly beside herself. Then he drew back and ripped her nightgown open all the way to the hem. He peeled it back. Her legs were spread, her arms above her head. All of her exquisite white self was displayed right before his eyes. He raised his face to the ceiling and said a prayer of thanksgiving.

He looked at her up and down, humming softly, even as he raised his hand, let it hover over her belly a moment, then leave. Her breath hitched. He rose and walked to the tea tray he'd left on the small marquetry table in front of the fireplace. He poured himself a cup of tea. He sipped it, then walked slowly back to her. He stood beside the bed, a teacup in his hand, looking down at her.

"Spenser."

"Yes, my sweet?"

She was breathing hard, her breasts heaving, a lovely sight, beyond what he could have imagined, actually, and that came as a bit of a surprise. She was trying to lift her hips.

He said, "That was stage one of your punishment. Did you like it? Appreciate its subtle magnitude? Applaud its name — not quite ecstasy?"

She just stared up at him.

He set down the teacup, sat beside her again, and leaned down, kissing her white belly. She heaved and moaned. He smiled painfully against her soft flesh, and whispered, his breath hot, "Now stage two." He moved down until he was lightly cupping her with his hand. He raised his head and looked down at her.

"Spenser."

She sounded as if she was in pain. Slowly, knowing she was willing him to caress her, knowing she was holding her breath, he lowered his head and kissed her.

She screamed.

She was his now, completely his, and she was in a bad way, his stubborn, big girl. He felt the pleasure ripping through her, felt the building tension, the urgency nearly crested. He lifted his head.

"Helen."

She was beyond herself.

"Helen."

She tried to focus on his face, but it was difficult. She wanted his mouth on her, something that only he had done to her, and it was immensely exciting and she couldn't begin to imagine how horrible it would be to go through life never feeling this sort of wild madness. And now she knew what it was and how it felt and how it made you just want to yell and yell, and continue yelling until you exploded or simply collapsed.

She felt his mouth on her again, hot, his tongue making her scream. And then, suddenly, he was gone.

She lay there, twitching and jerking and arching as far as the soft ties on her wrists and ankles would allow, until the pleasure gradually faded. She looked over at him as he sat in the chair beside the bed, drinking some more tea and reading the *Gazette*.

He wasn't even looking at her. She wanted to cry, but of course she wouldn't. She wanted to kill him, but of course, at the moment, she could not do that either. Perhaps she could curse him to death. But there were no words coming out of her mouth. She just lay there, feeling the pulses of pleasure slowly fade, leaving her empty and cold and ready to murder him. So that was his discipline. He called it not quite ecstasy, the bastard.

Objectively, his punishment was incomparable. It was a Level Ten, at the very least. Hollyhock bunches were nothing compared to this.

She wanted to stab him in his black heart. With her father's sword. She jerked on her left wrist. To her astonishment, she was suddenly free. She lay there and blinked. The damned tie had simply slipped loose. Now the other wrist. Surely she couldn't be so lucky as to free that one too. How had she moved her wrist just then, just before the knots had slipped loose?

She'd turned her wrist inward, then given a sharp jerk. She did it again. The knots slipped open over her other wrist. She did the same thing with each ankle. She was free. His head was buried behind the *Gazette*. He wasn't paying any attention to her at all.

She felt fury pump through her and a high degree of admiration and respect for his discipline methods. He had driven her to the brink of madness, then left her. Yes, it was very effective, but surely he could be watching her face, perhaps even teasing her. But no, the miserable wretch was reading. Very slowly she sat up, shook off the cravats, and without a word, with no warning at all, she jumped from the bed and onto him, flinging him backward. The *Gazette* pages scattered over the floor. The chair toppled and they fell over together, she on top of him.

24

She gripped his hair and banged his head several times against the rug. It was unfortunate that the damned rug was so thick and soft. She wasn't making any headway at all. She banged him again. "You bastard," she yelled right in his eye. "You wretched bastard. I think your discipline was disgraceful. I would rather be walloped on the side of the head with a beam. I would rather be forced to eat boiled turnips with no salt, which is a nice solid Level Three punishment. But not what you did, this despicable not quite ecstasy discipline. I hated it. Do you hear me, Spenser? I hated it." She smacked his head down again against the rug.

He was laughing.

She reared up, still beyond herself, and stared down at him. She banged his head yet another time. He was still laughing. At her.

"You made me wild and then you had the gall to leave me." She was sitting on top of him now, leaning over, her hands around his throat. Her ripped nightgown hung loose, nearly falling off her shoulders. "You clod, you left me and came over here to read your newspaper. A bloody newspaper. You even drank tea. I am going to mash every bone in your wretched body." She started with his neck. She was trying her best to choke him to death. She just might succeed.

Helen had very strong hands. Her breasts were nearly touching his face.

He grabbed her wrists and pulled her fingers off his throat. He grinned up at her like a man who had just filched a packet of silver and discovered, to his utter amazement, that it was gold. "Will you declare that I am the master of discipline? That you are only a very distant second to me? Just look at you, Helen, trying to kill the man who so perfectly disciplined you."

She stopped cold. She sat up on him. Her nightgown still hung around her, nicely open, and he just looked and slavered and enjoyed. "You're right," she said slowly. "It was a two-part discipline that was more than effective. It was devastating." She leaned down and kissed him. Then she bit him, then licked where she had bitten. She felt his hand on the back of her head bringing her back down to him. Because he had no shirt on, her breasts were against his warm flesh.

He kissed her wildly, without restraint for perhaps thirty seconds. "Oh, no," he said into her mouth, grabbed her arms and shoved her back up. Her eyes were slightly crazed, her lips parted, as were his.

"No, just stay there, Helen, even though you are crushing me into the floor. Now, dearest, I have to say this. You misled me. I had believed you possessed of one of the premier brains in all of England — at least that is what you led me to believe. I must reevaluate that now. Ah, I forgot that you are, after all, a woman, with all the drawbacks, all the problems, all the lacks inherent to your charming, albeit occasionally incompetent sex."

She started to come down to kiss him again, then she paused and frowned. "Whatever are you talking about?"

He shook his head, disappointment written all over his face. He sighed, then said, "Well, you see, that took you much too long."

She grew utterly still. She splayed her palms on his bare chest, a very nice chest with crisp hair. "What took me too long?"

But she knew, oh, yes, she knew. He loved her hands on him. He wondered if she could feel his heart speeding up. He said, "It's the little half flick that you do with your wrists, that quick turn inward, that does the trick. The knots just slip right off. Yes, it took you a very long time to find the answer." Then he reached up and cupped her bare breasts in his palms. "Just beautiful," he said. "Now, before you have your way with me, do you agree to marry me?"

She just sat there on top of him, her nightgown hanging off her, her hair tousled around her face, disbelieving what he had done to her. She had never known a more beautiful man in her entire life. All of him was beautiful.

"I mean this, Helen. No more ecstasy, no more insane desire. I won't make love with you again until you promise you will marry me."

She still just sat there, leaning into his palms

now, letting him hold the weight of her breasts. She closed her eyes. "I cannot."

In a flash, he threw her off him. She was on her back in the middle of the rug and now he was on top of her, lying flat on top of her so that she couldn't move.

Their noses were nearly touching. He yelled in her face, "Why the hell not? The truth, Helen, now, or I will tie you down again, and this time I won't build in an escape route for you."

She swallowed.

To his astonishment, tears were seeping out of her eyes, streaking down her cheeks. He cursed.

He rose above her. She immediately turned onto her side, bringing her legs up to her chest, and she cried. She stuffed her fist into her mouth. It didn't matter. The tears kept coming.

The discipline mistress of Court Hammering was lying on her side on the floor crying her eyes out.

He cursed again, leaned down and pulled her upright. "This will surely bow my back," he said, as he managed to pull her up and over his shoulder. He staggered to the large wing chair in front of the fireplace. He eased down into it, pulling her across his lap, holding her tightly against him. "No, sweetheart, don't cry. It shatters me. You know that a big girl shouldn't have to cry about anything at all. No, a big girl would tell me immediately what bothers her. I can tidy up any mess, Helen, solve just about any problem, strike down any person who is bothering you. Of course, first, you have to trust me."

He rocked her. Finally she dried up. She was hiccuping. He smiled as he kissed her hair.

"He's alive," she said, her voice muffled against his chest.

He blinked. "What did you say, dearest? You're thinking I'm alive and quite all right, even though I had to lift you off the floor and pull you over my shoulder and actually carry you over here to this nice big chair that thankfully holds both of us?"

He felt her draw a deep, steadying breath. He pulled her nightgown over her naked side. He eased her up. When she was sitting, her head lowered, her hair nearly covering her lovely profile, he said, "What's wrong, Helen? You didn't like my games?"

"Yes," she said. "Your games were exhilarating. The escape — that was very clever of you. If I had not happened upon turning my wrist in just that way, I wouldn't have found it. I would have felt very stupid when you finally showed it to me."

"Marry me, Helen. I'll devise new knots to tease you. I'll contrive a very special discipline for you on our wedding night."

She turned then, and the nightgown fell open. He resolutely kept his eyes on her face. Her eyes were red, her nose was red, and there were tear streaks on her cheeks. He gently touched his fingertips to her beloved face. "I'm not making love to you, roaring over you, all frenzy and madness.

No, I am containing myself. I am simply holding you, all calm and controlled, and your nightgown is gaping open, and your beautiful breasts not three inches from my itching fingers."

She smiled, but it was a pitiful thing, that smile of hers, and it fell away completely when she said, "I said that he is alive."

He said nothing at all. He didn't want to. He had an awful foreboding. He wanted to tell her not to say any more, but he didn't. He waited for the guillotine to fall.

"My husband is still alive. I received a letter about six months ago. I don't know where he is. The letter came from Brest, on the far west coast of Brittany."

He grunted. He had traveled through the picturesque town some seven years before, when the Treaty of Amiens was still holding together. "There's nothing there as I recall, except fishermen. Why is he there? Why isn't he here? What happened to him? Are you certain that it is his handwriting? What is the damned fellow's name?"

"Gerard Yorke, the second son of the First Secretary of the Admiralty, Sir John Yorke."

Well, that was a kick. "Isn't the First Secretary as old as that oak tree just outside the window?"

"Yes, at least as old."

He had to keep calm, keep a firm grip on things. There had to be a way out of this, there had to be. "Have you written to him? Or did you go to see him when you were in London?"

"I wrote to Sir John, telling him about the letter. He did not reply. I wrote him once more and enclosed a copy of the letter. He still did not reply. The day after Gray and Jack's wedding, I went to the Admiralty at Whitehall. He refused to see me. He sent his secretary to tell me that his son had died a hero's death and that he had nothing at all to say to me. He didn't know why I would send him a ridiculous letter that wasn't even written by his son. He said that since I had not even managed to provide my husband a child, I had no claim on him or on his family."

"He sent his secretary to tell you this?"

"Yes, the poor man was embarrassed to his toes."

"Why didn't you tell me this two nights ago at the inn when I poured out my soul to you?"

"Because at that moment in time I didn't want to marry you, nor any man, ever again. Just look at the one husband I did take on — he returns to haunt me and I never even liked him after about two weeks of being his wife." She shuddered at the memories, sighed, and looked down at her hands. "Maybe it wasn't even two weeks."

"I see. Why didn't you tell me when I had you here, all nice and tied down to the bed?"

She cursed. He was so surprised that he just stared at her. "Why?"

"Oh, all right, you will just keep pulling and tugging, won't you? Well, here it is — I wanted to see what you would do to me."

The woman would drive him mad, he thought,

staring at her, and he wanted it more than anything he had ever wanted in his life. He lightly ran his fingertip down her cheek and over her jaw. "You are so bloody soft. Did you like what I did to you?"

"I don't know if I should tell you the truth."

He hugged her even more tightly and said, "I have this feeling that you and I will come back to that again, later, probably many times. Now, have you told your father?"

She shook her head. "Why? There is nothing he can do. Besides, he never liked Gerard. I don't want to worry him. As for Sir John, perhaps he didn't know his son's handwriting all that well. But I did. It was his handwriting, or an excellent forgery. The main reason I wrote to Sir John and tried to see him is that he is the First Secretary of the Admiralty. He is powerful. If anyone could find out anything about Gerard, it is Sir John."

"And yet he didn't want to hear about it. He refused to see you. That seems odd, doesn't it?"

"Yes, and I don't understand it. His son's body was never recovered."

"What happened?"

"Gerard was killed aboard a ship that wasn't more than a quarter mile off the coast of northern France. One of the cannons exploded and set the ship afire. They couldn't get the fire out. Just about every man jumped overboard, including Gerard, who was the first mate. No one stayed on board, even the captain. The problem was that Gerard couldn't swim. Isn't that odd, a man in the navy who spends all his time on the water, and he can't swim? I have been told that many sailors can't swim. In any case, a severe winter storm then struck, but not in time to douse the fire on board the ship. I was told that only half a dozen sailors managed to survive the swim to shore.

"Sir John was the one who informed me of Gerard's death. I hadn't had any contact with him since that time. He never cared for me. Since I believed him to be an old curmudgeon, it didn't bother me. My father, as you can imagine, was bewildered that someone didn't like his beloved daughter. In any case, if Gerard did somehow survive, if he is alive, then I am still married. I can't marry you or anyone else."

He had managed to figure that out all by himself. It was quite a blow to the jaw. He sat there, holding her, tapping his fingertips on her right thigh, wondering how life, which had seemed so very simple and straightforward but moments before when he was caressing her with his mouth, had now flown yet again out of his control.

He cursed again. It made him feel a bit better, for at least a short time.

She collapsed against him then, her face against his neck. He closed his arms around her.

"If he is dead, as he is supposed to be, would you marry me, Helen?"

She said against his neck, her voice warm and

sweet, "The thought of awaking on a random morning with my wrists tied above my head and you over me, it is nearly too much for my brain to deal with. But you would have to promise not to 'not quite ecstasy' me again."

He laughed — there was nothing else to do. "No, I won't ever punish you like that again." He kissed her forehead and fell silent. "Well, perhaps for a little while, before I continued."

He fell silent then, looking beyond her to the white wall beside the fireplace.

"What are you thinking?"

"I am wondering how to flush the fellow out," he said. "You see, it makes no sense for him to send you a letter and then do nothing at all for six months. Something strange is going on here." He was silent again. Helen was stroking her palm over his chest. It was distracting. He grabbed her hand and pushed it down onto his thigh. That proved even more distracting. He released her and sighed, closing his eyes. "I know what we will do."

"How can you possibly come up with a plan within five minutes of me telling you about it? I have had six months to devise a plan and there isn't one."

"I see. If you didn't think of a plan, then one can't possibly exist. That is rather arrogant of you, dearest, don't you think? Perhaps a Level Six to punish you for this character flaw?"

She leaned close and bit his neck. Then she licked where she had bitten, and then a small, light kiss. He loved that. "I think you would enjoy a Level Six, my lord, more than I would."

He nearly swallowed his tongue. He cleared his throat. "The reason you didn't think of anything is because I wasn't here to stimulate you."

"What is your plan?"

He eased her up until she was sitting on his lap, her eyes level with his. He tweaked her nose. He lightly kissed her mouth. Her lips were soft from the cream. "You and I, Helen, are going to announce our engagement in every newspaper in London and all the environs. We will even send an announcement to all the newspapers in Paris. Society is above war, don't you know. We will give our wedding date as a month from today. We will hold parties and a big ball. We will enlist the aid of the Sherbrookes, also Gray and Jack. Everyone will be speaking of our nuptials. If Gerard Yorke is still alive, then he will come to you. He will have no choice."

She blinked at him. "That is a brilliant idea. Actually, now that I think about it, it wouldn't have been possible for me to come up with that plan because there was no one about for me to marry."

She beamed at him, and he laughed and pulled her tightly against him. "You will marry me, Helen?"

She stilled, and he knew she was worrying and assessing and worrying some more.

"If he comes to London?"

"Then we will do what we have to do," Lord

Beecham said, and wondered silently exactly what that would be.

"I don't want to be married to him, Spenser. Perhaps it is just better to go along as we have, not to put our hands in the hornet's nest. Perhaps I won't ever hear from him again."

"We will marry, Helen. We will not be lovers."

"If he is alive, then we can never marry, unless I divorce him. I cannot do that, Spenser. It would be a horrible scandal."

"We will speak of that again when and if the fellow shows up. If he is alive, he will come. If he isn't, then we will marry. If he comes later, then we will deal with it when and if it happens. If there is nothing else, then you will divorce him. If the scandal proves too great, then we will move to Italy, a lovely place. To Tuscany, I believe, our own snug little villa. You will buy a local inn and run it. I speak Italian and will teach you all the curse words. What do you think?"

"I think you are wonderful, but that isn't to the point. There is something you're ignoring here, and you simply can't."

"What is that, pray?"

"You are Lord Beecham. You must have an heir. I am barren."

"I have already given that all the thought it deserves. My nominal heir is a cousin, a sailing captain in the Americas. He's a good fellow, as are his sons. Don't worry about it. I want you more than I want anything else in this entire benighted world. Believe it."

"It isn't right." He said nothing more, just looked at her. She nodded, finally, then nearly leapt off his lap. "Oh, goodness, I forgot about the lamp. How could I possibly forget about the lamp?"

"I'm here with you and my hands are stroking up and down your beautiful back. How could you think about much of anything other?"

"I see. Thank you for that explanation." She turned to kiss him, but he held her off.

"No, Helen, I'm not going to make love with you again until we are wed. I am committing myself to you for the rest of my life. I have no intention of —"

He looked down at her breasts and swallowed. "You must help me with this. I am set upon a noble course, but I need help."

"If Gerard doesn't come by the time our wedding is to happen?"

"Then we will wed, just as I told you. Perhaps the letter was a forgery, for some reason that we will discover, particularly after we announce our engagement. Everything will work out, Helen. Trust me."

He was still staring at her breasts when she said, "He wasn't a very nice man. I thought he was when I first met him, way back in the summer of 1801. I was only eighteen and he was at least thirty — perhaps more, he never told me — and I worshiped him. He enjoyed that, I think. Since he was a hero, naturally he knew everything, and I listened reverently to every word out of his mouth. He swore that he adored me, worshiped me. He didn't care if I was taller than he was, it didn't matter. He was a naval hero, the pride of the Admiralty, a man who had fought against Napoleon in the Battle of the Nile in 1798. Lord Nelson promoted him for his bravery. Yes, of course I saw soon enough that I'd been dazzled by his reputation, by the illusion of a hero. But I really hadn't known him as a real man.

"But now that I have had time to look back on those two years we were together, I don't believe he did love me. He desired me, but he didn't care if I ever felt anything for him."

"He never gave you a woman's pleasure."

"You already know that he did not. But he wanted a child, desperately."

"But you said he was the younger son of Sir John Yorke, not the heir."

"That's right."

"Then why the immense drive to produce a boy child? There was no title or estate in the balance."

"I don't know. There is a lot of wealth in the Yorke family, but no title."

Lord Beecham sighed. "This is as puzzling as that bloody lamp and where King Edward stashed it six hundred years ago and why he stashed it at all if the damned thing was so powerful. And why didn't Burnell ever write about it being in that iron cask with the leather scroll that was itself ancient six hundred years ago?"

311

"He obviously never discovered its power. As to the other, goodness, I don't know."

He sank his chin onto his hands and stared down at the floor, at the way the planks seamed together, a habit of long standing, when he was thinking hard. "If Gerard Yorke is alive, why would he write to you now? So many years have passed with everyone believing him dead. You can't give him his precious child, he already knows that. Why does he care? What does the bounder want?"

"I don't know."

"Another thing. Why did he select you, Helen? No, don't try to convince me that you were the most beautiful girl available, that you were obviously the pinnacle of young, nubile womanhood, because that didn't really matter — at least I don't think it did."

"Perhaps he believed because I am so big and sturdy that I would birth boy children right and left, fill England with all my offspring. He really was very keen on children."

He sighed and kissed the tip of her nose. "I suppose that makes about as much sense as anything else, maybe. How wealthy is your father?"

"Not immensely. He is comfortable, nothing more."

"It has been eight years since you last saw Gerard Yorke. Is that right?"

"Yes. Right after the Treaty of Amiens was signed in 1803, he left. Some sort of secret mission. I remember him whispering to me of this

312

special mission in the dark of the night, and he sounded very excited about it. But then he was on a ship and it sank. What is so exciting about that?"

"Unless he was just aboard the ship until he left it somewhere to proceed with this secret mission of his. Was he a liar?"

"I don't really know. During our two years before his death, he didn't spend more than five, perhaps six, months with me, total. It wasn't much of a marriage. Surely it couldn't have been to him, either. We didn't know each other, not really. Why did he write me, Spenser? Why, blast his eyes?"

"We will discover that when he tracks us down in London before we have the chance to marry."

She tucked her head against his neck. "I don't want him to."

"Sometimes there is just no choice in life, my sweet. You simply have to clean up the mess before you can go on."

"There is something else we must discover."

He kissed her lightly on the mouth and said, "What?"

"We must find out who murdered Reverend Mathers."

"Yes," he said slowly, his eyes hard, "we must."

"I dreamed I saw the man who did it, but I only saw his back. He's evil, Spenser."

"We will find him," Spenser said and kissed her again, hard this time. And then he kissed her again.

25

He had held steady. He couldn't believe it. He was immensely proud of his strength of will. He was also so randy he thought he would grind his teeth to dust.

He'd had to button Helen's gown up the back, but still he had managed to hold firm. He leaned forward to kiss her shoulder blade, then bit down on his lip.

"No," he'd said aloud to the ceiling of the bedchamber. "I will keep to my vow."

"Who do you think you are, Galahad?"

Helen was irritated with him. Because he wouldn't make frantic love to her, three times in fifteen minutes? He just smiled. "In one month from now, we can stay in bed until we are smiling and witless."

"I suppose you are right," she said finally at least two hours later, when they were riding back to Court Hammering in the carriage he had rented. At his arched eyebrow, she added, "We will wait. We will find the lamp. We will discover if indeed Gerard Yorke is alive. We will find out who killed poor Reverend Mathers. In short, we have a lot on our plate. And to accomplish those things, we must have our wits about us."

"You mean that when I am loving you, you have no wits?"

"Not a one," she said and poked him in the arm. "And you know it. Indeed, you are proud of it."

When they arrived at Shugborough Hall, Lord Prith and Flock met them at the front door. Both were beaming at them. Lord Prith continued to beam even as they walked into the entrance hall, saying nothing at all.

Finally Flock said, "His lordship wants to know the result of Lord Beecham's outrageous strategy. Just imagine, kidnapping you, Miss Helen, to bring you around to his way of thinking. You will consider telling us everything now, Miss Helen."

Helen said to her father, "I received a letter from Gerard Yorke six months ago. Until we find out if he is indeed still alive, we cannot marry. However, we are planning to wed in a month. We will tell the world about our up-coming nuptials. If Gerard is here, on this earth, he will have to do something, and then we will see."

Lord Prith was impressed with this plan. "Naturally, Teeny showed me the letter, Nell, some three months ago. She thought I should know about it, smart girl. I nearly told Spenser about it the other night when he poured out all his frustrated passion to me, your dearest father. But then I thought, no, let the children deal with it. It is a good plan, my boy."

"Thank you," Lord Beecham said.

"Teeny is a superlative girl," Flock said, and

lowered his head mournfully. "She did not tell me about the letter."

"It will work," Lord Beecham said. "It must."

"I agree. Bring champagne, Flock."

"Why champagne now, Father?"

"One must always think positively, Nell. If we celebrate now, doubtless we will be celebrating the same thing again when you and Spenser are wedded."

"Is my valet still breathing, sir?"

"It has been a close thing, my boy. Flock and Nettle usually just eye each other and sniff, like two stray dogs in the same territory. However, it is Teeny who has stayed their more violent tendencies."

"What has she done?"

"She has informed them that she is going to marry Walter Jones. She told me, however, in private, that Walter is a ne'er-do-well and that she will have to teach him what's what. She told me that she has memorized all of your excellent discipline strategies, observed many of them and has selected the ones she believes will be most efficacious with Walter if ever he strays. She is fully prepared to use them."

Helen laughed so hard that Lord Beecham had to rub her back.

Later that afternoon, while Helen was at her inn in Court Hammering, seeing to her accounts and doubtless doling out punishments, Lord Beecham was working on the leather scroll in her small study. He was humming. The translation

316

wasn't going too badly now. Reverend Mathers had helped considerably. Poor Reverend Mathers. He paused, frowning. He would write to Lord Hobbs in hopes that he and his Bow Street Runner, Mr. Ezra Cave, had discovered something.

Lord Beecham looked up when Flock cleared his throat from the doorway.

"Yes?"

"My lord, there is a Lord Crowley here to see you."

"The devil, you say. What does that damned man want, I wonder? Oh, the devil. I will come now, Flock."

Jason Fleming, Baron Crowley, was in the drawing room, alone, standing by the fireplace. He was staring down into the empty grate. He turned slowly when Lord Beecham walked into the room.

"You wonder why I am here," Lord Crowley said without preamble.

"Yes."

Lord Crowley shrugged. "Everyone believes that I murdered Reverend Mathers. I did not."

"Why did you come here?"

"I came to see if you knew more now. He was murdered because of the scroll, wasn't he?"

"I have no idea."

"Come, Heatherington, there is no need to be coy. Damnation, there are men following me everywhere I go. I imagine that one of them is dogging my tracks as we speak, probably standing right outside that window, staring in at me. Lord Hobbs won't leave me alone; he continues to come by with his questions. He speaks to everyone I know. I know he believes that I killed Reverend Mathers. I did not kill the man."

"You believe then that it was Reverend Titus Older who stuck the stiletto in his back?"

"No, more's the pity. That silly old fool wouldn't have the guts."

"Then I cannot see that there is another available suspect, can you?"

"No, dammit, and that is what frightens me. I tell you, Lord Hobbs wants me hung and he wants to do it soon. He has spoken to everyone. I am not received. An opera girl recognized me the other night and refused to let me bed her, can you imagine?"

Lord Beecham could, but he didn't say anything, just shrugged. He frankly did not know what to make of this. Crowley coming to him for help? More likely, this was a ruse and Crowley was here to steal the leather scroll. But hadn't he already stolen the copy? He wouldn't need the original scroll.

Lord Beecham lightly flicked a small piece of lint from his sleeve. "I think perhaps you did it. You have a reputation for having a black soul. You are ruthless. You deal with scum. You are a luckless gambler, always betting, always losing, always in need of money. You have probably killed before, why not again? I cannot see your conscience pricking you overly. Yes, I can see

318

you doing just about anything to refill your pockets."

"Damn you, I am a man who looks for opportunities. But I didn't kill Mathers. Perhaps it was you who stuck that stiletto in his back."

"I suppose that is possible," Helen said from the doorway. "However, why would he kill anyone, Lord Crowley? He already has the scroll in his possession. You are a half-wit, sir. You are making no sense."

"Ah, Miss Mayberry. A pleasure, ma'am." Lord Crowley managed an elegant bow. "You are looking well, I see. Beyond well, really."

"Naturally," she said. "Lord Beecham, Flock tells me that there is a very nice man outside by the name of Ezra Cave. He is our Bow Street Runner, I believe, here, keeping an eye on Lord Crowley."

"I was mad to come here," Lord Crowley said, stomping toward the door of the drawing room. "You will not believe me, no matter what I say."

"Give us one good reason to believe you, Crowley," Lord Beecham called after him. "Just one."

Crowley looked back and forth between them, then blurted out, "Just perhaps Reverend Mathers wasn't murdered because of the scroll."

"Ah, now that is a rather unique way of looking at the business," Lord Beecham said.

"I don't know, not for certain, but I heard that his brother, Old Clothhead, as Reverend Older calls him, was fighting with him constantly. Perhaps he wanted the scroll, perhaps not. Perhaps he was jealous of his brother, perhaps he was finally pushed over the edge and stabbed him in a rage. He stole the scroll as an afterthought. Maybe he already knew it was valuable. That fellow also needs money. You'll not believe this, but he is married to a very young girl, and she is always encouraging him to buy her baubles and jewels. Yes, Old Clothhead sounds desperate. Surely he is an excellent suspect."

"Why don't you tell Mr. Ezra Cave what you just told us?"

"I done 'eard it all, milord. Sounds 'avey-cavey to me, but I'll pass it on, to 'is lordship, see wot 'e thinks about Old Clothhead wit' the sticker."

"Damn all of you, I did not murder Reverend Mathers. I did not even know that you met him in the British Museum!"

"Now, sir, ye'll burst yer liver if ye squawk like that."

Lord Crowley looked ready to commit murder now. He grabbed his cloak and cane from a stolid Flock and slammed out of the front door of Shugborough Hall.

"The strange thing," Lord Beecham said thoughtfully, stroking his long fingers over his jaw, "is that I believe the fellow. He's afraid. He's really afraid."

"But Reverend Mathers's brother, Spenser? Old Clothhead?"

"I don't think that's right either, but who

knows? Now, Helen, let us all have some tea and have Mr. Cave tell us what he has discovered."

It amounted to nothing much at all. Mr. Ezra Cave prepared to take his leave to return to London an hour later. "I got my fivers in all sorts of pockets, milord, and me ears plastered against all sorts of walls wot got blokes on the other side speaking in whispers amongst themselves. Something will pop out, ye'll see."

After Ezra Cave had left, Spenser and Helen looked at each other, each feeling the instant pull, the drugging desire. They both held to their places. It was a close thing. They would have leapt on each other if Lord Prith hadn't chosen that particular moment to stroll into the drawing room.

"Something I never told my little Nell here," he said to Lord Beecham, "but if I had to describe Gerard Yorke, it would be that he was a fraud. Oh, yes, I know, he was a hero then, and everybody believed him to be Lord Nelson's right hand. And perhaps it was true at one time. But by the time I met him in '01, it was clear to me that he was a deceitful creature, all decked out with ribbons and braid. This letter you got from him, Helen, it is what I would call a preliminary exploration. He wants something, don't doubt it. What he wants, I just can't figure out. I'm sorry, Spenser, but Gerard is alive. I can smell him.

"Look to your back. If you need help slitting his bloody throat, call me. Where is Flock?

321

Flock! Oh, there you are. I want you to rub my shoulders. All this excitement has left me stiff."

And Lord Prith walked out of the drawing room, Flock on his heels. They heard him say, "I wonder if one could mix champagne with some sort of sweet cream and perhaps have a perfect concoction to rub into one's shoulders?"

"Oh, dear," Helen said. She turned bewildered eyes to Lord Beecham. "I don't understand any of this."

"I don't either, but I believe it is time you and I returned to London. We need Douglas Sherbrooke. He knows everybody in the Admiralty. We have got to get to Gerard's father, Sir John Yorke. I'll send a message to Douglas, make sure he and Alexandra are still in London."

Lord Beecham walked to Helen, automatically raised his hands to touch her, then immediately lowered them, and took a quick step back. "No," he said, "no. Now, I believe that you and I should discuss what I have added to the translation on the leather scroll."

Rather than translating word for word, Lord Beecham pulled out several sheets of foolscap from Helen's desk drawer. "I have put together a narrative. There are still many concepts, ideas, words missing that Reverend Mathers scratched his head over. But what we have here, Helen, is the good beginnings of a story.

"No, please sit over there." He pointed to the settee, a good eight feet distant.

322

She sat on the edge of the settee, her hands clasped together, all her attention focused on him. He cleared his throat. "Listen, Helen."

26

" 'There was a powerful magician in Africa who divined that he needed a particular boy to gain something he wanted in Persia. He used guile and deceit and managed to lure the unsuspecting boy to a hidden place in the mountains, telling him that if he did exactly as he was told he would gain riches beyond belief. He sent the boy underground to fetch him a very old lamp that was protected by powerful gods who knew the magician and wouldn't allow him to come near, but the boy, the magician had divined, they would allow.'

" 'The boy took the lamp, but he wouldn't give it to the magician until the magician helped him out of the cave. Enraged by the boy's refusal, the magician sealed up the cave and returned to Africa. The boy would have died there but for the lamp.'

" 'When the boy emerged from the cave, he was changed. There was power in him that shone like a beacon, and all saw this power and knelt before it. It was rumored that the lamp appeared, then disappeared. When the boy had lived out his years and died, the lamp disappeared. Everyone believed the lamp was probably taken by the magician from Africa. It was not. That magician was long dead.'

" 'It was I, Jaquar, the old king's advisor, who

took the lamp. Even as I write this, I know that I will seal the accursed thing into this iron cask. I am sending it away, to be hidden forever, this history and warning with it. Leave it hidden, deep, without light.' "

Lord Beecham looked up a moment, and Helen said, "And somehow it came into the hands of the Knights Templar until the one Templar gave it to King Edward. Come Spenser, keep going. What did the lamp do? Why does Jaquar call it accursed? Why hide it deep, without light? Surely there must be something more?"

"There is nothing more that is important, just greetings and closings and what Reverend Mathers called more admonitions to the unwary.

"That's all, Helen. It is a history of the lamp, or whatever it may be, more formally written than I have translated, but in essence it is accurate enough. It was recorded in the second century before Christ, in Persia."

"It is very nearly identical to the tale of *Aladdin and the Magic Lamp* except for the ending, of course, and the warning from this Jaquar."

"Yes. It seems to me, then, that the history of the lamp was well enough known, widely enough spoken of, that it became incorporated into the *Arabian Nights*. We have verified the bloody lamp, Helen, but it hasn't helped us one whit to find it. I believe the only conclusion is that someone took it from the iron cask. When? Perhaps hundreds of years ago. Perhaps it was never even buried at all. Who knows? In any event, we know it existed at one time and that it was powerful and, according to this Jaquar, dangerous."

Helen was humming under her breath, a habit he recognized she did when she was concentrating utterly. She said, "But I wonder. How old was it before the magician from Africa went after it? Another one hundred years? Perhaps a thousand years older?

"How long was it buried in that long ago cave, hidden away, deep, and in darkness? Why didn't this Jaquar simply write down why the lamp was dangerous? And how did it end up in the storerooms of the Knights Templar?"

He rose and walked to her. He took her hands and pulled her against him. He said against her hair, "Forget the damned lamp. Who cares when it comes right down to the core of the matter? It is old, ancient, long gone from here. Listen to me now, Helen. I want you very badly. I am holding myself by the only single honorable thread in my body. Kiss me, Helen, then run."

"All right," she said, "if you are sure this is what you want," and kissed his mouth, his ear, his chin. "I will see you at dinner," she said over her shoulder as she raced to the door of her study. Her last glimpse was of him standing there in the middle of the room, breathing hard, looking like a starving man.

She wanted to come back to him, but she didn't. She knew this was important to him. She knew him that well.

For the first time she realized she was thinking more about him than about the lamp. It was true even though now they'd added its history and its warnings to their knowledge. Truth be told, the lamp was long gone, just as Spenser said. What was important was that they had discovered that it had existed, verified by an ancient text. She was pleased. She was ready to let it go back into myth.

She thought about the man she loved with all her heart, the man she wanted with every fiber of her being to wed. She thought of Gerard Yorke and knew to her very soul that he was still alive and that he would never let her go. She just didn't know why.

And she cried in the privacy of her bed-chamber and cursed the eighteen-year-old girl who had been so stupid as to believe herself in love with such a paltry man.

Spenser was so certain that everything would work out, but she just didn't see how it could.

In the early evening Lord Prith strode into the drawing room where Helen and Lord Beecham were talking, and announced, "I have a surprise for all of you. Flock, bring it in."

In walked Flock carrying a silver tray. "It is my newest experiment with champagne."

"Father, it's purple."

"Yes, Nell. I poured some grape juice into the champagne, just to give it that nice healthy color. All of you can try it."

"Father, Spenser and I are the only ones here, and he doesn't drink champagne."

Lord Prith heaved a deep sigh and held up his hand. "We will wait, Flock, until we have a more ample supply of palates." He sat down and leaned back, smiling at both of them. "Now, have you decided what you will do about Gerard Yorke?"

"We are just beginning our thinking," Spenser said. "And food will help."

Flock said from the doorway, "Cook has excellent timing. Dinner is served."

Over a splendid dinner of pork tenderloin with mushrooms, fish and capers in black butter, innumerable side dishes, including cook's specialty — eggs *au miroir* — and redcurrant fool for dessert, they decided that everyone would go to London the next morning. Helen and her father, Flock and Teeny, would stay at the Beecham town house. It was the first time the town house would welcome guests since three years before, when Lord Beecham's great-aunt Maudette had arrived with her ten best friends, all very old ladies, all of whom tatted and left their work in progress all over the house. Actually, looking back on it, Spenser had enjoyed himself immensely during those chaotic two weeks.

"Flock and I will be ready to leave tomorrow by ten o'clock," Lord Prith said to Spenser. He added, "Goodness, what with the Sherbrookes hanging about all the time, my little Nellie will be very well chaperoned indeed. Now I won't have to worry about you taking advantage of her, my boy."

There was another small bit of dead silence.

"And then," Lord Beecham said, clearing his throat, "Douglas Sherbrooke and I will go to meet with Sir John Yorke at the Admiralty."

"Yes," Helen said, "but you must be alert, Spenser. Sir John is ruthless and shrewd. I know that Gerard was afraid of his father. His father ruled not only him but his entire family with an iron fist. I do want to see what truths you manage to get out of that old curmudgeon."

Late that night Lord Beecham lay wide awake in his bed thinking about his life. It was at once extraordinarily complicated and very simple and as clear as a spring rain, and he smiled into the darkness. He remembered his words with Lord Prith just before they had all retired. "I have decided that you deserve to stay in the Dancing Bear's Room, in my town house," Spenser had said.

"An odd name, my boy. Wherever did that name come from?"

"Well, some fifty years ago, my grandfather had a trained bear and he kept him in the house. In that bedchamber."

"What was the bear's name?"

"Guthry, I believe. He did enjoy dancing with my grandfather. I was told that he died shortly after my grandfather did."

"I hope," Lord Prith said, "that they were not buried together."

"I understand that it was discussed, but I don't believe it happened. But you know, I have learned over the years that nothing in my family is ever what you expect." Except for his father, he thought, who was a thorough rotter, no doubt about that; but now, Spenser didn't flinch from it. He just dismissed it. It felt very good. He felt like a house that the ghosts no longer haunted.

As he was nodding off to sleep, Lord Beecham realized that life was fascinating, a thousand years ago and today. Who else had dancing bears hanging about in the past? He wondered now as he had when he'd been a boy, what it would be like to have a bear living in the house.

Beecham Town House
London

It was Claude, Lord Beecham's acting butler, who assigned the name "the War Room" to the large, shadowed study at the back of the house.

On Friday morning everyone was gathered around talking. Everyone had an opinion. When Ryder and Sophie Sherbrooke unexpectedly joined the company some thirty minutes later, Ryder simply stood in the doorway and said in the special voice he used for his fifteen children, which was actually a bellow, "Close your mouths or no dessert!"

That got everyone's attention. One by one,

each occupant ceased speaking and stared at Ryder.

Douglas Sherbrooke said, "Ryder, Sophie, welcome to London. Come join us. This is a conundrum both of you will enjoy. Ryder, did you know a naval man, Gerard Yorke? He supposedly drowned back in '03 off the coast of France?"

Ryder Sherbrooke frowned, looked thoughtful, stroked his chin, then announced, "I hope this doesn't distress anyone here, but he cheated at cards. He nearly got his throat slit over one incident where I was present. I remember him whining that his father never gave him enough money and that he was desperate. When he was asked why he was desperate, he said he was three months behind in paying his mistress. I remember he was a seedy fellow, complained a lot. Yes, I remember now that he reportedly drowned. What's this all about? What's the matter?"

And so the mix increased and the noise level escalated until Mrs. Glass, the Heatherington housekeeper, poked her head in the door and whistled, just like a man. "Claude has a slight cold and his voice isn't all that strong at present," she said once she had everyone's attention. "Who would like tea and cakes? No, don't speak. Raise your hands. Ladies first."

One countess, one sister-in-law of a countess, and Miss Mayberry all dutifully raised their hands.

"Good. Now gentlemen."

And so an earl, two viscounts, and the brother of

an earl all raised their hands. Lord Prith requested a touch of champagne in a subdued voice.

Sophie Sherbrooke said to Helen, "We haven't met, but I've heard a lot about you, from Alex, who wanted to garrote you before, but then she decided that you were just fine as long as you kept your distance from Douglas. Is it true that you are going to marry Lord Beecham?"

"Yes," Helen said. "But first as you have already heard, we must determine if my husband is still alive, and if he is, what sort of evil he is brewing. It is a horrid thing to have a husband pop up when he was supposed to have croaked it eight years before. It is particularly difficult since I want to marry Spenser."

"I see," said Sophie Sherbrooke, without blinking an eye. She could, after all, deal quite well with fifteen children forced indoors on a rainy day. "Tell me all about it."

Thirty minutes later, when everyone was eating cook's delicious chocolate puffs, peach fritters, and caraway seed cakes, Ryder announced, "Behold the new member of the House of Commons. That is why Sophie and I are here in London at this particular moment. I handily beat a very obnoxious paunchy man by the name of Redfield. I will now be representing Upper and Lower Slaughter and environs." He beamed at everyone.

"Hear, hear," Lord Prith said, and raised his crystal flute of champagne. "Er, are you certain you wish to do this, young man?"

"He wants to reform the wretched laws that allow for the terrible exploitation of children, sir," Sophie said. "He will succeed, you know."

They briefly discussed Ryder's Beloved Ones, the children he saved from dreadful situations and brought to live at Brandon House.

Plans were made, shifted, reevaluated. Ryder and Sophie decided to stay with Douglas and Alexandra. They were on the point of leaving when Lord Prith strode into the drawing room, Flock on his heels carrying a large silver tray.

"What is this, Father?"

"Ah, my dear, I believe we now have a suitable number of gullets to experiment on. No, don't look alarmed, Sophie, this is champagne."

"Sir," she said, "it's purple."

"Well, yes. It is something I have invented. You see I added some grape juice to the champagne to give it that healthy purple color. Splendid, don't you think? All of you will try it, if you please. Except you, Spenser, since you would turn quite green and ruin the evening."

Nobody wanted to, but everyone was polite, and so everyone drank the strange grape mixture with Spenser watching, a look of total revulsion on his face.

Alexandra cocked her head to one side as she lowered the lovely crystal flute after two small sips. "It is very different, sir. Actually, to be blunt about this, it is close to revolting. I think perhaps you should try something else to mix with the champagne."

Lord Prith looked hopefully toward Douglas, who mournfully shook his head and kept his mouth shut. When his eyes met Sophie's, he looked near to tears. Sophie cleared her throat, gave her husband an agonized look, and said, "I am so very sorry, sir. Perhaps it is the sort of grapes you used. Perhaps grapes from the Mediterranean region would work better."

Helen said, "Father, it is a good try, but Alexandra is right. If I were dying I would have difficulty drinking it even if I was promised that it would bring me back."

Lord Prith said, "Not even you, my little Nell? My daughter adores me, you see, and if she doesn't approve, then it must be very bad indeed. But wait — Ryder, you did not give me your opinion."

"Sir, I have found in the years I have been married that if I disagree with my wife, she refuses to give me her sweet smiles, as well as sweet other things. I am sorry, sir, but I cannot."

"I can understand your hesitation," Lord Prith said. "Ah, well. Flock, what was it that we called this lovely purple drink?"

"Grapagne, my lord."

"I do like the name. It has a certain cachet. Hmmm. What do you think of apricot with champagne?"

Evidently no one thought anything of it, since there was dead silence.

Both sets of Sherbrookes left shortly, everyone ready with his assigned task.

27

It was nearly midnight when there was a tap on Lord Beecham's bedchamber door.

He was naked, lying on his back in his mammoth bed, a sheet pulled to his waist, thinking about kissing the soft flesh behind Helen's knees, something he hadn't managed to do yet.

"Enter," he called out.

Helen floated in — no other way to put it, he thought, stunned, watching her glide toward him. She was wearing a crimson-silk nightgown with an even darker red dressing gown over it, and strangely enough, that incredible ensemble was not the least bit tawdry. In fact, it gave a man absolutely no hint as to what treasures lay beneath.

"Go away, Helen. I mean it."

"I will," she said, walked right up to the bed and stopped. "Do you like it?" She did a graceful twirl and the soft slithering sounds of all that fabric would have sent him to his knees if he hadn't been lying on his back.

"If you don't go away I will rip it off and examine it in the morning."

"I wore it to punish you. This is discipline, Spenser, a divine sort of discipline. What do you think — perhaps a Level Four?"

"Helen, I want you naked so badly that all I

can see is far too much red stuff for me to strip off you."

"Alexandra told me it was something a mistress would wear, a mistress who wished to seduce a very dashing, exciting, flamboyant protector. It was something, she said, that she would wear for Douglas, even though she was his wife. Sophie said Ryder would laugh his head off if she wore something like this and then he would strip it off her in a second flat.

"I thought about that. Well, I decided, we aren't married, and we were rather intimate, and so, does that make me a mistress?"

"No. You aren't a mistress. You are a lover. If you did not have any money, then you could be a mistress. Now leave, Helen."

She smiled at him, turned around, and walked back to the door. She said over her shoulder, one white hand laid against the door frame, "I didn't want you to think that I wasn't fully aware of you." Then her seduction fell away and she lowered her face into her hands.

He was out of his bed and was pulling her against him, all in under ten seconds. "No, love, don't cry. I would cry, but it isn't manly. There are certain standards that a man must uphold. Let me hold you, but please do not think lustful thoughts. Yes, all right, stop crying. We will deal with all of it, Helen. You and I are very smart indeed, and look at all our talented assistants. And now we've even added Ryder and Sophie Sherbrooke to our army. They are very resourceful. They have to be to survive dealing with fifteen children.

"Now there are at least ten people who know about the lamp, at least ten people who know about your blasted husband, who had better be good and dead. There are many more who know about Reverend Mathers's murder. Word will continue to spread. Things will happen. I have never believed in secrecy. It is having everyone know everything, that's the key. Then the truth will pop up. You'll see, dearest. No, please don't cry anymore."

She sniffed and raised her head. Again, he was struck by how close they were to having their noses touch. His big girl was right there in his sights. He wanted her very much. "I've been wondering if we also shouldn't just announce to the world that the scroll verified the existence of a powerful lamp. That the lamp had probably been hidden with the scroll. What do you think?"

"You're naked, Spenser."

He honestly hadn't realized it. He did now, and in less time than it would have taken him to remove an eyelash from his eye, he was hard and ready to leap. "Well, damn." He kissed her. "Go to bed, dearest. We have a lot to do tomorrow."

She gulped, then blurted out, "I slept with you knowing he was alive. I deceived you. I was dishonorable. I don't deserve you. I don't want to tell anyone about the lamp."

"Ah." He began rubbing his big hands up and

down her back. The silk slithered between his fingers. The feel and sound of that slithering silk would make a man of even greater will tremble. He shook his head. He got a grip on himself and managed to say, "Well, as a matter of fact, you did deceive me. So what? The blasted fellow has been gone for eight years. I would rather say that you couldn't help yourself, you had to have me, regardless of this hopefully dead bastard who may or may not have written you one single letter six months ago.

"You are not dishonorable. You are one of the most honorable people I have ever known. Now, if everyone knows about the lamp, most will simply discount it as a myth, since who would talk about it if it truly existed? Perhaps a few simpletons will go dig up anywhere they think the lamp could be hidden, not find anything except an occasional worm, and then it will eventually be forgotten. I don't believe that many people will believe that the ancient scroll had anything to do with the lamp. It is too farfetched."

She leaned forward, touching her forehead to his. "Still, I took you, and I realize that you really had no choice in the matter."

Now that was interesting, he thought, remembering how they had been sodden and shivering and miserable until they'd happened to touch each other in that dilapidated cottage with the rain pouring down not two feet away from them.

"Yes," he said, kissing her ear, "you took me, and I had no say in the matter at all. I remember

338

trying to tell you I didn't want you, but you just wouldn't let up on me. Stop it now, Helen — any lapses you are feeling in your moral character are just minor ones. But I wonder. Would I have made love to you if I'd known about Gerard? I can't answer that. I don't know."

"But that's why you don't want me now."

He closed his hands over her beautiful white arms and shook her just a bit. "That's not the truth at all and you know it. I want you all of the time, Helen. But the thing is, I want to know while I'm caressing you and kissing you and nibbling at your white neck that you are my wife, not my almost-wife or my lover or even just my partner. I want you for all of it, Helen. I want us to be married when we come together again. There's nothing more to it than that. What you and I are together is very important. It is forever. Do you understand?" He touched his forehead once again to hers.

"Maybe, but —"

"Now," he said quietly against her mouth, "you said you don't deserve me. That is a repellent thought. I also cannot accept what made you say it. It is nonsense and it makes me angry. Take it back — now. We'll keep mum for the time being about the bloody lamp and the scroll."

"All right." She sniffed. "Would you just kiss me one time? If you do, then I swear I'll run."

He kissed her and she ran. He stood there in the middle of his bedchamber, panting like the messenger who had run from Marathon to Athens, only to drop dead at the end. He wondered what it was this particular woman did to him. And he was very grateful for it.

Sir John Yorke was a desiccated old relic who was perfectly bald, had very frightening eyes because they had practically no color at all, and had a tic by the side of his left eye.

He was still very powerful. He was known to be ruthless and vicious when he perceived the need.

He was tapping together his steepled fingertips. The skin was loose on the back of his age-spotted hands.

He merely nodded to the three gentlemen. He knew all of them, not as friends but as powerful men, and that gave him no choice at all but to see them, to listen to them. He had no idea what they wanted. He looked at them, all young, healthy, well made. Their ranks were higher than his. They were all richer than he was. But the only one he truly feared was the earl of Northcliffe, who was still involved in the ministry for an occasional mission that a lesser man would not be able to perform. He was well connected to everyone of power in the government. As for his brother, Ryder Sherbrooke was newly elected to the House of Commons. He detested all of them. He had no choice but to deal with them, but then, thank God, they would leave. Good riddance to all the worthless bastards. He smiled a stingy, false smile.

He did not rise. "What may I do for you gentlemen?"

Lord Beecham said pleasantly, "We are here to verify that your son, Gerard Yorke, indeed drowned off the coast of France in 1803."

Ryder Sherbrooke watched those pale lashes flicker just once over the nearly colorless eyes. Got you, he thought, sat back, and folded his hands over his belly.

"Of course he drowned," Sir John said, his voice rising. "He was a hero. He would have followed me into the Admiralty had he survived. Your question is nonsense."

"Then how do you explain this?" Lord Beecham asked, handing Sir John the letter.

"Ah, I understand this now. My former daughter-in-law, has dragged you into this. I wondered what three society gentlemen wanted with me. You are acting on her behalf. Well, well, let us get it over with. This is not my son's handwriting. She knows that. My son is dead."

"Miss Mayberry believes that it is Gerard Yorke's handwriting," Douglas said, sitting forward, his eyes steady on Sir John's face. "She told us that you didn't know your son's handwriting all that well."

They heard the movement of Sir John's secretary behind them, but they didn't turn.

"She is wrong. Naturally I know his handwriting. More to the point, she is probably a liar. She needs money and thus she creates this wretched fiction. She did not produce a child for me — for my son — and thus she doesn't deserve any consideration whatsoever. Please inform her that I will not be pleased if she continues with this harassment."

Lord Beecham said very pleasantly, "I believe there is a misunderstanding here, Sir John. I wish to wed Miss Mayberry. With this letter from your son, it appears that she is not free, as she had believed for eight long years. We will require proof that he is indeed dead, else we will have to advertise in all the newspapers, speak to everyone we know, search out any friends of his, to find out the truth."

Sir John rose slowly, very slowly, because his hip pained him badly, nearly all the time now, and there was no reason for it, was there? None that his physician could find. It was just age, just bloody age. At least his blood was pumping strongly through his body, he could feel it pounding in his neck. "My son is dead, long dead. Wed Miss Mayberry with my blessing, Lord Beecham."

"I shall, sir. I shall also do whatever I can to ensure that he is indeed dead."

When the three of them were on the street in Whitehall, in front of the Admiralty, Lord Beecham was shaking his head. "That old man is wily. I don't trust him an inch."

Ryder said without hesitation, "He is also lying."

"Trust Ryder," Douglas said when he realized

that Spenser was unsure about this. "He has always been excellent at seeing through people."

Lord Beecham stepped closer to the iron fence surrounding the Admiralty as a carriage came careening around a corner. "You mean he knows his son is still alive?"

"Oh, yes," Ryder said. "He knows. But the strange thing is, he doesn't want anyone else to know. Now why is that, do you think?"

"Yes, and do not forget that Gerard was a hero," Spenser said. "He would have followed his father into the Admiralty if only he had lived. Well, hell and damnation. If he truly is alive, then I can't very well marry Helen. What will we do?"

"We will have to wait," Ryder said. "Just wait for the moment. Let us put announcements in all the newspapers."

"This is curious indeed," said Douglas. "Yes, we will have to wait."

Spenser didn't like it, but there was simply nothing he could do about it. He had prayed that Gerard Yorke was indeed dead. But now?

The three gentlemen adjourned to White's to ponder this more thoroughly and to ask every man who strolled by if he had heard from, remembered, or had seen Gerard Yorke after 1803. They knew that by morning Gerard Yorke's name would be on everyone's lips. While at White's, Lord Beecham wrote betrothal announcements to every London newspaper. The one he wrote for the *Gazette* was indeed splendid, filled with detail. Then he wrote inquiries for each newspaper requesting any information about the whereabouts of one Gerard Yorke, son of Sir John Yorke of the Admiralty. That should really please the old man, he thought. He offered a fifty-pound reward. He was rubbing his hands together, grinning like the devil himself after collecting a tidy number of souls.

Douglas and Ryder added their ideas. Everyone was pleased when all the announcements and inquiries were sent all over London by messenger.

When they returned to the Beecham town house, it was to meet Lord Hobbs in the drawing room — sitting much too close to Helen, Lord Beecham thought, his jaw clenching. I am jealous, he thought, and that amazed him. He saw Helen again in that incredible red-silk confection, saw Lord Hobbs trying to see her too, and it made him so furious he nearly attacked the man on the spot. Jealousy — what a very strange thing it was.

Lord Hobbs was once again dressed all in gray, and Helen, to Lord Beecham's eye, looked much too interested in what he was saying, the poaching bastard. He got hold of himself. He was being ridiculous. Jealousy was fine as an experiment, but he didn't want any more of it.

Lord Hobbs rose and was dutifully introduced to Ryder Sherbrooke.

"I understand you just took the seat for Upper and Lower Slaughter. My congratulations."

Ryder nodded. "I like all the gray," he said.

Lord Hobbs looked quickly over at Helen, and Ryder would have sworn that he flushed just a bit.

Helen said immediately once everyone was settled, "Lord Hobbs tells us that Ezra Cave believes Lord Crowley to be guilty."

"Yes," Lord Hobbs said. "I was fascinated to hear that Lord Crowley rode to Court Hammering to see you, Lord Beecham, to plead his innocence."

"Yes, he did." Lord Beecham looked directly into Helen's incredibly beautiful blue eyes, "Trust me on this. And I hate to say it, but I believe him."

Douglas Sherbrooke cursed.

Lord Hobbs didn't look happy. "He is a wicked man. Everyone I have spoken with confirms that."

"Yes, I know. But do you know, my lord, he told me he didn't think Reverend Older did it because he hasn't the guts. However, about Reverend Mathers's brother — Old Clothhead — it turns out that not only did he argue with Reverend Mathers, he also has a young wife who wants jewelry and such. Is it possible that Old Clothhead stole the scroll after he killed his brother because he thought he might be able to make money off it?"

"I don't know. I will look once more at the brother and his young wife. Who else is there, then?"

"Lord Hobbs," Helen said, handing him a cup of tea, "perhaps there is someone we don't know about who is overseeing all of this? Someone who is directing all this from the shadows, who is watching all of us, waiting to see where we will go to find the lamp?"

Lord Hobbs gave Helen a melting smile that made Lord Beecham grind his teeth, something that Ryder heard. He smiled at his wife, who immediately ducked her head so no one could see the grin on her face.

"That is an excellent suggestion, Miss Mayberry. A shadowy evil that directs and plans, that watches and waits."

"Yes," Helen said, "that's it exactly."

"It is a ridiculous suggestion," Lord Beecham said, his voice overloud. He jumped to his feet and began pacing the drawing room. "Helen, you haven't ever once intimated that you believed this could be the case. A shadowy character who is hiding his identity from us? Who is pulling all the strings? And we are just a bunch of puppets on a stage? Absurd. You drew that out of one of your silly women's novels, didn't you?"

"Oh, dear," Alexandra said. She rose, shook out her skirts, and walked to stand directly in front of Helen. "I have the beginnings of a headache, Helen. I need you to ask Teeny to dab some rose water on my temples."

"I will tell Teeny that she is needed," Flock said from the doorway. "I will at the same time make certain that Nettle is nowhere near her, causing mischief."

Lord Hobbs's eyebrows went up. "There appears to be disharmony here, my lord."

"Which lord?"

"Why you, Lord Beecham. This is your house, is it not?"

"Yes, and Miss Mayberry is my betrothed."

"Ah, yes. I see. A pity." Lord Hobbs rose. "I will continue with my inquiries. I assume all of you are well involved as well?"

There were nods from all over the drawing room.

"Have you discovered any more about this mysterious and ancient lamp that has more power than the devil himself?"

Lord Beecham opened, then quickly shut, his mouth. No, he would keep quiet about that. That was what Helen wanted. They shook their heads.

Once Lord Hobbs was out the front door, Helen turned on Lord Beecham and yelled right in his face, "Your behavior was very childish. You sounded like a petulant little boy. You deserve a Level Eight for that."

"What's a Level Eight?" Ryder Sherbrooke asked.

"They're speaking of discipline," Douglas said. "Level Eight is serious business. Just what is involved, Helen?"

"I won't tell you, Douglas. I will, however, tell Alexandra so she may use it on you whenever she

347

decides you deserve it."

"I want to know, too," Sophie Sherbrooke said. "I want to know all the levels. I want to torture Ryder. I want to make him howl."

Alexandra rubbed her hands together. "Yes, I want to know more about bindings and knots and ropes and such. Douglas is very forceful. He is also very big. I want him helpless. I want him entirely focused on what I am doing to him. Is this possible?"

"Oh, yes," said Helen. "All right, ladies, I suggest that all of us adjourn to Spenser's study. I will explain to you the disciplines I've developed that fit each Level. We can also devise new ones if you like."

"Well, damn," Ryder Sherbrooke said, staring at his departing wife. "What are we in for, Spenser?"

"A variety of punishments that will surely curl your toes."

Douglas said, "I must ask Helen to tell me the level of the exquisite discipline my dearest wife performed on me last week. Curled toes was just the beginning."

"By God, this is wonderful," Ryder said, rubbing his hands together. "I'm very glad Sophie and I stopped by, Spenser. I doubt we can manage to keep our minds focused, but perhaps you should tell me more about this lamp business before the ladies return, fire in their eyes and discipline plans overflowing their brains."

"She wants me helpless, does she?" said

Douglas, and he sat back in his chair, crossed his arms over his chest, and gazed off at nothing at all.

"Before we speak of the lamp," Spenser said, "let me give you several examples of Helen's discipline system."

"Ah, yes," Douglas said. "Then I will tell you what I came up with just last Saturday morning."

"What an unexpected pleasure this visit has turned out to be," Ryder said and drank his tea as he sat forward, all attention, not even realizing the tea was cold.

Spenser frowned at all of them. "I just remembered. We must plan our formal engagement ball. I want everyone in London to be here."

"Yes, yes, we'll do all that," Ryder said. "But first things first, Spenser."

28

It was the night before their formal engagement ball. The name of Gerard Yorke was on everyone's lips. Old gossip was resurrected, new gossip added to the mix.

Lord Beecham's drawing room was filled from morning until night. Everyone wanted to talk about Gerard Yorke and this fabulous lamp, and the murder of Reverend Mathers, but mainly everyone wanted to know everything about the magic lamp. Both Spenser and Helen told the same story, over and over. The lamp was a myth, a charming, titillating legend unfortunately with no basis in fact. No, the scroll had been no help at all.

There were scores of people arriving at the house who wanted the fifty-pound reward for information about Gerard Yorke. There were more scores of people arriving at the house who wanted the fifty-pound reward for information about the murder of Reverend Mathers. Helen held her breath whenever one of these individuals arrived — they were a scruffy lot, hats pulled low over their eyes, knives stuck in the bands of their none-too-clean trousers. Pliny Blunder, Lord Beecham's secretary, was kept busy from early morning until late at night reviewing each claim to the groats.

As of midnight tonight, three days after all the announcements and the inquiries had been in the newspapers, there were still no pertinent leads; apparently, none of the shifty characters who swore they'd just seen Gerard Yorke at the White Horse Inn just outside of Greenwich were telling the truth. And there was nothing pertinent either about the murder of poor Reverend Mathers. If there was one thing Pliny Blunder excelled at, it was ferreting out pretenders, liars, and just plain dregs.

There was also endless talk all over London of the magic lamp that no one really believed in at all, but it made for fascinating conversation, particularly since Lord Beecham, that naughty and very clever man, was involved in the business. London was having a fine time with the entertainment Lord Beecham was providing them.

As for his fiancée, Miss Helen Mayberry was glorious — all agreed to it, even those ladies, obviously jealous, who would say behind their hands that she was just a tad too tall.

Tomorrow night, Helen thought, as she sank deeper into the soft bed in her bedchamber that wasn't more than thirty feet from Spenser's bedchamber, curse him. Tomorrow night, and they would announce their betrothal. Where the devil was Gerard Yorke? If he was alive, surely he wouldn't wait until the last minute. Surely he had to strike soon. It was odd, but she didn't remember if he had ever shown much courage. Perhaps there hadn't been the opportunity.

It happened so quickly that Helen had no time to strike out or to yell. One moment she was sleeping soundly, dreamlessly, and the next a handkerchief was stuffed in her mouth just as a fist hit her jaw, knocking her senseless.

She thought she heard a man's voice say, "Good, we've got her now." Then she just drifted away.

She felt a pounding, a very deep pounding that seemed to fill her and make her want to scream at the pain it brought. She didn't want to recognize it, to accept it, but finally she had to. Her head was going to explode and there was nothing she could do about it. She gasped.

"Ah, you are going to wake up now, Helen?"

That voice — she knew that voice, but it had been so very long since she'd heard it, so long ago, a lifetime ago. And it was different now somehow, perhaps deeper and harsher, but she couldn't be sure.

"Open your eyes, Helen."

She did then, gasping again with the pain. She looked up at Gerard Yorke, an older Gerard Yorke, one who had lived hard. She knew dissipation when she saw it, and Gerard had not spent the past eight years in search of sainthood.

"How are you, my dear?"

"I knew you were alive, I just knew it. What rock were you hiding under?"

"Do you want me to strike you again? I suggest you keep your insults behind your teeth. Now, you wanted me dead, didn't you, Helen? Then

352

you could marry that womanizing rakehell Beecham. Actually I hadn't planned to come get you so very quickly, but I did not want to wait until after your damned ball.

"You wanted to flush me out. Well, you succeeded. I waited as long as I could, hoping that society would forget about me and the lamp, but it is just growing and growing. I have kept myself so well hidden that I even wondered if I could find myself. But it is over now. It simply hasn't turned out the way you planned."

"You came as a thief in the night, not as an honorable man, the hero, back from possible captivity in France."

"You are even lovelier than you were ten years ago, Helen."

"Why are you alive, Gerard?"

He sat back. He was more in focus now. She realized she couldn't move. She was tied down, her wrists tied in front of her, her ankles bound together. She was still wearing her nightgown. A blanket was pulled to her waist. Her feet were bare. It was cold in the room, wherever the room was.

He touched his fingertips to her mouth. She didn't move, didn't make a single sound. She wanted to bite his fingers to the bone, but she couldn't take the chance that he would knock her silly again.

"Yes," he said, his face too close to hers, far too close. "I didn't believe it, but it's true. You have become more beautiful."

She was afraid, but she would never let him see it.

"I have been sitting here, looking at you, wondering what it would be like to take you again. Ah, there was always so much of you to touch and caress. Now you are twenty-eight, a veritable chewed-up old spinster. No, I have that wrong. You are a widow, poor thing. Did you love me so much, dearest Helen, that no man after me could compete with what you had for such a very short time?"

"I was sad when I heard of your death, Gerard, but I will be honest with you. I had no more love for you than you did for me about a month after we were married. Actually, if I recall aright, I was quite disillusioned after about two weeks. You weren't the man I had believed you to be. You really weren't much of a man at all. All you wanted from me was an heir."

"That's right, and you never gave me one. Why else do you think I married you? My life was quite fine just the way it was, but I had no choice. I had to wed you. But then you were barren. Does your Lord Beecham know that you are barren, that he'll never breed an heir off you?"

"He knows."

He was silent a moment, studying her face. "You didn't tell him, did you, Helen? You lied to him. Just as you lied to me. He has no idea that you are not going to produce children for him."

"He knows."

He slapped her, not hard, but it did sting. "You have started beating women, Gerard?"

"It was naught but a little slap, Helen. Don't even try to pretend that I'm a monster. I never touched you in anger when we were together."

"No, you only touched me to impregnate me, never anything more, and that was perhaps more soulless. How could I have possibly lied to you about being barren? There was no way I could have known."

He didn't want to hear about that. "If you had known, you would have lied."

That was remarkable, she thought, but she said only, "You have been gone for eight years. A very long time. Where were you, Gerard? What were you doing? Your father believes you are dead. I sent him your letter, but he said it wasn't your handwriting. He told me not to harass him anymore. I never did like your father. He seems even more mean-spirited now than he did then."

He said nothing and she continued after a moment, "Lord Beecham and his friends went to see him. He swore you were dead, but one of the gentlemen believed he was lying. He said it was strange — your father knew you were alive but he didn't want anyone else to know that you lived. Now, why is that?"

"My father is the monster, not I. He has always been a monster. The ship did go down off the coast of France eight years ago. I couldn't swim, that was true enough. However, I managed to bind myself to a barrel. Eventually, over four hours later, the barrel was pushed to shore by the waves. I survived. I was also where I wanted to be, where I would be safe."

"What are you talking about? You were in France. They are our enemy."

"They are not mine."

"I see," she said, and indeed she did see. "Everyone said you were a hero. It was a litany your father sings to this day. Why did you become a traitor, Gerard? Oh, no, now I understand. You were a traitor even before that ship of yours went down."

He slapped her again. She didn't say anything this time. She began working at the knots on her wrists, very slowly, barely moving her wrists and hands.

Then he began to laugh. "You have changed, Helen. When I first met you, you were all of eighteen years old and such a curious and bewitching girl, so spirited, so filled with energy and enthusiasm. But you weren't filled with life, were you? All I wanted off you was a child, but you failed me. You have changed much more than have I. I am not certain what you have become, but I have been watching you for the past three months, and I have seen how you run your very own inn, how you still pander to that damnable father of yours.

"And then you took a lover, knowing that I was alive. That makes you unfaithful to me, your husband. You have committed, knowingly, adultery, Helen."

She looked at him straight in his very nice brown eyes that she had admired when she'd been eighteen. "There is absolutely no way you can possibly know whether or not I became Lord Beecham's lover. Was I not sleeping alone when you managed to kidnap me?"

"Well, that's true," he said. "But Lord Beecham is reputed to be a man of infinite charm. Why were you sleeping alone, then? Does he take you, then prefer to sleep by himself? Many men are like that. He had to have taken you. I have heard it said that he can seduce the chemise off a nun. You actually held him off? That is difficult to believe, Helen."

"He loves me."

"No, I don't believe you. A man like him feels lust, nothing beyond that. There isn't anything beyond that, anyway. He feels momentary pleasure, then he becomes bored and moves to the next female. Yes, I could bring you up for divorce to the House of Lords. Adultery. I could ruin your name, your precious father, and everyone would agree with me."

"Why don't you, then, Gerard? Then everyone could see you, see what you have become or learn what you always were. Yes, I believe that you were a traitor even then, weren't you, Gerard? Yes, take your wife to the House of Lords and let us see what happens. At the very least, you abandoned your wife. But there is much more than that. You are a traitor. Perhaps you will be hung by your neck." She worked the ropes that bound her wrists, slowly, twisting, back and forth.

He rose from beside her on the narrow bed. She watched him pace the length of the small room. The floorboards creaked under his boots. He was well dressed, tall, lean. Gray laced through his light brown hair, and lines scored his mouth. What had he done these past eight years?

He turned to stare down at her for a very long moment. "You are beautiful, so very beautiful, but I can't take you with me, Helen. I will leave you alive, however, if you will simply tell me where you have hidden this lamp. That's all I want, all I ever wanted."

The lamp. He wanted the bloody lamp? That's what this was all about? She grew very still. She smiled at him. "Do you mean you would never have come back if you hadn't heard about the lamp?"

"I wrote you initially believing that you would give me money to keep me out of your life. But then there was no reason for you to. You had not remarried. There was no other man you wanted. And so I really forgot about you. Then I learned about King Edward's Lamp. Then I learned about Lord Beecham. And I knew I had the leverage I needed. Give me the lamp, Helen, and you will never see me again. You can marry your rakehell."

This was very important, and she knew it. She looked at him silently for a good long time, then said in a very calm voice, "Gerard, I truly believed there was a lamp. When I found that ancient leather scroll in an iron cask, I prayed it was about the lamp, and it was. The scroll recounted the story you already know about Aladdin. Then the writer said it was to be buried because it was dangerous.

"Regardless, the lamp wasn't with the scroll. Someone had taken it long ago. When? I have no idea, but it is gone. Forget the lamp. To be honest, I have."

"Reverend Mathers was murdered."

"Yes, and the person who did it was hoping that the scroll told the whereabouts of the lamp. He killed the poor man for nothing."

She had told him the truth. There was nothing more she could do.

"I will kill both you and Lord Beecham if you don't take me to this lamp."

He was perfectly serious. He hadn't believed her. Well, she'd tried. She felt a spurt of fear, not for herself but for Spenser. No, surely he was prepared for Gerard Yorke to slither onto the stage. He wanted him to appear. He was waiting for him.

She smiled up at him. "Very well, Gerard. I will take you to the lamp. But believe me on this. It's just an old lamp. It has nothing at all to do with the magic lamp of legend. You will see — it is simply a worthless old lamp that does nothing at all. This lamp is nothing more than an old lump of gold. I found it in a vicar's attic. He had bequeathed all his belongings to my father, you see. Now, think. If I truly found this magic lamp, why am I here, bound, with you? Do you not think that I would have rubbed it and kissed it and even slept with it to learn its secrets? There are no secrets. There is no power. There is no magic."

"You lied about all of it, not just to me but to every one of those credulous fools in London. What I believe is that you have the lamp, you just haven't found the power in it as yet. If you had, it is obvious that you would be the most powerful woman in the world. I will find the power, you will see. Now, it is not that I don't trust you, but I am not a fool. I took not only you but also your dear friend Alexandra Sherbrooke. She is just across the corridor, all bound and trussed up, just like you."

Oh, no. Oh, no. "How ever did you manage to get your hands on Alexandra? She sleeps with her husband, not alone, like me."

He actually gave her a whimsical smile. "I worried about that, I can tell you. But do you know what? I was prepared to cosh her husband on the head, no hope for it — I knew it would be more than dangerous, but I couldn't see that there would be a choice. But then, all of a sudden, there she comes floating down the front staircase in their house, on her way to the library to fetch a glass of brandy. She couldn't sleep it seems. I nearly laughed myself sick from the luck of it. And so I have her and there's nothing you can do about it, Helen."

Douglas would awaken, Helen thought, he had to. Alexandra would be gone. Surely he would wonder where she was. Surely he would raise the alarm.

"You have told me truth and lies, Helen. But I know one truth — you found the magic lamp. Now, if you try to deceive me again, if you try to trick me in any way, the lovely little countess will die."

"I am wearing my nightgown. Surely I cannot take you to the lamp like this?"

"I brought both you and the countess some men's clothes. It will be easier than dragging you about with all those women's skirts. I am going to reassure your friend while you change, Helen. She is already wearing her men's clothes. They are not such a bad fit, actually. I changed her while she was still unconscious. Unfortunately, you woke up before I could strip you down." He rose then. "Hurry, I want to leave soon."

He leaned down and untied her wrists. He seemed not to notice that she had worked them nearly free. "You may untie your own ankles. Hurry."

Helen was free in a trice. She changed into the men's clothes in three minutes flat. All the while she was thinking furiously. Alexandra. She had to be careful not to get Alexandra hurt.

She drew a deep breath and waited, just behind the door, the chamber pot in her hands.

When he came through the door, he was pushing Alexandra in front of him. He said in a loud voice, "Stay back, Helen, or I will kill the little pullet here. Obey me. I want no tricks from you or she is dead. See my gun is right by her right ear. Come out from your hiding place."

Helen brought the pot down on his head as hard as she could, and that was very hard indeed.

He went down like a stone.

"All right, Missy, 'ey! Wot'd you do to Mr. Yorke? Ye cracked 'im on 'is poor 'ead, ye did!"

Alexandra said in a clear, calm voice, "Who are you, sir?"

"I'm the cove wot this cove paid two quid."

"Fine. Now I will hire you. You will have five guineas once you see us back to London to our own houses."

The gaunt-faced little man looked down at Gerard Yorke, then at Helen, who stood a good eight inches taller than he. "I guesses there be no choice."

They made it to the front door of the small cottage. Helen's hand was out to turn the knob when it slammed open. There was Sir John Yorke standing there, a pistol in his hand.

"I knew you would fool Gerard. He has always underestimated women. What did he do, leave you? Yes, of course that is what he did. And you laid him flat, didn't you? I looked at you when you were but eighteen years old and I knew you were strong. I knew you would grow stronger over the years. And you've also become dangerous. Move back, Miss Mayberry, or should I say Mrs. Yorke?"

362

29

Gerard Yorke came into the small front room that held only two rickety chairs and a rough-hewn wooden table. He was holding his head and he was groaning. He staggered into the wall and then leaned against it, trying to get himself together again.

"You useless fool," his father said. "You couldn't even capture a single woman."

"Of course I could. I did. I captured two women, not just one. You can see them both. They are standing right here. Bad things just happened. Bad things always happen when Helen has any say about it." Gerard shook his head and forced it up to look at his father, who was holding a gun on Helen and the countess of Northcliffe. Gerard's own villain, that lantern-jawed individual to whom he had given two whole quid, was hovering just behind Sir John Yorke.

His father just looked at him as if he wanted to kick him. He wasn't surprised — it was the way his father had always looked at him.

Gerard said slowly, trying to get his wits together. "How come you to be here? You followed me?"

"Yes, naturally. I finally found you just two days ago. I have been waiting for you to make a decision about Helen, and you did, you bloody little ass — the wrong decision, but you have never made a right decision, have you? You should have just stayed dead, remained gone from England, remained a hero in your family's minds, but you didn't. Now just look what has happened." Sir John turned then and smiled at Helen, for no reason she could think of, and that smile of his made her shrivel inside. What was going on here?

Gerard shook his fist in Helen's face even as he collapsed even more against the wall. "I tell you, Father, I could not stay gone. And this wasn't my fault. I had to leave Helen alone so she could dress. I had to fetch the countess of Northcliffe from another chamber, and when I brought her back, I pushed her into the room in front of me. I even had a gun pointed at her head. The room was dark. Look now, it is barely dawn. I saw something that should have been Helen lying on the bed. How was I to know that Helen had that chamber pot and was behind the door? No man could have imagined that. I didn't have a chance."

"What is the meaning of all this?" Alexandra asked, looking from the old man to his son, who was still breathing hard, still holding his hand to his head. "Who are you, sir?"

"Ah, my lady. So you are Douglas Sherbrooke's wife." He gave her a slight bow. "Your husband is a cocky bastard I greatly admire. He is a genius at strategy and has proved

364

it many times over the years. I suppose my son here brought you along as leverage against Helen?"

"Yes, I did," said Gerard, pushing off the wall and finally managing to stand straight. "And it will work. Helen is fond of her. They are great friends. I have but to point my gun at the countess's head and Helen will take us to the magic lamp. She already said she would, once I threatened her friend here."

"A lamp," Sir John said, marveling at his son. "You actually believe that foolishness that is all over London? Are you an utter fool? There is no magic lamp. It is all fiction, an interesting tale invented in Helen's fertile imagination. Everyone is enjoying gossiping about it. It means nothing. Don't you realize that if there were something that important, some ancient relic with strange powers, no one would know about it? It would be kept a close secret."

Helen looked at him and smiled inwardly. Spenser had been exactly right. How could anyone possibly believe in something purportedly magic when everyone knew about it?

Alexandra went to stand by Helen, making Sir John laugh. "Just look at the two of you together. You are a giant, Helen, an oddity, a freak."

She grinned over at him. "At least I am not so old that my skin is spotted and hanging off my body and my teeth are all rotted."

He took a step toward her, raised his hand, then slowly lowered it. He looked down at his hand for a moment. "You were not so impertinent when you were eighteen," he said slowly.

"And you were not so openly rude — though you were older than death even back then. I remember as well how you looked at me and how you did not want your precious son to marry me."

Sir John shrugged. "I knew you wouldn't hold him. I knew you wouldn't give him a child immediately, as he claimed you would."

"What do you mean, I wouldn't hold him?"

"Even then, my worthless son was already searching out ways to make more money. I bought him the commission, hoping, praying he would change. He could have followed in my footsteps. But he didn't. He got an excellent dowry from your father, but it was gone in a month. And what did you do? Nothing. You believed every ridiculous lie he told you. But I knew you would change. I knew there was grit in you, a strong will, but you just didn't change quickly enough to be of any use to me. Yes, I was right. Just look at what you've become."

"No, Father," Gerard said. "Her dowry lasted two months. It would have lasted much longer, but I was cheated. It was Jason Fleming, Lord Crowley, who cheated me. I wanted to kill him, but then he left to go hunting in Scotland, the conniving bastard, and I could do nothing. And Helen refused to get pregnant." Gerard gave his wife a malignant look. "All I wanted from you was a child, nothing more, nothing less, at least after your dowry was gone. But you wouldn't give me one."

"I am very pleased about that," Helen said. "Incidentally," she said to his father, "I was only eighteen. If I had been as smart then as I am now, do you believe I would ever have attached myself to your toad of a son? Not very likely, sir. He turned out badly enough. I cringe to think if he had, instead, turned out like you."

Gerard, unlike his father, did not have much self-control. "Don't you insult my father, you worthless woman!" He was on her in an instant, his arm drawn back to strike her. Helen just shook her head as she raised her knee, struck him hard in the groin, then sent her fist into his neck.

Gerard howled, clutched himself, and fell to the floor, hitting the wall. He didn't know whether to rub his crotch or his neck, both hurt so badly. He kept swallowing and moaning as he rocked back and forth. Finally he whispered, "Father, look what she did to me. Kill her. No — just wound her. You can kill her later, after I have the lamp — but maybe not. She is my wife, after all. I will think about this. Also, if she knows you will kill her, there is no reason for her to take me to the lamp. And I swear to you, there is a magic lamp and she knows where the lamp is. She finally admitted to me that she has it. I want that lamp. She said there is no power in it, that if there were, she would have struck me dead with it.

"But she is just a woman, she doesn't know anything, except how to lie. Oh, God, I will die now." He was gasping, leaning over, holding himself.

"I don't know how you can talk with that blow to the throat," Helen said, not moving, just watching the effects of her handiwork. "Much less talk so we can understand you."

"Thems were fearsome blows ye planted on 'im," said the skinny little man in such an admiring voice that Alexandra stepped forward, shook her fist at him, and said, "Would you like to be next, you little sot?"

"Sich words from a countess. It be a disgrace."

"Be quiet. Hold your place, my lady. Now, what is your name?"

"Alexandra Sherbrooke."

"No, not you, I know who you are. Him, the little villain."

"Me name's Bernie Ricketts. Yer son wot's lying agin' the wall over there moaning give me money to get them ladies. I knows locks, and I twists them and kisses them until the doors open like a dream, I did, and in yer son goes, all free like, into both them bloody mansions. Then I keeps the watch so nobody can come and nab us. I did everything right, I did. Yer bloody son, that one didn't give me enuf money. The big 'un there, all blond and beautiful she be, but at the core o' things, she's a killer."

"Yes, I can see that she is," said Sir John Yorke. He looked bemused at the outpouring of all Mr. Ricketts's confidences. He shook his head. "Now, all of this has been amusing, but I have much to accomplish before the new day breaks."

"The new day has already broken," Gerard said, trying to straighten, trying to speak above a whisper, because now his throat hurt very badly. "What do you mean?"

Sir John looked his son over, his eyes dark and very tired. "You know, I tried to kill you once, Gerard, and I failed."

"No," Gerard said, "no, that's impossible. You may be sinister and no one really knows what you do or who you are, and I know that you beat my mother to death, but you're still my father. You wouldn't kill me, would you? Surely that isn't right."

"I didn't beat your mother to death, you idiot. She fell from the balcony of our house, nothing more than that. As for you, you were my son and I had hopes that you would make something of yourself, but you didn't. You are a wastrel. You are utterly worthless. You became a traitor to your country. There is nothing lower than a traitor.

"Naturally I would not let you ruin our family's name, but you managed to survive the ship's exploding and somehow get to shore."

"But you didn't make the ship sink. Even you couldn't manage that, Father."

"No, I hired one of the sailors to hit you on the head and throw you overboard, quickly and qui-

369

etly. Then it would have been over, and your reputation of being a hero would be safe. The family would have been saved from disgrace.

"It was all arranged, but then there was the accident aboard your ship and it exploded before the sailor could find you. And then you were safe with your masters and I couldn't get to you."

Helen and Alexandra looked at each other. Sir John had fully planned to have his own son killed?

Helen said, "You honestly wanted to kill him because you discovered he was a traitor?"

"Yes, Helen. Gerard wanted money, and so he got it the only way he could. He betrayed his country. He went willingly and quickly over to the French. I don't know how many secrets he sold to them, for he had the run of the Admiralty, as you can imagine, since he was my son. I discovered what he was quite by accident. The idiot left some papers he had stolen in his jacket pocket. His valet found the papers and brought them to me. I had no choice in the matter.

"I did my best by him. I puffed up the dispatches, had him made a hero, and then when I learned what he really was, I planned to kill him. There would be no dishonor for anyone. But he survived.

"Now, tell me, Gerard, was it indeed just the money that made you a traitor to all your family, to all that your father holds dear?"

Gerard remained on the floor. He didn't look at his father. He looked at Helen, and there was murder in his eyes. "It was just a few ridiculous

370

battle plans, the location of some troops and ships, names of towns where there were supply lines stored, that I sold to them, nothing of much importance. I gave them some names of men who were spying for England. Nothing much, again, I had to do very little.

"Of course I needed money. I had a wife. I had to support her. I had to pretend to want her after her dowry was gone. If I had only gotten her pregnant, then you would have given me half my inheritance. That is what you promised me."

Helen looked at her husband and wanted more than anything to have his damnable throat between her hands. "Are you saying that that was the only reason you wanted a child? To get money from your father?"

"It was a great deal of money — ten thousand pounds."

Helen just stared down at him, so much pain filling her, all of it pain for the innocent girl she had been. "But my dowry was ten thousand pounds. You spent that in two months. What was another ten thousand? Nothing much at all. You pathetic worm." She raised her leg to kick him, then stopped. "I only wish your father had come to me when he realized you were a traitor. I would have helped him destroy you. I would have knocked you overboard myself."

"You couldn't have," Gerard said. "You are a woman. They would not allow a woman on board ship."

"Your mind," Alexandra said slowly to

Helen's husband, "astounds me."

Gerard preened.

Sir John gave Helen a look then that she didn't understand. Was it admiration? No, surely not. He said slowly, "All of that was true, Gerard, but Helen is barren. And then because you have no honor, you became a traitor. Now, why did you write to Helen after eight years?"

"Dammit, I had to have money. When I heard about this lamp business, I decided to wait until she found it. Everyone in that stupid provincial town she lives in — Court Hammering — everyone speaks freely of it. Everyone believes she will find it, and very soon. I believe she has already found it.

"She had Lord Beecham with her and they went to this cave and came out with this strange iron chest. I knew the lamp was inside it, it had to be. They kept it close. They were secretive. Then Lord Beecham hared off to London. I knew they had found the lamp."

"Listen, you idiot, if I had found the lamp and the lamp was magic," Helen said very precisely, "I would have made you disappear with a mere snap of my fingers," which she then did, right in front of his face. "But I didn't make you disappear, did I? I couldn't, unfortunately. Listen to me carefully, Gerard. *There is no magic lamp.*"

"You told me there was," Gerard said. "You told me not above an hour ago that you would take me to it."

"I lied."

Sir John said then, "Enough about this ridiculous lamp. Of course she lied to you, Gerard. She wanted to escape you, and she would have if I hadn't come.

"It is daylight now. I must hurry. Helen, I am sorry, as strange as that may sound, but you and your friend here must die. I wanted only to kill Gerard, once and for all, but I was unable to catch him alone."

"You would kill three people?" Alexandra said, her voice incredulous. "Only a monster would do that, a monster who was truly evil, all the way to his soul. And to kill your own son? To prattle on about your honor? You are unspeakable, sir. You deserve to rot in hell."

"I say, guv, the lady's right. Ye ain't much of a pa, and these purty littil pullets — well, ye shouldn't pop them, guv."

"Shut up, Ricketts. Now let me think. How will I do this?"

Alexandra moaned, clutched her belly, and fell to the floor in a dead faint. No one moved for a split second, then Helen cried out, and went down to her knees beside her friend. "Oh, God, Alexandra. What is wrong? You must wake up, please."

"That was quite well done. You can get up now, Alexandra."

Sir John closed his eyes for a brief moment, then slowly turned to see the earl of Northcliffe and Viscount Beecham and two men he didn't know, standing behind them in the open doorway.

"I thought you were keeping a watch, Ricketts," Sir John said through his teeth, so furious he almost choked on his own bile.

"No, guv, not since ye came along and caused all the ruckus."

"Helen, are you all right?"

"Yes, but come here quickly. Douglas, she grabbed her stomach, then fainted. What is wrong with her?"

"Nothing at all," Alexandra said, got to her feet and gave her husband a big smile. She swept him a curtsey. "Welcome, my lord. As always, your timing leaves me breathless."

"Well done, Alex, well done indeed. You gave us the distraction we needed. I'm proud of you. Now, don't move while we see to these villains."

Douglas walked up to Sir John Yorke and twisted the gun out of his hand. He then held out his hand to Ricketts, and the little man, cursing under his breath, gave it up. "The knife as well," Douglas said.

"Ye knows too much, ye does."

Douglas handed both guns and the knife to Spenser.

"Go hug your wife, Douglas. These marvelous specimens aren't going anywhere at all."

Sir John said to his son, who looked both relieved to be alive and terrified because now he had been caught, "I should have just hired someone to shoot you. Now look at what you have done, you incompetent little sot. You couldn't even kidnap the women without having the men on you in an instant."

"Actually," Lord Beecham said easily to Gerard, "your father is right. We were on you in an instant." He added to the father, "We held back once we saw you following your son. We wanted to find out what was going on."

"He was going to murder all of us," Helen said. "Alexandra is right. He is a monster."

"She's a lying bitch. I am not a monster." Sir John ran at Alexandra. His son stuck out his leg. Sir John went flying. Gerard heaved himself against Spenser, knocking him sideways into Helen, then leapt through a rotting window that was covered with a thin sheet of wood. The wood splintered and Gerard was lost to sight.

Lord Beecham straightened, shook himself, and said calmly, "Mr. Cave, would you and your partner please fetch Mr. Yorke back here? Thank you."

"Certainly, milord. Come along, Tom," he said to his partner. "Let's catch that sniveling cove traitor."

Lord Beecham watched the two men run out of the cottage. Then he said, "As for you, Mr. Ricketts, you just lie down on the floor and clasp your hands behind your neck. Now."

Bernie Ricketts stretched out on his stomach on the floor.

Sir John staggered to his feet. He was holding his left arm.

Douglas released his wife, then walked slowly to Sir John. He calmly took the old man's neck between his large hands. "You were going to kill my wife. She is right. You are a monster. It is you who do not deserve to live. Your proud name, sir, won't survive this day. You will be remembered as a cold-blooded murderer, a dishonorable man whose son was a traitor."

"It is my turn when you are finished, Douglas," Spenser said. "Don't kill him just yet."

"No, I won't. I want him to stand in front of all the men in the House of Lords. I want everyone to see the sort of malignancy that exists in the highest levels of our government." Douglas shoved Sir John back against the wall.

Sir John threw back his head and yelled, "No — you cannot tell anyone. I have spent my life fighting for the honor of England. No!"

Ezra Cave came through the front door at that moment, a knife in one hand and a gun in the other, and in front of him he was shoving Gerard. The father looked at the son, disheveled, pale, blood streaming down his arm. He yelled again in fury and threw himself against Douglas. Douglas tried to grab him, but the old man, quicker than a snake, jerked away from him, grabbed the gun and knife from Ezra Cave and turned it on his son. "I should have killed you when you were born. Your mother was a sniveling fool and that was just what she birthed." And he stabbed his son through the heart.

He jerked the knife out of his son's chest and

used him as a shield.

Ezra Cave grabbed his partner's gun and fired. He missed — not that it mattered, since Gerard was already dead. The bullet hit the wall beside Sir John's head, shredding the wood, sending splinters flying. Sir John let his son's body crumple to the floor at his feet and waved the gun wildly about in front of him. "No, none of you come at me. Just stay right there." Then he threw his head back and yelled to the heavens, his voice thick with failure and rage, "I have done my duty to my country. I have executed a traitor. It makes no difference that he carried my blood. I have devoted my life to England. History will judge me an honorable man, a man who never shirked his duty, a man who gave his life for his country."

Then Sir John turned the gun to his mouth and pulled the trigger. Blood gushed out of his mouth and the back of his head exploded. Both his face and his head were crimson with blood. He didn't make another sound, collapsing where he stood, over his son's body.

No one moved for a very long time, just looked at the old man sprawled over his son, as if covering him to protect him.

Helen said then, "This is too much, Spenser. It is just too much." He saw the blankness of shock on her face and a dreadful sorrow in her eyes. He drew her against him and held her close.

But what Spenser was thinking was that

Gerard Yorke was dead, finally and truly and irrevocably dead. He wondered in that moment, if he ever managed to get himself admitted into heaven, what Saint Peter would have to say to him about the thoughts in his mind as he held his future wife tightly against him and looked at her husband's dead body at his feet.

30

Spenser Heatherington, Seventh Baron Valesdale and fifth Viscount Beecham, and Miss Helen Mayberry were married in St. Paul's Cathedral. There were five hundred guests present, many of them there to trade gossip about the fantastic lamp that of course didn't really exist, that was only a titillating jest played on society by Lord Beecham. Ah, but what a fascinating tale it was — a magic lamp that had been in the possession of King Edward I, who had hidden it from the world, for whatever reason. Everyone had spoken of it, guessed at its whereabouts, granted it various powers. Ah, it had passed the time so pleasurably.

There were at least fifty guests there because they liked Lord Beecham and believed the lovely Helen Mayberry would make him an excellent wife.

As for the bride's father, Lord Prith was in his element. Sophie Sherbrooke had told Helen that Lord Prith was giving samples of a new champagne concoction to guests on the sly as they came into St. Paul's. Sophie said it had a blue tint. Helen just laughed and shook her head. She wondered if perhaps this time he had mixed blueberries with the champagne. What was he calling it? Bluepagne? Or perhaps Chamblue?

Bishop Bascombe performed the ceremony, his deep, melodious voice booming out into that huge cavernous space, touching everyone there, making even the most cynical of those attending forget about what their friends were wearing, and warming them to their toes.

It was a lovely service, all said. The huge reception held at Lord Beecham's town house was magnificent, no expense spared. And some asked behind their hands, not in seriousness, of course, if the magic lamp had provided all this bounty. After all, both the lovely ceremony, all those guests, then the food served at the reception, were surely more than could be planned in a year, much less a mere month by a mere mortal.

Yes, surely one would have to have the services of a magic lamp to have such a splendid wedding on such short notice.

Ryder Sherbrooke was saying to Gray St. Cyre and his new bride, Jack, "Did your husband tell you my only marital advice?"

"Yes," Jack said, stood on her tiptoes and kissed Ryder's cheek. "He did. You are a brilliant man, Ryder. I can see why Sophie adores you even when she is planning to discipline you."

"What's this about discipline?" asked Gray St. Cyre, an eyebrow raised.

Lord Beecham came up in time to hear them. "And what is Ryder's brilliant marital advice, Jack?"

"Laughter," she said, giving her husband a wink. "A man can always seduce his wife with laughter."

And that, Lord Beecham thought, was true enough. He looked over at Helen, standing next to Alexandra Sherbrooke. He didn't even see Alexandra or the sublime décolletage that displayed her beautiful bosom. No, he saw only his new wife. His wife. At the advanced age of thirty-three, he was at last a married man.

Helen Heatherington. The alliteration pleased him, tasted delicious on his tongue. She was more beautiful than a simple man deserved. She was dressed all in pale-yellow silk, yellow silk ribbons threaded through her hair. She wore a diamond necklace around her neck that he had given to her the day before and small diamond drops in her lovely ears. He simply couldn't stop staring at her, and knowing, knowing all the way to his soul, that she was his and would be his forever. His wife, so tall and willowy and graceful, and strong as a bloody ox. He wondered, as he watched the two ladies talk, if they were exchanging more discipline recipes. He hoped that Alexandra was giving his new wife exciting new ideas. Probably so. He imagined that Douglas was hoping it was Helen giving Alexandra the new ideas. The ladies appeared to have very fertile imaginations, at least that was what Ryder had told him the previous week, a fatuous grin on his face. He'd said that Sophie was absolutely brimming with wicked notions, eager to test each one on him. The ladies had even brought Jack St. Cyre into the discipline fold. Gray would shortly be cross-eyed with pleasure. Sophie had announced that Ryder was always one to try something new, particularly if the something new promised to be administered with wicked abandon.

As for Gerard Yorke, all had gone smoothly in that quarter, thank all the heavenly forces involved. He had been found in a back alley down near the docks, stabbed, his possessions stolen. They had all discussed burying him and just forgetting him, but Lord Beecham knew that there would always be questions, sly looks, particularly since they had let the gossip rip through society that Gerard Yorke just might very well be alive and need to be found.

Lord Beecham had wanted no whispers that a man should not marry a widow if there was even the slightest chance that the husband were still hanging about somewhere. No, he had to be dead and there had to be a body. He wanted no questions, no doubts.

Well, Gerard Yorke had been found, and quickly. He was dead. Many had seen his body. Lord Beecham's dearest Helen was indeed a widow. So all, thank God, was well.

Had Lord Beecham been responsible for his murder? Not many people even considered it a possibility, for which he was profoundly grateful. Douglas and Ryder and Gray St. Cyre had done a good deal of talking after Yorke had been found. Their reasoning had been this: After all, Lord Beecham could have simply killed him and buried him beneath an oak tree and no one would have been the wiser. He would not have left him in an alley where he would be found. That made no sense at all. And everyone in society agreed. Thieves and murderers abounded at the docks. It was one of these dreadful blackguards who had murdered poor Gerard Yorke.

But the death of his father, Sir John Yorke, First Secretary of the Admiralty, shocked everyone. It was said that he was so saddened by his son's murder, never even knowing that he had still been alive all these years and surviving in secret for reasons no one knew, that he killed himself. He put a gun in his mouth and pulled the trigger. Father and son were buried side by side, on the same day, by the bereaved and shocked Yorke family.

People spoke of nothing else but Sir John Yorke's suicide for a full week. The parties involved said nothing at all.

Then people spoke of nothing else except the magic lamp for a full week.

People didn't really speak all that much about the murder of Reverend Mathers, surely a good man, and it was a shame that someone stuck a stiletto in his back, but after all, who was he anyway?

He remained very important to Lord Hobbs and to Lord Beecham. Lord Hobbs could not prove to his own satisfaction, however, that Lord

Crowley had murdered Reverend Mathers. Nor could he wring a confession from Old Clothhead, Reverend Mathers's brother. Helen firmly believed that Gerard had killed Reverend Mathers, but still, they could not be certain. It was damnable to Lord Beecham, but there was nothing he could do about it.

"I have a toast!"

Five hundred pair of eyes looked toward the bride's father. Lord Prith, a giant of a man who was of vast good humor, proud of his daughter, and seemed genuinely fond of his new son-in-law, stood on the dais in front of the orchestra hired for the reception.

He lifted an elegant crystal flute of champagne. "My beautiful Helen has married a fine man who will give her his all. He will continue to give her his all even as the future eventually becomes the present.

"I wish all of us to drink to their happiness and their immense and endless regard for each other, a regard that surprises even a fond father."

Helen burst out laughing — there was simply nothing else to do. There was no one like her father. She wished she was close enough to kiss him and hug him for a brief moment, to tell him again how much she adored him, but she was standing beside her new husband, and so she just laughed and waved at her father, who much enjoyed being the center of attention.

The crowd loved this unconventional toast given by the unique and quite eccentric Lord

Prith, whose manservant had tears in his eyes as he passed around glasses of champagne to the guests. No one would know that Flock, the manservant, was weeping not with the joy of the day, but because his Teeny had married a certain Walter Jones just two days previous in Court Hammering.

The toast and the manservant's tears for his beloved Miss Helen and her happiness, were spoken of for a good three days after the wedding.

At exactly 3:57 in the morning, long after all the guests had departed, Lord Beecham lay upon his bride, wondering seriously if he would survive his wedding night, which was only half over. His beleaguered heart was going to pump itself right out of his chest, but before that, he would probably suffocate because he, very simply, could not breathe. He pressed his forehead to his bride's. "It's all over for me, Helen."

It was the fourth time he had loved her.

"It should be." She managed to purse her numbed lips together, finally, and lightly kiss his neck.

"I did it. I succeeded." He hauled himself up and managed to balance himself over her, so exhausted, so replete with pleasure and love for the nearly unconscious woman beneath him, with her beautiful blond hair all tangled around her face, that he could have wept with the power of all those wondrous feelings settled deep in his heart.

"Helen, this was quite an accomplishment. We did it."

"Hmmm?"

"Four times, Helen, not just three. I have managed to break that miserable sameness, that triad cycle that seemed to have us by the throat."

"We could have stopped at two times, Spenser. That would have broken the cycle too. We could have stopped after one time."

"No, that would have made me less of a man. A man must always strive to achieve even greater strides. I have strided tonight, Helen. But I fear that I cannot strive more."

He dropped down beside her and pulled her against him. He managed to kiss her hair. He was unconscious in the next drawing of a breath. As for Helen Heatherington, Lady Beecham, she simply lay there, pressed against her husband, lightly stroking her fingers down his chest. She didn't have the energy to do more.

She rested her palm on his belly. "There is something I must tell you, Spenser."

He snorted in his sleep, managed to pull up his head, and kiss her ear. He fell on his back again, but not to sleep. She had his attention.

"I wanted to tell you earlier, but you were so intent upon extending our lovemaking horizons that I didn't want to distract you."

"You could not have distracted me. No man could be distracted if he had you, dearest."

"Yes, you would have been utterly distracted.

You would have fallen off the bed, you would have been so distracted."

He actually managed to come up on his elbow as he gently shoved her onto her back. He leaned down and kissed her mouth, then said, "All right, tell me. Distract me if you can."

"I'm not barren. Evidently I was just unable to become pregnant with Gerard. The physician told me this sometimes happens. We are going to have a child, Spenser."

He looked down at her, blinked a couple of times, then flopped onto his back. In the next moment, he slid off the bed onto the floor.

One week later

Lord Beecham awoke to Helen's soft mouth on his cheek. Nothing unusual in that. He loved it, and he was becoming used to it. He was so used to it that if she didn't kiss him every morning, he knew he would miss it desperately. He would probably whine and beg.

He sighed and turned toward her. Nothing happened.

He couldn't seem to move. Now this was odd. She kissed him yet again, her mouth soft and warm against the whiskers on his chin. He was immediately interested, but that was nothing new. And so he tried to bring his arms around her, but his arms wouldn't move.

His eyes flew open. He saw his bride smiling

down at him, her expression so sweet, so tender, and that beautiful mouth of hers touched him yet again.

He said slowly, trying to get his wits together — not an easy thing when he wanted her, something that happened with very little delay. "There is something very wrong here, Helen."

"Yes, I know, my lord." She kissed his left ear. "You are now my prisoner."

She was right about that. He was lying sprawled naked on his back, his arms tied over his head, his legs spread and his ankles tied as well.

His eyes crossed. "Fate is a remarkable thing. Helen, my dearest, what if you had never even seen me? What if, by some awful quirk of fate, I had never even seen you? What if you had never decided to hunt me down?

"No other woman would do this to me. Ah, Helen, kiss me again, or shave me first, then kiss me, and don't stop."

But she didn't kiss him or shave him. She laughed and stood beside the bed, her hands on her hips. "Oh, no. This is retribution, my lord. Remember when you tied me down? This is revenge."

"Ah, if I flick my wrist inward, will my bonds slip away?"

"No. I don't know how to tie a knot that would do that. I fear that you are completely at my mercy, my lord. No escape for you unless I allow it."

He thought he would expire of unrequited lust at that very moment. He cocked an eyebrow at her. "Will you beat me with a bundle of hollyhocks?"

She gave him a brilliant smile. It was then he noticed that she was wearing a thin silk nightgown, just a single layer of soft silk that was thinner than the film of sweat on his forehead. It was pale cream. He watched her ease one strap off her very white shoulder.

He gulped and felt himself respond, instantly, fully. "What level is this?"

"I haven't assigned it a level yet. I must conduct the experiment first, then evaluate my results." The other strap fell off and the gown slowly slipped over her breasts to fall to her waist. "Perhaps it will prove not to be an efficacious discipline. Perhaps you will simply close your eyes and fall asleep again. Perhaps even snore."

"I am dying here, Helen."

"That's good. Just be patient. Just let me tease you a bit more into oblivion." She looked down his body, came down beside him, and began kissing him.

He arched up, sucking in a roomful of air, his heart speeding up so fast that he knew he would embarrass himself if she continued. "Helen, you must stop. It is true that I am not a very young man, that one would expect me to have gained more control by my thirty-third year of male life, but it isn't true. You must stop or I will leave you and that isn't a good thing to do to a beautiful woman who also happens to be your wife.

"Stop, Helen. Ah, your mouth is so very warm —" He groaned and heaved at the straps around his wrists. They gave just a bit.

She stopped then, and he wanted to weep. His brain was fogged, his eyes were filmed with lust and monstrous need. He saw her stand by the bed again, saw that creamy silk nightgown slip over her hips and pool at her feet. She was all his, this beautiful, devoted woman. He wanted to breathe his last breath with her beside him.

"I am so full of feelings for you, Helen, that they are all jumbled in my poor brain. Just know that I have waited for you all my life. And finally you jumped me in the park and saved me. I love you, Helen. You won't ever forget that, will you?"

"Oh, no," she said. "I will never forget. You will not doubt, ever, that I worship you to the ends of my very extremities? That I would do anything to make you happy?" She leaned down and touched the knots on each wrist.

In an instant, his wrists and ankles were free and she was on top of him and he was inside her, and he wondered even as he lost what little control he had, how many decades a man could survive such pleasure without crumbling into dust.

"It is at least a Level Nine," she said into his mouth. "At least."

And he wondered what a Level Ten could possibly be.

31

Eight Months Later
Shugborough Hall

Jordan Everett Heatherington slid into his father's hands in the middle of a Wednesday night, howling loud enough to make the physician in residence laugh and rub his hands together. "Well done, my lady, very well done indeed. And you, my lord, my congratulations on the birth of your son, although I thoroughly disapprove of you being here, in this very room where your wife has labored long to do her duty by your line. But you did insist, and thus I had no choice in the matter.

"However, pushing me out of the way to receive your son in your own hands is highly irregular. I disapprove. You might have dropped him. And then where would you have been? Your son should have been received by my hands. No, none of this is done. I do appreciate you allowing me to remove the afterbirth, not a pleasant thing to do, but as a physician, I had no choice."

Lord Beecham looked down at his son, looked at the physician, and shouted, "Flock, come in. Ah, yes, there you are, lurking over there by the door. Do take Dr. Coolley downstairs and give him a glass of Lord Prith's newest concoction."

"What is that?"

"It's a mixture of mashed apples and champagne. I believe he calls it appagne. He wanted to create something special for the blessed event. He has been working very hard at it. I hope he is still conscious."

"Eh? What is that you said, my lord? Appagne?"

"You will discover soon enough, sir." Helen watched her husband carefully hand his son to the waiting midwife, who was crooning to him even before she held him close.

"My love," Lord Beecham said, as he sat down beside her. "You are brilliant, perhaps even more today than you were yesterday."

Helen certainly did not disagree with that. After she had been bathed by Teeny and dressed in a fresh nightgown, she fell into a dreamless and deep sleep for the rest of the night.

Toward morning there was a huge storm. Trees were uprooted, rock avalanches ripped down cliffs. Helen slept through it all.

Two weeks later, when Lord Beecham and Helen visited the cave, they found that an entire wall had fallen inward. In that small opening they saw a strange light.

It pulsed, Helen thought, pulsed with a soft yellowish sort of glow. The light seemed to go on forever, extending back into the dirt wall as far as the eye could see.

"What is it?"

"I don't know." Lord Beecham reached his hand toward that light. His fingers closed around something solid, something very warm, something that felt as if it were somehow moving, but it wasn't. It pulsed against his flesh.

"Helen," he said very quietly, "I have found something that shouldn't be here, something that isn't like anything we have ever known." Slowly, very slowly, he grasped the object between his hands and pulled it toward them.

It was a filthy old lamp.

Neither of them said a word. They could only stare at the thing. Helen ripped off a long strip from her petticoat, and Lord Beecham lightly began to rub the lamp clean. Some minutes later, they saw the dented old gold of its surface. The lamp was small, not longer than two of Lord Beecham's hands, fingertip to fingertip, perhaps as tall as one of his hands, fingers extended. It was immensely heavy. Lord Beecham handed it to his wife.

Helen cupped it in her palms. It didn't seem quite so heavy now. "The lamp," she said, tears in her eyes. "I cannot believe it was here all the time. But why wasn't it in the cask?"

"Maybe as an extra protection in case someone, like you, found the cask. It must be the lamp that King Edward the First received from the Knight Templar."

"Or perhaps it was originally in the iron cask and it removed itself further inside the cave wall. Yes, it is the lamp, and it is so very warm. There is something alive about it, something that makes little sense to me, but it must, to someone."

"It was hidden in the dark," he said. "Very deep in the cave wall. Perhaps it was hidden there for more protection or more likely, I believe now, to keep it buried." It made him want to withdraw, to forget anything like this damned lamp that wasn't of this world, that shouldn't be here, held in Helen's hands, looking all sorts of benign, when he knew, he simply knew, that it held more power than was wise.

"It isn't real, Helen."

She was stroking the lamp. She sat down on the cave floor and held it close to the branch of candles they had brought into the cave with them. She tried to lift the golden lid that was shaped like a small onion. It didn't move. It seemed all one piece, even though there was a dirty seam. "What do you mean, it isn't real?"

"I don't know. I just said it. What do you want to do with it?"

She said without hesitation, "You remember how King Edward laid the lamp in the queen's arms when she was so very ill? And she survived? I want to see if it will help Mrs. Freelady. I visited just yesterday, and she is very near death."

Lord Beecham didn't think that was a good idea, but it was Helen's lamp and her decision. Mrs. Freelady spent the night with the lamp held to her chest, Lord and Lady Beecham in the next room. When they looked in on her early the following morning, she was dead.

Helen said nothing at all, just took the lamp back to Shugborough Hall. Word got around, as

394

word always did, that the lamp had been found.

Late one night, not three days later, three men tried to steal it. Lord Beecham awoke to hear Flock yelling at the top of his lungs. He shot one of the men in the arm, but the fellow's cohorts managed to get him away.

He lit candles and stared at the bloody lamp that sat atop the mantel in the drawing room, just sat there, all old and dented and harmless-looking. He rolled his eyes and went back to bed.

The lamp had done nothing save sit there since they had found it. It didn't pulse or give off any light. It didn't disappear and then reappear again, it didn't do anything remotely remark-able. Lord Beecham was beginning to believe that he disremembered any sort of magic attrib-utes.

It was just an old lamp. If it had ever been magical, that magic was long gone.

Only two days after that, an old woman tried to steal the lamp. Lord Prith tucked her under his arm and carried her away. She never stopped yelling that the lamp was evil and she had to de-stroy it.

So many years, Helen thought, as she stroked the lamp. So many years she had searched for it, and now that it was hers, it appeared to be ex-actly what it was — an old, dented lamp with nothing at all magical about it. It didn't disap-pear, or change shape even once. It just sat there on the mantel, looking decrepit. But all the writ-ings, warning of this and that. Why, really, had

King Edward buried it? Nothing about the damned lamp made sense.

There were no answers. King Edward hadn't found the answers either. The lamp simply sat there on the mantel through two more attempts to steal it.

32

Two Months Later

It was early spring, the wildflowers just beginning to bloom, the air soft and scented with salt and pine trees. Lord Beecham stood just behind his new wife on the promontory, his hands splayed over her now flat belly, looking out over the sea, watching the storm come closer. The waves were whipping up, huge spumes of water striking the black rocks just off to the left, sending arcs of water thundering into the air. Birds shrieked and wheeled in the air above them.

He kissed her ear. "Did I tell you that I have already bought your Christmas present?"

"Christmas is still nine months away."

"I dream of sitting in front of our Yule log with you at my side, opening your present. Perhaps there is some champagne in there. Perhaps your father will concoct a special Christmas drink. Perhaps it could be champagne mixed with smashed holly berries. A lovely red color."

She was still laughing when he said against her ear, "Have I told you recently that I love you?"

She turned slowly in his arms and kissed him full on the mouth. Her breath was warm and sweet. "Not since this morning, just before you fell asleep again, and I'm not really certain that

397

you even knew what you were saying. I had quite wrung you out, my lord."

"I have been wrung out so much since I met you, Helen, I have decided that a man who manages to find a woman who fits perfectly against him and knows discipline — all levels of discipline — is not only the luckiest bastard on the earth, he is also the one with the biggest smile on his face, at all times."

"All that," she said, and kissed him again and again, her hands roaming over his back now.

He kissed her hair, pulled her close, closed his eyes and rubbed his cheek in her hair. "Jordan is now sleeping through the night, a blessing, I say. Your eyes are all bright again." Then he gave her a dazzling smile. "You know, dearest, Jordan is quite perfect, even his yells sound inspired, at least according to the vicar, who paused in the midst of his sermon on Sunday to listen. I was thinking that perhaps he is in need of a brother or sister. What do you think, Helen?" He kissed her mouth, and added, his breath warm against her flesh, "No, not right away. Even if you beg me for another babe immediately, I won't let you have your way. We will wait at least two years, all right? Now, how many babes would you like to have?"

She kissed him back, loving the feel of him, the taste of him. She loved him more today, this very morning, than she had even the day before. It was amazing. "More babes, Spenser? I don't know. My father wants a half dozen, he told me.

What do you think? Can we attempt that many?"

He actually shuddered, and she knew he was remembering that very long night he had spent while she'd tried to birth Jordan. He said finally, "I don't know if I can survive that many more births, Helen. I had an awful time of it. So many long hours I suffered through. Perhaps my memories will fade a bit and I won't dread the birthing so very much. Yes, we will decide one babe at a time. I want a girl this next time, just like you. Well, perhaps she will have my brain, and that will make everything perfect, don't you think? Ah, I just felt a raindrop land on my cheek, dearest."

"The rain — it's wonderfully warm. But you're right. The storm is almost on us. In a few minutes it won't be so delightful."

He thought a moment, then grinned. "Let's go into your cave and wait it out. Just perhaps I can convince you to make the smile on my face even bigger. Let me tie the horses beneath those trees to wait out the storm."

It was the cave where they had found both the iron cask and the lamp itself. They hadn't been here since Lord Beecham had pulled it out of the cave wall.

They stood in the entrance of the cave, watching the storm finally strike land. Thick sheets of rain came straight down, forming a gray veil between them and the world outside. They could hear the roiling water smashing against the rocks. There were no more birds screeching and wheeling about. All was quiet, save for the crashing of the waves, so rhythmic, steady, predictable.

"Are you cold?"

Helen held her arms over her chest. "No, not really."

"Thank you for Jordan. He looks exactly like me."

"Not much fairness there," she said, "but since I think you are the most handsome man in all of East Anglia, it is all right."

She turned in his arms and smiled right into his beautiful eyes. "I wasn't ill for a single day with Jordan. Mrs. Toop told me it was because I somehow managed to make you sick for me, only you were too proud to admit it. She said it was a charming discipline that, as far as she knows, no one else has yet discovered."

"That's it exactly. I retched up my innards while you blissfully fattened up and ran my life. Now, I heard yesterday that you had to go all the way to a Level Six punishment with Geordie."

"Yes, the idiot got drunk and grabbed one of the guest's maids. He tried to maul her."

"Did she want to be mauled or not?"

"I asked her most particularly about that. She told me that she is still considering her feelings in the matter."

"Ah, if she deems him a clod, will you let her inflict some of his punishment?"

"Oh, indeed. Her eyes sparkle when she even thinks about it. I fear she will deem him a clod simply because she wants to conduct the discipline. She wants to punish him herself, and, I imagine, she also wants to examine what he was mauling her with more closely."

"A bunch of hollyhocks? Will you strip poor Geordie down to his skin?"

"Oh, yes. All the village will come and participate. I believe that the squire and his wife wish to make it into a party. The vicar loves lobster patties, and he has announced that he will provide them to everyone who comes. Of course, only the women will be allowed to whip Geordie. They do it with so much more finesse than men. They tease and stroke ever so delicately, and poor Geordie will moan and groan, much more than last time."

Lord Beecham rolled his eyes. Lobster patties at a discipline party presided over by the vicar, whose wife would probably be wielding a bundle of hollyhocks. He had never realized how exciting living in the country could be.

Lord Beecham removed his jacket and they sat on the floor of the cave, kissing, talking, worrying a bit about the horses, when Helen said, "Something is different, Spenser."

"Different? What?"

"I just noticed that there is wax here on the cave floor. Why would there be wax?"

"Why don't you stay right here and think of new disciplines for me? I will just walk back into the cave and see if perhaps someone has been sleeping here."

He heard her muttering as he walked toward the back of the cave. Then he stopped cold. He couldn't see a foot in front of him. He had no candle. He began to laugh as he walked back to his wife.

He stopped abruptly and stared at Reverend Titus Older, who was standing over Helen.

Water was dripping off him, but he looked triumphant, joyous. What was going on here?

"Reverend Older," Lord Beecham said as he carefully stepped toward him. "It is raining. Is it not strange for you to be out strolling in this inclement weather? You wished to see us that badly? This is an odd visit, surely. Perhaps you would like to tell us why you are here, in this cave?"

Reverend Older pulled a gun from his capacious coat pocket. He aimed it directly at Helen.

"Lord Beecham, such a pleasure, my boy. Come and join your lovely Amazon. Yes, that's right, just sit right there beside her. I wasn't sure that I should come in on you. I feared that you would be in an intimate way, if you know what I mean. Not that there is anything wrong with that, don't misunderstand me."

Helen eyed that gun he held, then focused on his face as she said, "What are you doing here, Reverend Older? You haven't, by any chance, been sleeping in this cave, have you?"

"Well, yes, my dear, for the past three days. You see, my once-sweet wife-to-be, Lilac, has kicked me out of her bedchamber. She doesn't want me anymore. She has even told all her friends that she doesn't wish to marry me, and thus I was forced to come here, to Shugborough, where I heard you were still in residence."

He paused a moment, looked around at the grim walls of the cave, and sighed. "This is not a comfortable place. Even with six blankets I could not get completely warm at night, you know? There is just something about the insides of caves, even small ones like this, that freezes the bones. But I came here because I heard this was where you found the magic lamp. I hoped that perhaps I would find another lamp, perhaps a sister lamp. What do you think?"

Lord Beecham and his wife just stared at Reverend Older.

"Not again," Helen said.

"I didn't find anything, of course. Now, why are you in residence here, my boy, and not back in London?"

"We both like it here. I see no reason for Helen and me to go to my country estate in Devon just yet. Lord Prith likes to have us staying here with him. Why did Lady Chomley not wish to marry you, sir?"

Reverend Older sighed deeply and rubbed his fingers across his forehead. "The sweet lady discovered I had, er, temporarily removed one of her brooches from her overflowing jewelry box. I had lost a wager, you see, and as a gentleman, I had to pay it. Actually, she had postponed our wedding several times over the past months.

Perhaps she distrusted me." He sighed.

"Very unreasonable of her to rid herself of you," said Helen, and Lord Beecham saw the calculating gleam in her eye. He knew that gleam well. She would tackle the good reverend in the next two minutes. He was terrified and pleased. But he couldn't let her have her fun. No, he couldn't take the chance of her possibly being hurt. It curdled his belly. She was his wife and Jordan's mother.

"What do you want with us, sir?"

"I want the lamp, my lord. Nothing more, just the lamp you and your wife found here. Oh, yes, this bloody cave is becoming quite famous. I know that others have tried to steal the lamp from Shugborough Hall. I am smarter than that. I waited until I got the two of you alone. Now I will hold one of you here whilst the other returns to the hall and fetches the lamp back to me."

Lord Beecham said, "Yes, we do have the lamp. However, it is simply a very old lamp. It does nothing at all. It just sits where you place it. There is no magic to it."

"I am a man of God. The lamp was meant for a man like me, not for common Philistines like you. I have the spiritual depth and the incredible insights of a true churchman. The lamp will guide me to further greatness. The lamp will perform for me."

Lord Beecham said slowly, "I don't know what you mean. Did you say 'further greatness'?"

"Very well, I was speaking prematurely. The lamp will guide me to beginning greatness. Greatness has eluded me until now. But with the lamp I shall find my way. I shall perform feats not even dreamed about."

Helen yawned, then cocked her head to one side. "I cannot imagine any greatness springing from you, sir. You are a villain, nothing more, and a thief — just ask Lady Chomley. Did we nearly catch you in your hidey-hole?"

"I was watching you on the promontory. When you came here to escape the storm, I followed. As I said, I have great insight. I knew that the storm was meant for me, that it would force you here, that you would then give up the lamp to me, its rightful possessor."

Helen yawned again. "It is nasty weather, is it not, Reverend? And you are an elderly man. It is likely you will catch an inflammation of the lung. Let us go now. You will return to London. You may not have the lamp. Go away."

Reverend Older frowned. "I don't like this," he said slowly, looking from Helen to Lord Beecham. "I had not expected you to be so very rude to me. Now, my lord, you will return to Shugborough Hall and fetch the lamp. I will keep Lady Beecham here with me. I will not harm her if you are quick to bring me back the lamp."

Both of them just looked at him.

"I must have the lamp, else I will be in dire straits."

"Dire straits happen, sir," Lord Beecham said. "That is a pity, but you may not have the lamp. Go away."

"You force me to violence, something I abhor." He raised the gun and aimed it directly at Helen.

"I say, what the devil is going on here? Who is this old fellow who has the gall to aim a gun at my dearest daughter?"

Lord Beecham wanted to cheer at his father-in-law's unexpected arrival. He did smile. He took Helen's hand in a firm grip and held her still. "Good day, sir. This fellow is Reverend Older. He has come from London to try to steal our lamp."

"You mean the lamp that a good dozen people have tried to filch over the past few months? That old dented lamp that probably isn't worth the filching?"

"Yes, Father, that's the lamp. We have told him that he cannot have it, that the lamp has no magic, that it has nothing at all. We have been truthful with him."

"It is you, Lord Prith?" Reverend Older said, turning slowly. "How do you come here? You are wet to your marrow, sir. I want the lamp. It will perform miracles for me. Now get in here, stand beside your daughter and Lord Beecham."

"Oh, I don't think so," Lord Prith said. He called over his shoulder, "Flock, you were right. We have come across yet another villain who is up to no good. He has a gun and he is pointing it at my beloved and beautiful daughter. What do you want to do?"

"Kill the blighter," said Flock, peering around Lord Prith's shoulder.

"This is enough." Lord Beecham walked right up to Reverend Older.

"Stay back, my lord."

"Listen to me, sir. You cannot kill four people. It would not be good form, particularly for a man of the cloth. You have claimed to be a man of the church, a man with profound insights. Well, prove your greatness. We have told you the truth. There is no cursed magic in the lamp. Now you need to go away."

Reverend Older looked as if he would burst into tears. "It isn't fair. It is so very difficult to be a good man, a godly man, a man to be respected through the ages. Ah, it was just one silly brooch and the old cow rained abuse on my poor head. And then there was Reverend Mathers. He refused to have anything to do with my very nicely devised scheme. I had no choice. Oh, I am undone."

Lord Beecham felt his blood run cold. So many months had passed, and no one had learned anything about who had murdered Reverend Mathers. Lord Hobbs had given up. Reverend Older had done it?

Helen just stared at him in amazement, unwilling to believe what he had said. "You are the one who stuck that stiletto in poor Reverend Mathers's back? You are the one who murdered him?"

But Reverend Older didn't answer immediately. He was staring down at his wet shoes and shaking his head. Then he said, just above a whisper, "I liked Reverend Mathers. He and I were friends once, a very long time ago. But he wouldn't tell me anything. What was I to do?"

33

There was dead silence.

Lord Prith simply closed his hands around Reverend Older's neck and lifted him off the ground. "You pathetic little man. And you are, you know. Very little, too little, and just look what you have done. You are a sniveling cretin. Flock, what shall I do with this murdering nitwit?"

"I already told you, my lord. Kill the blighter."

"No, Father, let me take his gun. Loosen your grip a bit, his face is turning quite blue, although as a discipline, it has produced an excellent result." Helen removed the gun from Reverend Older's limp hand.

"Flock," Lord Prith said, "tie the fellow up."

"What with, my lord?"

"Use your scrawny imagination, Flock."

It was Lord Beecham who removed his cravat and tied Reverend Older's hands behind his back. He looked down at the man and said, "What shall we do with you, sir?"

"I suppose I must meet the hangman, my lord."

"You murdered an excellent man," Helen said. "You stuck a stiletto in his back. You are a vile person."

"Yes, ma'am. You are right. I now accept your

judgment. I am a foul menace."

"I say kill the blighter."

"Well, I am the local magistrate," Lord Prith said as he eased Reverend Older down onto the cave floor. "Stay there or I will kick you off the cliff."

"I shan't move. Actually, I do not believe that I can move."

Lord Prith announced, "I will have him locked up in my cellars. We have no local gaol of any kind. Then we will decide what is best to do with him."

And so it was that Flock gave Reverend Older three blankets, food, water, a large branch of candles, and a chamber pot, and locked him in the wine cellar, with the warning that if he drank more than one bottle of wine Lord Prith would hang him himself, without a trial.

"I shall deport the man to Botany Bay," Lord Prith said later as he handed his newest champagne concoction to his daughter and to Flock. "I doubt he will survive there long, if he even survives the voyage. Come, won't you give it just a small try, my boy?"

Lord Beecham stared at the strange color in the beautiful crystal champagne glass and actually shuddered. "No, sir, but I shall watch my wife give it an excellent test."

Helen gave him a look that clearly said she wanted to boot him out the door. But she took the glass handed to her.

Lord Beecham watched her take a tentative

sip. He watched her lick her lips, then take a longer drink. Then she smiled and held out her glass for more. He actually heard Flock moan with pleasure. Goodness, what had Lord Prith poured into the champagne?

"Oh, my, Father," Helen said, once she had downed her entire glass. "This is wonderful. It is the best mixture you have ever discovered. What ever did you mix with the champagne?"

"Something I just hadn't considered before, my dear. Even to me it sounded too dreadful. But it isn't bad, is it?"

"It is ambrosia," Flock said and poured everyone another glass.

"What did you mix with the champagne, sir?"

"Well, my boy, it is only orange juice, nothing more, nothing less. I am pleased that finally I have achieved greatness with the grape. Yes, orange juice and champagne. Now, what do you think we should call this wondrous new drink?"

Lord Beecham said, "Oranpagne?"

Helen said, "Chamorange?"

"No," Lord Prith said, frowning as he shook his head. "We need a name that will tease the senses, sound soft and inviting, something not tied directly to the ingredients. Yes, a name that is altogether different."

Flock was staring outside. "The trees are so very beautiful. Soon they will be full and green again, not a thing like the champagne, my lord, but yet, drinking it makes me feel at once mellow, pleased, and a bit droopy, just the same result as when I look at those trees yon that will be beautiful in but a couple of months. Why do we not name the drink after a tree?"

"You wish to call this drink an oak?" Lord Beecham said, raising an eyebrow.

"Or a pine?" Helen said.

"No," Flock said, his voice dreamy now. "We must be more poetic. What is a poetic tree?"

"I know," Lord Prith said. "Why don't we call this drink a willow?"

Lord Beecham thought about that for at least three minutes before he slowly shook his head. "It is close, but still not there. Another tree, Flock."

Flock looked off into the distant trees and meditated. "I've got the perfect name for this incredible drink, my lord. How about calling it a mimosa?"

"No," Lord Prith said without hesitation. "That is not a name to stick."

"We will use it only until a better name comes along," Helen said and stuck out her glass. "Another mimosa if you please, Flock."

There was another attempt to steal the lamp that night. It was three local boys.

The next day Helen said, "I simply cannot live life knowing there is a thief around every corner. This time it was just boys. What if one of them had been hurt? We must do something."

Lord Beecham said, "I thought about hanging it in front of your inn."

Helen brightened. "That is an idea. My inn is

412

King Edward's Lamp. It would be only fitting to have a lamp hanging out over the front door. Ah, if only everyone didn't know we have the lamp. It's too late now to do that, but it is a wonderful notion."

"Then, there's just no other choice, Helen." They looked at the lamp, but the thing just sat there, doing nothing. No pulses of warmth, no soft yellowish light. Had it all been a dream?

How could this dented old lamp have been the basis for Aladdin's tale?

And so they carefully wrapped the lamp in soft, warm clothes and put it into the iron cask. Spenser could not bear to hide the scroll again. It was a historic find. It was meant to be studied by scholars into the future.

They buried the iron cask in a meadow about one mile east of Shugborough Hall. They buried it very deep. They did not mark where they had buried it.

No one would ever find it.

In the years to come, they remembered the lamp only when they received letters from scholars asking to examine the leather scroll. Or when Helen chanced to visit the graveyard and pause at Mrs. Freelady's grave.

Local people made up tales about the lamp to while away the long winter evenings. But even they, after a time, forgot that it had ever sat atop the mantel at Shugborough Hall. It passed into local lore.

Lord Prith ceased experimenting with his fine

champagne, saying that the mimosa was perfection itself and he could not hope to outdo it, although he could not like the name.

And, over the years, to no one's surprise, one of the Beecham children's favorite stories was "Aladdin and the Magic Lamp."